The Married Land

Charles G. Bell

Fomite
Burlington, VT

ISBN-13: 978-1-944388-48-5
Library of Congress Control Number: 2020936246
Fomite
58 Peru Street
Burlington VT 05401
www.fomitepress.com

12/10/2022

The beauty of the course of this world is achieved by
the opposition of contraries, arranged as it were by an
eloquence not of words but of things.

AUGUSTINE, *City of God*, XI, 18.

To our great originals

I WANT TO SPECIFY THE DEBT implied in the dedication:

From the unpublished journals of my father-in-law, Samuel Mason, I have drawn material without which I could not have realized the Adam Woodruff of this book.

From the unpublished memoirs of my mother-in-law, Carola Middlemore Mason, I have put together the Graftons and the English scene.

From an unfinished autobiography by my own father, Judge Percy Bell, I have derived the early life of Gerald Byrne.

To my mother, Nona Archer Bell, I owe as much material, including a poem and letters given as Octavia Clayborne Byrne's.

These four characters are celebrations of admired originals. Yet even they are *fictional* celebrations. For example, Judge Byrne, as tragic focus of the book, is given more urgent reasons for dying than my father had, the debacle of his life and tension of his marriage are considerably heightened.

The rest of the book has no relation to fact. The traveler is not me, but a kind of projection out of William Blake and Tom Jones, nor are the events of his life mine. It is true there is a Mill, which I know through the hospitality of my wife's great-aunt, Mrs. Francis Stokes, and it is true that Uncle Steward gets his interest in machines from Uncle Frank; but otherwise Steward and Hester Cope are quite made up. I can only apologize for appropriating a loved place, moving it from Maryland to Pennsylvania, and re-peopling it to its harm, as the polar needs of this book required.

So, in general, if I have made the Quaker society somewhat stiff and the Mississippi one somewhat explosive, it was to serve the structure and has no bearing on any existing society in Mississippi, Pennsylvania, or elsewhere.

In short, with the exception of family biographies freely altered and here acknowledged (acknowledgment to the memories, since the writers are dead), this book is purely and simply a piece of fiction, and as the formula goes, no resemblance to any actual persons living or dead is intended.

Among my obligations I should say that I have proceeded as Ghiberti did with the model for the bronze door: I have set up in the marketplace and welcomed counsel. A list of all the friends who have helped in the making of this book would exceed a hundred names. I record ten who have given much of their time, and let thanks to them extend to the unnamed: Erich Kahler, Galway Kinnell, Jim Gilbert, Diana Bell, Lois Clark, Ann Worthington, Josephine Haxton, Walker Percy, Diarmuid Russell, Craig Wylie. Also, since my briefcase was stolen in Versailles, with the MS. in a critical stage of its development, there might not have been any novel but for the devoted sleuthing of Lulix von Simson, who must therefore share in any credit or blame. Finally, there is Yaddo, a kind retreat, in which much of the actual writing was performed.

. . . an Historiographer discourseth
of affayres orderly as they were
donne . . . but a Poet thrusteth into
the middest, euen where it most
concerneth him, and there recoursing
to the thinges forepaste, and diuining
of things to come, maketh a
pleasing Analysis of all.

SPENSER, Letter expounding
The Faerie Queene

Contents

1 ~ The Waking

Before the waking comes the dream —

At Woodruff Farm, when Daniel and Lucy walk out together, they make the descent through hemlock woods to the spring under the rock. They go down on their hands and knees, their reflected eyes meeting, and then their lips stir the water. To drink from the dark earth. A strange communion — the basin charged with assault of last year's leaves, a leopard frog leaping off stirring the mud, a few water bugs, newts and blind worms. But they knew do no harm. Not for all their kicking and staling in the pond. So one drinks from underground, and it is cold and clean . . .

That was in Maryland. Here in Mississippi, in this Delta, there was no rock, and though the whole place was afloat with water, there was hardly a clear spring.

Daniel Byrne waked with the dawn in the heat that had hung through the night, a windless presence. He stretched, hunting a position on the lumpy mattress his aunt Betsy had put in this side of the house when she fixed it up for renting, though it had been vacant now for more than a year. Through weeds and althea bushes light entering the stale cave.

Staring into the murk, he traced patterns on the wallpaper, mildewed where the roof had leaked and been patched time after time, patched and never repaired, everything kept hanging together that should have been razed and rebuilt solid . . .

He closed his eyes to break that meandering, to focus on Lucy's waking.

It would not be at Woodruff Farm. They had both left there the same day, she north with the children to Pennsylvania, her great-uncle's country place, Cope's Mill, Daniel south to Mississippi, Aunt Betsy's, to this.

> Dear One: I have been looking through Uncle Steward's albums at pictures of old family times, a happiness revived which makes me sad. When you and I are together again, I will not be able to talk of Daddy and the things so close to me. But here I can apologize. He has been too much a part of me to make me the adaptable wife I should have been. He and mother were truly one. I had thought of marriage like that, tenderness, devotion, sharing. Because of this I fear I have fallen down. I am sorry, for I love you.
>
> LUCY

Remembering that sad little letter, her Quaker testament of self-search, he tried to realize her, his opposite shore, to which again and again he must build airy suspensions. What was he reaching for, stretching, as from pole to pole, over gulfs of water and fire?

Whatever it was, it would not be at Woodruff Farm. He must summon up the Mill, near Philadelphia. Well, he had slept there enough to know that also, to close his eyes on these grimy stains, or with them open in the gray to relive the other waking.

The white-walled, clean-smelling room, casements wide on the eastern morning . . . The bed is high, four-posted maple, so high that rolling over you can look through the window and down onto the mill creek putting off mist to reflect the first light. Lying there by Lucy in the familiar morning, he sees her rise, throw back the sheet and stand: the gray-green eyes, the mouse-soft hair, the deft figure

in the homemade flower-printed gown, loose-hanging, connubial
... But now she is solitary, he a thousand miles away in the moldy
house, watching her as she goes to the basin in the comer, freshens
her face in spring water, and turning, walks onto the balcony over-
looking the maple-shaded lawn. The hill, sloping down to the race,
the stone outhouses, the garden. The hired man goes the rounds,
dusting and weeding. The Irish maid walks from her apartment to
the house. The cook parks her car and enters the kitchen, from
which shortly the fragrance of coffee and toast, or maybe at this
season fried apples with wheatcakes will summon to breakfast.

Nothing will be changed, not by a sickness or heart attack, not
even by the death of one loved and grieved for. The order will go
on unbroken, the proprieties, the social forms, as surely as Uncle
Steward's clocks will be wound, will go on ticking.

In the last luxury of the lumpy bed, Daniel stretched, thinking his
day must begin too.

The phone would ring about an apartment or the carpenters, and
he would have to run over into his aunt's shuttered bedroom, not
knowing in the dark whether she has staggered to the toilet in the
night, too late not to mess the floor. And when that is cleaned up
and the colored woman has come and they have got breakfast, he
must go back to work clearing the desk or the front bedroom, or out
to attend to the property, or to buy the day's groceries at the store.

— The chrome and glass fluorescent-lighted supermarket flashes
in the corner lot, where once the Blandon house had stood, in which
he had courted the mild Emily. The pneumatically controlled door
springing back as he steps on the pad reveals heaped row on row of
processed, sterilized, emulsified and vacuum-packed foodstuffs. He
clangs a shiny wheeled vehicle from an interclasped array of them and
turning back the strapped seat built for baby, starts down the long
aisle, looking among fruits from Oregon and lettuce from California,

frozen fish from the Banks and lobster tails from Africa, with hundreds of brands of soft drinks boasting genuine artificial color and flavor, and chickens grown under mercury light, whose feet have never touched the ground, fattened with injections and dipped in antibiotics for preservation, and bread white as Kleenex, made of flour thoroughly reduced and reconstituted, with thiamine and wheat germ added, and calcium propionate against spoilage, so that not even a mold can grow on it, much less a digestive enzyme — as he searches for the things on his list, always present, under the image of the spring and the bright externals of the store, below the ordered shelves and the vanished house where he courted a vanished girl, yawns that other ground at which his soul labors.

(The encounter of day, reconnoitered in waking; foreseen and remembered as real as the deed. There past and future merge, smeared in present: *To make the actual conditional and the conditional actual, to blur the distinction.*)

As he tries to fix on Lucy, the spring, the Mill, the vortex will open; like breaking through the surface of a puffball into the choking brown spore case, he will wallow in all this, not in the physical objects only, but in their effluence, even his thoughts succumbing to that style; its web of parentheses, as if some demon of the place had laid hold of him and was ranting through him, the turgid rhetoric of the South boiling in him like a river —

The old woman, his aunt, home from the hospital, as decayed as the house, as hopelessly, and he to draw her back, to solve the problem for which there was no solution and no right way, every effort at clearing and ordering, even if that were possible, being against her will: "Don't do that; don't touch that; I'll get to that tomorrow."

A tomorrow postponed four years, with apartments unrented, bills half paid, insulin bungled and diet not adhered to, everything jumbled and out of hand, and not a square inch of the place but was loaded and treble loaded with junk that should have been discarded — all the fragments of past lives treasured with the maniacal avidity of an old spinster clinging to what she had as if it would give her what she never had, clutching at objects, mere objects, with the desperation of a dying solitude.

That desk now which he should have cleaned, but she opposed: "Not today, Dannie; I'll get to that tomorrow" — papers and souvenirs laid down in a matrix of disturbable dust, the ghost that could wake when stirred, haunting the nose and mind — *that desk, that drawer:* LET THE OBJECTS BE NAMED —

An ivory-tipped splintered pen with which Betsy Byrne had written the letter fifty years ago, refusing the only man to offer himself on the sanguine altar, Fran Dudley, immigrant hardware clerk, whom the mother — the delicate small woman, often rapturously praised, but domineering, spiteful, in her Colonial Dame pride, rooted in aspiring and childhood inferiority, having been looked down on in Kentucky by others whose houses and history marked them as higher and whose rank she had enviously claimed — made her reject with this pen, and so seal herself in the maternal spinning, where she had withered, first under the living influence in spirit, and now, the mother long dead but Betsy hanging on in miserly crankishness, in these late house-and hospital-unravelings, thinking the old woman alive again, neglecting her food, talking of the mother, searching for the mother — as then in spirit, now in body — withered . . .

(The cloudy rhetoric beating in his mind like fever.)

Three Christmas tree balls with the stems cracked, dimmed with dust, saved from the faintly remembered past when there was a family to celebrate the season, for the unimaginable future when she would resume those festivities — though for the past ten years she had fled town for the holidays, leaving, yet bearing with her, all sentimentally wept-over memories of joys that were hardly such when they existed, and of the changes that had made them cease to exist, riding the Greyhound buses south, north, east or west, to friends, cousins, the nephew, anywhere, hotels, loneliness, anything, to remove herself from what she carried along — she who was now too weak to travel, and even at home would hardly trim a festive tree with these dust-dimmed but glistening, stem-cracked balls.

The third object, the fourth and fifth, a chance collocation: *the thirteen dusty rattlers from a rattlesnake's tail,* and beside them *the smooth-textured mahogany-brown buckeye* brought as a talisman from the East (they did not grow in the Delta), a luck piece, a charm; yet what luck could this bring against the thirteen warning clappers of a snake's malice? — and fifth, strangest of all, *one of those little Christmas apples picked up somewhere in Catholic travels* — snake and charm tied together in the deepest myth the folk mind or myth-creating Lord ever hit on for our curse and blessing: a shining rose-and-gold-skinned apple, the fruit to which the snake led in the fabulous garden; but behold, a mystery: a little hinged door in the bit cheek of the fruit, opening to a cave, a stable in miniature, with Mary and Joseph and the baby between admiring beasts, a tiny golden baby . . .

But the rattles were most in evidence. It was only they which the craggy-faced Savannah had seen the day before when Aunt Betsy was on the porch, and Daniel, snatching a furtive moment to assess the darkness, had opened the drawer, and been called away by his aunt's thin lost piping: "Dannie, Dannie," and had gone to calm her, and been called back into the house by a wilder alarm: "Misser Daniel, Misser Daniel, come here, Misser Daniel! They's a snake's rattlers in this drawer; Lord save us, they's a snake's rattlers."

When he got there Savannah was standing off pointing at the desk as if at any moment the original snake would rise from its recesses. He walked to the drawer, his eyes hazy with the change from light, rustled among the papers, groping. She jumped further back, her voice sibilant: "Don't touch em. Don't stir the dust off em. You go blind. That's why she can't see. You keep rattlers like that around, you go blind as a bat."

But his sight, at least for the present, was coming back, adjusting to the gloom. He found the rattles, grappled with them, raised them rustling in his hand: "You mean these? They're no harm."

Savannah flung her arm before her eyes, shrinking away: "Ole Mrs. Byrne, yo grandmother, she was stone blind. Miss Betsy's almost blind. And now you goan be blind too. It's all come from the rattlers." And she fled the room . . .

That was it, to flee, clear out, to leap over the perpetual opposition of their bloods —

"And when thy mother came from England, Lucy, as thee must know, it was against thy Grandfather Grafton's will. He said thy dad should comeback alone and get a job and house and be set up in life. But thy dad, our Adam, said he'd been thirty-three years and wasn't set up yet; why should he wait any longer; he and Meryl could get set up together. As it turned out, he was right, because the adventure appealed to Meryl, apart from their being in love."

The crisp Quaker voice possessed the room, like Lucy's, though not as warm; it was her father's sister, Aunt Chris, telling of old times:

"We had found a run-down farm for sale, in Maryland, near Swallowfield, where he used to go as a boy — but thee knows that, it's where thee lives, only it's been fixed up since, thee can hardly imagine what it was then. We sent him a snapshot of it, and he showed it around Grafton Hall as if it was one of the mansions in paradise. He told the Baronet: 'See here, Sir, I don't want your money, not a penny of it; all I want is Meryl; but I want her now.' And he flashed that photograph.

"I suppose Sir Thomas had never seen anything so shambly, with the house unpainted and the privy to one side (what thy dad whitewashed later and called the White House), and a big gully in the front yard. He held out for a long engagement, until Adam could come up with some more adequate provision.' But thy mother was an independent lass; she had read Ibsen and Bernard Shaw, and believed in her rights. She told thy granddad his ideas were so ancient they might have stepped off the Ark, and Adam kept nodding and saying it was a dreadful waste of time, not to mention the money. Time, of course, was what Sir Thomas was after. But Meryl wouldn't give in; so he disinherited her, at least for a few years."

It was a voice only, heard or remembered, but it revived the scene — not Woodruff Farm this time, not even the Mill, but Steward Cope's townhouse in Germantown — long since swallowed up in Philadelphia. There Lucy will stop for lunch or tea after seeing Uncle Steward in the hospital.

"I must say, thy dad was one of the world's drollest sights in those days. He'd come over from the Friends' Service Camp in France, and he had only one baggy suit with the pockets full of rocks he would pick up, or birds or animals he had killed and was planning to stuff for his collection. Thy mother said he pulled some kind of a jumping mouse on her father almost the moment he was introduced, and expected the Baronet to be delighted. For a joke she called him the Duke of Vallombrosa or Abruzzi or something of the kind, and he called her his Duchess, and when they would meet in the great hall in the morning or walking the lawns or gardens, they would bow to the ground like orientals and salute each other with those titles.

" 'Good morning, my dear Count of Abruzzi,' she would say; and he, 'Good morning, my beloved Duchess' — their noses practically rubbing the ground."

Aunt Chris's voice was yielding to Cousin Samuel's, his tones modulated and soft, with something almost like a lisp, but natural and pleasing. "Has thee heard the story of that, Lucy? It was later, at thy farm. They kept up that ritual of salaaming. Thy dad had been out to get a haircut, and thy mother was walking along the lane when she caught sight of the car coming through the woods. She stood in the middle of the road bowing and scraping, her head bent down so far she couldn't see, until the car stopped almost on top of her, with no laugh or 'Hail Duchess.' She looked up thinking something must be wrong, and it wasn't the Duke of Abruzzi at all, but the milk inspector, with his mouth open, wondering what could be wrong with Mrs. Woodruff."

Yes, Lucy would have heard; even Daniel must have shared in it somehow. How else could he be resonant with it now, tuning in on the voices, which brought with them the place, Springmount, the essence of Cope?

There was a whole spectrum of houses, ranging down in orderliness from the east: from Grafton Hall in England, the Jacobean manor where Lucy's mother was born; through Springmount, Uncle Steward Cope's town house; out to Quaker Mill, his country place; then south with Lucy's father, over the Susquehanna, to Woodruff Farm; then all the way south with Daniel to Mississippi, those decaying houses: the Ionic extravagance Daniel's father, Judge Byrne, had built for a bride who did not require that, or to impress a mother who failed to be impressed; and on the other side of town, this older Byrne house where Judge Byrne and Aunt Betsy had grown up, and in the grime of which Daniel lay. If you wanted to sink lower, to attach an infra-bass to the known diapason, all you had to do was to get up and walk three blocks westward to any of Aunt Betsy's Negro cabins, Winnie Bloomer's, say —

Winnie would open her frog mouth, tilting her face up sideways, and say, "When you goan gas me, Misser Dan?"

"Gas you, Winnie? Don't you know the law'll be onto me if I go around gassin people?"

"De law, Misser Daniel? I mean put me some gas in dis here house. Ah'm tiaahd uh choppin wood for dat old chuk stove. An you better brace up mah kitchen while you on de job. Look in heah. Iss all wobbly."

He gropes in through the dense air and gives a trial jump in the middle of the kitchen floor. It is like jumping in a tree house, everything swaying and dancing. The dishpan on the table slops up a tidal wave and spills on the floor; the pans clatter on the wall; and Winnie Bloomer breaks out: "What you doin, Misser Dan? You cain't jump like dat. Have dis house down on our heads. Now when you goan gas me, Misser Dan, and when you goan brace dat dere flo?" —

But it wasn't Winnie's he was after; it was the opposite, the Eastern pole. Let him try again —

Uncle Steward's was the largest house in the Quaker enclave of Springmount. Like Aunt Betsy's it was old-fashioned and possessed by the past. Only it was half again as old, three times as large, it had never been made into apartments and had never run down. It was in a stem honest style, 1845, gray granite, no gingerbread. It commanded a height over Wissahickon Creek, north of central Philadelphia. A lawn punctuated with fine trees sloped down to a stone wall crowned with an iron fence. There were hemlock, maple, beech, a Norway spruce whose trailing limbs had rooted at the comers and begun to grow up themselves, minarets around a hundred-and-twenty-foot spire. Flanking the gate stood an ash and tulip poplar, the towering clean trunks seeming to contend for size.

If it was afternoon there would be cars parked and a group of relatives come to ask after Great-uncle Steward. And though Great-aunt Hester would probably be with him at the hospital, Aunt Chris and cousin Kathy Swain Aldrich would be on hand, and there would be iced tea and cakes under the maple. The talk would not dwell on present misfortune; a few words about the patient, pious hopes, and the Friends would reconcile themselves to being cheerful. Since the scattered clans gathered largely for weddings, heart attacks and funerals, the conversations before and after were almost indistinguishable, quietly jovial in either case, stories from uncles and aunts about their youth and the Friends' Meeting of old days.

If Aunt Hester was away, that would clear the road for some account of her doings. She had been born a Cope; Uncle Steward was her second cousin; it had been a kind of marrying into herself, a reinforcement of peculiarities that seemed to go with the name. Though in most things she was the soul of efficiency, she had quaint crotchets. Cousin Samuel, of the Germantown Trust, who looked after her stocks and bonds and made up her income tax, might describe the trials and splendors of that great checkbook, which she had turned to a kind of journal, jotting down urgent thoughts that struck her when she should have been filling out the stubs. There was one stub on which she had written the date but had got no further, waylaid into this meditation: "Feb. 20. Alas, 20 years ago today, old Silver, our dog, died." On another she took off from the signature, copying it over with increasing size: "Hester Cope, Cope, Cope"; and then in capitals: "COPE. How I love that name."

Tales of Monthly Meeting long ago, where the stern little ladies in black capes had popped up after every speaker: "I agree!" or "That Friend speaks my mind." And when the tedious old "minister," Lucy's Great-great-uncle Gabriel Pendle, asked release of the congregation, by which was meant their blessing to represent them at the Boston meeting, or wherever his zeal was taking him (that was "Greater-than-our-Lord" Pendle, who used to rant about pernicious books and pernicious clothing, crying in his shrill voice: "The women show too much skin to the men!"), Aunt Hannah Cope, spinster, who had begun the drift to Maryland seventy years ago by buying the farm called Swallowfield, quoted scripture with an air of such approval, she seemed unaware of the venomous allusion: "Our dear friend requests release," she said, rising. "1 would like to quote on this occasion the words of our Lord at a certain place in the Testament, where he said: 'Loose him, and let him go.'" And the intense little ladies jumped up affirming: "And so say I," and "That Friend speaks my mind." . . .

But today Lucy was at Springmount, and the talk would have come round to her parents, Cousin Samuel passing it back to Aunt Chris, who had begun: "Thee can be sure, Lucy, they had a hard time those first years, until thy grandfather relented and settled something on Meryl. One weekend I went down to see them. As I drove in the lane, Meryl was out trying to round up the pigs and get them home. It was as if Christ had sent a legion of devils into them; they were missing the bridges and wallowing in the stream. Meryl had taken off her shoes and was running behind, driving them into the lane. 'If Sir Thomas,' I thought, 'could see his favorite daughter playing the barefoot pig girl.' But that night at the log fire we laughed and told stories and roasted chestnuts — thee knows how it was; thy father could live in the old way better than anybody else in the world."

As if Adam Woodruff had risen from the earth he was committed to and stepped into the room, the man Daniel had known such a short time, but who had gone on living in his mind and in the house, a presence shared among them — had he died at all? or only withdrawn to the privacy from which he would come again — from his pine wood or the treasured small valley of virgin timber where Broad Creek went down to the river and oaks and hemlocks grew in a mist that seemed to breathe from hundreds of miles to the north — or from any of the fields or guarded second-growth woods where he botanized, collecting ferns and flowers for skillfully made presses — all those files of artistically mounted species and varieties with Latin and popular names and places of picking, poetic allusions, a treasury, of ordered love and lore: under a fem arched like a Chinese design across the page: "*Cystopteris fragilis,* Upland Brittlefern, growing in the spray under the falls above Kilgore's grist mill. June 2, 1945," and in pencil below: "Site since destroyed" — the old man who had preserved into smiling age a young man's body, face, blue eyes, like Lucy's gray ones, another species than the fierce vindictive or staring blind eyes of Daniel's grandmother and now of his aunt — as if he had come into the room, his corduroys swishing, to squat by the fire Indian fashion, as he had done at countless campfires, cooking hardtack or stirring coffee, to crouch there on his haunches, glancing at the quietly loving English wife, the children, nephews, grandchildren, anybody returned to the wonder of the farm — Thanksgiving maybe, or in the cold of the Christmas holidays — he too returned, but from nature, like any of its phenomena, a field of grass, say, that ripples in the wind, his face rippling with shy revelation, a moment's talk before retiring to his study, to the ferns and annotated books and designs for furniture or wrought iron or weaving — as if Adam Woodruff had entered the room to crouch a moment, glancing and talking, telling of his boyhood.

(As when you have taken quinine and your ears roar with it, roaring and boiling, a muddy flow: Sunday visits in the already shuttered house, the grandmother's voice insistent, as the searching blind eyes probe the boy, then leap to the father: "Have you heard about Mrs. Walters, son? She's broken her hip." — "I'm sorry for her, poor woman. At her age there's not much hope of recovery." Against the grandmother's snort: "Hmph! I have no intention of wasting my sympathy on her. She comes from the lowest hill people; she's lived beyond her means, like others I know; she drinks and she dopes and she's an unfaithful wife. Don't tell me. Mrs. Walters! I never cared for Mrs. Walters..."

It was the wrong childhood. Cover it up. Go round about on the other.)

Adam Woodruff grew up in Springmount. His great-grand-father, the first of the name, bought it before 1800. It was then a sixty-acre farm. The level land to the north and east had since been sold, but thirty acres of sloping park and woodland remained. The eighteenth century whitewashed stone house had descended through four generations of Adam Woodruffs, until Lucy's father let it go to Aunt Chris, abandoning it for Maryland. But long before, the estate had become a Quaker corporation dominated by the energetic Copes.

The first Cope was a sea captain of whom lively stories were told: When he was boarded by pirates, he did not fight. It was against his principles. But he encouraged the men. As a pirate was climbing up the ship's side by a trailing rope, he whacked it off, and leaning over, called to the man in the water: "Friend, thee has more need of that rope than I." Years later he surprised a burglar at his house in Philadelphia, stepped into the room cocking the big flintlock: "Friend," he said, "I am going to shoot right where thee is standing." And he blasted off into the space from which the obliging friend had departed.

The second Cope took over his father's ships, but as a merchant. During the Revolution his vessels sailed past the British blockade as if protected by the Lord. The scarcity of goods at the time did not diminish the profit of the trade. An admirer of Ben Franklin, this "Poor Richard" Cope had tempered the Quaker faith with so much optimism and common sense that Fox and Penn might hardly have recognized him. He was acquainted also with the first Adam Woodruff, who as steward of the Mount Airy Hospital, was breaking new ground in the gentle treatment of the insane.

The third Cope, Ezra, lived in a time of Quaker faction. He dropped his father's worldly enlightenment, at least on the surface, assuming a piety of the dourest kind. But beneath that front he was a shrewd old skinflint, and as one of the founders of the Pennsylvania Railroad, could hardly help adding to the family fortune. When he was about forty years old, he married Patience, young niece of the first Adam Woodruff. That was his entrée into Springmount.

As the Cope tribe grew, various granite piles of severe dignity appeared at convenient distances through the woods. Ezra, called the Pious Moneygrubber, built the first before 1859; it was the largest, in which Uncle Steward now lived. Another Cope, Aunt Hester's grandfather, built about 1860. By 1870 the Moneygrubber's son had married a Pendle, so "Greater-than-our- Lord" built the somberest house of all, paneled throughout in dark chestnut wood. Finally, Jenny Cope Aldrich built near the end of the century. The Prices (a sad comedown for one of the Cope girls) never made the grade. They lived in rather grubby street houses in Germantown.

The whole estate was walled in; there were common woods and pastures, a stream and waterworks, a skating pond, an ice-house — even, for a brief time in the 'seventies, a private school. Here the families lived, rather sheltered from the world, entertaining hordes of relatives in the summer. The children played mostly among themselves, sometimes, in the end, intermarried. Thus Lucy's grandmother, Martha Cope, was a grandchild of the Pious Moneygrubber and his wife Patience, a match to which Lucy could trace her way along either line.

This was the Springmount of which Adam Woodruff, squatting by the fire, gave curious glimpses.

Of Christmas and Thanksgiving in the Copes' state rooms, where he, being small, with a delicate voice and repertory of songs ("Sewanee River" at the head of the list), would be set up on the table like the Giant's harp, to sing for the company.

Of kindergarten in the city he hated — coats in the hall, lunch baskets in the cupboard; songs about violets and daffodils swaying in the breeze; then strips of colored paper to be woven through sliced cardboard sheets. While month after month, on the ornate walnut shelf at the back of the room, waited the mystery, a large lump of peacock coal — until the door opened and a silver-haired gentleman entered with a "Good morning, children," went to the shelf, picked up the lump, and gave a tedious lecture on the economy of coal, and of this peacock coal in particular.

Three years of kindergarten. Then primary. Work; despised discipline, sometimes whimsically broken. Picture Sally Goodhue, now a staid mother, the pigtailed small mischief passing this note: "Come around after school and let's talk about babies and piss and those things." Observe dignified old men of the Facing Bench come to life, like any other group of laughing boys, calling Adam to a hollow tree: "Look what we've got trapped in here." He bends and receives in the eye a stream of urine discharged by Cousin Samuel concealed in the dark hollow.

Touches enlivening the recital, not altering the man's judgment: the long winters, the sterile city. Protesting, he appears with his little brass cannon under the trees behind the Pendles', loading her up with gunpowder and pebbles and firing from ambush on his great-aunt's chickens. They jump into the air squawking and flapping, while Aunt Rebecca Pendle sallies to the rescue: "Pernicious boy!"

The sterile city, the waste of time . . . And only summers to keep promise, to fill the spirit another way than in Meeting. He would travel then, through rolling Pennsylvania farmland, south (south for the summer!), over the Susquehanna, to that middle ground — Negroes, tales of spooks and hants, throaty laughter — in which his Great-aunt Hannah, for some obscure Cope reason, had purchased Swallowfield — in that warmer looser land where he was to settle at last.

The red-faced hired man met the flame-belching train, frantically reining the horses, tobacco juice trickling from the comer of his mouth. Hooves clomp over the loose boards through the long dark tunnel of the covered bridge, the little square of light beckoning at the end. Then comes the dust- raising ride along the river, past the old lime kiln, over the haunted Pedlar's Run, and into the lane at Swallowfield.

Aunt Hannah and Aunt Jenny, who have come down earlier, lead him into the cool hall. There is a smell of fresh matting on the floor and of apples in the Chinese bowl on the table; and Aunt Temperance, an African princess, shuffles in with the red bandanna on her head, grinning and bowing welcome. He carries his things to the bedroom upstairs, and at the washstand by the window pours spring water into the white basin, washing off the stains of the city and train and road — a baptism, a ritual — while the farm air flows through the window, and the bobwhites whistle in the hedgerows in the evening sun . . .

These were the river hills where Lucy and Daniel lived now, following in Adam Woodruff's traces, except that Lucy was seventy miles north, Daniel a thousand south, while the old man, who had stepped into the firelit imagined room, gave his secret withdrawing bow and gesture of the hands, as if he gladly presented you with all that was not to be told, communication being doubtful at best — under the bow and wave, he retired, leaving the backdrop against which, so evoked, he had appeared: the lawn at Springmount, and his sister, Aunt Chris, continuing the story of his married years —

(As a short-wave radio blurs bands and the loud program you are trying to get shut of bleeds through into the quiet one: *Stoneware jars, dried peas, old beans, flour, grain, grits, swollen cans, bargain-bought vegetables, pineapple, soup, stale precooked macaroni, stinking lard, unwashed greasy skillets, mouse nests, droppings in the drippings, crap on the wrappings* — but you tune it out and the quiet voice reestablishes itself.)

"Adam didn't know anything about farming, though he could pick up any kind of trade. But he had curious ways of learning.

"There was the stump of a dead locust in the back yard, and the morning after I got there, Adam decided to root it out. I must tell thee, Lucy, for a Quaker and a pacifist, thy father had more love of guns and explosions and dynamite than I could ever understand; and at that time he kept an outhouse on the farm loaded with dynamite sticks.

"He got a post-holer and hollowed under the stump, keeping the entrance as small as he could. Then he loaded it with dynamite and stopped it up tight with a fence post hammered in with an ax. Meryl and I were in the kitchen doing the dishes; we had no notion what he was about. The thing was built like a cannon. When he touched it off there was a big explosion; the stump heaved a little and settled back like a sow, but the fence post tore through the air and went crashing through the clapboard wall of the kitchen. It passed like a bombshell within a foot of Meryl's head and hit the other wall so hard it brought down the plaster.

"We heard a yell from outside, and here came Adam dashing in at the door to see how many he'd laid low. I was at the window, and when I saw the stump heaved up and the mortar hole smoking: 'Is thee crazy, Adam,' I said. 'Think what thee might have done.' But Meryl began to giggle; Adam broke into a sheepish grip; and the next thing I knew, she was in his lap on the chair and they were whooping with laughter."

"The first time they went down there" — that was a midwestern voice; so it would be Cousin Samuel's wife, Kathy Swain Aldrich; she had come from Iowa into the clan, but she treasured their legends — "they borrowed Swallowfield from Aunt Hannah. Their second honeymoon, they called it. They rented a horse and buggy from a livery stable in Germantown and drove down. The horse was used to company in the livery stable, and when they stabled him in the empty barn at Swallowfield, it seems he never slept, for loneliness and the scampering of the rats.

"They kept him going all day, driving over the farm, comparing it with others round about, trying to decide whether to close the deal; and at night the horse got no rest, until finally his ears were hanging over his face like a mule's and he was stumbling along in a daze. They didn't know what was wrong with him. Then one of his shoes came off and they had to take him to the blacksmith. There were other horses there, and it must have seemed more like the livery stable, because as soon as the blacksmith went to work on the fore foot, the horse fell asleep, and being off balance on three legs, he tumbled over on the blacksmith. Tools went flying, and a whole barrel of nails got knocked over and rolled every which way. Adam said you never heard such a noise and cussin. That horse was a wreck when they brought him back."

"Adam would have been a wreck too," said Aunt Chris, "if it hadn't been for Aunt Hester." . . .

(From the first Aunt Hester had taken Meryl in charge — the American aristocrat welcoming the British one. Uncle Steward, indeed, had gone to New York to meet them when they landed — partly to invite Adam back into the plant. It was in New York that Meryl saw her first colored mammy, and whispered: "Oh look at the wonderful Nigger Lady" — to be cautioned by Uncle Steward: "My dear, we do not use the word Nigger here; and we never call them ladies."

Digressions. Let Aunt Chris continue.)

"As thee must have heard, Lucy, thy mother had been to a cooking school her last year in England, but it was a school for the genteel, and all she learned was to make a suet bag pudding. Adam phoned from Swallowfield the first night after dinner, groaning about a stomachache. So Aunt Hester and Aunt Hannah got together and sent off the Priggs."

"The Priggs?"

"You know, O Wild Pig."

(Yes . . . Aunt Hannah had christened him after reading Oscar Wilde, and a name like that was bound to be corrupted. The Copes had helped his grandfather to freedom, concealing him under the shrubbery in the greenhouse at Springmount. Well, it was the old slave's descendant, O Wilde Prigg, with his wife, who arrived at Swallowfield the day after the telephone call. He was dressed in long black tails, sky-blue pants and white sneakers and he appeared before them, bowing for service.)

"But what do you do with a colored servant?" Meryl asked Aunt Hester later, after Adam had hired a maid; for being English, she was puzzled how to handle her.

"It's simple, my dear," said Aunt Hester in her regal way (she couldn't have been over forty-five, but already she had the grand air). "All thee has to remember is to give her everything thee despises to do."

Daniel heard the story twenty-five years later. Aunt Hester had received him with cool condescension in her state parlor, and he wondered if strict application of the rule in her case might not have led to the colored girl's being concubine to the husband as well as maid to the wife. But that was not the kind of question one addressed to Aunt Hester . . .

But the voices now, with the scene itself, were trailing off and drifting away, as if that Colored eruption had brought Daniel back to the flood plain of the Delta, back to the waking which involved him in all the rest, the house, the desk, that eternal drawer —

Sixth: *A ring of old keys,* extinct patterns that fit nowhere, unlatch nothing, symbols without evocation, tunnels of a cave turning and winding and affirming the maze of loss and inconsequence — the haunted round ring of various molecule-by-molecule, hour-by-hour and year-by-year rust-transformed iron and moisture-and-mold-greened brass inoperative keys, once opening houses, lost rooms, coffers, hearts . . .

And here, side by side in the drawer, were *three gold wedding rings,* each inscribed with the name of the gentle bearded grandfather, Daniel Byrne, to his beloved Hilda; so that seeing them lying there, and knowing something of the history, how she ran off as a girl and came to the Delta and raised her children and fell out with her son for marrying against her will ("Miss Clayborne, indeed — hill-born! What do we know about her, but that she works in an office, which no decent girl . . ."), how she lived ten years in the same town without speaking to him, even when his first child died, though she sent him her legal business by mail, secure at least he wouldn't charge her (why Daniel could remember when he was in second grade and they were clearing up matters of relation, and each pupil was to write down all the kin he had in town; he had listed only his mother and father and brother and sister, while the teacher insisted: "But you have an aunt and a grandmother in Delta Landing," and he with sharper insistence, uncertainty not being a Byrne weakness: "No ma'am, I don't have any aunts anywhere except in the hills, and no grandmother at all"), until the father rose to his chief folly, ran for governor against Gyves — Hilda Byrne thinking: "If he'd stayed with us and done it shrewdly, he'd have won, but now he won't, and I'm glad." Gyves, who lived up to his name, shackled and fettered the state and left Judge Byrne like Hamlet's "mutines in the bilboes"; and then Daniel's grandmother, who had never weakened when her son's own flesh and blood son died, weakened, feeling this sorrow more intimately, she weakened and invited them, and they began to go for the long sessions of rocking on the porch and talking Sunday afternoons . . .

(The visits to be repaid at Christmas, Thanksgiving and the glorious Fourth, when the grandmother and Aunt Betsy would come to dinner in their black robes, but not of penitence, to sit eating and talking with the father and children, ignoring Daniel's mother — as that time one July when they were asked after the meal if they would care to look at the garden, and Aunt Betsy, bending to some foliage, said to the grandmother with customary assurance: "Well, here's portulaca"; and Daniel's mother, gently, but with the mystical distance that vexed them more than rage: "It looks like portulaca, but I think it is sedum." — "It is portulaca" — the thin-featured old woman, sightlessly piercing the intruder, the upstart, spoke, only to her daughter, the familial creature, as if they were alone, the emphasis barely admitting an assertion to be denied: "It *is* portulaca.")

Seeing the rings lying together so negligently beside the rattlers and the buckeye and the letters in the drawer, one asked: "Why three, Aunt Bets, why three?"

The answer: "That was always a bone of contention. Mother would say: 'I never had a wedding ring. I hardly feel married this way.' And Father: 'But I gave you one ring; in fact, I've given you two.' And she: 'Never. I never had a true wedding ring.'"

(The symbolic copular . . . Daniel had heard: his namesake, the wandering photographer, old enough almost to be the girl's father, with no fixed home or place of business, and a mystery about him which turned out to be another wife, unmentioned, in the north, divorced, and a son by that marriage, later to descend the river, exploding into the tidy home of a jealous small Kentucky beauty.)

"So Father would buy her another. 'Here's a ring,' he would say, 'a real gold wedding ring. You see, it's engraved *Daniel to Hilda*. It's the third, so don't say you never had one.'

"And would you believe it, she would lose that ring again. I never could understand how she lost so many. She would forget about it too, though she wasn't forgetful. She would say: 'No, I never had a ring at all, not a true wedding ring. You never gave me one.' That was always a bone of contention . . ."

Aunt Betsy's voice droned on, applying a stroke now and then to a landscape adumbrated by years' attendance at such' recallings — the chair rocking land creaking, the voice tired, almost vacant: "always a bone of contention."

When suddenly, pulling herself together, between sternness and alarm, as Daniel drew the drawer out, aiming to empty it: "Don't bother with those things now, Dannie; I don't feel like fiddling, with that drawer today."

"I know you don't, Aunt Bets; but I'll do it for you."

"You leave it alone. I can't depend on you. You'll go back up east terrectly and there'll be nobody left to see to anything but me. I'm the only one, and I'll do it; but I can't get to it until tomorrow . . ."

He lay in the dawn, thinking of another waking —

Thinking how strangely, under a likeness of aim, the two regions were in fact different: Mansions, memories, family, something called tradition revered in both; but in that East it was an unbroken heritage of stable goods, where in this South — broken time after time since the old war, crossed and recrossed by violence and social upheavals in which the first were always boiling under and being made last, old families shattered to frayed ends, drunkards, river bums, squatters, mad suicides, as the crass urgent trash rose to engross estates, stocks, stores, in a brief arc of parasitical glory, to rule in their stead, building showy new mansions in cleared swamps or on the conspicuous leveled tops of Indian mounds, the old homes in the center of town declining to apartments, like this, barely sustaining a nucleus of junk-cluttered rooms where gentility of the last age hoarded what in the East had functional being: letters, canceled deeds, paid-out mortgages, treasured irrelevancies of a life so whelmed that only the flash of genius could atone, the combustion which now and then bursts from degenerate lingerings — papers and legends handed down like heirlooms from, father to son or maiden aunt to nephew, ignited, leaping into the flame- shapes of a world-historical fable — in this South, except for such poetic fruiting, all else on that horizon spelled features of a single loss, meanderings of a bayou that coils on itself and arrives nowhere — except as the whole landscape, in one blast of insight, burns in its darkest windings a calligraphy of fire, the mere ruin become its own transcendence.

He lay in the dawn, setting his shore of dry rot and flame against that other of decently ordered goods, into which Lucy was waking, though in grief, and he asked: by what redeeming road had he found an entrance to her country, the clear directional streams, the preservation that is sane, ceremonious humanity sustained by safe inheritance, stocks and holding companies managed by boyhood Quaker friends or children of second or third cousins, honestly efficient schoolmates from Westtown, Haverford, Swarthmore, meeting Sundays in Germantown or at any of the country crossings, returning to the center for weddings and too often funerals, upholding the dignity of a whole neighborhood of eighteenth century well-kept houses and rich farmland with woods, wheatfields, pastures, cattle, groomed horses, a people doubtful of egoism, wildness, the passions — almost, despite their eccentricities, stuffy —

Yet that order had accepted him, made a hearth at least for his burning, for his vision to project itself, softened in that air, and on the shelter of those walls, to become the saving flicker — a world suspended between space and flame . . .

Clarity, vignettes caught in confusion, luminous as the mother-of-pearl lining of a shell . . .

Daniel and Lucy had parted on good terms and for valid reasons, but their parting, the separation of half a continent between them, was more than an accident in their relationship, more even than an enforced penetration of origins. It was an actualizing of something always latent, some specter the waking raised, necessitating an ultimate encounter — the harrowing of hell.

Daniel faced the day with three questions — The first arose from the image of the spring, that mystery of water out of earth; it was addressed to the heart: *How to bring clarity from the dark house, the opening of its dens?* The second was asked of the mind and followed from the first: *In the face of all the dens would reveal, how had a bridge been possible from Woodruff to Byrne?* The third, neither the heart nor the mind could answer, but only time: *When would he be with Lucy again?*

2 ~ The Calls

CHANCE WILL BOW to the symmetries of form. It was strange, but the two calls had come on the same day . . .

"For God's sake, Lucy, where is my mask?"

"Your gas mask? You had that with your first wife, in Europe."

"You know what I'll need down there, don't you? I mean my swimming mask, the only mask I've got."

"Do you think you are going to the coral seas, Daniel?"

"I might as well swim if I get a chance."

"And what will you see with a mask, in the Mississippi River?"

"There's blue-holes, Lucy."

"Blue-holes — as blue as pea soup. Don't be a fool, Daniel. You've got to get on a plane."

"All right, all right. What clothes have you packed?"

"You don't have to paw through them that way. What do you want? Your heavy sweater, in case it gets cool some day? What about your ski boots? You can ski on the levee if they have an August snow. You'll need your painting stuff too, and a library to work with in your spare time. And a trunkful of those unfinished manuscripts, because some time in the middle of the night you might wake up with an idea for one of them."

"Hot tamale, what a girl. But I've got to have my paints. I'll narrow the books down to three or four."

"Well pack them yourself. I've done the clothes. There's everything you need, so don't rumple through them that way."

"Don't, don't, don't. You sound like old Nobodaddy." He caught her around the hips. "But what lovely hills and ledges, like the hanging gardens of Babylon."

Whether he was going to accomplish anything serious in his art, nobody could tell, but he had a lusty talent for rhymes. They popped out of him any time, along with syncopated tunes. He broke into one now, kneading her rear:

> "Oh the ladies have their asses where they set;
> We call them little assets.
> (*Le mot francais est*
>   *FESSE*)
> So when we get aggres-
>   sive and we want to tup,
> We catch them by their dress-
>   es and we say:
>   Fess up, fess up, FESS UP!"

On these occasions, Lucy would assume a Quaker shock, drawing herself up for a moment, like Aunt Hester — until she began to giggle.

"For the lord's sake, Daniel, what's the matter with you? Can't you think of anything but ladies' fesses and that stuff?"

"What *stuff?*" he says, shifting his focus. "What *stuff* are you talking about?"

At this moment the phone rang . . .

Daniel's call had come earlier. He had been out in the pinewood tearing honeysuckle and poison ivy from the openings where the Scotch Pine had caught the borer and died. He was going to clear the whole space and set out fresh trees. Lucy's father had planted this hill of pine, and Daniel treasured it, as he had the old man.

He was pulling and hacking, dripping with sweat, talking as he sometimes did when he was alone, a Southern vein of oratory he had learned from his own father, except that where Judge Byrne had made a mark with it over the state of Mississippi, Daniel kept it for a private joke: "Three-leaved bastard" (heaving a hairy root of poison ivy), "you throttled my father. I know you of old. You're Gyves, the governor. You spread the itch and give the blotches. Demagogue, shyster. I pull you out by the roots (eradicate!), tear you limb from limb (deracinate!) destroy you leaf and bole (extirpate!), crush you into nothing (annihilate!)." With gloved hands he wrenched the vine from the tree and threw it into the clearing.

"And what's this, so elegant?" (Heaving and grunting.) "Washington imported you like a flower for a garden. Freedom, equality and honeysuckle. You're the sweet hypocrisy that smothers the colleges. Is there no way to get the earth clean?"

Lucy had come from what they called the schoolroom to answer the phone. She was trained as a teacher, and used to work the children a couple of hours a day in summer, to make up for the public schools' waste of time. The children objected; the first week there would be tears and flapdoodle, then they would settle down.

She told the operator to phone back in half an hour. She walked through the rose garden to her father's toolshop to ring the firebell, schoolbell — whatever the big bell was that he had put there when she was a girl to have them called from play and himself from the farm.

The sound goes over the green slopes. The cattle in the north field lift their heads, chewing the slow cud, ruminant: "The bell of some god-bull?" Behind the field the thirty-year-old pinewood looms like a wall, almost black, hemming the horizon. The waves go surging through the branches, creeping into the densest brown-stained depths over the needled ground. Daniel will hear. But she calls to the children to go on with their reading, and then, with her loose stride and shoulder-length light hair flouncing behind her, she sets off to meet him.

They have always walked the farm together and lingered in the pinewood, and when they come up from the pasture onto the walnut knoll, they like to sit down and look back over Broad Creek Valley, where the hills fold and clasp into each other. They have done it since their courting days, when Daniel, under suit for divorce, would come from the city to this quiet, a weekend maybe, and they would wait on the hill, Sunday evening, minding the time, feeling in the sun's descent, the descent of solitude, as if soul was being drawn from soul.

She had loved this farm almost too much, and without his insistence might have given it up. After the hurricane and loss of her parents, it had seemed a ground of death, choking her. She would stretch full length in the grass remembering how she had helped her father set out those pear trees, or how he had made them a ski jump on that hill, or how they would lie under the black cherry tree watching the bees coming and going to the hives. While always in the pasture under the walnut knoll stood the dwarf tabletop pine, older than their records, where the new double grave had joined the colonial old ones.

Whatever was warning Lucy away had attached Daniel to the soil. After the funeral they had to put the place in order whether to keep or to sell. It was while he was working with the others, clearing the debris of the storm, sawing up fallen trees through the day, and at night helping to sort out and divide books and possessions, that something had taken hold of him, something breathing from the land, relics, journals, artifacts and mementos, a presence not only of that man, but of the pastoral life he had formed — as if the dead were coming back, stemming a break in the soul's formation, requiring new bodies they could train and ride — to Daniel it became unarguable: Woodruff Farm was not to be abandoned.

"I can't face it," Lucy told him. "My brother won't and my sister won't. They know better. They have other lives. And you have the University."

"The University! I've wanted to chuck it for years."

"But you're a born teacher; you love to teach."

"All right. I like to teach. You know what I say: it's a pleasure too frequently indulged in, and may prove habit-forming. I've· got other things to do."

"But not on a farm. You don't know what farming is. Besides, it hurts me. I think all the time about Mother and Daddy."

"In time you'd be glad of that. But I won't argue with you. If you have to leave, we'll leave."

Then she had the dream.

It was like a plain occurrence. She was sitting in her father's study. The fireplace was not laid for a fire, and to prevent heat loss the wide chimney had been stuffed with paper, of which a piece or two hung down, yellowing. There were no books. The empty shelves had been painted in contrasting loud colors; magazines were on some and gewgaws on others. Where her father's picture of the hemlock woods had hung was a garish tray of imitation hammered copper with a machine-punched design. The secretary and ladder-backed chair were replaced by a chrome and enamel office desk; and in the corner a wide-screen television set was crowned with a metal aerial rising toward the ceiling. It had ousted the dovetailed cedar cabinets her father had made for his flower and fern collection.

She remembered why she had come. It was to pick up those cabinets which had somehow been left behind in moving. She remembered, and at the same time knew it was a fool's errand; they would not be here.

Then she realized she was not alone. The place was haunted. Sitting in the study, the floors creaking around her, she diffused in time and space, like ripples. She was approaching the house past the silted pond; the door was opening; the cook who had stayed on like a property transferred with the land, was embracing her tears. At the same moment she ranged ahead, over the knoll and down the valley where tulip and hemlock were crashing in the wood, choking the spring with twisted branches. There was a sighing over the fields and a ghostly unquiet creeping in the rooms.

She got up and started for the study door. There, at the head of the stairs, she saw her, Sibyl, the new possessor, as she had seen her once at a window, looking out, hypnotic. It was Sibyl, and not Sibyl; for before Lucy awoke, in the first dawning of her faculties — still involved in the dream — she recognized that it was someone else, any alien woman, the breakthrough and abandonment overtaking the farm.

The desolation in which she came to herself was not from the actual Sibyl and had little to do with her, it arose from the dream's prophetic character, as if there was a foreseeing also of the possible, the farm that was to be, whenever she would weaken and sell.

She waked to what she was defending against that overthrow. The doves were cooing in the distance. Lying in the calm, she assessed the alternates: not only the farm, there was the alternate Daniel, teacher of art or philosophy, department head perhaps, if he would compromise that far, the harried professor, wishing he had followed his instincts and art; there was the alternate Lucy, entertaining new faculty members at dinner or tea; and of course the alternate children.

She made the decision, took up the farm in her third of the estate. What capital remained was enough, with care, to keep the place going. The problem from the first was whether she could stick it. Now, as she walked across the pasture to meet Daniel, her eye followed the slope to the gnarled trunk and wind-blown dark umbrella of the tabletop pine. The wheel had come full circle; there was also a renewal from the graves of a good past.

She remembered the turning point. The nightmares of the first winter had come to a head in the spring. The car would be rushing toward a cliff or into the sea, she struggling with her father for the wheel; or they would be falling, the water closing over them; she would wake gasping for air. Often, settling into sleep again, she would swerve into the same dream. She got up in the dawn and walked out of the house and through the field. Her mother's snowdrops and crocus were pushing up here and there. She sat down by the grave, dry under the covert of the pine, while the hills took the light around her. She knew it was a mistake; they had to leave.

Then a wren came and sat on the gravestone. In the brightening air beyond the tree she saw a pigeon hawk, a rare bird her parents had watched for. It circled and swept off over the woods. The branches, through the mist, showed the first plum color of spring. She sat motionless. A little way off, as if they had condensed out of dew or air, two rabbits were playing. No, they were not just playing; that was a dance. She had never seen it before; but she recalled something her mother had told out her, of going as a girl in the spring meadows of England and seeing the hares dancing in the fresh grass. Now close to her came a mole, his coat almost silvery, smooth and shining. He was rooting under the grass stems with his flat nose and did not notice her, though he was scarcely a yard away.

It was as if her father and mother were there, among these, the living, telling her there was something she must cling to, that they were part of it, that she was and the farm was. So that morning had ushered in another age, fabulous childhood revived, under the richer textures of being a mother and wife.

Daniel saw Lucy as she reached the fence by the stream, where the pasture touched the corner of the pinewood. She was climbing the weathered planks nailed up in place of a stile. She saw him too, and stopped with one leg flung over, the wholesome mound of generation pressed against the top board. He was dressed in his blue jeans, a long-sleeved work shirt and canvas gloves. Strangers took him for her brother; he was built like her, shapely and compact, with a firmness of muscle and looseness of joint, a certain swing in his walk, that took her under the omphalos with a love sweet and sisterly, yet rich with desire.

He strode up the path through the mottled shade. She waited on the fence. He threw a leg over, sat against her, lacing her with his arms.

"It's the phone," she told him. "Long distance. From Mississippi."

He groaned.

They climbed down and started for the house, their arms around each other, their steps in time.

Daniel had heard of the accident three weeks before. His friend B.J. had phoned: "Thought you ought to know. Miss Betsy just went through a led light at the bridge highway. Some guy hit her, and they say she's gone to the hospital half dead."

But when Daniel had phoned the hospital: "Nothing but a sprained shoulder and some bruises," Dr. Fisher had said. "The car seat went out with her and broke her fall. She'll be out of here in a few days."

"Look, Dr. Fisher. I'm giving lectures in Baltimore for a month. If I have to call them off, I will, but it's the first chance I've had to tell those people what I'm up to. If she's all right, I'd rather come when they're finished."

"That'll be fine, Daniel; come when you can. We'll take care of her. Miss Betsy's one of my oldest friends."

"If there's any problem, let me know."

"Surely, Daniel. No trouble. The injuries are minor."

Daniel had written comforting letters and got no reply, but that was as expected. He let no news be good news. In five days the lectures would be over; he was planning to fly down.

"Did the operator say who it was?"

"No," Lucy told him, "just Delta Landing."

When the phone rang again it was not Dr. Fisher. That was to allow him more gumption than he had. It was one of the nurses upset about not getting paid. She had got Daniel's number and was reversing the charges to find out how they were going to collect for their time. The nasal hillbilly whine which, in the migrations of the Great Depression, had thrust itself into the Delta between the re-fined planter speech and the melodious drawl of the Negroes, came creeping over the wire —

"Hit's a shaime how Miss Betsy's gone down. She's not in her right mind any more. Dr. Fisher didn't want to let her go till she was better, but she's been gittin worse all the time. In her head I mean. Some nights they have to strap her down to keep her in the hospital."

"Strap her down! No wonder she's out of her mind. Why hasn't she gone home long ago?"

The cautious whine: "Well, Dr. Fisher said she wouldn't look after herself; said he wanted to wait for you. But maybe he should a let the Colesons take her . . ."

"The Colesons? Who are they?"

"Don't you know the Colesons? They live in one of Miss Betsy's duplex houses. Mr. Coleson been her jackleg carpenter a long time, patchin up her shanties. They wanted to take her home and look after her until you could git down. She'd a done better. Miss Betsy's right fond of the Colesons. She asts for him at the hospital. First she asts for you and then she asts for Bud Coleson. Evy day."

"Well, I'll be coming along. Just keep those nurses on the job. But give up tying her down."

Silence. Then: "Sometimes we had to put a little strap round her, or she'd a been out the window in the night. It's her mind that's botherin her."

Daniel phoned Dr. Fisher, but he was out. The operator would call back.

Lunch was at twelve. In the summer they ate on the screened porch under the big sugar maple. It was shady and cool. Like everything on the farm the maple tree was a focus of memories. Lucy's father had tapped it when Lucy was a girl — though they lived almost too far south for that. He had boiled down the sap in an iron cauldron at the fireplace in his room. The branches reached up to the porch upstairs, and at night when she and her brother had been put to bed, they had made a lark of climbing out one tapering branch to the ground. Their own children were just beginning to try, Hester egging Mardie on.

The trestle table had been made by Lucy's father from walnut logs his father's firm had floated down the Susquehanna. Grandfather Woodruff had shared with the Copes in various ventures, but the most lucrative had been timber. So the money Lucy's father had inherited at his mother's death and had applied, with the Grafton money, to keep the farm a sanctuary and bulwark against spoliation' — of which Lucy's share had been devoted to the same end — was partly derived from denuding vast tracts of land in the valleys of the Appalachians. The rivers had floated black with trees in those days; there were log jams and thundering thaws and the violence of the loggers; and out of it had come stocks; bonds, money, the farm, and as it happened, two russet-colored logs, which Adam Woodruff had begged, cured, sawed, converted through the years into furniture: a crib, the trestle table, a Dutch cupboard, a delicately poised sideboard, chairs and a chest, all of his own design.

They had finished the potato soup and were starting on the salad, with cheese sandwiches warmed in the copper covered pan over a flame wick, when the phone rang. The connection must have been made. But for Daniel, the association of Dr. Fisher with midday, summer, eating, plugged in another line, which sent him to the phone growling.

What he fished up was a meal in the pilastered Mississippi dining room of his childhood. A visitor from the North was being entertained. The windows were wide on the languorous summer. The ceiling fan was ambling its lazy round; on the sideboard the small fan swung a feeble beam. The silver pitcher of ice water was beaded with a cold dew. As Judge Byrne raised it to pour for the guest, his voice boomed out, defying the lethargy of the somnolent air. He was narrating the local sagas, not of political youth and high endeavor this time, nor of experiences in Europe, but of the Flood, when the

St. George of Delta manhood fought hand to hand with the river, the whole land wrapped in the slimy folds. The battle was recounted like Homeric song: the levee a forest of tents and a blaze of torches at night — the struggle for food, shelter, clean water, vaccination against disease. The hosts were catalogued; there was praise for the heroes, scorn for the foolish and small.

Among the latter crept in Dr. Fisher, timid, pale, in charge of the Board of Health. Judge Byrne had confiscated a warehouse of food and drugs, but Dr. Fisher stalled, preventing distribution, saying they lacked authority.

"Waiting for the government," cried Gerald Byrne, "while women and children were hungry and typhoid might strike at any hour. There is a point at which caution becomes cowardice and evasion a crime, and Al Fisher has spent his entire life toeing that mark."

The memory. And now the voice, guarded, allowing that Miss Betsy was in poor shape as far as her nerves went — physically fine, but not otherwise.

"Why haven't you let me know?"

"Why Daniel, we expected you down here from day to day."

"I said I'd be about a month. I had no notion she was still in the hospital. Why didn't you let her go home?"

The stern act, self-righteous: "See here, Daniel, I'm her doctor. When she was lying there knocked out on the pavement, they asked her 'Who's your doctor?' and she cried out 'Dr. Fisher'; so I had to look after her."

(Sounds like a charity, thought Daniel, like a great big lovely charity.)

"She's your aunt. I guess you want her to have the best. She can afford it, can't 'she?"

"It doesn't seem to have done her much good, is what I'm saying."

"No, at the moment something else has got to be done. You should have been down here already to take charge. Why the bills haven't been paid, and the houses aren't looked to, and Miss Betsy won't pay the nurses, You can't persuade her to write a check. Something's got to be done."

(Give up, thought Daniel. The guy has just brains enough to make out a bill.)

"I'll be down tomorrow," Daniel shouted, and hung up.

Then he phoned the museum and put off the last lecture.

And next the airport.

Lucy had gone upstairs to pack for him. She always did his packing, bought his clothes, polished his shoes, took care of things he would have neglected. When Daniel had finished his sandwich, he followed her up; they began ragging each other about the mask and then about fesses; and where it might have led, Lord knows, if the phone hadn't rung again.

Daniel got it, but it was for Lucy, from Philadelphia. He stood by, anticipating trouble. It was clear at least from the first tones: the metallic sound in the earpiece, then Lucy's solemn voice: "Yes, Aunt Hester . . . I'd been worrying . . . I don't know. I had a dream . . . I'll come up. But I have to get Daniel on a plane, tomorrow . . . It's his aunt, in Mississippi. We'll work it out . . . I'll come as soon as I can."

She turned to Daniel in tears. Grief stirred the old resonance. This was her father's uncle, patriarch of their clan, who since her parents' death had assumed a fatherly role. "It's Uncle Steward," she said. "He's had a heart attack. He may not live."

Daniel would have found it hard to elicit tears. Uncle Steward was one of those men whose very limitation is the perfection of their powers; there was no breach in his soul's wall. At eighty-five he was still running a millionaire business he had built up from scratch, managing the Mill estate, keeping its water-power generator going and looking after what amounted to an arboretum on the grounds; he was on the board of directors of what was formerly the family bank, and was the mainstay of two Quaker colleges and leader of charitable causes. He never let any of these things interfere with one another, or let his wishes or his conscience interfere with them. Even during the war, when his electronics firm was doing a largely military business, neither that fact nor the profits it implied shook his Quaker self from its always healthy appetite.

This blend of power in balance Daniel admired; but to love Uncle Steward asked something more. Lucy, who had grown up in that orbit, saw another man.

She remembered Christmas and Thanksgiving gatherings at the Mill or at Springmount. After an overpowering turkey dinner with cranberries and pies and all the trimmings, the menfolk would go into the study to smoke cigars. She had not considered it strange that her father, drawn in Uncle Steward's wake, was talking with the boys and smoking the big cigar; she never asked why he was so eager to get back to his farm and woods. Her attention was fixed on the door of the study. She was waiting, with the other children, for Uncle Steward's return — not only because he would laugh and romp with them, or lead the group singing with his big clear voice: at these reunions he always had a pocket full of silver dollars, fresh from the mint, and as the children watched, he would go around the room, dipping and exclaiming, reaching into a child's coat here, a trouser-cuff there, or under Lucy's blond soft hair, tickling behind her ear — each time resurrecting, by some sleight of hand, a shining silver dollar, which he would slip with congratulations into the child's paw.

Better even than the money were the times when they would cluster around him and he would draw his marvelous old pocket watch from his waistcoat. It had a fly-back gold lid on one side that opened to the time, and another on the back that revealed a crystal, behind which all the jeweled works were ticking away in geared precision. It was a watch that could strike the time, not hours and quarters, but any time. You had only to punch a little button at the side (every child got to punch it) and it would whir a little and then begin to sound, lively as a rooster, a low gong knocking out the hours, then another one, higher, telling five minute intervals since the hour, and last a high tinkle, numbering the minutes beyond. It was best to do it in the evening and late in an hour; then it would strike say eight, and eleven for the fives, and two or three tiny ones, and you would know that it was almost nine. You would know it by the sound; even if you were lost in the darkest night, you could punch that button and put yourself back in the frame of time.

It was curious, Daniel thought, that Lucy's best memories of Uncle Steward should be of bright dollars and of a time-telling gong. But for Lucy, Steward Cope remained the pattern of what a man should be, enlightened, kindly, of inexhaustible energy, God's image and masterpiece. He was all of that, Daniel would have agreed; still, there was one small lack — or how could you call it a lack when it was only the perfection of his powers . . .

Lucy was in tears.

"Why don't we go right now?" Daniel said. "Today. Drop me at the airport. I'll get on a plane, don't worry. I dare them to keep me off."

Lucy could tell from his look that he would. She could not be sure of the method; she could only infer it would be irregular, pushing, distasteful. She was almost as glad to be going in the other direction, not to be a party to the crime . . .

— As in Bach's violin Chaconne or the solo cello suites, the single voice cannot sustain the pedal point, so it becomes intermittent, the music plunging again and again to the ground over which its flourishes are made, Daniel would be flung forward in time, or if he was already there, his backward reaching would yield to the recurrence of that day's climactic separation, waking in his aunt's house, going out to buy food —

He will be scanning a shelf of gaily wrapped homogenized breads, looking for something of plain ground wheat.

"Well if it isn't Daniel Byrne." The silly little voice tinkles around him.

Raising his eyes and detaching himself from the mind's two images, the reflecting spring and the opaque drawer, let him focus on the lace-clad, powdery, plump object before him, and see what he would have thought impossible here — impossible because it was too perfect, she came pat on her cue, as if through all those years, while her house was torn down and this Food Fair was built around her, she had haunted the same spot where he courted her on the Empire sofa, in that room situated about where she now stood — though if she was a ghost, she had enlarged like the Faustian dog swollen to a hippopotamus; so that only the suggestion of the place and the familiar bright whine of the voice, with no doubt some cast of features almost lost in flesh, gave her away, Little Emily, once the mildest and slimmest sweet thing in the Delta.

He had heard of her marriage and forgotten it; she had moved to the suburbs, though of course she would return to this store; but he had not seen her since he could have clasped his two hands around her waist, his fingers touching in front and the thumbs, almost, behind, and been glad of the excuse to hold her, whom now he could scarcely have engirthed with both his arms. He had loved her for years, his eternally enshrined and virginal beauty, loved her with such tongue-tied devotion, that he would spend the whole week with his friend B.J., who was as gone on the sister, planning what they would say and do, and even practicing on sofa pillows how they would embrace those dear girls and smother them with kisses, telling them all the passionate things one can so easily say to a sofa pillow, and then Friday, when the dating time arrived, he could never break from the routine of playing cards, driving out for a coke, or at best sitting on the Empire sofa holding hands, his heart jumping with unacted resolve, to blurt it out once and for all: "I love you Emily, marry me, though I'm only fifteen," and have her melt in his arms — until he would leave, so fed up with small-talk and vicious with self blame that he would race the car, swerving at the comers, or those rare times when there was ice, brake and cut hard, so the black sedan would go spinning down the midnight deserted wide street.

And here was Emily, fulfilling the suggestion of the place, asking how he was and where he was located, and after just such bland exchanges as might have transpired a quarter of a century ago, getting around to Aunt Betsy, when at once, carried on the rush of the subject, she assumed a certain narrative verve: "You've brought her home! They say she was a problem at the hospital. I went up to see Tot not long ago — you remember Tot Bass, Ingram now — well, she had her appendix out. I didn't know Miss Betsy was still there. I was walking down the hall. It was hot and the doors were open, and there she was, sitting in her room, so thin it was pitiful, and a great big nurse by her, looking like a bulldog.

"'Are you still here, Miss Betsy?' I said. I don't think she recognized me. 'I'm little Emily, Daniel's friend.' 'Well how are you?' she said, 'And where's Daniel?' as if she expected you anytime. 'Oh he'll be coming along,' I told her.

"Just then Dr. Paul was walking down the corridor looking to his patients. She wasn't any of his, but he stepped in. 'How are you making out, Miss Betsy?' he said. 'Well who are you?' she said, staring him in the face. 'You know me, Miss Betsy; I'm Dr. Paul.' 'Dr. Paul? You're not Dr. Paul,' she said; 'Dr. Paul is a young man.' 'I'm Dr. Paul, though, Miss Betsy,' he said. 'Neither one of us been young for a long time.' 'Well, you don't look like any Dr. Paul to me,' she said. 'What's happened to you?' 'Nothing, Miss Betsy; I'm all right.' 'You'd better go to bed, man. You look like you're at death's door.' As a matter of fact, he's got cancer, but nobody mentions that. So all he, could do was tell her: 'You're looking fine,

Miss Betsy, you'll be out of here soon.' Which he's been telling everybody for the last thirty years.

"When he left, Miss Betsy turned to me like she was going to tell me a secret. 'That can't be Dr. Paul,' she said, 'because Dr. Paul is a year younger than I am; and that was an old man.' And then she said she had to go home to her mother, she was supposed to get ready for a party that night somewhere out in the country, and how brother and Ida Lake were going to come for her. I declare, Daniel, she thought she was a girl again . . ."

"Well, she's all right now she's back home," Daniel said. "That hospital would drive anybody crazy . . . Hope to see you again Em'ly."

They drifted apart, a small object detaching itself from a bale of lace — Little Emily, his love.

His eyes fell back to the shelf of bread; his mind to Woodruff Farm, the spring; and then to the house, the desk, the drawer:

Three gold wedding rings, and then —

Tenth: *One ripped-out clipping* from a local paper of 1905:

> The week's round of social gaieties was concluded Saturday evening in a most delightful manner by Miss Betsy Byrne at a progressive euchre party. The house was brilliantly lighted and converted into a perfect bower of roses, delicate pink, white and yellow blossoms in great profusion being gracefully arranged in parlor and dining room, while gorgeous American Beauties lent their rare loveliness and fragrance to the reception hall The columns, doors and mouldings were effectively decorated with a cut-out cloth design of red and yellow flames, an ingenious play upon the family name. At the climax of the evening an ivory and gauze-fan was presented to Miss Cornelia Ireys for the highest score, and a silver-mounted pearl paper knife to Mr. Lyne Archer for the greatest numbe' of progressions. Near the midnight hour a delicious supper was served in three courses.

And torn out with the clipping in the same column, a random ad: "Fluid Extract of Root Bark for Chronic Dyspepsia. A thin spirituous liquor of not unpleasant bitter taste."

So Daniel. While Lucy sat on the lawn at Springmount, hearing the Quaker talk of old days, talk that could summon from the almost-past a countryside of green farms and stone-built houses, with the cognate Friends who possessed them —

"Didn't they live over in Westchester?"

"No, that was the Walms. Bernie was on the other side, cousin Becky's brother-in-law. He had a creamery on Flourtown Road, and sent butter to Philadelphia. Father used to visit there. A cow put her foot in the pail once and old cousin Bernie knocked her on the head with the pail and said: 'Thee will, will thee?'"

"He was the one who had the balky mule. It stopped in the middle of the ford, and Father heard him say: '1 shall not smite thee, neither shall I curse thee; but if thee don't move, I shall twist thy damned tail.'"

"I remember the place. The house burned when I was a girl."

"No, that was the barn; the house is still there. But how can thee remember? That burned before thee was born."

"Oh no, I was four years old."

Lucy also could break through this, pursuing her private quest of the missing Daniel. And her search, like his, could lead astray, into the lion's den from which somehow he had escaped — what he had been in the old days, when he was hardly Daniel at all, but Sampson with Delilah, Ahab with his Jezebel. Venturing into that space was circling the funnel of a web where the crab presence laired. But Lucy was winged, almost immune. She banked by, skirting' the vortex, caught a glimpse of Daniel lounging on a tuft of moss under a hemlock tree, saw him and smiled, while the surface of conversation recomposed around her —

"We miss that old Germantown crowd. 'See the little wood over there,' Cousin Gideon used to say as we drove past his old place. . (He had been born a twin and the other one died.) 'Over there is buried little Joshy or little Giddy, nobody could tell. It might be him and it might be me.' "

"He's the one who was so lively with the ladies. Old Gabriel Pendle had him read out of Meeting for wearing a red tie — Pernicious Clothing. And when he married his second wife, they both had children before, and as the new ones came along, she would say: 'Thee must go out, Giddy, and put things to rights. Thy children and my children are fighting with our children.' " . . .

There was a contrast, surely; that much was clear; but it was not clear what the contrast was. If her people were as crazy as his, how were there separate shores? Yet Daniel lay on the swampy side and saw the gulf yawning, and across the way, the promontory, as distinct as it was far. There was a cleavage like dark and light, though not like that nameable — shadows on a cave wall, hard to define.

3 ~ The Two Roads

As Daniel got out at the airport, Lucy slid over behind the wheel, while the kids bounced up into the front. Corny, the yellow cur bitch, quivered her hind quarters, thought better of it, relaxed and sat down. Daniel kissed them, all but the dog, took out his bags and crossed to the entrance. He waved. The car merged with others, passed out of sight.

He knew her road by heart. They had taken it often enough weekends or holidays for the same visit under better circumstances, the road she also had taken as a child — a farm girl driven by her parents to Quaker boarding school or to reunions at the Mill or in Germantown — the same road Daniel was coursing over in his thought, the quiet back road her father had preferred and which they hardly deviated from.

It crossed the Susquehanna at the dam. The old river lay below, the swift stream broken by rocks and islands, rapids plunging and veering through potholes and into eddies. Upstream was the planners' version, the long lake between wooded hills, winding out of sight to the north and west.

— Daniel pushed through the airport door and stood in the luminous central hall, taking his bearings, a snag, a towhead in the eddying stream —

Woodruff Farm lay above the dammed part of the river, and there were trees from which, climbing, you could see that sinuous blue inversion of sky — in May perhaps, through the lyre-shaped leaves and yellow wax blossoms of the tulip trees — like an Italian lake or Norwegian fiord, flooding the lost country.

— There is something in us that regrets change ... But what are we longing for? The traditional lost way, or deeper and wilder, the holocaust where all ways, all traditions, are drowned?

Adam Woodruff had made no bones about it. He had loved the primeval river, that had sucked down saw-logs, canoes and people — the water under a full moon glinting at the riffles, murmuring south among dark islands; he had imagined it rising to fling off its puny master, and go sliding to the bay unshackled, as it had done for thousands of years.

How could a man so rooted in order sustain the cult of daemonic nature?

It was another thing for Daniel to espouse hurricanes and volcanoes. He was born in the Delta outpost of that abandon, had defied police and authority wherever he could; so that, without his father's influence and the remains of pioneer sympathy to fall back on, he'd have landed in jail instead of college, Europe and art school . . .

As now, knowing he would be overweight, he crossed the waiting room, set down his typewriter and painting satchel by the wall, and carrying only the suit case, started for the counter to weigh it in.

Lucy, spared these wiles; went her way, the familiar road yielding to the motion of the car . . .

Across the Susquehanna, and now east, a long narrow pike cutting down into sharp valleys, the land, like the road and houses, this far back from the main highways, almost unchanged, except at intersections, where tumorous cellulations crept in: cinderblock picture-window flats set down from magazines in any scene or landscape; but mostly it was the narrow blacktop, straight as a street, over streams with the lovely names: Octarara, Little Elk, Brandywine . . .

Take it easy here on the steep hill; this is Cope leap: a little bridge and railroad crossing. Uncle Steward was once coming the other way, full tilt, taking Lucy home from school. He sped down the hill singing his favorite song, about the Grandfather Clock; he hit the railroad embankment and took off, sailed over the creek without benefit of the bridge, came down with two broken springs on the far side. But he went on in good voice; like the clock itself, he never missed a note.

Penn's Grove, the last crossing. Daniel's thoughts stopped, as in traveling they stopped the car, as Lucy's father had stopped before them. White oaks of great girth and height soar over the meeting house. The soft green of the local stone blends with the shaded lawn. Under the porch are two doors with simple pediments — male and female, made he them. Grateful, after years' absence and deaths, this leafwoven continuance — the air under the gray-barked pillars holy as the enclosed space of prayer. Lucy would stop inevitably, silent, waiting for whatever pervades such a texture to well into the crannies of our asking. Then she would drive on, past the boarding school entrance, and beyond, the main fork: town or country. The right winds through thicker traffic into the center of Germantown; the left draws back from the clotting into a region of fine country, saved for a time by the coincidence of tradition and money. Coasting down the old tulip woods to the rocky stream, hemlocks black over the water, she will take the private drive past the mill and along the race, the Mill-house coming into view through maples on its garden knoll. It is Uncle Steward's retreat from the city, a place of happy gatherings, to which she comes, bringing grief to grief, anxiety to an expected dying . . .

Working up in a long queue, Daniel arrived at the ticket counter of the likeliest line to Memphis, only to be told there was no place; everything was filled, with stand-bys already issued for the flight. If he wanted a stand-by, he was welcome, but so many were ahead of him it didn't promise much. He stormed about a car wreck and a dying aunt; then took what he could get.

Of course, if worst came to worst, there was always the bus or train, a ride of thirty-six hours.

He knew that one by heart too. He had been coming up east since he was a boy, coming and returning, as if some urge of his being drove up that ascent — ascent because the gravitational South would not relinquish its hold. In childhood it had been the father whose thrust could never break him away, would only launch him with the whole family every summer from the sun-baked flood plain, over the Yazoo and through the red hills, where the mother's people lived spread out on broken-up Civil War farms or in the dried-up towns, lived in an age before the modem, drawing water from wells or pumping it at the back stoop and carrying it into the houses, to porcelain pitchers in chipped washbowls — no electricity then, almost no cars, one telephone among all those relatives, and that a crank job on the wall, grinding as hard as if old Alexander Graham had made it — and still the bumpkin horror of this thing of the devil, the aunt's story about the cousin talking in a thunderstorm, his mouth open at the phone when the ball of fire rolled out, rolled into his mouth and he swallowed it and died — up from those hills over the battlefield of Shiloh where the mother's father had fought with the saber now hanging on the Delta wall, on through Tennessee, the hills rearing into mountains, the huge impoverished Smokies, up over the divide, round hairpin turns in the rutted gravel, and into the Shenandoah, the beautiful valley, estates of leisure and tradition taking form around them, Daniel's father breathing the cooler air, the nobler past, battlefields with names from history books, the reference changing now from the war in whose shadow they always lived to the benign one, where Judge Byrne's heart moved as his car advanced among its relics — homes of great men called by an enlightened constituency to the leadership which was their due — he breathing the calmer scene, expatiating, fulfilling his nature, though he could only fulfill it in a tourist's projection, these summer dashes year after year in swifter models of cars — northward up the Shenandoah and over the Blue Ridge to the University of Virginia, the college he loved best, as he grandiloquently phrased it: "one of the few academies of learning that thoroughly look the part" — on north, over the more and more mansion-sprinkled and university-endowed earth, through great historical cities, a trek ending somewhere by the rock-hemmed, fog-bearing sea, with scallops, lobster, fish, cold nights, and colder dips in the salt-stinging waves — and then the descent, the inescapable reverse journey, like a rocket from the height of its night flight turning, gathering momentum, plunging to its ground, the damp plain of their first spuming, down the last line of hills, with even a sense of weary gratulation and home-coming, under the steaming air, to the cotton-rowed, wood-and-marsh-streaked flatness of the land, the blistered towns, and then by the Mississippi the more spacious, oak-shaded Queen City, the broken proud remnant of the always dying South, the queer South, into which the father's father, plying a photographer's trade up and down the steamboat-gilded river, had chosen to settle, and settled in that choosing the destiny by which a grandson, facing another of countless returns, bought his ticket, saw it marred with the bradded-on slip in red, making it for this flight conditional, most likely useless, and told himself, with the willful lawlessness he had drawn from that south and west: "So help me God, I'm going to get on that plane."

He had lived with Lucy long enough to feel her with him at any moment, an inner monitor. He saw her drop her eyes and shake her head. Hers was another orbit, a journey to a milder terminus, the car gliding up the maple drive to the side entrance of the Mill.

It was hard not to imagine Uncle Steward, in the rosy flush of octogenarian health, surging from the house to meet her, his white mustaches, bald head and sharp eyes, something in the rightness of his dress, suggesting an English peer on his land — though in other ways he was not at all the aristocrat, a plain Germantown Friend, rather boisterously amused at the spectacle of his own success. If he exemplified a joy, and evidently he did, it was of job after job tackled with verve and finished with precision.

Almost a proof of the identity of opposites, thought Daniel, to put him beside Betsy Byrne — both activity, but in contrary phases, as under the sway of cross-purposing stars.

— It was handy to get things into categories, to get them paradigmed and displayed, like that rowed table of flights where Daniel searched for the gate number the public address had just announced and he had failed to hear: —

There had been the Woodruff line of Lucy's family, which went back to gentle Quaker settlers from the time of the Revolution. They had married gentle and borne gentle children, never too many, for they married late in life — a son mostly, and two daughters; and the son assumed the father's name, and for three generations his placid character, even (to judge by journals carefully penned and preserved) the same meticulous, almost feminine hand.

There was Adam Woodruff the First, who might indeed have been called Steward, since that was the title he bore as warden of the Mount-Airy Hospital. The mad folk used to be brought in chains to be lodged, as was the custom, in cellar rooms. But he would meet them at the gate, saying: "Strike off the chains; I won't have them in chains." Then he would offer his arm with a courtly gesture: "Won't you please come in with me, sir — or madam?" To soothe mania was his occupation; at the same time it made him a man of substance; as if the calling to help others would naturally reward the helper. It was he who bought the farm of Springmount.

There was Adam the Second, who turned it into a corporation, and Adam the Third, who clenched the deal by marrying Martha Cope. They were two more quietly prosperous citizens, trustees of orphans and visitors of schools.

But a change had begun. Already the third Adam's speculations in timber were under Cope tutelage. And now Cope blood flowed into the placid stream, sharpening the character and with it the calligraphic style. That was the other line leading to Lucy's father — Cope — which might itself have formed a pole to Woodruff, though both were contained within the wall of Springmount.

For all his force, Uncle Steward had never left that containment. What he wanted was a flaw, divine madness, some saving disease. It was as if he had never sensed what is called the Human Condition, did not know what it meant and did not care, had never seen tragedy or read one, though they might have been enacted all around him; as if all suffering had rolled off that shiny head and washed itself from those blue eyes like rain off the slate roof of his own barn (that expanse of "little blues," slates as precise as tiles and joining in a coat like a black snake's skin). He was a daytime phenomenon, the bland face that confronts the sun. Where he kept the skeletons of the unconscious, whether he was built at all over those dens, nobody could tell.

Could such reasonable energy be an energy at all, or only in Blake's phrase, its outward bound? This was hard to get straight — such satanic fascination with power, and no awareness that there had ever been a Fall.

One could not lose sight of the boy in his summers at Swallowfield, walking over the bridge to the flint mill at Conowingo to feast on the machines, memorizing the motions. And his wife, Aunt Hester, had watched in amazement, when they went to the Yellowstone, how Steward took to the place. In those journals of hers (for they all kept journals, even when they were on a car trip west and she recording: "This is a life of freedom and rest high up in the Rockies miles from all the demands of life" — though you had only to read on to learn that Uncle Steward was standing on a granite boulder up stream tirelessly lashing the water with his line, catching trout they could broil for lunch, while she, her "escritoire" opened on a rock before her, was keeping up with her correspondence and continuing that detailed account of their idleness, or maybe writing the month's checks and putting comments on the stubs), she had described how Steward walked around the park for hours exploring all the geysers, leaning down and dipping his fingers in one side, then walking around to see if it was just as hot on the other, licking his fingers for the mineral content, while she wondered: "What can anybody see in so many boiling puddles, poking into each as if it was different from the rest?" She felt only a vague fear, as if the whole region, poised on fire, might blow up at any time. They had to return again and again, even to get up before sunrise the day they left, to watch Old Faithful do its stuff.

It was not the passionate aubade and phallic white jet of that great eruption which drew Uncle Steward to finger the water and taste the salinity. It was the clockwork of the thing — that nature here was already self-controlled; his mechanical spirit was roused, asking: "Since this thing is, practically a machine already, to what use can it be put? Are there no cogs it can turn?"

His fascination was with the harnessed powers of his own Mill.

So he must have been troubled by the other phase of Quaker being, that the Christ he worshipped on Sundays had some devilish fiery quirks. If he had tried to forget that, he would not have had to go to Adam Woodruff for a reminder. His own first cousin, Nathaniel Pendle, would have done. For even Uncle Steward's birth was polarized; the mystical and fanatical blood had broken in through his Pendle mother . . .

The table of flights and arrivals Daniel studied on the wall loomed up, column upon column, the categories displayed:

There were the passive Woodruffs and the active Copes. The Copes again were dividing: Uncle Steward with the clock-men, and in the other row, the Voice-of-God Pendles. And the Pendles were yielding to the cleavage (the rift in Quakerism itself), reformers and mystics, men of works and men of prayer.

The family could be exhibited like that chart. And now dotted lines of cross-relationship were shooting through the structure. The second

Woodruff had made clocks. Woodruff and Cope met in that daily dependability. As if Uncle Steward was a radiant, from which, backward and forward, the worldly virtue shone, fringing the most mystical cloud with a practical emphasis on deeds.

The plane was on lane five. Daniel slipped across the room, picked up his unweighed bags, and started down the spiral ramp . . .

Spiraling . . . Let the design be laid on a cylinder, since its **end** returned to its beginning. What else but the mystical light at the far right had bathed the gentle Woodruffs on the other side, conferring a blessing on their house, trade and garden, a Biblical sanction on their prospering in the world?

The whole outline rose from the surface where imagination had sketched it, shifted and regrouped itself, forming in air a whirling plasma (the propellers of that plane taxing over the field), some Heraclitean vortex of formulable being; and as always the four elements began to differentiate themselves, symbolic positions in the flow —

For the clock men were earth, and the mystics air (vessels of *Geist, pneuma,* the *inspired);* they defined the long axis, and across it was the other: active-passive, the daemonic being fire, and the yielding, water . . .

Daniel approached the flight gate and saw the two lines separate, sheep and goats, these with reservations, those mere stand-bys. He caught the picture. Pausing a moment, setting down his bags and turning to the wall, unconcernedly, with the instinctive want of compunction selfhood breeds, above all in the South — the creative will arrogating to its own right and wrong — he bent back the brad, removed the red warning from the otherwise undistinguished ticket, crumpled the slip in his pocket, took his place in the luckier line.

The plane rounded the wing of the building; wheeling for position; the propellers roared into a dying action. Dust, trash, papers, leaves, rose, whirled among the passengers; coats fluttered, hats were caught at, eyes blurred.

As if, the door of the Mill opening, a great wind had blow through, setting the whole tribe like leaves aflutter: and there would be Lucy's great-great-aunt, Rebecca Cowgill Pendle, whose quieter sister brought the fanatical blood into the Copes — for today or tomorrow, at the Mill or in Germantown, Lucy would open such a parlor door and be confronted with all the cognate hordes, some in the flesh and some talked of, so it would be hard to distinguish the living from the dead — Great-great-aunt Rebecca, rushing forward with her butterfly net and the white cork hat she wore to the Amazon or on that last great safari in Africa, about the time Teddy Roosevelt went for bigger game (her collection in the Philadelphia museum). But it was not gaudy insects that lured Rebecca Pendle over the world. However much the Quakers' suppression of color drove them into nature, birds, flowers, it was a nature translated into spirit; she chased the winged symbol, to which she would refer in her first-day raptures, invoking all champions of metamorphosis: Thoreau, with his bug in the table, that hatched into a butterfly, for Dante, with those *vermi nati a formar l' angelica farfalla*; and she could quote them all, if it came to that.

Her brother, Gabriel Wistar Pendle, might as well appear, since he could come from the grave as forcefully as she could. Let the door be flung back and he be lugged in by two sober-suited Friends, as when he refused to stop talking in Meeting and was toted out crying *magna cum voce* — and whence his nick-name — "Behold! I am greater than our Lord. He was carried by one ass, but I am carried by two."

As for Gabriel's son, Nathaniel, he might be there indeed, in the flesh and alive, a concentrate of the eccentric trend, as if to leave Uncle Steward entirely of the other following. Though such separations could not be perfect. Even Uncle Steward's love of clocks used to erupt in something almost like chasing butterflies — those hunts over the East for any antique assemblage of cogs that would keep a tally on seconds, minutes, hours, or if possible days, months and years: like the huge astronomical clock he installed in the gable of the Mill, which practically took two men and a boy to keep it going; and of course Nathaniel Pendle's caprice had to rest on some shrewd base, or it wouldn't have stayed solvent as long as it had.

In the actual parlor, Cousin Nathaniel might be standing, lanky as Ichabod Crane, in his primitive Quaker clothes, so drab you'd wonder where he dug them up, unless you knew they were ordered from a London tailor at considerable cost. He would be haranguing Aunt Hester about the Cope plant, and how they not only paid taxes to support the cold war, but, he had been informed, produced inertial pilots which were affairs of the devil, designed to destroy bodies Christ had intended as temples of the living God . . .

But in his legendary guise, blown with the other leaves on the roistering wind, let him come in hawking souvenirs at the University of Pennsylvania football game, with his peddler's license taken out for the purpose and a basket of knickknacks he had made to sell: banners and fall leaves preserved in wax, and carved wooden puzzles; and on his head one of his trick arrow hats, the feathered shaft out one side and the point from the other, as if he had been shot through the skull (was there ever anybody more Quixotically pierced with the arrow of God's love than this Pendle?) — peddling, and preaching too, though he had no license for that, then starting off clear around the stadium to give a biscuit to a dog of his acquaintance, and talk with him in thees and thous.

The Prices too would be there, inescapably, for the whole region was grubby with Prices, the lowest of the clan, but with the same proprietary rectitude, an absurd false dignity in their case — Cousin Abe, the Smyrna Merchant, as Daniel called him, of the red face and big nose, full of talk about his candy business —as if all that Quaker gift for trade should have culminated in a Syrian huckster or wandering Jew . . .

("What is it," the traveler asked, "that Quakers believe in?" And was told by a native of Germantown, no doubt an ancestral Price: "Well, friend, they believe in First Mortgages and Irredeemable Ground Rents.")

Cousin Abe would be telling how such and such a drummer, whenever he came in to settle, said: "You're the Price we have to pay, aren't you?"

"Get it?" Abe would bray, slapping his thigh: "The Price we have to pay!"

Then he would discuss makes of candy and which one chalked up the best profits. It would turn out to be Butterfinger, naturally: "Gives the best rake-off."

("What is it those soldiers on those atolls are fighting for? To get back to America. And what does America· mean to those soldiers? The comforts of home — with *Butterfinger!*" A wartime radio announcer's voice, Daniel taking it up in a vexed refrain: "Oh it's Butter — Futterfinger, we are fighting for today.")

Or Abe's brother would be sitting with him on the sofa, as they had sat one night at Woodruff farm when they took the trouble to drive down for a visit, and Lucy's father left Meryl to make the responses (though they were his kin), and stalked up to bed grumbling aloud: "I'm not going to sit there all night and listen to those damned bores." Abe would be telling what he liked for breakfast: "What I want first," he would say, "is a good glass of tomato juice. Cuts the phlegm." And Ben Price would remonstrate: "Oh Abe, don't say phlegm. Not phlegm, Abe. *Mucus.*"

And there would be more, such a lot of originals that a polarity with the Byrnes or anybody else would seem to fall apart, not to mention finer differentiations within the clan. They would be mixed, intertwined — not copulating exactly, not in the parlor — even in their imagined state they remained proper Friends, some of whom wouldn't use a one-syllable word like "phlegm" if "mucus" could be hit on — but breeding in sanctified marriage, crossing the strains, so that Daniel would almost despair of his analysis . . .

— Consider that family tree, which was sure to be spread on the wall of whatever room they were in: a fat trunk with branchings in every direction, long bare stems for the men, ending in feather dusters for

women, and out of the female dusters more bare stems of men protrud-
ing. One did not quote Joyce: "My uncle has a thing long; my aunt has
a thing hairy," because that was bad form; but one looked and noted at
the peripheries how details had been added in small handwriting with
dates and names, crisscrossings of a family sometimes weaving back
into its own vine; so Daniel would have despaired of that simple division into the streams of Woodruff, Pendle, Cope, and their meeting in
the pool of Lucy's father — except that, ludicrously and impossibly, it
seemed to fit . . . As if vitalism and teleology were true; as if that tree of
life were instinct with pattern, purpose, its half-accomplished goal . . .

The line moved; Daniel moved. The ticket was torn out. He leaped
up the aluminum stairs, trying to make those excess bags look light;
he greeted the stewardess as if she was in on the deception and ought
to enjoy it. Going to the front of the plane, he took a seat by the window, settling into the foam rubber recess, hardly expecting a hue and
cry, but scheming how to meet it if it came.

He waited, while people piled aboard, filling every place, before
him, behind, at his side. He waited. The girl went around again counting heads. Suspense. Then the port was slammed; the propellers
turned. He was facing the Delta as he must face it again and again . . .

In the grocery store, Daniel approached the checkout lane as
Emily left. At the same time, a woman, skillfully poured into a low-
cut dress, would come from the manager's booth with a slip of paper.
Leaning down to talk with the cashier, let her exhibit the alley between well-preserved breasts. It is not the breasts so much as the in-
spection of the face they occasion which brings him up short, almost
laughing, the whole thing impossible, a comic opera; this can only be
Ginny, looking better than anybody would have believed.

The recognition this time will be his, and with none of that lace-
wrapped cool; they almost fall into each other's arms. She too is

married — to the manager — whom she helps with the books. A businesswoman! While Daniel rakes up another Ginny —

She had been a turning point in his life, or rather one of those turns he had failed to take, that might beckon later in a stage scenery of cross-roads and exits, as if there had been some way of swerving from the course that swept him on, the romantic lunge for the infinite under female flesh, to make a green goose a goddess and sacrifice the heart on its cackling altar — thus the affair of Ginny displayed itself, far off and silly, in its bright foolish style, an old funny paper uncovered in a bin, say the Katzenjammer Kids.

It was in the time of the ideal Emily — though the pressures of body had brought him to cast seed in whatever field or wood, shed or room solitude took him in — and he would have carried it on to machine or beast or Tiberian baby, any dumb or inanimate thing to be used surface to surface without the commitment of soul to soul — a time of practicing on pillows, as if that would help assault the heart's angel; so his purity was more than make-believe, it was the floating fragment of a cleft desire.

And here Virginia, who had won nicknames from Ginny to Vagina, anything but the virgin one of her christening, called him to her porch as he passed: "Hey, Dannie, comere a minute; I wanna ass ya sumpn."

She was a strapping big girl now and really put together, though he hardly saw that, measuring beauty on the scale to which he was born — those genteel girls dated and admired because their mothers had been, though no better of face or flesh than others who waited a call into the magic circle, and ended by calling what they could get into their little circles instead —

And he was a striding lithe charmer in his puritanism and pride, which were his nature only — well grown, angel-faced — as he leapt up the steps and stood by her side, proud and unconscious of his pride: "Hi, Ginny, what is it?"

Living so near, but she over the social tracks, almost in an outhouse of his residential temple, and being of the same age, they had always been together as children, and had signalized the places of their meeting, one time or another, with games of look and touch (having heard of a copulation hard to be effected) which children can be so precocious in. When they were told on or discovered, Ginny's parents did nothing; his nailed up the secret houses and forbade their meeting. When the prohibition broke down, his mother used to worry, not foreseeing that Southern adolescence would accomplish what she had failed to do; he was fifteen now, and had hardly looked at Ginny for years.

He would drive downtown to worship his true virgin; but this so-called Virginia, in the pause almost at his back door, went unregarded.

She had other talents that had perverted her name. She could run more like a boy than a girl, except there was a certain grace. Teachers make curious projections. If some fatheaded boy shows a freak talent for math, multiplying and dividing at sight, it is rumored that a new Einstein is hatching in the school. So Ginny was supposed to be training for the Olympics. At a recent field meet, while Daniel sat in the grandstand with Emily, Ginny had run the hurdles, tripped and hit herself on the first one, got up and finished the race, taking second prize, then run twice more without complaining, though the pain must have been considerable, for she had broken two ribs.

She had just recovered from this accident; the bandages were off; and she sat looking at Daniel's glowing face as he stood on the porch in front of her, where she could have taken him in her bare arms against those bouncing unbandaged breasts. She smiled. "Come on, sit down a while. Nobody's here. I hate to be alone."

Her family had come from Iowa when she was a child; they were Polacks too; Daniel's father would picture them on the sledded ice. Daniel sat down, though his way of yielding was a denial.

"Do you remember when we were little and used to play in the goldenrod fields and had secret houses?"

He remembered. The drying of his mouth was a measure of her meaning, the revival of those days when sex had been simply what it was. "Mm-hm." His lips did not part.

"Tell me, Dannie, do you think we did anything real? I know we played look and that stuff, but did we do anything bad? . . . Fun, I mean?"

His eyes fell.

"I mean did we ever put it in?"

"I don't know," he said. "I guess not."

"We were too little."

Silence.

"But we're big enough now."

Silence.

"Let's do it now. I'd like to. Nobody's here. Why don't you come in the house?" She gave him a Yankee classless look, mixed with a sex she could not make romantic, though she could run hurdles and break two ribs and go on without complaining.

"Ginny," he said, "I got to go. I told somebody I'd meet em at two-thirty."

He left and walked a mile to sit in the swing under columns like his own and talk devotion to pale Emily. And the unknown future rose like thunder in the Delta heat: chivalric ideals and autoerotic compensations converging in a whirl flesh could not withstand, the turning point he had already turned — as he sat there, swept forward, eyes at train windows looking through their own reflection to strange landscapes and the strangers of that wandering, until the first impulsive dark married Isolde, silk tatters of the — South and breeding trailing about her like robes she had torn to be more sadly voluptuous, would take him in her arms and teach him the mysteries of tragic love . . .

He had gone off and sat with Emily — though only for a couple of hours; because that had been Sunday, and he was obliged to meet his father at Aunt Betsy's, his grandmother's then, where they had also sat on the porch rocking and talking — as Aunt Betsy was no doubt sitting now, twenty-five years later, still expecting his return.

"So long, Ginny; I got to go."

"Come out to 1015 Lee Avenue," she said, "and see us while ya're here."

Too late. Though he rendered a silent tribute: "If I had it to do over, it wouldn't be Emily." Of which the consequence followed: "A course of education which would have eliminated Sibyl." Daniel then, like Antony: "Would I had never seen her!" And as Enobarbus: "O, sir! you had then left unseen a wonderful piece of work which not to have been blessed withal would have discredited your travel." Himself then, baffled. "Besides, if you drop Sibyl, how do you get to Lucy?" — the conclusion following: "Let it stand," with the condition: "For it is hard to affirm anything but what you are."

The glass door opens. From the air-conditioned supermarket he swims into the Delta heat, headed for the house, the desk . . .

What boils up in the cesspool?

The eleventh item: *A broken nutcracker* with which his grandmother had cracked pecans from the small-nutted but sweet pecan tree planted by his grandfather and enjoyed together in the days when this was still a home, before their son's marriage to a woman from the hills had turned always venomous propensities inward and destroyed the meager yet once fire-lighted convivialities of an already ill-matched family.

The twelfth: *A bundle of old letters* bearing testimony to that time, curious indeed for one who now sealed himself in the prison of the house — letters saying:

> . . . I cannot tell you how much I enjoyed being with you
> in your sweet and hospitable home. Don't ever give it up.

It means too much to your friends to come there where everything is so restful and peaceful. And O the inexpressible comfort of feeling safe with a person, so certain that a faithful hand will sift the chaff and grain together, keep what is worth keeping, and with the breath of love blow the rest away. I shall never find other friends to take your place, and when I need you and send for you, I hope you can come. There must be a time some day, although my heart fails me when I think of it . . .

And at Springmount —

"When Cousin Gideon's boys grew up, they'd been out one night raising Cain somewhere, and came home just before dawn. As they were putting the horse away the old man walked into the barn. 'Well, sons,' he said, 'it does my heart good to see you at the chores so early.'

"He got asthma in his old age and thought he was going to die. He called all the family together and they sat with him waiting. He said some last words and went to sleep. In the morning they crept in early to see how he was. Well, he was out in the back yard, feeding the chickens . . ."

"Thy dad used to play there as a boy, Lucy. He had graduated from peppering Aunt Rebecca's hens with his little brass cannon. He had rigged up some bombs with iron pipe and gunpowder, and he went into the pasture to make war on Cousin Gideon's cows. The bombs were flying and banging and the cows were kicking up their heels, when Giddy rushed out to see what the matter was. As he got there a bomb went off under his favorite Guernsey and lifted her right into the air. Thee can believe thy dad didn't go' back for several years. . . ."

Lucy listening poured the tea. She drank and looked into her cup at the leaves. She had gone to a gypsy at a carnival once who stirred the leaves and told her: "Beware of a dark woman and a fiery man."

Lucy had not inquired into Daniel's passions, past or present. Some Quaker gift of silence kept her uninvolved. In that, as in most things, she was the opposite of Sibyl, who could never let anything rest until it had been pursued, if possible, to a lacerating conclusion.

But Lucy did not have to be inquisitive to pick up things in the course of the years, as they traveled in the summers to get Daniel's child, Octavia, or to take her back to New Orleans; she had seen Sibyl once, standing at a window staring out at birth of their first child, wishing them joy of their bastard; on Daniel's first art show, a newspaper photo of one of his paintings with a scathing analysis in terms of Oedipus; and four years later another, in almost the same words, about a different picture, as if Sibyl had been repeating that accusation over to herself through the entire interval. And though Lucy had not met her, she had seen Sibyl once, standing at a window staring out at her, an expression of veiled tightness on her face, as if she was making a spell, which did not seem, however, to have taken much effect.

But Lucy was human. If her waking restraint did not give wonder the runaway rein, she slept, like everyone else she had waked sometimes with the sense that a dream was real. Daniel had heard her once, moaning, then sitting up in bed crying out, and he had sprung up himself, flicking on the light, and had seen her, in the grip of something hardly her own, twisting the sheet and crying, while his own voice, still half from sleep, sounded: "Lucy, what's the matter?" — but in terror; for it came like a curse and reversion: that he had waked again in those early years of the other marriage out at Ozark College in the drab apartment for which Sibyl had gladly surrendered her widow's jointure with all amenities of clandestine Europe — that tawdry town among college instructors complaining of their salaries and scheming for advancement — jealousy, bickering — when Sibyl's nightmarish fears, with pregnancy and after Octavia's birth, had grown upon her, and Daniel had waked night after night to her increasingly deranged cries . . .

"Lucy, has thee seen the journals of thy three times great- grand-father Cope? I've been typing them out, as I told thee before. He was the Revolutionary merchant, an admirer of Franklin. I'll show thee a volume."

Cousin Kathy steps over to her house and brings the notebook, through which Lucy turns:

> "Laugh and be fat" is an old adage, as if one had nothing to do but laugh and forthwith have his sides thick with butter and lard. Though I have laughed much in my time, I have a precious thin covering on my ribs; but I am ready to go on trying. Surely I will weep as little and laugh as much as possible, whether it makes me fat or thin . . .
> A pious Quaker father past his prime, on good terms with his wife, has been discovered after months assiduously engaged in the monstrous act of seducing a girl of 14. The true cause of this maniacal rashness seems to be the pestiferous influence of novel reading. His wife has long taken this trash from circulating libraries, and for relaxation he has copiously imbibed of its poison . . .

— As if Prospero had waved his wand, and the terrors were exorcised — out of us. Novels, the Devil, Sibyl, drink, labeled and in place: beware the pestiferous causes.

Poor Sibyl. Dreams had made her the monster of which, as with all infection, she was only another victim.

4 ~ She's a Driver

The plane took the runway south. It seemed with the body's beginning to travel, the mind had already arrived. The surprise might have been that his aunt's accident had waited until now, that her supreme gesture of independence, her driving, had not long ago become the pit into which she had fallen.

Was she a type of something — the South, decadence? What could eccentricity typify but itself? "You, with your historical trends and bridges between shores; it's poppycock; she's Betsy Byrne, or if anything else, she's old; age is ubiquitous." The skeptical voice, to which the other answered: "Yes, but there are trends: species, entelechy, *Zeitgeist,* styles. Madmen have represented history. There are drifts in the particular, symbolic riders, always doubtful, always *there* . . . "

There she was over the decades, from that time two generations ago, when she got her first bouncy little red Dodge and learned, more or less, to jerk it around town, swerving and stalling, but never stripping the gears, never, by some ludicrous chance, traffic being thin and slow, quite hitting anything; until she was cited in the newspaper among Delta wonders: "Miss Betsy Byrne has driven the same car fifteen years and never had an accident" — she ignoring the touch of malice, so confirmed in her self-esteem, she never saw the other cars slam on brakes when she strayed to the wrong side of the road, or heard the horns and cries as she stalled at intersections — fell out in fact with one of her friends for venturing to warn her at a cross street of an approaching car, turned on her furiously with: "You let me drive, will you? I'm perfectly capable." And never took her out again.

She bounced that Dodge over town, her little form puffy and pasty-fleshed, streaked with powder as if she'd thrown herself in the flour barrel, and wearing the black lace of what amounted to a perpetual mourning (the clothes, it seemed, along with the mother's opinions and everything else but her meticulous housekeeping, taken over from her and enlarged); they were together in the car, that arrogant Kentucky belle, blind now and fierce, a mere wasp of a woman, and beside her the daughter, pasty-fat, propped up with pillows beneath and behind, so that she seemed in her bosomy inflation to be blown up against the wheel, that wheel which always, in the nervously energetic manner of her walking and talking (tiny fretful steps and short exclamatory sentences full of so's and very's), she jiggled and wiggled from side to side, as if the only approved method of driving a car was to keep it swerving like a stalking cat, an unpredictable progress from which it might dart off at any moment in any direction.

Daniel remembered a ride the whole family took, soon after the reconciliation when they tried to be a family and went with both cars on a common outing, this time to the low dam and locks on the Sunflower River, the banks dense with oak forests and the water racing with fish. His father's car had gone in front with the grandmother, Daniel and little Gerald; Aunt Betsy came behind with his mother, Hilda, and her school friend — these consigned in an abortive effort at sociability to the risk of that driving. They were creeping along a narrow strip of concrete road with gravel shoulders, the pride of the country, over the wide flat land through the hot air. The fields of rowed cotton succeeded one another. The bordering masses of wood blended into an horizon on all sides that moved as the cars moved. Now they were bumping down from the concrete ribbon, one wheel on the gravel shoulder, to meet an approaching car; and again on the other side to pass a cotton wagon. Now a couple of cars were coming, and on their side of the road, blocking the shoulder, was a stalled Model T, a Negro peering into the engine. So they had to pull over and wait behind while the other cars got by. The grandmother leaned out in her self-righteous fury and scolded the man: "Why don't you get that wreck off the road?" (Though there was no place to move it to but the flooded ditch.) "As if you had any right to a car I anyway; you Colored Man!"

The concrete road had played out. Also the gravel. Under a summer shower they were crossing a swamp on a built-up hard embankment of buckshot mud. Hilda had shifted to the larger car, pleading car-sickness. So Daniel was on the spot, with his mother. But he liked it. Aunt Betsy, following the Willys Knight, which was already skidding a bit, would slide clear across the road, almost into the ditch. "Whooee! Almost got me that time!" she would shriek, gambling as always against dangerous gods. Flinging the wheel over, she would skid toward the other slippery edge, and there: "Whooee! Almost had me again!" would fling it back as before.

Thus she graduated from the Dodge to her second car. The mother was dead now; the daughter lived on in the stingy solitude the old woman had spun her in. A black robed, graying form, propped up, her pinch-nose glasses on her head, she went swerving at somewhat faster clip in the green Buick. She was more forgetful of the gears, would put on the brakes without the clutch and jerk to a stall, or start from a stop without shifting out of high. The fenders too were showing signs of the increased hazards of the road. Her sight was worse, at night impossible, but she refused to surrender the wheel to anybody, nephew, brother, hired help or friend — assured, even as she scraped and dented the cars parked by the curb, of the matchless skill of her newspaper-cited handling.

Daniel remembered: on a summer's visit how she had driven him to tea with one of her friends, the Impeccable, and finding the house on the left, had crossed over the crowded street and parked in the wrong direction, and then starting up afterwards, had gone ahead on the left, the cars honking at her, until she reached the corner, where the sign forbade a U turn, but she made one anyway, beginning on the left of the road and swinging clockwise, to wind up still on the wrong side, going the other way, while traffic in all four branches stopped dead, honking.

Her reputation went on increasing, deepening the irony of that first citation, as police fines and revoking of licenses failed to arrest the always more perilous trajectory. The law knuckled under, as it will in the deep South before the defiance of female eccentric age.

Her driveway backed onto Bolivar, one of those more and more trafficked ways, into which, without warning or a rear-ward glance, she would come tail-first any hour of the day or night, bumping over the sidewalk and roughly hacked-out curb, between concealing masses of crape myrtle bushes, backing into the road and cutting left or right, in either case occupying both lanes, stalling as a rule before she could shift gears and grind off to a jerky forward — why she had grown as famous in the town as the Sirens or Scylla in the legends of the Greeks, one of those father-to-child expounded dangers of the place .

He remembered about then, with the wartime influx of airmen to the base, overhearing (it was at a summer party, and a native youth had come back in uniform, with his northern wife) the wife complaining — for they lived down Bolivar: "I don't know what to do when I go by that place. Half the time some old woman comes backing out of there. I honk and try to get by, but I don't think she hears me. I get so nervous coming there I start praying: 'Don't let that old woman back out, Lord, don't let her;' because when she backs out I don't know what to do."

"Honey," said the boy, "there's things you've got to learn about this town, and it might as well be now. That old woman you talk about is Miss Betsy Byrne, and when she backs out of that drive, I tell you what you do. You pull clear out of the road, clear out mind you, and cut off the engine. And if you want to go on praying, it can't do any harm."

Miss Betsy sold the Buick and came to the third car, the blue Studebaker with the automatic shift. That took care of the shifting and stalling — which was better and worse, for in her increasing feebleness and diabetic forgetfulness, she might have had to quit driving if she'd gone on struggling with a clutch and gears; but with this car all she had to do was give it the gun and it would go; and she gave it more gun than she should, and more often.

Though she did cut out the night business. "No," she would say, "I'm afraid I don't see very well at night." She wouldn't tell you how she learned that. It was one fall evening on her way home from visiting a country friend. The best she could do at night was to follow the red taillight of the car in front of her, but this turned out *to* be a cotton picker, working late. When it left the road and veered into the field, she lit out after it down the embankment, and mired in the furrow; so they had to get a tractor to haul her out. "I don't like to drive at night," she would say shaking her head. "My eyes are getting bad." But of course she was perfectly competent in the daytime.

It was no longer the pneumatically inflated form propped up and juggling the wheel with excess of energy. She was actually lean —the surplus that had fattened her gone to blood sugar. The hollow face, as the outward energy decayed, was assuming by sheer loss the secret fierce demonism of the mother. The pillows had long since disappeared. She was unbuoyed, shrinking down into the seat almost out of sight, the eyes too, retiring into the sunken face. Yet still she drove around to her houses, collected rents, or sometimes, when they were threateningly overdue, paid the bills for water, light and gas.

By now her glasses were recurrently lost in the house which had become a quicksand of objects stored and misplaced, into which anything laid down sank without trace, so that though she bought a new pair every few months, she was mostly without, and couldn't see to read her mail or the newspaper, or to transact the simplest business or maintain the necessary checks on an environment that would otherwise, from carelessness if not design, cheat, bungle and overcharge at every turn of the road.

She came into the water office with a purse full of random bills paid and unpaid and asked the clerk to put them in order and tell her what she owed on all her houses. "I can't do it," she said; "I'm ashamed of myself; I've always done it; but now I can't see."

"Why, Miss Betsy," they said, "if you can't see, how'd you get down here?"

"Oh that's nothing," she said. "I drove my car."

And when one of the crew of bosom or bosom-fallen friends she had gossiped and quarreled with since childhood and written cards to on all her bus tours over the nation, asked her in the same connection: "But Betsy, if you can't see, how on earth do you drive?" she had countered (one could have thought a year and never have hit the answer that flowed off her tongue with the bright unassailable defiance of her being): "Well, I only drive out on bright days . . . "

Daniel kept his eyes on the window as the power thrust bore him back into the seat. The ground whirred. The bumping and lurching went air-smooth. Descents and returns stretched in a series back into childhood, indistinguishable. It was here, settling towards the delineations of the city, that he had laid aside the Delta after the last return, here, where he shouldered it again, the buildings going gray in the mist below him.

And now, like one of those things called up in the mind where it had waited all along, unnoticed, as if you were sitting in a twilight room and a voice sounded, and you would turn, startled, and see by the window a form emerging, the puffy po-white form and pasty scar-cheeked face, one eye knocked asquint in some undivulged feat of heroism or folly, a look not unkind, but shifty — Daniel had said on the phone he did not know the Colesons, but he only needed the connection to bring it back: Bud Coleson, like something transported from Dickens down the Mississippi, over the gullied clay hills to the Depression Delta, and slowly in the war boom that followed, finding work, claiming to be a plumber, though he might as well have said electrician, or carpenter, or jack of all trades, earning enough at least for himself and his leathery, lean, officious wife and increasing family of kids, and then by the chance of renting one of Miss Betsy's houses, coming, out of fondness, and self interest too, that loyalty of the Southern poor to some heir of tradition and pride they serve, yet hope one way or another to get something out of, becoming her hanger-on, fixer of all breakages and shiftless maintainer of her property — Bud Coleson, the man, and now the voice, the drawling low voice: "Yes sir, Miss Byrne's a driver; she's quite a driver."

That had been when Daniel first found out anything about his aunt's property. She had been secret as the grave until a year ago when she broke down and said things were vacant and she couldn't get around the way she did, she wished he'd see what should be done. So he went to the insurance company for the list.

"Daniel," said Mr. Laurence in his doddering old voice that had been too soft years ago, and that got more secret as he got older, until you had to lean forward saying: "What's that, Mr. Laurence? I can't hear you."

"Daniel, I wish you'd think about the insurance your aunt's got on those houses. She won't listen to me, but something's got to be done."

They took the schedule and drove around. First they parked on Walnut Street. "You see that, Daniel? She's got that house insured for twenty thousand dollars, a four-apartment house, it says, furnished. I like the premiums, but my company won't let me keep that house insured that way. And the furniture for five thousand. There's not a stick of furniture in it. It's been vacant three years, every window is broke and the doors are off the hinges. And now the roof is falling in. That's not a house, that's a ruin.

"I tell you how it is, Daniel." He lowered his voice as if this one was too hot to bear repetition.

Daniel crowded up: "Louder, Mr. Laurence, I can't hear you."

"You know Miss Betsy's not as clear as she once was. She's been after me to sell some of her property. Well, I had a good offer on this lot — three thousand — because nobody's going to buy it except for the lot.

"'Mr. Laurence,' she said to me, 'don't talk nonsense. I want to sell that house, I don't want to give it away. I wouldn't take a bit less than twenty-five thousand dollars for it. That's a big house, with four apartments in it.'"

"'Miss Betsy,' I told her, 'that house is in bad shape. It would take thousands to get it where it would rent, and the best thing would be to tear it down and start over again.'

"'Oh sha! Mr. Laurence,' she said, 'that house don't need a thing but a little paper and paint to spruce it up. That's a fine house. You tell your buyer twenty-five thousand.'"

They drove on. One place Daniel thought he had Mr. Laurence. Two little trailers had been run into the yard behind a duplex house and hitched to the light and plumbing and rented for a while, when you could rent anything. They were a wreck now, the roofs off and weeds inside, and there along the outer wall the boards were charred — My Lord, they were charred; those houses had burned, and they were insured each one for three thousand dollars with their furnishings. "We'll put in a claim right now," Daniel said.

Mr. Laurence shook his head. "Those trailers fell apart," he whispered. "They were empty for years and the boys tore 'em apart. They weren't insured against boys. Then the grass was burned and that smoked the walls. Burning weeds is what did it. You couldn't collect on 'em. They aren't worth insuring."

"Look here, Mr. Laurence, you can't have it both ways. If they can be insured they can be collected on, and if they can't be collected on, she shouldn't have been paying premiums all these years."

"I been telling her to drop those premiums, haven't I?" Mr. Laurence almost raised his voice. "You know she won't change a thing. That's why I had to talk with you. It's doing her no good to have insurance on that junk."

"You mean all the premiums she's paid are lost, and she couldn't collect if the houses had burned?"

"If she'll cancel the insurance, I'll get her back some of the premiums. I told her so, but she won't sign a thing."

In desperation Daniel went to the colored houses, which were at least rented. At the first house, he got on the trail of Coleson. The tenants all knew Daniel, even when he didn't remember them. This was Winnie Bloomer, as broad as she was tall, with a droll face, elfish, no doubt, in her youth, but spread now into the likeness of a great frog. She worked for Lawyer Hargreaves and was one of the best cooks in town.

"Misser Dan," she said, "you see those steps? I hate to fall down and break a leg on those steps. Can't you get me some new boards there? And I wish you look at my bathroom. Mr. Coleson pertend to be fixin me a bathroom. He a nice man, but he don't know no thin tall bout no bathroom. He done got it so low you have to go down squattin, like dis here."

She went backing off from him, bent over, bracing herself with one hand on the chair, her belly swagging between her knees, breasts like hams, the monstrous buttocks going lower and lower, as she heaved and grunted with the strain, looking up at' him with grotesque, unvoiced question. "Yes suh," she said, "you have to go way down on that bathroom. It's a mess."

The word bathroom had thrown him at first, but the demonstration was enough. He walked around to the outhouse, a latrine once, fitted up now with water as the city required. (That was during the campaign of a few years back when Segeen Wright was engineer, and the local paper had written: "We believe this situation is going to get cleaned up, because Segeen Wright is in charge, and as everybody knows, he is not the kind of a man to let his end drag.") So Miss Betsy had dug up a secondhand toilet with a long pipe and pull-chain, and Mr. Coleson had set it in "a chunk of cement before he thought about flooring the place. He built the floor in afterwards, running from the sill of the door, which was six inches off the ground, back around the toilet base, the boards cut out hit-or-miss to fit there, so what was left of the toilet was not a foot high, like a toadstool half our of the ground.

Winnie flung open the door, turned to Daniel and wrinkled her fat face: "Dah," she said, slapping her thigh. "You laughin, Misser Dan. Ain't dat sumpin? Mr. Coleson call that a bathroom. He the limit. You got to go way down . . ." And she backed off again, squatting. Daniel left her with promises.

Late in the afternoon, at the last shotgun house, he found Bud Coleson putting on a ripped-off screen door. He had rebuilt the door partly with the old wood that would go to pieces in no time, partly with patches of the lowest grade of splitting pine. Now he was screwing it on the jamb, but he had set it so low there was an inch above where flies and mosquitoes could make a freeway, and the thing was dragging at the bottom, so there was no way to open it over the rough floorboards without catching it again and ripping it off the hinges.

"Hadn't you better put it higher?" Daniel asked.

"Should be a mite higher, I reckon," said Mr. Coleson; "but 'tain't worth movin now."

"I'd move it though," said Daniel. "It'll get ripped up that way. Why don't you set a board under it while you screw it on, and then when you're done it'll be off the floor?"

"Sure," said Mr. Coleson, "ony I didn't find a board handy."

Daniel looked under the house. There were two bundles of termite eaten flooring. He pulled out a board. "What's all that lumber doing under there, anyway?"

"Lumber?" said Coleson. "Oh, that. Gonna be used to fix the floorin. It should a been did before now, but I haven't got to it, ony workin nights and on weekends."

So they unscrewed the door and in three minutes reset it, while Mr. Laurence stood by and watched. He was one of those planter offshoots who had taken up insurance in the Depression, — and you'd no more have expected him to screw on a door or drive a nail, even into his own house, than you'd have expected an angel to hoe cotton.

But he went on talking, in his dying tones, to' be cranked up now and then by Daniel's proddings. And being agent also for Miss Betsy's automobile policy, he mentioned her driving:

"You know, Daniel, she oughtn't to be allowed in that car. They tell me the police have taken her license away, but she goes right on. If my company finds out about it, I'll have to snatch that policy out from under her."

It was Mr. Coleson's turn: "Sho nuff, Daniel" (they called him by the first name like a boy, because his aunt did, and in fact the whole town), "she ought to be kep off the road."

"Who's going to keep her off?" said Daniel. "I can't, and you can't, and I don't imagine the law can, either."

Mr. Coleson shook a gray face: "No, I reckon she'll keep on. But she ought to be stopped. She's liable to git killed.

"It was jest yestiddy I was comin from work and I see Miss Betsy limpin toward her driveway, the car grindin like a sawmill. She went out wide like she was going to turn in, but it wouldn't turn, so she angled across traffic slow and parked against her curb headin the wrong way, where you can't park anyway, even headin right. I said: 'Now, Miss Byrne, they're goin to give you another ticket parkin there. Why don't you go in the driveway?' And she said: 'I can't turn in. I don't know what's the matter with it, but it won't turn.' So I looked under it and the steerin rod was bent all out of shape. 'Who'd you hit, Miss Byrne?' I ast her. 'You've done hit somethin.' 'No,' she said, 'I never hit anything at all. I backed over some trash up there and a stick or somethin caught in it.' 'No stick goin to bend it like that,' I said. 'Where was that trash?' 'Oh back yonder a piece'; she waved her hand. I figgered it must be at them nigger houses of hem back up Bolivar. I got a hammer and straightened out the steerin rod. Then I put her car in the drive and turned my truck around and went up there. There was a nigger in front of the first house. 'Did Miss Betsy Byrne run over some trash up here?' 'Trash?' he said. 'She run over a plow.' She had backed plumb up over the curb and onto the yard and gone clean over the plow backard and forrard and drug it a considerable piece, trying to turn around, and not even knowed what she hit. Yes sir, Miss Byrne's quite a driver. If you don't look out, she'll git killed."

They had all cautioned and warned, but she had gone on with her jaunty reply: "I only drive out on bright days." Except the Sunday she drove herself to church, her friends having phoned they would come for her, but she unwilling to depend on anybody but herself — that day seems not to have been quite bright enough. So she moved toward the intersection where blindness, eccentricity and defiance of age limitation and law, baited their traps against her.

Which was it that prompted her to drive through the stop light at that busiest corner? Had the newfangled green arrow for the right turn, beckoning simultaneously with the flaring red, blurred on the merely physical organ? Or was she thinking of those houses vacant and falling to pieces, on which she was always waiting for some tomorrow when she would wake with the old energy and get them spruced up and rented again?

Or was it a temporary shock from the diabetes and too much or too little insulin? For she injected herself whenever she thought of it, or when she could find one of countless old needles mislaid, or get out to buy a new one; and if the insulin so taken was irregular and the doses at best guessed at and blindly groped for, the food which was to have balanced it was even more haphazardly administered, cooked up for herself — opened from any of the rusty cans that had accumulated through the years in the pantry, and mixed with old rice or com meal or grits left in five-gallon glass screw-top jars by the mother, and now so moldy that the malodorous unscrewing of the lid would have turned any stomach but hers — fried on the stove that had lost its oven door and had no broiler, so the only place to cook was on top, and the only utensil any way operant (the rest on the floor under the sink or stove rusted out and filled with dirt and spider webs) was a clumsy skillet with a convex base, which would have been rusty too if it hadn't been protected any time this last fifteen years with a deep layer of roach-traversed rancid grease, into which she had thrown her bacon, eggs, stale rice, grits, old canned tomatoes, whatever else she could locate, to fry on the back-burning leaky jet and call it a fit diet for one not only afflicted with diabetes, but guessing at the doses of insulin required — would it be any wonder if returning from the new church at the edge of town (if a body couldn't pray with any better success than that, Daniel thought, why bother?) she should miss a red light, or a dozen of them?

Or could it have been her determination to pay no attention to these novel devices and changing rules of the aftercomers to a town she had once been at the center of? She did not submit to any of their regulations. "Young man," she told the cop who whistled at her for jumping a red light, "don't you ever let me catch you blowing that whistle at me again!" — bawling him out while the traffic waited.

She would never put a coin in a parking meter, and the police, after leaving her summons after summons and revoking her license with no effect, had got to where they recognized her car, and left it alone, even the immigrant greenhorns on the force, admired her in fact, as officials with any of the unregenerate man in them always will those who ignore or defy their social rigmarole: "Hello, Miss Betsy. You know you should put a coin in that meter. That's what it's there for."

And she with a start: "Is there a meter? I didn't know. We never had meters in town before. So many changes. Well, I only parked for a minute."

"That's all right, Miss Betsy," he would say. "How you feelin?"

Worst was along the main avenue of the town. In the old days it was wider than the traffic needed, and cars parked diagonally to the curb. But as traffic increased one had to park alongside, as in most places, and the marks and meters were spaced that way. But she would never do anything but slant her nose in to the curb as she had done for twenty years. Maybe it was inability (power and will being hard to separate), since she could hardly have wormed into one of those marked-off lateral spaces if she had tried — backward or forward. But she never tried. So it was defiance as much as incapacity. And when the police took after her about it, it was the same story, call it intransigence or failure to understand what was being talked about: "No, officer, I never park that way. I've parked like this all my life, and I'm going to keep right on."

"Well, Miss Betsy, you know you're supposed to get up there inside those lines and put a coin in that meter."

She: "I can't see the lines. They change the lines all the time. So many changes. I'm too old to change now. But I won't blame you. You're new to the force, aren't you? How is Judge Harper? Give him my best."

Judge Harper had been dead for years.

So it might have been sheer intransigence, one could not tell. And of course she would remember nothing. She would not have seen the car coming fast from the left strike her amidships, stave in the door and the whole driver's side of the car, tear the seat assembly from its moorings, burst out the opposite door with the thrust, and hurl her, along with the seat, clear of the car, through the air and onto the pavement on the far side — except she would fall half on the seat, and so preserve herself for what the phone call had announced to Daniel a thousand miles away in the quiet of Woodruff Farm . . .

Announced: and initiated this voyage, through a window of which he peered, observing: the plane's reflected interior, lights, travelers. Also the self: mouth, nose, eyes, separate pools of vision. Approach. They merge: one cave of sight, one great cyclopean eye. That is what you see through. And what you see is a tundra of cloud, from which the Appalachians roll up in long folds and ridges.

The conjunction caught him. He remembered a pool, not one of those cloudy blue-holes of the Delta, but away from there, on a summer trip long ago, in the Ozarks perhaps, or these Appalachians — clear water between rocks, a surface of mirrored limestone and trees, a sky broken with leaf shapes.

From the branches something falls to the water, insect or seed pod, sending out luminous ripples, a diverging iris, into which rises a vortex of flesh, subliminal Grendel through a plane of reflected earth, defining the complementarity: facet and depth, pattern and *dynamis* . . .

What energy was stirring under that mottled surface of a world, cresting beneath him like a wave?

5 ~ The Dark Love

Long ago he had known that his life must wear the aspect of
two landscapes superimposed, as if the foreground were Poussin or
Claude, luminous, calm, and behind it El Greco — that turbulence
through this peace. And now with the propellers' motion (the plane
lifting up and setting its nose on one after another of countless impal-
pable cloudy rests) foreground and background were changing places:
the boiling colors of blood, slate blues, copper greens, zigzagged at the
lines of collision with sulphur lightnings flaming in the darker flame;
were coming forward, surrounding him; and beyond, receding into a
dream, were pastel geometries of hills against a classic sky.

And of course the two profiles were there, the two women, spirits of the place: he and Sibyl on the winds of hell, and juxtaposed,
Lucy — the healing that was dawn on the shores of purgatory, and
might be something of the empyrean. But as he tried to focus on the
foreground which he had just left — the gray-green smiling eyes and
mouse-blond hair, the little widow's peak — all that escaped him. He
was inundated under black waters of hair turnbling from the other
to him, over him, about him, as the Nofretete form with the slim
conical breasts bore down, covering him in its sway.

He was ready to admit that the heart is always suspended, like the
world between Yin and Yan, the psyche between love and destruction.
There were poles of energy, the leaf and the flame — the rush of entropy
and whatever counterurge buttresses against the stream. Everywhere

the primal cleavage reappeared: plant and animal, grazers and hunters. When he was a boy, the ambivalence had shown itself in woman.

A summer afternoon. His mother had read to him for a while, *Myths of the Golden Age.* Memory reinforced by photographs presented her, sometimes standing, especially by the river, or on their summer trips looking over the sea, tall and serene, in the Greek style gown she or the age inclined to; or they would be sitting together, the long oval of her face lifted, as it had been that afternoon, when he begged for entertainment and she read, and then recited some of the poems she loved, "Daffodils" and "To Night," her eyes filled with the mystery that removed her from the world — until finally, having things to do, she told him to go out and pull grass for the guinea pigs.

It seemed he had spent a third of his waking childhood pulling grass for those squeaking animals. He went out, and found Sarah, the mulatto woman they had working for them, already there, cleaning the runways and giving the pigs fresh water. He came up behind her and sat down listlessly, pulling the long Bermuda grass that grew by the flowerbed.

Then he looked up.

Sarah was doubled over from the hips, her legs spread, knees bent, not asquat, but almost, scrubbing the fouled concrete with a bristle brush. Her dress stood out in a cone, wide of the mark. What he saw almost alarmed him, a medical anomaly, an unnatural wound — like a whirlpool under a matted rock, so drawing, the soul flung out arms to lay hold on the tangled roots of some fig tree over the abyss.

Two thoughts struck him: of birth (for the swaying pocket seemed ready at any moment to be reamed out by a full-sized issuing human head) and of begetting; while the latter entrained its fierce speculation — his eyes groping the furrowed dark, his thought measuring beside it his own diminutive whiteness – like throwing a bean into a lion's mouth, or as the Negro tale had it: "Rastus, how does you content that woman?" "Well suh, Ah jus sticks in mah haid an wiggles mah years . . ."

He had experienced them both. It was not a question of skin color. His mother had given birth, and this one had crooned lullabies. It was a tossup which he had seen. And whatever names one used — ideal mother and earth-maw — did not signify, or explain how the loves of his youth and maturity were alternations in that field — changes from light to dark and back to light — yet each gathering more of the antithesis into itself — weaving.

No doubt there was a proper order of time. Taken first, the devouring love could be carried along, a serum against later infection. As he told a poet friend who had married a motherly gentle girl and then gone wild for a guitar-playing siren, and who came to him, as to a man divorced, for sympathy and advice: "How can I advise you? You've got the whole thing exactly backwards."

But nobody can be cocksure of his immunity. After all these years, what was throwing him back, into the sphere of that influence, that power sweeping over him, rising to such a resonance?

Two things, right and left, both coming into focus at the window —

He did not have to turn his head to fix on the right-hand one or smile to invite her; she was already leaning across him to look out, the passenger he had not previously examined, a young woman, redolent of desire and a vague perfume. Having seen whatever trout of the depths she was hunting for, she drew back into her plate, giving him her eyes: "I'm sorry," she murmured.

While he, between defense and generosity: "Won't you take the seat by the window?"

Generosity, because it was his way to throw himself into situations as into a mountain stream, and on journeys most of all, islands in time, to welcome the castaway. But he was also tugging at the reins, since reason went into operation with the impulse, telling him he had seen something like this before: "Yes," he thought, "this is where I came in" — stems of the old bungles buried in time, sending up shoots again; so the only small progress was like that of a rat in a maze, a series of particular avoidances, to board up some openings and mark them with a sign: "Tried, and not worth it." For she was obviously calling.

He had only to go to a little theater in New York or Washington, or to any of those smart stores of the Georgetown variety featuring local avant-garde artists, to observe the type, meeting a lover-boy or strolling in search of a soulmate — that was the style of her looking, this woman, as obviously divorced as the aunt he was going to see was an old maid, divorced or ready to be — while Daniel hammered the sign on the alleyway: "Tried, and proved BLIND."

Ten years of burning blindness.

(The stage had been set long before, that void between Emily and Ginny; now the cue was spoken; and who should appear from behind purple hangings but his queen of sorrows — call her the first synthesis — Sibyl.)

Such dark windows of eyes had declared her his almost at the first moment of her walking, beautiful and sober, with a husband obviously drunk and obviously estranged, into the party his father's friend Major Evremond had given in Daniel's honor at the officers' quarters of the old fort on the outskirts of New Orleans. He was staying there a few days before sailing on a freighter for his art fellowship in Rome. Sibyl was one of those women whose hearts do not open halfway, and he at that stage of absorbing Blake and believing impulse-is-all, when nothing seems more tiresome than the moderation that is partly dead: "Those who control desire do so because theirs is weak enough to be controlled."

She spent most of the evening on a footstool at his feet or on the sofa by his side. Later they crossed the columned court to the levee and sat on a stone bench over the river, which was sweeping boats, barges, lights, under the moon and stars to the sea.

He sailed in possession of kisses, tears, protestations, everything but his chief need, the enjoyed flesh of a mistress; though there would be schemes for that, or rather, as romantic love required, for marriage: pressed flowers, letters, eternal vows, a gray feather a dove dropped as it flew past, which she had wished on and passed to him for his wishing, which he tucked in his drawer, a keepsake to be sighed over, sentimental as a girl — until she would break away and join him, leaving the poor chump of a husband to drink himself under the heaviest of tables, one of those marble raised tombs of flood-plain New Orleans.

She had a fair income as long as she did not marry. It was spring in Rome. Could a better arrangement have been found for two people needing to exercise their passions? Or a woman more richly abandoned, to give an arrogant young artist the Francesca he required? Later, when they were fighting over the child, he would stand in his rented room like a man gone crazy — or at last painfully sane — hammering his head with his fist and mouthing in his father's style: "God crucified! how dumb can you get, not to know the difference between romance and marriage, or that if nothing is better for the violent young than to get experience on each other's flesh, nothing is worse than to cloak it under a sacrament, to bring actual children into the pretense of a home, subjecting them and society to the miscarriage of your blundering chemistry?"

For they had quarreled from the first. He thought of her as possessed, not knowing how far he possessed everything, merely by his way of being: the books he read were the great books, the pictures he enjoyed the great pictures, he had no patience with any others; he would have no radio, no records but of early music, no liquor but wine; she must scorn movies and society as he scorned them; and he would hardly go out without a book in his pocket or a sketch pad in his hand.

Fights, voluptuous returns: "He was sorry," and she: "She was to blame, he was a saint, a god." But when the wildness of their relation had almost torn it to pieces, what did poor Sibyl imagine but the impossible white-picketed lawn and tidy bungalow in wooded suburbia, and a man entirely hers; so blaming the tension of two Roman years on their chief blessing, that unmarried condition, what did she require but to throw off income and everything, to settle down and keep house on what Daniel could earn, to get children, not just to talk about it, but swell and be gravid, worry about one's looks, to have morning sickness and varicose veins; and what should he do but plunge in with open eyes, guessing the future but saying with the reckless pride of all romantics: "I can take anything" — though years later, in the solitary room, beating his head with his fist or against the wall, he would ask: "Yes, but could she, could the child betrayed before it was born, could society, the country, the time-tormented gods?"

Because marriage had not helped.

And that settling down, not in wooded suburbia, but in the hillbilly southern town, on a teacher's pittance, those weary years of the war — could that have solved anything? Ozark College: how they went out one winter night, walking to a concert already late, Daniel holding Sibyl's arm over the slick places, but at the same time drawing her forward, until the furies came between them, apologies boomeranging into fresh rounds of the fight. How she broke away and ran, but fell with a groan on her great belly, and he in a storm of penitence kneeled above her, as if he had killed her and the child, but she pushed him away: "Don't hurt me any more than you have already. Go away; let me alone." Yet if he had gone the blame from her and himself would not have been less but more.

It was at this time that he noticed the increase in her fears. Her mother used to threaten her when she ran away from home with tales of a wicked house where men would pen her up and do nasty things. And a nursemaid had told her something of a bloodsucking erotic Dracula. One night early in the summer, before the screens were put in, she had waked with what must have been a Luna moth flopping around the room. Perhaps she had been dreaming of the other, perhaps the whole thing was half dream; but by her account the great fuzzy thing flew down in the moonlight beating at her throat.

After all, she had come to him in fears. First it had been her husband, the silent man with heavy brows — a hunter too, and the house filled with guns and knives — of whom she had been afraid; and she had spun the web so convincingly in the tears that fell by the turbulent river that Daniel had taken it at face value, had carried her alarm with him to Europe. Though, as it turned out, it was the man who died, if not by knife or gun.

When she joined Daniel abroad the fears had withdrawn to their sleeping center. The trivial sally into common life was the apprehension of being spied on, so that even their kissing had to be hid. Daniel entertained no extravagant hopes of marriage, but he had assumed this one worry might let up when their couplings were legitimatized.

But as her pregnancy advanced, she would wake in the little apartment where they slept in the double bed, wake from nightmares, clutching him in terror; and sometimes it would be the landlady crouched at the paper-thin partition listening for their stirrings, or to pick up hints of the earlier marriage Sibyl tried to keep buried; or a more sinister male figure would be hunched at the window threatening enormities, or the spider would have crawled out into the room and Daniel would have to get up and turn on the light to show there was no such thing hanging in the corner over her head; but still she would not be sure, and when the light had gone off it would have to be flicked on again for the same demonstration. After her fall, which did her no physical harm, other worries appeared, fears the child had been killed, that it would be born maimed — new fears which merged, as she approached her time, with the vampire, the gossipy spies, the armed man.

She had a long hard labor. Daniel tried to read to her, but she could not fix her mind on anything he inclined to. She had returned to a childlike dependency (one of her disarming recurrences), her face in its Madonna mood, an oval of mourning beauty, a Florentine Mary who foresees her sorrows. Daniel sat with her for hours, mostly in silence; they held hands, waiting.

After the birth she could not sleep. Her wishes began to pin themselves on going back to that grim little apartment where they had never been happy, but which beckoned now, a place of privacy and rest. With wide eyes she motioned him close: he had to take her from the hospital; the doctor was plotting against her, the nurse would not bring her the child, they were going to take it away. He must get her home where they would be safe.

He took her as soon as he could, with a day nurse to look after the baby. But still she did not sleep. And now the landlady and the man at the window and the spider came from the shadows, began to ally themselves with the harsh-voiced nurse, all plotting against the baby, making Sibyl nervous, spoiling her milk. The baby got colic and cried until it was put on the bottle.

When Sibyl picked it up, she trembled for fear of dropping it or sticking it with diaper pins; yet she wouldn't trust it with anybody else. She must have thought it was like the flame of a candle everybody is huffing at, or like the child in a fairy tale that will die from the prick of a needle. The third day at home she dropped it indeed, taking it slippery from the bath, having told the nurse to leave it alone; she dropped it with a thud and it cried a long time. The candle was not blown out, not much dampened; but Sibyl went to pieces.

There must have been a corner of sanity left in her, because she consented to go away. For weeks Daniel rode to the private sanatorium to see her, but always found her worse. Now it was these doctors who were practicing against her, and what she accused them of (whispering with backward glances) were the perversions she might have been used for in that nasty house where her mother had threatened bad girls would be shut away. At the crisis she would not eat or speak; she could only sit staring with eyes of accusation, sobbing and twisting her dress. Until the doctors advised him to stay away.

Slowly she began to mend, but from that time on there was a sense in which Daniel had become the enemy, the one who has spied and knows too much, the man at the window with knife or gun. And though he could hardly have admitted it, even to himself, there was truth in that. He had spent more than four years in Sibyl's college, and he must have begun to wonder when the diploma would be conferred.

Of course, one can always learn more, or learn again. As now from the woman at his right leaning over him, the same offer was being made, the door opening for another lesson, assuming another was required: CLASSROOM AVAILABLE. Thank you!

But that was only one of the forces meeting at the round plane window, the crosscurrents driving toward Sibyl, this woman smiling as she withdrew was the right-hand influence, but the landscape itself, to which Daniel, carried in the woman's wake, leaned, was the other, the left, and sinister.

They had launched out over the mountains, and there it lay, between thunderheads, the Appalachian Art School, in the valley by a dammed lake, the long dormitory; the dining and lecture hall, with faculty cabins trailing up the stream into the woods. Closing his eyes he could have felt his way in the dark up those paths, or looking down with eyes open have named the peaks, traced the walks, the trail tunneling through rhododendron, where he had gone with Marlene, the pasture under Spruce Knob where he found Sibyl with Heinrich; that was the setting for the final act. His term with Sibyl had been ten burning years, years of war and shifting jobs — from Rome to Ozark College, then east to the city and out to Appalachian, a single summer, the ninth, but enough — the disruption of that rank affair.

It was a place made for disruption, a school of European exiles and American misfits, expatriots come home — "to Carthage I came, burning." All the factions were there: socialists, idealists, opportunists, queers, and at the war's end, when hopes that had pulverized themselves in Europe came here to set up camps and cells, whether in Chicago or New York or out in the mountains, last rallying places for those inflammable dreams.

And, by God, how he had rallied! He couldn't, have done it any better if the impulse of fire had been what he was born to yield to. Had not the passionate Marlene, on whom he was to prove the contention, told him so?

They were standing in line to give blood. It was a self-help school, so everybody had to take a turn in the kitchen, and for that the state required a Wassermann. The nurse was ramming the needle into each sufferer's arm, pulling out the plunger and copping her test tube full of blood. When she came to Daniel; she jabbed it in and started to draw the plunger, but the whole thing came apart; the washer slipped off the plunger, the plunger fell out, blood spurted over the nurse and the others. "You see," Marlene told him, "you can't even give blood like other people, but there has to be a mixup and explosion."

That was after his diary had been confiscated by the students, precipitating a row that might have shaken the place apart, except the plate was used to such shakings, one could almost say it thrived on them . . .

Where to begin? There was no thread to catch hold of in the jumble, to pull out, leading from one thing to another in an ordered progression. It seemed the character of his life and thought to knot and coagulate this way — like catching a snag fishing and heaving up the bottom of the lake. Perhaps it was that which had driven him into painting, to exhibit the tensile field in simultaneous exposure; as the map of corrugate sinuations over which the plane's shadow was darting, the mountain scene, triggered this tangle of experience. Curious how that labyrinth, remote from him there, had been his, had been him. It was an exotic hothouse where his native violence could go to seed. The entity called Daniel Byrne had engaged in that action, and detaching itself, had entered its later phase. Even those characters lived in another context, requiring not a sequence but a volume — The Death Throes of the West.

Flashes would rise — Vronsky, rival art teacher, with a growing class of summer smart dabblers. Vronsky did not trifle with traditions of art, representational techniques, the great artists. He would set up a broom, broken glass, chicken wire, strips of metal, a tin can; the students would sit around, glancing at his canvas and making scritch-scratch, always scritch-scratch, to be exhibited every week in the dining hall. The power of the great Abstract was its revolt from the bourgeois norm, but for a pack of middle-class Americans who couldn't paint a cabbage to sit around a Russian exile, doing scritch-scratch, seemed laughable. Daniel decided to supply the antithesis. He taught history, skills, disciplines. His classes dwindled. When the faculty met for periodic discussions of results, Vronsky, with glowing satisfaction, would announce of almost every student: "Came with no sense of art, began with academic sketches, by the middle of term understood something of design, before the close was awakened to value and form." While all Daniel could report was: "Might have done better with application," or "Lost interest about mid-term and neglected assignments."

There was only one beside himself who had come from that condition into this, without even a metamorphosis, as much at home in one as in the other. It was von Loewenstein, rock of a lion and a Levite, one of the true Jews, the priestly cast. It was he who had got Daniel invited to the school in the first place, and who was coming to give lectures and concerts there. He was a product of all that European speculation and splintering, but he carried it and contained it, turned it into wisdom — Geist. It was Loewenstein also who would come to Woodruff Farm to be best man at the reconstructive phase, the marriage with Lucy.

When Daniel and Sibyl exhausted Ozark College and moved east, it was the eighth year of their ten. Commuting to the metropolis now, working in war physics, but aiming at art and philosophy, Daniel had gone to a concert (one of those meetings. of the tiny cult in the great city) where a tousle-haired intense sage played the Art of the Fugue. Drawn by the man's face, an amalgam of beast and angel, the mystery of the sphinx with the patience of a Saint Bernard dog, Daniel went up afterwards and asked, in the German he was always practicing, something about predictability and surprise in the fugue and its Hegelian parallel, law and freedom in history. He got such an answer as confirmed his appraisal of the face. When he suggested that they read German together, Hegel or perhaps Goethe: "Both," cried Loewenstein, "both."

Their sessions began, weekly penetrations into the text, then soarings and departures, Loewenstein pacing the book-heaped room, glancing at the floor and ceiling, not absently, but with the determination of a man calling up demons, his face working, his hand tugging at tattered hanks of hair, as in the labor of birth, the words stammered and then rushing out grandly mouthed; it was a droll sight, so droll that Daniel could hardly listen; until he would get up and pace also, his eyes on the floor, and then he could hear only, while insights opened and spread around him like realms of light; for there was no one else who could talk like Max von Loewenstein.

But the others at Appalachian, lord, they grew in a lushness of their own, saprophytes rooted down there, where a blighted chestnut had fallen; they could no more have been transplanted into the present than Indian Pipe into Meryl Woodruff's garden. It was almost absurd to try to pull them up, and yet one must, though they shriek like mandrakes —

"Heinrich! Heinrich!" It might have been Gretchen's cry, but it was Sibyl's. And here came Heinrich Vogel, another of those banished Germans, of the old romantic strain, but fallen — young, wild, disruptive, leaping like a roe or hart onto Sibyl's mountain of spices. For she had made the same mistake twice, gone for the same liberation, only madder and more unstable, a Germanic concentrate! of whatever had first lured her to Daniel and soured her on him by the end.

It was the view of Appalachian that called Heinrich to mind, but he had entered their lives years before, at Ozark College. Exile and flight to America had slowed his formal education; he appeared in the Humanities class; but outside of it, Daniel had learned more from him.

They would sit on a bluff over the fall woods, and as sunset burned on the stream, Heinrich would voice Holderlin's cry for one God-summer: "Nur einen Sommer gonnt ihr Gewaltigen." Daniel would take it up from Faust, the vision of winging after the setting sun; and as he reached the ebb: "Ein schöner Traum," Heinrich Vogel would spring to his feet, spreading his arms against the radiance, crying: "Gefühl, Gefühl ist alles."

Daniel's mother had loved the romantic; that was Daniel's origin. He had left it a while for the primitive and medieval, anything impersonal and sharp. This was his return, to his birthright, in a way to her, though she would have repudiated some of the consequences.

For, of course there were women. To whom Daniel's blend of idealism and innocence made him curiously subject. Also, he was in need. Sibyl would take him imperiously when she wanted to, and then set him wild by days or weeks of denial. Moreover, she was jealous, and long before there was any cause.

Or had there always been cause? Those years of quarrel and agony, when he prided himself on his fidelity, had she seen through all that better than he did, and known he not only wanted loves but was bound to have them? Her intuition must have told her he was waving the unconscious flag. And if he began to back water and hold off, sighing in his pride and virtue, what was that to her? Could it give her the yard and picket fence around the white frame house in the suburbs?

She may not even have realized how hard he backed water. Could anybody have credited how naive he was? He did not know that women will fall for any halfway demonic man, that they had been falling for him since his teens and wanting him to take them, the experienced ones knowing what they wanted and maybe hinting, without getting anywhere, the innocent ones not knowing, and ready to resist a little, but wishing he would begin. And he, being of the innocent, was in their boat, wanting it and half suspecting they wanted it, but not willing to sanction his desire or trust the symptoms of their response. So he hung around, fanning a fire with those asking eyes, never breaking the barrier between small talk and revelation, hand and flesh, lip and lip, member and orifice.

Scores of times it would happen, with students, young teachers, married women, while they were listening to music or walking, swimming or drinking wine at the table, their eyes would meet his and he would be aware: It's a message; I could take her hand under the table, or touch her body swimming, or turn from the sunset and kiss her, or simply say "I want you," and she would yield; she is asking me. Then doubt would come, and he would say: "You damned fool, do you think the whole world is in love with you? You have no notion what she wants, nothing but projections of your own desire." So he would look his longing and they would look theirs, and both sides would go on waiting. But the time was coming when the veil of innocence would inevitably give way here and there, and gradually it would be forced upon him that in almost every case where his prompting had told him such and such, it must have been pretty nearly true. "But haven't you known it for years; surely you must have felt it," one would say, and then another, and finally another. Yes, he had known it for years, if only he had known that he knew. That was why Sibyl had a right to be jealous, though what she accused him of hadn't happened; and besides, if she had the right, it didn't do her much good, since its exercise pushed him toward what supposedly she was trying to avoid.

If this was a Faustian affair, Heinrich was hardly a Mephistopheles — only a companion Faust. Gretchen's, however, were plentiful; they were more or less everywhere. Daniel looked at least as young as his students, and Sibyl's jealousy had already indicated which ones were drawn to him, so it could have been a student; but his moral sense overworked itself in that matter. The students, after all, had not sent themselves to college, it was the parents; one was hired to teach, not to breach them; there seemed to be a contract seduction might betray.

No, his first affair came from an adult class. Adults had enrolled on their own and paid their fee. If one of them wanted to get something in addition to the regular instruction, what was he doing but giving her a bargain? Naturally, he would not have put it that bluntly. Indeed, in a second-string sort of way, he fell in love. And it took years to develop, and always under an accusation which urged in that direction. The woman was about his age, a separated wife, living with her parents at Ozark College and looking after her child. She joined the music and poetry groups forming around Daniel. She was also of German descent, and it was in communion with Goethe: "Nur wer die Sehnsucht kennt, weiss, was ich leide" (None but the yearning heart knows what I suffer), or with the lonely songs of Schubert, that the main damage was done.

They had to be secret, of course; there was not only Sibyl; the girl's husband would have used any evidence against her. And Daniel was just impractical enough, after a summer and glorious fall of weekly hikes and swims and reading poetry and their sighing and dreaming at each other, to break through, Lord knows how, by accident or nudging, to final intimacy at the dead of winter; and for a meeting place they had nothing but the romantic nature they were so fond of, the woods under the clay bluff, with about a foot of snow on the ground and more falling. Though it seemed they could have melted their way through mountains of ice and not have lost fervor; since Sibyl, for all her languorous appeal, was slow at the game, where Manda, his first revelation of what varied delights there were to the palate, was lissome, mobile, quick, and iterant as a young rabbit or sparrow.

That was the first consummation. There were not many more. Not half enough for Daniel to be appeased. Manda's family moved West; she went along to get a divorce. Then she got a job with the Y.W.CA. in social work and stayed out there, even when she had to change jobs because of Sibyl's intervention.

For there were letters. Sibyl got one from Daniel's box at Ozark College about the beginning of summer, when he was no longer going there every day. It was at the same time that she had begun to take so many solitary sunset and moonlit walks — tempting June, when Daniel had only the snows of winter to look back to — that one might have wondered if she was not up to something herself, or perhaps showing it for the first time, since Daniel was home from classes. But he had plenty on his mind already, with her teasing him for weeks: "Tell, tell; why be a coward? Tell the truth; it won't be as bad once you admit it." Finally she made her surprise offer: "You tell me, and I'll tell you." He didn't give it much weight. His trusting her was the overflow of his arrogance: could she love anybody but him? But she kept on: "Tell, and I'll tell. I've been doing something too." While she fondled him.

For of course they were in bed. She had chosen a moment when the revelation might seem a part of sexual play. In the confusion of desire, so toyed with, he confessed. She took it with superior calm: "You see, I told you so." She began to pry into particular details. At last, as if it added to her charm, she told him she had been having an affair with Heinrich for more than a year.

Daniel's first reaction was disbelief. He thought she was teasing. Then she marshaled her documenting particulars. Since she had never been troubled by his jealousy and had been alone as much as she wished, she had not had to fall back on woods in deep snow. She told it like a story from the Decameron, for the titillation of desire.

From his mother Daniel had learned that jealousy poisons the soul. He had thought he was beyond it. He could not have guessed that the fact of infidelity would seize on him with such physical images: Othello's "cistern for foul toads to knot and gender in," would make him ready to destroy what he had presumably loved. After all, he had been unfaithful himself.

Or was it outraged justice, that where he, who had offered Sibyl more passion than she wanted and been tormented from the first by her jealousy, should have done nothing for years, and in fear and trembling seized a brief moment in a snowfield; she, with too little sex to spare, and freely trusted, should have been taking her ease in bed all that time?

She slid beneath him, turning her slow voluptuousness into a taunting demonstration of what she had done; and the acts which talked of might have stirred passion blasted it being real, left him in the withering of desire, impotent, his hands at her throat, her head forced into the pillow; he was strangling her. She gave a choking cry. He came to himself, got up, dressed, left the house, left the town; he just went away.

In the Arabian Nights the king traveling from his wife's adultery takes comfort from other cases. Daniel hitchhiked to the mountains, carrying nothing but a sleeping bag, which he threw down in the fields wherever night took him. Misery is a fraternal order of which Daniel wore the badge. There was the traveling salesman who told how his wife had run off with another man. He had drunk himself almost to death. Then a friend took him to a revival and Christ brought him from the grave. "Brother, are you saved?" But the blood of the lamb did not flow as easily for Daniel; besides, he had to get off at the crossroad. Next was a trucker with bushy brows and hollow eyes. He sized up Daniel's trouble right off, then talked about his own wife: "Sure, feller, she's at home fuckin her ass off right now. She does it whenever she gets a chance. They're all alike. Get some good tail yourself and get her off your mind. You can always get better tail than what a wife will give you."

Daniel spent two nights in the mountains, living on bread and cheese, puffballs and wild strawberries. He slept on a table rock and watched the mists in the morning flow like glaciers through the valley. By that time he was at peace. He hitchhiked home. At peace — though it must be added, he did not intend to cohabit with Sibyl.

When he returned he weakened, because Sibyl was desolate. Heinrich had gone to California to see the Pacific break on the rock headlands. He had some kind of allowance from a Jewish father in Mexico, which he supplemented by picking fruit as a migrant worker or sponging on people he ran into, in the end I camping out on the beach. And being still an enemy alien and neglecting to advise authorities, he got the F.B.I. on his trail. Then one night, for no reason but the love of fire, he kindled a colossal blaze of driftwood, and when the coast guard saw it from miles out at sea and assumed it was some traitor to democracy (if they were right, it was in a subtler sense than they knew) signaling Jap subs, they closed in, and found Heinrich dancing in a loincloth, worshiping the primal god. That was how he landed in jail.

By this time Sibyl was well along toward another depression, sleepless and threatening to kill herself. Daniel went into action, roused a handful of faithful congressmen, his father's old friends, and shortly had Heinrich out of jail and before the court of appeals to pass on his citizenship. Daniel even went to the court as chief witness, and using oratorical powers his father also had left him, achieved extraordinary success."

As he considered the appalling record Heinrich's pursuit of the limitless had made on the page, and asked how a sober judge could be brought to overlook all that, even to sympathize with it, the answer came in a flash: Huck Finn. Every American boy: had shared in that hatred of authority; the cop, the magistrate, the hangman, must have dreamed of life on the river. Heinrich was reconstructed in the Mark Twain image (perhaps they were related historically); and before long, robed authority was laughing at the spectacle of a young man kindling a bonfire on a beach without once thinking of the coast guard, or that his own motives, as a wandering alien, might be doubted. Innocent he was. Fine boy.

"I submit, your Honor, that this kind of impulsive individuality has been the foundation of free America, and remains the life blood of the American dream." Things were put on the right road.

When Daniel got home from the hearing (his new home, that is; he had lately changed jobs and was in the East, grinding at war research), he found a letter from Manda in San Francisco. Another was enclosed, written by Sibyl to the Y.W.C.A. director, the evidence on which Manda had lost her job. It accused her of immorality and of breaking up a happy home.

The home was not made any happier by the rebound of this message. "How can anybody love a person who does things like that," Daniel asked, "at the same time that I've told Lord knows how many lies for your Heinrich?"

"But you like Heinrich," Sibyl said. So he gave up; though he advised her that he was finished with the sexual phase of their relation. }

He might as well have said he was going to give up eating. She took a new tack: tears and penitence, flapdoodle, caresses. Daniel held out. Finally she came into the bathroom when he was drying after a shower, tore the towel from him, went down on her knees, kissing him everywhere, murmuring she loved him, she needed him. Inevitably he responded, and they began again. They even contracted to be faithful to each other. As far as sex went, they never had it so good; though there was always the undercurrent of their hating one another. Perhaps that contributed to the success in so ambivalent an affair.

Winter came, and Heinrich was heard of through friends. He had landed a job as Master of Sports at a junior college. Skating with a boy and girl, he ventured almost to open water far out in the lake, the boy following, perhaps dared to follow. The ice gave way. Heinrich scrambled out, the boy didn't. The school authorities, no doubt, felt the captain should go down with the ship. It was under this new cloud that Heinrich began to wander the world again. And wound up, some time in the spring at Appalachian Art School. Of this, Daniel was not aware.

They called him the "back-door boy." He had persuaded a farmer to let him live ill an abandoned chicken coop up in the mountains. He had a knack for decoration and handicraft, and before long that dropping-littered shanty was a livable place. Then he began to come down to the school and borrow books. Next he sat in on some art classes, and, it was said, tried to seduce the model. Soon he came for a meal or two. At each break — through a mild attempt was made to stop him. Finally he picked a lot of cherries, and taking them to the kitchen, asked the cook to bake him a pie. At this point the Dean served an ultimatum. Heinrich retired to his shack. That was not long before Daniel and Sibyl arrived, with their little girl, a fine example of married bliss, pledged to a renewal of love and constancy.

To do Sibyl justice, she must not have known where Heinrich was. And the summer at the art school was none of her arranging. It had been managed by Max Loewenstein, their new friend — or rather Daniel's friend, since Sibyl did not like him. She played the Madonna role so consistently, it upset her to think anybody had peeped behind the curtain. And Loewenstein was already too close to them not to have had revealing glimpses. At which he had shaken his tattered head, as if that was precisely the way it had to be, and he knew because he had gone through the same thing himself long ago. But Loewenstein was giving lectures somewhere else first and did not arrive until August. By that time Daniel Byrne was the center of an uproar.

As he looked down at the cloud-shadowed foldings of that landscape, the school, the negligible dot on the hill where Heinrich had lived, what stamped it with malign suggestion was his own involvement there. What he had shown himself then, for all his change, must still have its roots in his soul. Sick. . . After nine years together he and Sibyl had swapped infections. He had drunk her jealousy; she had absorbed whatever poison he had married her to unload. But their sickness only made them more a part of that horizon, devils in some hell described by Spengler. That diary Daniel kept on the typewriter in his office, writing at it from time to time, rolling it back into the machine when he went out (until the students saw it and touched off the fireworks), that prying dissection of the place and people — was it a human document? Or how could he have written it?

Strange reports I heard before I came. "So you're going to Appalachian?" a colleague asked me. "I hear the relations between the faculty and student *body* are good there."

On the crowded local train, chugging up into great wooded mountains, were the normal travelers, red-necked farmers, and the others: Scheherazade with sweater tits and yearning eyes, a boy beside her with hair as long as a girl's, strumming on the guitar — as if Greenwich Village had released its ultimate products.

An overblown Jewish girl, Lydia, I accosted in the aisle with the prophecy of her destination, a familiar word that opened me to her. She joined a party the first evening taking a moonlight walk. I felt sprightly, ran up a cliff, climbed a tree or two. We were talking German. She took my arm, pulling me behind the rest, calling me *du*. She wrapped her arm around my waist, whispered me Daniel, and blowing like a porpoise, walled moonlit eyes at me.

My big surprise was to look down the dinner table that day and see Hyde Hanrahan, my best student from Ozark College. He had taken some G.I. money and followed me. He's a big man, but only twenty and without experience of women. He has started out, with a colossal show of stomach, to test every girl in the camp. The other night we had a talk and he gave me the benefit of his researches.

First he tackled a plain sweet girl named Mary, the obvious non-Semite of the community. After a day or two he got the notion she might fall in love with him, so he eased up, his aim being lower. Next he fell on Frieda, the "hint and run" girl. I had thought from the provocation of her remarks she must be as experienced as the Whore of Babylon, but it turns out she is eighteen, perhaps innocent, certainly inept. Hyde went into her room (they all have private rooms), put one hand on her stomach and said: "How does that feel?" "It tickles." He lowered his hand. "How does that feel?" "It makes me want to belch." "And how does that feel?" He lowered it another span. "It makes me want to go to the head" — a term for the toilet stool. "Well go to the head then!" Hyde cleared out.

So he came in another bad moment to light on Lydia. Having seen her in action, I can believe that in less than half a minute the door was locked, the light extinguished and she stretched on whatever couch or divan it is she keeps there. Hyde swore it was with terrible revulsion that he kissed and paddled the creature, but paddle he did, and might even, in the costly itch for knowledge, have gone further, but in a lush moment she fell blowing like a whale (Amen, say I): "I love you, I love you; I've only loved once before, but I love you." At this Hanrahan, who can't take a goose too high, leaped off, the bed, and blurting out that he was a bad man to fall in love with, tore from the room.

A few days later, having got up his courage again, he asked a sturdy Russian Jewess to go nightwalking. He guided her to the deep hole in the creek. On the spur of the moment they agreed to swim nude. A thunderstorm broke, and Hanrahan's first passion was consummated in the flux of water and under barrage of lightning

I ran into Lydia the day after Hyde told me all this, and thought I would get her version. "What do you think of my boy Hyde?" "Hyde Hanrahan?" she cried. "I hate him. I hate men in general. The idea of physical contact with them is repulsive to me. But with Hanrahan I thought I could have a true friendship. Then he tried to ravish me. Would you believe it, he's tried almost every girl in the school. He quotes reams of poetry and then falls on them. I mean really, it's too much. He came to my room yesterday. Before I knew it he had locked the door and turned off the lights. At first I was swayed. He threw me on the bed. Then I fought him off. Now I despise him."

"All right," I thought, "I'm here to teach her." "Look," I said, "if you act the way you did the first night with me, men will think you want something."

She broke into tears. She was not like that at all. She had only loved once and could never love again. He was a college friend, and it had been beautiful, but he was killed. "In the war?" I asked. "No," she said, "he broke through the ice at school."

There are circles in which the same people turn up again and again. "With Heinrich Vogel," I exclaimed.

She staggered. Her hatred of Hyde was nothing to what she felt about Heinrich. How had I known him? What a ghastly coincidence! She began to weep and confess her troubles, adolescent pretenses (though people die of pretenses), feigned Lesbianism and a thousand things. But she tells as much to any patient ear. So my original diagnosis, *nymphomaniac*, has lost its first two syllables. Her father, I observe, is an Analyst.

That was where the page had been left in the typewriter, turned back, Daniel thought, so it wouldn't be read. The account had arrived at Heinrich, though without revealing that he was in the chicken coop back in the mountains. Neither Daniel nor Lydia had been aware of that. She was to hear it in a few days, but by that time she would not have told Daniel. Because she was one of the students who walked into his office to get some art materials (he allowed that), and noticing the page turned down in the machine, rolled it up, eager to see what their favorite teacher would be writing. Needless to say, he did not remain their favorite for long. They had hardly read a paragraph when a deputation was sent to bring in other students; and, to make their proceedings legal (the rules of residence being theirs), they got a quorum and had a polity meeting on the spot, at which Daniel Byrne was declared an enemy to the community. They then searched his drawer and confiscated the journal.

The next thing he knew, he was called onto the carpet by the Dean. An unequal match took place. Daniel was not only declared a sex maniac, a slanderer of his pupils and a traitor to the school — he may have been all that — it was proved from his emphasis on "an overblown Jewish girl," a "Russian Jewess," and Mary, the "obvious non-Semite," that he was anti-Semitic. Dean Stein, American Semite, seemed hardly one of the true Jews, and how could one convince a false Jew of one's not being anti? Because in his case, one was. If one said: "But I love Max Loewenstein like a father," the response was: "That's what all anti-Semites claim, that their best friends are Jews. I tell you as long as you know your friends are Jews, as long as you make the distinction, you are against them.".

"My God," said Daniel,"then the word Jew has no place in the language; and it would be the same with Catholic, Negro, Southerner, or Damned-Yankee. But that's poppycock. I interest myself in the background of my friends." But the only telling argument was a left below the belt, which Daniel flung out again and again, that this charge could only be made on the basis of stolen papers, which nobody had a right to take, keep, or read; and that in everything he said, the Dean was pandering to immorality.

Daniel did not invoke the latest piece of evidence, that he was drawn to the Bohemian gypsy-Jew, Marlene, and it wouldn't have helped, because even if she'd been his wife, which he wasn't aiming at, he'd still have called her Jessica, my Jewvenile, or sweet infidel. Besides, he hadn't got any further than looking into her brown orbs and recalling he must be loyal to Sibyl, even if she'd begun again with solitary walks, while he kept Octavia in the office. It seemed clear that Sibyl had not taken up with anybody at the school, and Daniel didn't think she'd reached the stage of the lady in the *Arabian Nights,* who went out to couple with a bear. As far as virtue was concerned, he was back where he started from.

"You see," Marlene smiled mournfully, "you can't even give blood like other people, but there has to be a mixup and explosion.

"Of course," she said as they walked to his office, "I've never seen the journal. Several of us refused to read stolen papers."

"That's a blessing," said Daniel. "But you might as well. It was left on my desk this morning with student comments in the margin." He handed it over.

"Yes," said Marlene. "We had a meeting last night. It wasn't easy." She read. "It's a summer crowd," she told him. "You should come in the regular term."

"I doubt if there'll be much demand for that."

"No," she said. And then, "This Heinrich you write about, have you seen him?"

"Heinrich Vogel? How would I see him?"

"He's been around the school for months, living in a chicken coop up in the mountains."

"Heinrich Vogel? Where does he live?"

"Up the trail past your house. It's strange you didn't know. About a mile and a half. In the saddle."

"Heinrich Vogel — in the saddle. Well I'm damned."

The next day, at Loewenstein's first noon concert of Bach, Daniel sat by Marlene. Changes are revealed. At an appropriate moment in the music their hands met, and his was drawn out of sight under the pleatings of her skirt. That night, as they lay hidden in the densest covert of rhododendron: "I'm afraid of Sibyl," Marlene whispered.

And then "I want you again." Daniel did not explain how their act was warranted, but the thought that Marlene, who had worked in the underground against the Gestapo, was afraid of Sibyl made him laugh as he rose to possess her.

But there was one small item he had not sufficiently considered. He had gone to the village and bought devices for the occasion, and it was hard to conceal the residue from Sibyl's prying. She had a way of searching through everything. Her own affair didn't seem to make her better, but worse. It was a hard spot for her. She was trying to slip away whenever she could to be with Heinrich; yet she didn't want Daniel to know he was anywhere in the neighborhood. She couldn't afford to be divorced, because Heinrich had nothing to live on, and besides, for all her hints, he hadn't proposed. Yet for all she knew, Daniel might be planning to ditch her for that Bohemian. He would have told her if she had asked, but she couldn't have believed him. They had set up conditions which made communication impossible. So she stewed. It was always "that hot Gypsy" or "that old Jew-baby," and "don't think I don't know what you're up to, because I've got ways of finding out."

Then Heinrich went away. Sibyl couldn't discuss that either; she wasn't supposed to know he'd been there. He said his father had died in Mexico; but she suspected he might be walking out on her. It was true, however, and in a few days he was going to return better off than he had been before, with a settled income, though not a fortune. But not even Heinrich knew that beforehand; so how could Sibyl be calm?

As for the means *contra natura,* Daniel canvassed his office the night he left Marlene, trying to think where they could be safe. What he hit on was an empty container for cactus phonograph needles. It had been lying around since before he came. He loaded it up and threw it in the bottom drawer of the desk. If she found it, he could say it wasn't his. Next day he went on a walking trip with Hanrahan. That was a perfectly bona fide walking trip. Maybe both of them were tired of women and wanted to get their minds on other things.

But the affairs of women did not cease just because two males left the school. As it turned out, Daniel had underestimated Sibyl's check on his drawers and secret places. She found the needle packet in the drawer the second morning. She recognized at once that she had seen it lying on top of the desk before. Who could tell what Sibyl thought? — "Curious it should have been put there" — or did she open it and know? Anyway, she left it in the drawer. And happening later into the music room where some students were playing records: "Don't use that old steel needle," she said; "it's hard on the records. Come to Daniel's office and I'll get you some thorns." A group followed her.

She pulled out the drawer, caught up the container, thrust it open. The condoms sprinkled over the floor. If she had known, she gave a good imitation of surprise. "You see what he's up to," she cried, "telling me he was faithful."

Students came in; the room almost sustained a second polity meeting, this one a solemn inquest into the comings and goings of Daniel Byrne. Sibyl was so obviously innocent, so beautiful, so betrayed, there was nobody who did not sympathize with her, sympathize and squeal. Living in such a close community, someone had seen Daniel and Marlene steal off to the woods at such and such time and return a couple of hours later. And somebody else had seen them do so and so. Every phase of the affair came to light at the moment that Marlene walked past the door. Sibyl called to her in that sweet but charged voice, like the air under a magnolia when the barometer falls. Reluctantly, Marlene came in. The students fell back.

It was not clear what happened. Some said Sibyl ran at Marlene and clawed her face, others said she only accused her and that Marlene tried to stop Sibyl's mouth. But by all accounts they had it out, tongue and claw; Sibyl called Marlene a whore and said she was breaking up that famous "happy marriage." Marlene said Sibyl was a demon bent on destroying Daniel. But the sympathy was with the wife, the true and beautiful, who proved her distress by going into hysterics, saying Daniel was deserting her and she had no place to go. She ran out of the building toward their cabin with an incoherent cry that she wouldn't live this way, she was going to kill herself.

The students hardly knew how to grab a faculty wife (short of a polity meeting), and the only adult there, Marlene, must have hoped the resolution would take effect. Anyhow, she was too beat up to interfere. Also the Dean came in and Marlene had to explain things. That was the start of her looking for another job; so her fears about Sibyl turned out to be well founded.

By the time the place was roused enough for people to walk up to the Byrnes' cottage, apply a timid knock at the door, and finally open it and walk in, they found only the child; playing quietly.

Everybody was alarmed. The students were marshaled and began to search the woods. Each had to ask what the business was and be told the whole story; so by the time Daniel came in with Hyde Hanrahan, he was practically met by a lynching party. But he had a notion where Sibyl might be, and in the stress of the moment he revealed it. They followed him up the trail to Heinrich's shack. The door was wide. Sibyl lay stretched on the bed poignantly beautiful. An empty vial of sleeping pills was beside her. But her case was damaged by the note clenched in her hand: "Heinrich, why did you leave me? I love you."

They carried her down in silence. The doctor, who pumped out her stomach, said she would not have died in any case. By morning she had slept it off.

The next night, when Daniel came from Loewenstein's lecture — those radiant lectures, assuagement of a grim time: the sage seated at the table in the rough pine hall, rustling through volumes of notes, then burying his head in his hands and lowering his voice as if talking to himself, with the sad wisdom of one who has endured the whole of the Western hope and ruin, tracing "The Crisis of Art and of Man" — after the lecture and a walk in the valley, the moonlit mountains melting into mist while Loewenstein quoted an old geography he had studied as a boy: "Die Nacht is ja die schonste Tageszeit" . . . "And surely night is the fairest time of day" — when Daniel came down, as from the eighth sphere, to "this little threshing-floor," he went to his cottage and found Sibyl gone again.

Only when he had raised the alarm was he told that Heinrich had returned. He said he would go up alone. But he motioned to Hanrahan. "Hyde," he said, "if she's up there, anything might happen. You'd better come along." He was shaking as in a fever, torn between fear of her killing herself and what must have been the suppressed desire — both given a final twist by what he thought likely, that she would be in bed, having another bounce on his time. "My God," he said, "if she could just run around without leaving Octavia and taking pills and turning the whole place topsy-turvy, it might not be so bad."

But if she and Heinrich had been at it, Daniel was too late this time to catch them. As he and Hyde reached the pasture, they met the others with a flashlight, on their way down. "1' was coming to see you," Heinrich said. "We've got to work this out."

The four of them went back to the shack. They had hardly sat down when Heinrich blurted it out. "Why don't you let her go?" he said. "We want to marry."

Daniel's eyes widened in' the lamplight, widened and shone. He said nothing. He was like Saul struck with the great light. Let her go. *Let her go.* LET HER GO.

Heinrich glanced at Sibyl and interpreted the silence. Could any man relinquish her? And then from Daniel broke a weird laugh. Profanation of the temple; flatulence at the altar. Even Hyde was startled.

All those years Daniel had been tormenting himself over Sibyl and her with himself, thinking he loved her, was jealous of her — thinking God knows what; and all because he was tied to her and didn't know how to get loose. And now Heinrich, who had been his worst betrayer, was going to come like the angel of the Most High, and open that prison gate and get in there, clang it to, and lock it again on himself. "Let her go; we want to marry."

Daniel thought of the child. "Sure," he said, recovering. "What else? But see a lawyer. There'll be problems." He got up, giddy. "Goodnight." He waved Sibyl back. "You needn't come down. Don't worry. It's different now."

But they had only gone a little way when her light flashed behind them, and the self-conscious Madonna voice, a little tight with posing, called: "Wait. I'm coming." For she would not trust them. They could witness against her. There was plenty to fight for: the child, money, her terms. As much as possible to tie Daniel up so he could not marry again. "Don't think you can laugh and have it your way." She spoke from her room before going to sleep, one of those utterances she would whisper and deny, hardly admitting herself that she was like that. "I'm going to make you suffer."

All that net of experience, the untellable detail, lingered in the landscape, to be released by its grooves from the involutions of the brain, where the whole must have existed in tensile simultaneity.

The evocation was immediate. It was just as the school and little lake were slipping away in the mist that Daniel turned, not to the reincarnated Sibyl traveling at his side, but to his notebook, scribbling something about the polarities of water and fire. Fire, because whenever he thought of Sibyl wandering off into those mountains, the students beating the woods for her, he saw it, as once in his boyhood on a summer trip, when they drove out at night to a viewpoint among such ridges, and looked across a valley to a slope up which miles of fire-tongues were leaping — a memory so old it seemed ancestral, yet live enough to assault the other, setting the forest of Sibyl's wandering into such a blaze. He turned from the window and wrote the equation as in theory it would run: "Water is to fire, as plant to animal, as lamb to tiger, as woman (see Goethe) is to man. But the last formulation is too much contradicted by experience."

He scribbled . . . The woman looked on and then interrupted: "Are you a writer?"

"Partly," Daniel said, "but I'm more of a painter."

"I love painting," she said. "I love everything to do with the arts: music, writing. I knew you would be something like that; you look more free. I like that freedom;"

"Yes," said Daniel

"Are you stopping off in Memphis?" she asked.

"For a while."

"I think I'll stay overnight." Her lids closed like curtains.

"I have to take the next plane."

"That makes me sad," she said.

If he had not spent years catching on to that sort of thing, it would have seemed the expression of an innocent regret; one would not have been surprised if she had passed over a scribbled paper with First Corinthians turned into a love confession: "And now there abideth faith, hope and love . . . but the greatest of these is love."

Daniel found himself apologizing: "I've got an aunt who's dying. I've got to be there."

She caught the remoteness. "Are you married?"

He was not trying to lead her on. But the mountain scene had left his mind so possessed with Heinrich and Sibyl and the seared time before he met Lucy, it was as if he had lost her or she had never appeared. "I've been married," he said.

"Then you can give me some advice," she told him. "I'm going to Mexico for a divorce."

"I know," said Daniel.

"What do you mean? How can you know that?"

"I didn't know it was Mexico." Her face was a study. Daniel went on. "But what you need isn't advice; it's a husband."

Her laugh was not without a trace of nerves. "I told the truth anyway when I said you weren't like other people."

"Yes, and that's why I wouldn't be good for you. You don't remember it, but we've been married before. And it didn't work. I was looking out the window just now at the place where you and I separated ten years ago. Why start the same thing again? You're hydrogen, look for oxygen; don't mess around after potassium. What you need is somebody quiet and steady. Stability . . ."

She leveled at him: "You don't know anything about it. I had stability. I had the stablest business man in Baltimore, and the dullest. I'd rather fight than that. I want somebody I can go wild about, a poet or painter, a bullfighter, a confidence man."

"Well God help you." He protested too much. "It's the same damned thing I've had to say to somebody else. You should have started at the other end. You've turned the whole thing around bass-ackwards."

She wheeled from him with the imperiousness of Sibyl, a gesture of hurt beauty that drew the sympathy of every man within range —

Like the time they went to the concert together but quarreled before it began and she rose with her head high and her shoulders back and the dark veil incredibly enhancing her mystery of sadness, and paced out of the theater, as if she would go to the cloakroom and take poison or measure the streets in offended innocence looking for a bridge over dark waters — so regally sad that every man in the theater grew aware of her, their souls swept in that transformation of the sexual vortex, not even asking who was at fault, the question a profanation of the heart's urge — until Daniel, under hostile eyes all echoing his own self-blame, tried to follow; but she had slipped off, and he went home to wait for her, thinking only how the shoulder-length black hair, where it was caught in the silver clasp, issued at the nape of the neck as a stream from a gorge, falling ebon waters —

So she rose, this other woman, and walked down the aisle to the smoker at the back of the plane.

While Daniel, turning to the window, began to grope, as through a great darkness, toward Lucy.

6 ~ Pioneers

It was like grofing for someone you have left behind in port, when the furrowed ocean is before you. Over the strip-mined ridges of the Alleghenies he was headed west and south — the drift of his blood through generations. He gave himself to that gravity . . .

"Come here, Dannie, I want to ask you a question. You'll have to think now, because it's a riddle, a D.A.R. riddle. Listen: 'What capital won the battle of New Orleans?'"

Judge Byrne gave Aunt Betsy a look of long-suffering which in fact declared impatience: "Lord, Betsy, you might as well give up. Dannie can't tell the Battle of New Orleans from the Battle of Waterloo."

Daniel gawked into the trees. "Is it Napoleon, Aunt Bets?"

"Suffering Mother of God," the Judge groaned, "to be cursed with a feeble-minded son."

But Aunt Bets was pushing on doggedly: "No, Dannie. It has to be the capital of one of the states in the United States, and also the name of the general who won the Battle of New Orleans."

"There are forty-eight states, Aunt Bets; and I don't know who won the Battle of New Orleans."

Not even Judge Byrne could have put it more succinctly.

"It's our native state!" she cried in triumph.

"Ma'am?"

"It's Jackson . . . Jackson, Mississippi."

"No use, Betsy," said the Judge; "he doesn't have any notion who Jackson was."

"Well, look, Dannie, here's an easy one." Daniel's look ranged the cottonwood tree. He wished he was up there, though he wasn't partial to cottonwoods. She changed her mind. "No. Little Gerald can answer this one: 'What capital was used by David as a weapon to kill Goliath?'"

Gerald wrinkled his precocious plump face and studied: "You know, Aunt Bets, he used a sling."

"That's right, dear; but what was in the sling?"

"A rock, I guess . . . Oh . . . I see, I see. It's Little Rock."

Judge Byrne beamed: "Chip off the old block. Did you hear that, Daniel?"

A murmur, vacant as from the trees.

"And here," said the aunt, "is one for Hilda." (The poor girl had been saddled with the grandmother's name, in a vain hope of healing that old estrangement.) "She's so far along in school, she should be able to guess the hard ones. Listen, Hilda."

Hilda was leafing through a magazine, — as always on these onerous Sundays, withdrawn as far as possible from the visit.

"Listen — 'What capital exercises a wise and constant care over earthly creatures?' "

Hilda faced the aunt. She looked too much like her, like those dreamy pictures of the other's adolescence, except she had cultivated a level business stare, as if she defied the gushy family image to exhibit itself in her. Her eyes never blinked or lost their green bored defiance; she looked straight ahead a moment, not seeming to think, and then in an icy voice (it was this D.A.R. stuff she hated above all things): "It's Providence, Rhode Island, Aunt," she said; "but I dispute the care."

(You would have thought she was botched for life, bearing the brunt not only of the grandmother's name but of the drive the grandmother had bred in Judge Byrne, and lacking Daniel's protective thickness of skull. She was studying all the time to make the A's they demanded; so with adolescence she got unhealthy and pimply plump, hardly ever went to parties or had dates.

"Now Hilda," her brothers would say: "no matter how many people tell you you're ugly, don't worry, because *we* love you." When hairs grew under her arms, they pointed and giggled, talking about "black hairs under the shoulders," until Hilda threw a tantrum, and the mother told them to stop that vulgarity or she would call the father. Then they changed the words: "Daniel," Gerald would say, puckering his face, "do you know where there are some little black bears under boulders?"

Nobody could have imagined a pioneer liberation would come to the rescue and get Hilda out of there, least of all while she was sailing east with her mother to visit Daniel abroad. But a ship's officer, Bjame Vig, one of the small dark Norwegians, fell in love with her. They met afterwards, wherever they could, though Judge Byrne fumed. It was wartime, and Bjame couldn't get a release, until finally he jumped overboard in New York harbor and swam ashore. The Judge must have thought it was time to act. He phoned a senator he had helped long ago, and in a couple of days Bjame had been yanked off Ellis Island, rushed to Canada for a visa, land was in Delta Landing with the unblushing Hilda for a bride.

Having fished him up that way, Judge Byrne made it tough for him. He could hardly have thought anybody was to the Byrnes born. For example, he had inherited from his father big hanging ears with lobes like dewlaps, which he used to pull when he was meditating. He had got the notion from somewhere that those bloodhound lobes were a sign of character. Bjame had no lobes at all, but curious little ears that ran straight and thin into his jaw.

"I can't understand it," the Judge said to Daniel; "Bjarne seems a nice fellow, but have you noticed his ears? How can you trust a man with that degenerate ear?"

Then the squirrel popped up in the toilet stool and bit Bjame on the tail. The plumber said it must have fallen in the vent, squeezed its way through the water trap and come up in the stool. In any case, there was Bjame, blocking the way. The squirrel tried to scramble out, biting and scratching, and Bjame jumped off the stool with a yell that fetched the house. For maybe three minutes everybody stood at the locked door listening to a racket like wrecking the place. Then the squirrel found a crack under the window, and Bjame opened the door, as shaky as if he'd had a fit.

"What's going on in here?" said the Judge.

"A squirrel in der stuhl," said Bjame. "It gnaws my romp."

"A squirrel?" said the Judge, with a look of total disbelief. "In the stool?"

"Not much wonder," he told Daniel, "with that bad degenerate ear. Well, Hilda's made her bed; she can lie in it."

But if Hilda, as she put it, "had buttered her bread and had to lie in it," she wasn't planning to do it around Delta Landing. She and Bjame gathered up what money they could and went to the Argentine. That was fifteen years ago. Apparently they had done well. At least a case of wine arrived for Daniel every Christmas . . .

Though nobody, watching her ten years before that, as a girl, seeing the level stare she gave Aunt Betsy, or hearing those icy tones, would have dreamed she could slip out of the noose — she seemed overlaid from the cradle, and no mistake — "Providence, Aunt, but I doubt they care.")

Judge Byrne had stood enough for one afternoon. "Fine riddles," he said, "but we've got to get home." And tactlessly: "I promised to take Octavia for a drive."

"But there are so many more," said Aunt Betsy. She must have memorized the whole D.A.R. exercise. She began to rattle them off without waiting for answers, coming to the curb as they piled into the car: "What capital started out to find a new world? What capital is a minor surgical operation? What capital is a modem dance?"

While little Gerald, their pet, to whom they would feed candy until he was sick, leaned out of the window as the car drove away: "Goo bye Gunmuddy, goo bye Aunt Bets —" waving his plump arm.

That had been when Betsy Byrne, as the most active D.A.R. woman in the state, was bound to push her lineage back in all directions until, by hook or crook, she latched onto a Revolutionary soldier at every branch and headwater. Lady archivists were set to work in the state libraries of the East. "All families are related in the end," one of them wrote. "Only give me a lead, and I will produce what you want." Hardly a principle to inspire confidence. Yet the outlines of what emerged were clear and the inference extraordinary.

In the old days, Daniel could not have cared less. But a few years back, when he had brought his family down, Aunt Betsy, though she could no longer read them, had laid the genealogies on the table, as much as to tell Lucy: "This is the kind of American stock we stem from." Daniel leafed the pages, idly at first, then with quickening interest, astonished to observe that each of those pioneer lines, the Boones and Byrnes, the Baines, Clarks and Cravens, had come from around Philadelphia, Quakers often, families taking their origin from the same region and ambiance as Lucy's. But where her people had stayed at home, bequeathing good lands, heirlooms, documents, trades or professions from father to son, his were seized by a curious unrest. The Woodruffs, the Copes, even the explosive Pendles, had somehow been contained. But these others had gone out like rivers, down and out, underground, or through the tenuous rift of bigamous and illegitimate connection — a line of dots and dashes, a few question marks on the page — south and west, through Pennsylvania, Ohio, Indiana, backwoods Maryland, Virginia, Kentucky, Tennessee, wandering from generation to generation.

Though, Lord knows, there was something ironic in the fact that all that pioneer dynamism should have landed them on the floodplain of the Yazoo-Mississippi Delta, the lowest and laziest, the most liquidly dissolving landscape in the world.

Yet there was a fitness in it too. The drive that had crested in Daniel's father, tragic by its outwardness, had not stopped there; it had gone inward, ricocheted from that horizon — not simply of water, but of flood — the river "chthonic and daemonic," which Daniel was still fighting and using for an impossible achievement of art . . .

Invoke the great images, world-codifiers: the cave wall of shadows, the garden in the desert, the mill on the stream, the stable of birth, the network of the blood . . .

He had seen a chick embryo projected on a screen, channels of flow and return in a substance that gropes into form, nature in all its parts alive . . .

Thunderheads boiled up, soaring turbulencies the plane banked around, or now land then, setting its jaw, plunged through, lurching. Valleys opened under lifting clouds, dammed lakes of the T.V.A. Then the endlessly rolling expanse of hill and pasture, moist evening, sunset after rain.

The luminous projection of America he took from the roaring air foil spread itself into the historical landscape, a topology of spirit. Her people had been at the center and his in the flow, hers directors and his agents in a circulation which had opened continents without and within. The cooperation was unconscious. They had started together, and some pushed out, had organized the peripheries, something had gone with them and something had flowed back. If Daniel could not exhibit the deeds and leases, he knew that, like Thoreau, they had started out with somebody's axe. So they went to the woods and began chopping down trees. In time the trees floated down the rivers back to the center, 6 percent compound interest on the axes. What went out again was powder and lead, salt, clocks maybe, books, even college degrees for returning sons. By the time the watershed was crossed and the rivers would not float logs east- ward, the tribute had turned to specie credited in New Orleans. But there was tribute. If Quaker Mill and the estates of Germantown had stayed green and quietly opulent, it was because lumber, coal, hemp, skins, tar, were flowing in from those subtly indentured others out there brawling in the wilderness . . .

The first wave had passed, the wildest, unsettled heroes, Boone and the rest, who breached the passes. It had yielded to the second, stabler but tawdrier: half-settlers who squatted a few years in the clearings, built larger cabins and raised a few crops, then drifted on, on the tide that had brought them. So the second wave yielded to the third: litigators and jail builders, men who dispossessed Boone of his Kentucky lands. Still, it was raw men in the raw towns, pockets in a wilderness where squatters fought through fever and chills, doctoring themselves with mountain whiskey against sicknesses of winter, and of new lands. There were Indians in the forests, their dogs barking through the night, or when the Indians had withdrawn across the river, they were expected to return. The one-room log cabin, later enlarged, to which the Baine women used to come home to give birth, had been an outpost in the "dark and bloody ground."

Daniel's grandmother had the stories from her grandmother: that Sunday at dinner, how they heard the repeated cry; how they fled to the stockade; how, looking out, they saw boatloads of warriors paddling in, a bloody human scalp lifted at every prow. From far off one watched the dance, spasmodic leaps and curvettings, saw guns and tomahawks brandished, muscles bulging under vermilion war paint; one heard the yells clashing pitch on pitch. A remote relative had been caught in the corn patch, scalped, his clothes parted among the warriors . . .

Danger had not prevented the coming of more. They arrived every year, ancestors and collaterals, converging toward Gerald Byrne's future cradle. Generally they were destitute, families who could carry their earthly possessions on a single wagon, in a wheelbarrow, or on their backs. They had trudged out the Lancaster Pike or the East-West Road to Pittsburgh, or over the Cumberland Road to Wheeling, and had floated down on the Ohio, veering south or north, as chance deflected them, to Kentucky or Indian Territory. Until the north country rose to anguish again as Tecumseh roused the tribes to the war of 1812.

All that time the branches were converging, meeting, marrying, jockeying into position for unforeseen future conjunctions. In the neighborhood of the great house where the Virginia gentleman had lately butchered a slave and got himself shot before trial, a Baine son had married a daughter of the Cravens. He was boasting how his pappy cowed the Indians twenty-five years before. Captured with seven others, he had run the gauntlet unhurt, and catching up the last two braves, had knocked their heads together and thrown them over his back. Then he jumped high in the air, kicking his heels together and crowing like a rooster. The chief had spared him and taken him into the tribe. At about the time of the wedding, and near the same place, an ancestral Byrne squatted a few years, having fled with a crowd of refugees over the Ohio, leaving burnt-out cabins and abandoned stockades on the Wabash . . .

The first generation of the Republic . . . In Germantown there was Adam Woodruff, bowing and offering his arm to patients of the asylum: "I won't have them in chains!" — then going home to Springmount to keep his "Diary of the Weather and other Occurrences," a testimony to sweetness and light, precisely filling the ruled pages of commonplace books, to be left to his son, and to his son, of the same name, who would continue the journal in almost the same hand:

(N.B. In cold weather I take the state of the Thermometer from 5 A.M. to Sunrise: In warm weather from 12 O'clock Noon to 3 O'clock . . .)

Jan. 8th. 30 degrees. Clear and rather windy. Went to the city for a quarter of beef, raisins, currants, etc. Robert threshing wheat. Sent the wheat to the mill and brought the Indian meal I sent yesterday. Received from Neighbor Comfort a cartload of wood ashes for soap, also I 1/2 lb. of twine for tying grape vines, on condition that I will give him a bunch of grapes next fall. Took Mary Cooper from the Asylum and brought her here to board for some time . . .

This day I am 45 years in America. I then had no acquaintance with any individual in the country excepting the passengers that landed with me. Glory, Honour, Praise and Thanksgiving be unto the Most High forever and ever for preserving me and blessing me with the many unmerited comforts I now enjoy, Amen and Amen! . . . Mary Cooper and Sarah went with me to Meeting. Mary began to preach! . . .

Went to Monthly Meeting and took Mary Cooper back to the Asylum . . . Sarah and I went to the Asylum to see Mary Brown and Mary Cooper. The former we saw, but the latter was not suitable to be seen . . .

With the turning of the carefully penned pages, days and years passed, a gentle recurrence, while Adam Woodruff recounted the equable changes in the weather, the particulars of his doings and prosperings: how he planted a row of raspberries along the east side of the garden, or some fine flower seed, Violet Tricolor Heartsease and Double Columbine, given him by a horticultural friend; how he sent a valuable lecture against the Iniquity of Slavery to Squire Wilson, one he felt solicitous to keep from evil; how he engaged May Butler, a black woman, to wash clothes. One day he was appointed by the court to look after the property of Susan Clarkson, a lunatic, amounting to upwards of nine thousand dollars; another day he was chosen trustee of such and such school. This week he bought a house, or sold one and invested the money; this first-day he rode out with his beloved wife, Sarah, to the top of Chestnut Hill and along the County Line Road, fine open country.

As he pruned his grapes or spread manure on his garden, or took his telescope out to observe sunspots, it seemed to him, no doubt, a life dangerously environed:

> This day I have been 48 years in this country, and in no year since my arrival have I known so much embarrassment, so much swindling and Robberies accompanied with Murders as in the last. O Holy and Merciful Father, preserve me from the wickedness so prevalent in this country, if it be thy Holy Will.

The Merciful Father did a pretty thorough job. It is true the grandfather clock stopped from time to time and Adam II had to come by to get it going, but that was a pleasure for both father and son. Also merchant Cope died and was regretted, and his son Ezra married Patience, an event which may have been regretted as well, though it helped Adam II into banking, and the invasion of Springmount did not come while the first Adam was alive. One evening Adam's sister came by with "a pressing importunate letter" from her son at Westtown, entreating permission to come home, "on account of a Dysentary that had got among the schollars," But the Lord preserved him through that affliction. There was one indentured child who proved immoral and had to be taken back to the almshouse, but "a female child, said to be innocent, about 7 years old" was supplied "on trial for a month." The greatest excitement occurred when son Adam's stable was broken into and his most valuable horse stolen. But the horse was brought home next day, and the thief lodged in Norristown jail.

Violence was kept on the peripheries, falling now and then, in the shape of fire, on some other Quaker's factory or barn. Always the fire was set by "some Child or Children of the Devil," or "some infamous Villain or vile Incendiary." As if nature did not commit that rape in the land of the righteous. One of these Sons of Satan would give a party with music, drink, even fire-rockets, and if the rockets were not enough, then the whiskey-inspired fiends incarnate would do the work, and Whalan Whitman's hay house with ten tons of hay and a quantity of oats would be consumed:

> Whalan Whitman being a Sober Young Man and keeping no liquor in his house, rude boys and men went to a Tavern kept I am informed by Wm. Wilson, and caused buckets of Whiskey to be charged to W. Whitman, and many of the boys at the fire became intoxicated thereby. A Melancholy Contemplation, that by setting a Barn on fire, and by a Tavern keeper's giving out Liquor without the Owner's order, wicked boys will be induced to other such acts, in order to obtain more Liquor by the like evil courses.

Death in this pious Arcadia was subdued to the temper of the place. In Adam Woodruff's diaries it announces itself by a slow change in the writing. Diminuendo. Though many ruled leaves were waiting, with spaces ready for Date, Mercury, Rain, and the rest, the hand draws back from entering them, contracting its letters into smaller and smaller compass. As if the soul begrudged any more room to the petty affairs to be recorded: the body's feebler state, friends coming on the newly organized horsecars to visit, a last trip to the Asylum to see Mary Cooper, who had been in and out through all those years . . . and of course the doctor's coming to prescribe pills. "But my reliance is on a better Physician who will ease me, I hope, in His appointed time, in that Place where the Wicked cease from troubling and the Weary are at rest." The last entry, after telling of increasing pains in the stomach, discharge, the doctor's call — the letters microscopically reduced, shrinking from existence — trails away: "A light and refreshing Shower fell last evening between 7 & 8 O'clock." The next entry is in the scarcely distinguishable hand of the son . . .

Good Quaker wives and mothers, with serviceable lives and holydyings — Patience Comfort, Adam's niece, having endured forty years with the Pious Moneygrubber, began to realize: "Behold the Bridegroom cometh," and her heart responded: "Go out and meet him in the gate." She called her children and grandchildren and nephews to her side. To her son, Albert, she said, smiling sweetly: "My darling son, try to walk in Wisdom's ways. I want you all to be solid substantial characters. I firmly believe that Quakerism is primitive Christianity." And to Leah Pendle, her son's wife: "I believe thee has been a visited child. Be a strength to my son. Avoid the small vanities." And to Elsie and her husband Price (he was to be the grandfather of "the Price we have to pay"): "Don't become too much absorbed in the world. Mind the still small voice." Then to her daughter Hannah: "My precious child, beware of the little foxes that spoil the tender vines." Now she turned to Adam, son of her beloved cousin, perhaps more warmly than to her own: "Once when thee was a little boy, Adam, I stayed at home from Meeting with thee, and was graced with a visitation in which I was assured that thee would be preserved from every evil. That promise remains with me." Finally, to all those gathered around, she spoke: "My dearly beloved. If you are energetic and careful, you will not want. Your Heavenly Father will look after you. Seek the Lord and learn his ways."

Pain now and bodily prostration increasing upon her, she said: "I hope I am not complaining. These moans are for release from the distressed body."

Feeling herself near the crisis, she cried: "Where is my husband?" And then: "But he can do nothing for me." Taking her hand he asked if there was anything she desired. "Nothing," she replied, "but the wine of the Kingdom."

She closed her eyes. After she had slept for some moments, she stirred. He said to her: "My dear Patience, I believe I have been favored while thee slept with an assurance of thy acceptance." She looked at him earnestly and said: "That is a comfort to me, Ezra. I will lie down now, and be at rest."

. . . Maybe the pilot knew what he was doing, but he had overshot Memphis, as if he'd lost it on the map; but now he saw it, as who didn't; he pulled up on the reins and went banking down over the extended scurf of the city and the great bridged river, one wing aimed at the half-moon and the other digging for the water, the motors bouncing like a woman's bubs.

"My God, he flew too far; we've crossed the Mississippi."

Streaked brown and gold with the late sun, the river, with that whiplash of the snake it was always being compared to, crawled, launching itself from Cairo and the north, cutting through the low clay hills, to spill out between levees into the Delta, the mottled plain that stretched with sinuous wave markings, lakes and bayous and figure-of-eight brush strokes of swamp, down and down, further than the sight, until it was swallowed in a burning haze of air. Earth, air, water, fire. And the greatest of these is fire . . .

It was a long way to go, banking and groping, when what one wanted was behind.

But he was on the way, getting nearer, speeding up the reel of the pioneers, repeating that phylogeny. He was settling, with the Boones, the Byrnes, and the rest, toward the present. They had made half a century since the last sounding. This was the 1870 gilded, violent river, down which Daniel's grandparents came from Kentucky, headed for the Delta, yellow fever, the little town, a few lamps flickering in the forest.

Come so far west and south, they were no longer conscious of the eastern indentures and checkreins; still, they were part of the old circulation — with lumberjacks in the Alleghenies, the immigrant raw blood, fighting, whoring when there were whores, and logs jamming the streams, in spring breaking their own impediments, crushing through splintered: walnut, oak, white pine, hemlock; the mountain topsoil washing off the rocks, polluting the bays — while in the bank at Germantown sat the calm, sweet man, third of the gentle Woodruffs, smiling. It was his land; he had hired the furies, but far off; his house was quiet, his family ordered, praying and "theeing" and never a raised tone — a visited child he was, preserved from every evil. But Daniel's people had been out there, in the back country.

The boat was loaded in all classes. There were Irish louts coming to tote earth in wheelbarrows to dike new plantations against the spring rise, so trees could be burned off and cotton planted and fortunes made and lost, and gentleman planters pretend to revive antebellum days, building mansions and living high, sending their children east to college and their wives every summer from the heat and mosquitoes to the White Mountains or Cape Cod, or going with them for winter trips to New York to hear grand opera; there were Jews traveling south with their wares, or with nothing but their native wit and maybe a book of Schopenhauer or Heine, bound to light on their feet in Vicksburg or Yazoo City or Delta Landing, and in twenty years own the best store in town and make doctors and lawyers of their sons; there were carnival men going down with tricks and games to fleece the Negroes who worked the cotton; and side-burned gamblers to cheat the Irish, elegant swaggerers with a flash of rings and pearl-handled pistols, whom even the fightinest Irishman knew enough to leave alone; there were saloonkeepers to open houses for the gamblers and the Irish; and carpetbaggers dreaming of starting plantations and getting waited on hand and foot by Negroes they had helped to free. Among the rest came Daniel Byrne, with his traveling studio and cameras and a Kentucky bride, she bringing such baggage and household goods as could be extracted from a family more proud than rich, and outraged by her marriage.

The low whistles throbbed as the side-wheels beat down a river that still flooded most of the Delta land, filling bayous that meandered out to the Yazoo and back into the Mississippi at Vicksburg. There was not a hill in all that country, except for Indian mounds; but the banks of the river and of the oxbow lakes were a few feet higher than the rest, and here farms were appearing in a forest of cypress, water oak, water gum. Not a tenth of the country was cultivated; and if a man wanted to hunt, why he could take off from Delta Landing, put in a boat at the Hushpucanna Bridge, and paddle for days down creeks and bayous flowing one into the other: Hushpucanna, Rattlesnake Bayou, Black Bayou, Deer Creek, the Sunflower River, the Yazoo — nowhere a cleared field, but swamp, canebreak, or the virgin hardwood tangled with grapevines and trumpet flowers. There were fish in the water: bass, white perch; goggle-eye, brim; turkey in the brakes, black and gray squirrels in the trees, deer drinking in the shallows, bear on the headlands, and now and then a panther stealing off with its prey. Through this jungle Daniel Byrne came with his child-bride, on the tinsel palace of a side-wheeler, among the younger sons of the old America and the lawless loud riffraff of the new.

The story had descended with the generations: how the open deck at the front of the steamer was filled with chairs and tables and a bar handy, so drinkers and gamblers could get together. How Daniel Byrne left the sweltering stateroom the last crowded night south of Memphis and walked forward. The space surged with a drinking, smoking, chewing, yelling, gambling crowd. They had spilled beer and whiskey, and between spitting tobacco and the young men throwing up, the floor was a loblolly. Now a quarrel broke out over a card game; it spread and became general. In a few minutes the whole forward deck was a melee of wrestling and slugging bodies, wallowing in the stinking mire, while officers ran about, calling the crew to pry the drunks apart and put them to bed.

Young aristocrats of the Delta were in that brawl, would have counted it a point of honor to be nowhere else. But Daniel Byrne was a Yankee photographer, and it was too dark to photograph. He turned and went back to his cabin, his bride, the impounded female force that was flesh of his flesh.

As the current of energy buttresses against its own descent, the westward torrent is always eddying, forming in itself pockets of eastwardness, tradition and pride: As the East to England, to the East, Kentucky —

The only state more vain of its heritage than Virginia, and with less cause: 1870, it was already a white fence country of racing yearlings and trotters grazing on bluegrass, the columned house in the distance, and Ye Olde Tavernes in Paris and Lexington. Hilda Boone Baine, now Byrne, had brought that past in the set of her face, the ambition that would sour on her — as if she had been born with a silver spoon hanging out of her mouth, in any of the peerless mansions built by westward kin of Patrick Henry or Thomas Jefferson; as if all those life-sized figures standing stiff in the Mayfield cemetery, their horses and pets carved in white marble around them, buried together in Christian ground, had been the relatives she almost claimed — she who was in fact a runaway daughter of struggling hillbillies with petty-bourgeois connections: one learned schoolmaster, of whom the only relic Judge Byrne could find later was the Virgil in the outhouse of the ancestral cabin, half devoured by the nether-mouths of the unlettered — burn fodder; and one considerable landowner, Uncle Elisha, captain in the Civil War, Union side, who organized a company of horse among his friends and relations, with a loyal Negro slave as orderly, and got them all killed off by an idiotic stand on Pilot Knob in the hills of the Buffer Zone.

And Oh the lauds one must hear about this cousin of an uncle, and the letters coming from home-abiding relatives: "Today I gave Uncle

Elisha's uniform and company roster to the Museum in Belmont Park, where they will be admired by visitors from all over the world. I did so hate to part with these priceless heirlooms, but I could not keep the moths out. I comfort myself that such treasures will have the glory of being seen."

Daniel's grandmother had brought it all with her and would swing onto it, as to the tight-lipped photographs in the bedroom; she would interrupt a Sunday talk on the horrors of Bolshevism with some more immediate ground of woe: "Son, have you heard about the Durwood mansion? The Durwoods have torn down their old house to keep from paying taxes. Lura says there's nothing left but the columns. How can the country keep on this way? And the Durwoods! I'm shocked and ashamed." Judge Byrne would sit, hearing it probably for the third time, thinking of his own unpaid taxes, while the spirit of his father shook his silences: "What are the Durwoods to us or we to the Durwoods that we should weep for them?"

This was the woman who waited for Daniel Byrne in the side-wheeler's close stateroom, demanding what that fight had been: Were the men of good family? Had he got to know any? If she had been a man, she would have been out there holding some poor scoundrel by the scruff of the neck and shaking him. But Daniel Byrne was more like what he must have descended from, those Quakers of the gentle kind.

Like among unlike meets with unlike fortune.

As he returned to his cabin, whatever he thought unspoken: "Those of good family are wallowing in their vomit on the floor" — he must have been marked already as a man who would fail.

They had descended the river, down there, where Daniel Byrne, grandson, watched the left wing banking and thought of another river, the Susquehanna, like a blue lake from the trees of Woodruff farm. He pictured it in the old days, log-jammed, and in the Germantown bank, modest, kindly, Lucy's grandfather, investing the profits that would revert to the farm. At the other extreme, Hilda Byrne, sparing and scraping, began to buy the houses Aunt Betsy would inherit and squeeze until they were dry. In the East again, Uncle Steward, a boy, walked from Meadow Farm over the covered bridge to Conowingo Mill, to watch fascinated, first projecting how Cope energy and Pendle fanaticism could be geared into the clockwork of a millionaire business.

The two rivers were highroads to the present union; Betsy Byrne and Steward Cope appeared as living links between that 1870 and now. After all this travel, Lucy and Daniel were reaching their stations, he the Delta and she Quaker Mill. She would be standing with Aunt Hester over the rose garden, talking of Uncle Steward.

Suppose Daniel could take her road, as in thought he had done, he would still find himself at the gate, outside, groping for a key, Indeed, if Uncle Steward was the link, what was needed was not a key, but a battering ram. If Lucy was of that stand, so impervious to fire, how had she yielded to the assault of Byrne?

7 ~ The Wedding

Uncle Steward had done what he could to prevent it. In the rose garden over which Lucy might be standing, looking from the balcony, he had talked with her, that Easter morning, in the spring and morning of her love.

"But how do you know you love him, Lucy? My dear, how can you know?"

Uncle Steward was the more determined to hold her because, of his own children, two had married so badly — so inexplicably considering their upbringing and background; and what it had taught him was not that the family needed some inoculation against the devil, but only that Lucy, whom he loved like his own, was making the same mistake Seth and Gretel had made; and that his obligation, by bitter experience, was to warn her against such an obvious moral castaway as Daniel Byrne.

And now, as if Daniel had taken Lucy's place on the balcony, a silent witness, and she had strolled into the past with Uncle Steward — she young and fresh, with the innocence of the once-born, he proper and well-groomed, the ideal Quaker gentleman, his strength and looks finely preserved into age — she was standing by the box hedge, while the old man looked down at her with loving concern, trying to assess how impulsively childish she was going to be.

That was the day Uncle Steward had first met Daniel, though he had heard him rumored about for some time, Daniel, the haggard one, with his cowlicked hair uncombed, blurting out arrogant opinions on philosophy, music, art: Daniel, still suffering through the shipwreck of his first marriage and an ugly suit by his wife, begging at the gates of virtue like a ragged Pariah —

"Of course he needs you; he needs somebody at least; but don't confuse love and pity. We pity the insane, we don't throw ourselves into the madhouse."

"But it's not what you think, Uncle Steward. He's not pitiable. I love him."

"My dear, how can you be sure? Take time. You need someone from your own walk of life. You can't live with violence and intemperance."

They walked from the garden down the gravel path between pink and white dogwood and along the race under the English limes, Uncle Steward growing more tender and at the same time more stem. "Lucy, I love you like my own child. I've taken the trouble to look into this. I've been to his college to ask about him. Our kind of people say he's no good: one of these crack pots who thinks he's a genius and fumbles everything. And he's not so young. If he's going to do anything, he'd have given signs of it by now. But he's lost his job and he's lost his wife. That's two strikes against him. Why should you be the third?"

They had gone out of sight under the trees. It was only a voice, the quiet ordered voice heard and imagined, possessing the inner space of Daniel's world, the South, Aunt Betsy's tumbled house to which he was flying, and on the other shore, across from it, the Mill, the path, the rose garden, the mowed fields and woodlot — that voice possessing it all — hardly a voice even, but the proprietary soul of Steward Cope, the order that would outlive his demise — as if he had now replaced Daniel on the balcony, to survey what was his, while Daniel, possessed too and appropriated, a strange identity, found himself gazing down at Lucy, not with his own eyes, but with those Quaker gray ones, looking at the small delicate girl, so gentle but so determined, and wondering, while the bald and white head shook: "Is there no way? Is she bound to be like her father?"

Uncle Steward had seen that look of naive recklessness in such eyes before, in 1917, when his nephew Adam, a man with mechanical genius, who could have done wonders in the business, gave it up, ranting about the money mills of Germantown and the Quakers who slaved in them, and went off, bumming in the pine barrens. It was only the grace of God that in the foreign adventure which followed he had met Lucy's mother. Otherwise he might still have been living in a squatter's camp instead of on a Maryland farm which had almost the air of an English estate.

What Uncle Steward had hoped from Lucy was the social sense of her mother with her father's homely truth. As he saw in her face the radical innocence he had seen thirty years before, he weighed the miscalculation . . .

"If it's not pity," he said, "I can tell you what it is. One look at him and I know. It's passion, what you young people call sex. And that's a worse ground for marriage than pity. Pity is at least of the soul. You're sexually involved with him, isn't that the truth?"

They had been meeting in Philadelphia for half a year, not exactly in secret, Lucy wasn't capable of that; her family knew; but Daniel was under suit, so except for his landlord and friend, old Loewenstein, no one else was told. They would meet in the downtown station, get on the suburban train, and off again out by the park. The places were so large it was like open country. They climbed a slope and crossed a field. There was a little pond. They stood a long time on the dam, their arms around each other, and looked through thawing ice into the water. They did not need to talk. They saw a muskrat slide under the ice, leaving a cloudy trail.

They took the winding road down into the park, slipping by houses where they must not be seen, Lucy waving off there in the distance, some gray stone pile on a hill: "That's where my great-uncle lives," or a Colonial one across the way: "That's where my father grew up."

They felt safer when they came to the woods, the stream, a rocky valley, with bridle paths and trails and the old tearoom by the ford. Daniel reached in his knapsack and brought out the round bottle of Chilean Riesling. He had forgotten the corkscrew. He said he would pound it open, he had done it before. He wrapped his scarf around the base. Holding it with the mouth down he beat it against a tree. He explained how it worked, how it always worked: "Pressure waves are focused down the bottle onto the cork." Though as he said it, he wondered: "What are you talking about? With a regular bottle, yes. But this one is round, with a little cylindrical neck. So how can anything focus?"

The cork did not move. It should have been creeping out. He pounded harder. All at once, in an oval window of the curved bottle side, opposite the point he was pounding, the glass broke; a piece sprang out; the wine ran gushing, aromatic.

"Lord," he cried, "I've busted it."

Then they saw the window, clean and round, a glass cork those famous pressure waves had pulled. He held the bottle up. It was open but intact, miraculously intact, beautiful, ready to be drunk. He tilted it up.

"Don't cut yourself," she said.

Like drinking from a glacier. "It's not sharp. Try." She took a sip. It was an old wine, almost too old, but with a great tang. "We can't recork it," he said; "gulch it up."

They went swinging down the path, drinking from the window of glass . . .

"First time she went riding they gave her a horse that had been a hunter, and when they came to the ditch he sailed over. She went spinning through the air and lit on the ground and lay there yelling: 'I've got a compound fracture; I've got a compound fracture.' You'd have thought she was proud of knowing it, because we'd studied that stuff in hygiene." Two college girls were coming behind them on horses. Daniel and Lucy moved aside. They could see and hear but at a distance, rapturously removed, in windowed privacy, a glassy bubble of air.

"As a matter of fact, it was a compound fracture, and her leg was in a cast for a long time. When she got up courage to ride again, she came down with a bunch of us. 'I want a slow, safe horse,' she said. Well, they brought her one that had absolute cobwebs on him, and so low arid swaybacked he just dragged. 'Prudence,' we told her, 'what's the point in riding at all if you're going to get a horse like that? ...'"

The voices drifted away as Daniel led Lucy from the path. They slipped into the woods, climbing, then along a moss-covered ledge, hanging rocks above and a drop below, to a sort of hollow above the stream, almost a cave. The trees were hemlock, flecked with thawing snow. Sometimes branches would spring up and a shower of flakes would drift down, bright in the air. It was deep with hemlock needles below, warmed and dried in the sun, a russet bed under thawing trees.

> O love that in our embers
> Is something that doth live,
> That nature yet remembers
> What was so fugitive ...

They finished the wine and lay back, hands laced, smiling at the sky.

She had explored such paths before, even at Quaker boarding school, but not to this terminus, never to this cave under hemlock, this opening to the new things he had taught her, as she had taught him the ways of muskrats and the names of trees. She was caught; it was passion, the longing for total embrace never to leave her ...

And here was Uncle Steward asking if she was sexually involved. The gray eyes Daniel had usurped took the shock of her smile. "If I weren't, Uncle Steward," she said, "I wouldn't be thinking of marriage."

"Won't you learn from those who are older? You needn't give him up. But wait. Take time."

"I'm twenty-four, Uncle Steward. I've turned down people before." He knew. She had refused his favorite nephew among others, a Pendle, her third cousin. "But now I'm sure, and I won't change."

"Lucy," he said, "I had planned to put thee in my will" (he had operated so much in the world it was not often he slipped into the Quaker form, and Lucy had abandoned it since childhood), "with my own children; but I can't see my estate shared with this Daniel."

"You shouldn't have said that, Uncle Steward. My love for you has nothing to do with inheritance, and your love for me will just have to make the best of Daniel."

You would have thought she had no doubts; and maybe she didn't, in her heart, though Uncle Steward's warning necessarily echoed in her head. But she pushed on.

And, of course, as it became clear that the thing was not to be averted, Uncle Steward, like the other relatives, made the best of it; whatever he intended to do about the will, he provided a suitable gift and came to the wedding. There was none of that Southern passion of Daniel's clan: "I'll take my toys and go home," or: "If you marry so and so, I'll never speak to you again." No, they had come to the wedding, and the forces, once and for all, had been displayed.

The marriage could not be in Meeting, the Friends would not sanction it; so it was to be at Woodruff Farm; and to avoid traipsing down to Lucy's father's hemlock valley and really putting the seal of nature on the thing, it was to be in her mother's garden, which was at least a work of art, in the English tradition, the larkspur arched over by the clustered wisteria.

And there on the velvet lawn by the silver maple stood the shock-haired groom, stood or slouched (her lounge-lizard Lucy called him), in a linen suit that didn't fit, that was not — Uncle Steward heard in amazement, for Daniel broadcast it — his own, but lent him by his father-in-law to be married in. So he had come without any decent clothes, maybe in his blue jeans, with his underwear and the shirt on his back, no money and not much promise of any, and with even the gall to joke about it (sitting under the tree with Lucy, tucking her silky hair behind her ears, calling her his "hairy heiress" and once letting loose with some doggerel, sung Mississippi style, about "Honey, honey, I love you for your money, but honey don't you poke, poke, poke me in the funny bone so"); there was the alimony and support to pay on his previous bungle, and just the hint of a job in which he said he wasn't much interested, because he wanted to write or paint, Lord knew which, it was all a confusion.

And here came his aunt from the swamps of Mississippi, the only relative who appeared on his side (he had a mother down there somewhere, but she wouldn't travel), Aunt Betsy, who would travel anywhere at the drop of a hat, and who had ridden all that way on the Greyhound buses, and got off tottering and tousled and talking interminably about how she had sat in the front seat all the way . . .

(As she would come year after year when they were married and living in Chicago, stay with them a few days and then whirl off on a cruise around the nation — though Uncle Steward would only hear that later and thirdhand.

It was the police phoning: "Are you expecting an aunt?"

"Lord," Daniel thought, "they're going to deliver a stiff one." For he had met the bus and she wasn't there. "Yes," he said, "I've been waiting for her. What's the matter?"

"Nothing," came the voice, not so much reassuring as reassured — of course these city Yankees would think she was crazy — "We just had to check. We'll bring her along. Yeah, she's O.K."

When the patrol car drew up in front of the house and the crumpled little figure was boosted out, thanking the officer in her categorical brisk way, sure enough, it was Aunt Betsy, but she staggered as she walked to the house, listing to port like a waterlogged vessel. Daniel had never seen anybody walk like that, like the tower of Pisa, that far heeled over, toppling along thinking she was going straight up — it must have been her balance conked out by days and nights pounding her ear; so she'd have been funny if anybody had felt like laughing. Daniel ran forward to grab her, but she was perfectly capable.

"Where's your baggage, Aunt Bets?" he asked.

"On the bus."

"What bus?" he said. "I met the bus."

Stopping in Memphis and Kentucky to see folks in the day-time, she had gone on three nights riding: "But it was so nice. 'Driver,' I said, 'I don't like any seat but the front.' And I saw so many towns, such fine country."

Coming into the city, early morning: "Driver," she insisted, "you've passed the place. I want to get off on the South Side."

"No ma'am, we haven't got there yet."

"I said my nephew lives on the south side, driver."

"I know, ma'am. We still haven't got there."

"Well, I've got to stop, driver. I have to go to the bathroom. And besides, you've passed the place."

She had gone on arguing and telling him to stop so she could ask the way and go to the bathroom, and he had gone on telling her they would be at the terminal in fifteen minutes and he wasn't allowed to stop off schedule that way, until she had cried out in agony of body and soul: "I'm leaving this bus, driver, whatever you say. You stop this minute and let me off."

He pulled over to the curb and she tumbled off without her bag, which was stowed under the bus, and with hardly her wits about her. Walking into the first store, she demanded the toilet. Then she asked after Sixty-third Street and found herself way short, as the driver had said. Meanwhile the bus had gone.

You'd have expected her to phone her nephew and take a cab but Aunt Bets never dropped a nickel into any device if she could help it, and she hadn't used the pay phones since they began to take two nickels instead of one. As for taxis, she religiously avoided them.

She walked out onto the street and flagged the first police car that happened along. In fact she put herself in front of it, so it had no choice but to stop.

"Officer," she said, "you've got nothing to do but drive up and down all day. Take me to this address. It's my nephew's, and I'm lost."

She was sitting on the sofa eating her breakfast while she told this. It was characteristic that she finished the food before she began to nod. Then she slumped forward. Daniel caught the plate as it slipped from her fingers. "Here it is," he thought: "old lady rides three days for visit, has heart attack on arrival." Then he realized she had only dozed off in the middle of what she was saying.

Daniel's desk was in that room. He worked most of the morning. She never left the sofa. She would start up every now and then, pull herself together, and cry: "Goodness, I almost went to sleep," and go on talking, working back from the trip to problems at home: "Such poor workmen, so ineffectual and insolent, if I hadn't been in a jam, I'd have ordered them off my property . . . And so many sewers stopped up; one roots and two squirrels. The squirrels put nuts in the standpipe and go down and can't get back. I have two more stopped up now, and I'm afraid it's the squirrels."

She would slump again in the middle of a sentence, as if you'd hit her on the head with a brickbat. She rallied for lunch, surprised how fast the morning had slipped by. Then she wandered around, still listed over, asking if she could do anything. Sitting back on the sofa, she tried to talk, and passed out for the afternoon.

As it was getting dark, she came to with a jump. "Goodness gracious! What time is it?"

"So late!" she exclaimed, struggling up. "I must have been asleep. I've got to get to town. I have a ticket for the play."

"But you can't go down there by yourself tonight. You're worn out."

"Nonsense. I'm perfectly fresh. I ordered a ticket weeks ago."

"But you have to eat."

"I'll get a bite on the way."

She tilted out of the house, stumbling along with that physical machine that didn't look as if it would get to the comer, though the will would have made it to the moon.

She returned at midnight, the short quick steps almost dragging, but the voice tireless, praising the tawdry play: "Lovely costumes, such lovely costumes. Bright scenery . . . So glad I could see it. Very fine effects."

As in a few days, when she could walk without too much heeling over, she would start on the rest of her cruise — the itinerary made at her insistence by the staggered clerk in Delta Landing: "Leave Chicago 4: 20 A.M., see Madison, arrive Minneapolis 5:00 P.M., sightseeing tour, night Hotel Van Dyck; leave Minneapolis 5:45 A.M., arrive Bismarck, N.D., 4:40 P.M., Tour, night Hotel Dakota; leave Bismarck 9:05 A.M., arrive Livingston, Mont., 1:00 A.M., Hotel Parks; next morning 9: 00 A.M. begin Yellowstone Tour — two days; lv. Livingston 4: 20 A.M., lunch Glacier Park, arr. Banff 1: 30 P.M., etc. — out to the north Pacific, south and around, a jaunt from which she would return with chromo cards and souvenirs to clutter up her house and show her friends — rocking and repeating: "Such a fine trip. And I rode in the front seat all the way.")

She had come to the wedding, staggering with the same cock-eyed defiance, though this was in the country and she didn't have occasion to flag a police car. But it didn't require that for Uncle Steward to get the general idea, while she stood there in a dress she too might have borrowed, it hung on her in such a way, and her face and withered gorge and even her pinch-nose glasses splotched with powder and set on her nose awry, talking about the trip and her houses: "So impatient with the squirrels. I'd cover all the pipe tops with screen if the workmen weren't too worthless to climb up and put it on" — and then for a climax giving Lucy a box of twenty identical cheap baby dresses bought at a fire sale in Delta Landing, to be put aside, as she said, for a rainy day: "Such pretty little dresses, and such a bargain, I couldn't resist them, though they're a mite soiled from the fire."

While on Lucy's side, in the absence of the more eccentric Pendles, was a whole neatly dressed and sedately human clan, heirs of a long tradition of decent values and civilized virtues, who drove down in their polished dark Buicks from Germantown; and friends of the family, who lived in country houses between Philadelphia and Baltimore, and visited and kept up a culture, as if they were still independent gentlemen of Jefferson's America or Jane Austen's England; all gathered in their white cords to drink (the old Quakers tea and the country gentlemen spiked punch) and talk about polite subjects.

Until the bridegroom jumped in with all fours, taking up something one of the young cousins, a literary man, said about an English playwright, Daniel countering the general tenor of acclaim with an outburst of scorn that might have been taken for personal jealousy, though he had never met the man: "Christopher Fry! He's a charlatan. All that pseudo-Elizabethan verbosity; and people pretend to admire it . . .I was asked last year to read in a play for a ladies' club; somebody was sick and I was to fill in at the last moment. I never heard of the play, but said I would."

Uncle Steward looked at Daniel, wondering: "Will he never use anything but the first person pronoun?"

"And it turned out to be this Fry thing. I couldn't read through the first scene by myself, but it was too late to back out. Luckily a friend was getting married that day, a young poet named Hanrahan, though it didn't turn out a lucky marriage for him; so I drank enough champagne to be half looped . . ."

Uncle Steward looked at Meryl, and her face was a study. The strange thing was, she was drawn ·to Daniel, as she had been to her own crackpot, Adam; but whenever Daniel opened up like that, her affection only supplied the basis for a tension, of which the counter-tug was British outraged propriety. Lucy felt the same thing, bur in her it was borne down by a younger love; even her father recoiled a bit, though with him it was not the want of convention; that was all right; it was the ego, his own eccentricities being always retiring.

Everybody stood there while Daniel blasted off like a volcano, until, remembering that she was hostess, and to salvage the feelings of any more tasteful lovers of drama, Meryl spoke, her usual sweet tolerance turned, by Daniel's pontificating from a chair he didn't hold, to a kind of chilly remoteness: "I grew up with the Frys. It's an old family. And though I have not read the play, I must say that the Frys do not produce charlatans."

But Daniel took up even that, crying: "Literary and personal morality are different things. The sweetest old lady in the world can write the most dishonestly sentimental poems." Until Lucy took his arm and led him away.

Thus they approached the wedding. Lucy had been around to all the churches in the neighborhood, trying to get somebody who would take them on; but whenever a preacher found out that the groom had hardly got his divorce from another family, he repeated the counsel of aged wisdom Uncle Steward had given in the garden, until finally Lucy's father went out to the backwoods and dug up a poor redheaded Baptist, who received a donation and came along, glad to officiate. He stood talking with Aunt Betsy, and Uncle Steward felt how right it was this pair should have got together, they might almost have been born for that meeting.

Then the best man, Daniel's spiritual father, old Max Loewenstein, came down the steps from the house, and Aunt Betsy pitched forward to shake his hand. She had met him on earlier visits, and for some reason this queer pair had always been fond of each other. Once at her special request, he had taken her by and introduced her to Einstein; she had talked with that great sage about the Greyhound bus and squirrels in the plumbing, and had got him to autograph a current biography, which she had later shown to everybody who was anybody in Delta Landing; so on her side it was an admiration that would never die.

Uncle Steward staggered again, under a new blow, simultaneously telling himself: "Two of a kind, another perfect match," and: "Hold on, I've seen that man before."

Loewenstein had driven down in a battered old Ford and had rushed into the house to dress. But he might as well have left it alone, since he couldn't have looked any drabber before he changed. It was a hot day in Maryland June, but he was heaped around with a black winter suit, slung over a messed shirt and tousled collar, with a tie like a rattail that had either been knotted way round at the side or had slipped there. He was at least as old as Aunt Betsy, and though he had a powerful face, it was by virtue of something intense, a bit wild and crazy, as if you had turned on a flashlight in the forest or ghetto, and he had poked up his head, his hair as long as Einstein's, but affected with some capricious scalp disease that brought it off in big patches, so there were bald spots here and there shining through mats of uncombed black and gray.

Still, it was an unforgettable face, and Uncle Steward had only to glance at it to bristle with recognition, while the best man, who was being introduced to him, stared, groping in a detached way, as if there was something puzzling in the case, he hardly knew what or why. "We've met," said Uncle Steward, with the patronizing boom. "Aren't you Dr. Loewenstein, who stayed with us at the Mill when you first came from Austria?"

Recognition dawned also in the other now, though of things far off, seen through a veil, too distant to evoke warmth or resentment. "Well surely. Mr. Cope. I felt something in the face. How are you? And your excellent wife? Couldn't be here?" (Aunt Hester, whose instinct against miscegenation went so far that even in eating she kept her vegetables methodically raked into separate piles, from each of which she took a precise little bite, and re-formed the heap before moving on to the next.) "Not well? I'm sorry. So you are going to become a relative to my dear friend?"

"It seems so," said Uncle Steward. That was an awkward direction. "What is it you do for a living, Dr. Loewenstein? I'm afraid I've forgotten."

"I am a philosopher, Mr. Cope, or a composer; for me philosophy is composing, and vice versa. I was with the New School, but now I have a small grant. What our friend Daniel proposes to do with paint, I am doing with music. We stand very much in a relationship to each other. The secret of these forms is the emergence in them of the new symbolic language; or you could say the very old symbolic language. In my case it returns directly to Pythagoras and the magic of number . . ."

"Of course," said Uncle Steward. "How could I have forgotten?" For it could go on for hours — on that original visit, it had — for days, interrupted, it seemed, only by demonstrations at the piano and the punctuations of sleep. How could he have forgotten indeed?

Daniel began to put the thing together. He had heard the story before, but had not made the connection: the Copes, the Mill. So that had been Uncle Steward, seen through foreign eyes. And of course Aunt Hester.

Being patriarch of one of the great Quaker lines, Steward Cope was up to his neck in worthy causes. His mere presence on a charitable drive gave it an air of smiling success. During the Hitler time, when so many refugees were running from Europe with nothing to live on, he had taken his share as guests at the big mill house with its outlying dormitories, where, with the numerous tribe of family and visiting relatives, there was always room for a few more.

Aunt Hester joined in this enterprise with the same spirit. Uncle Steward could advise marriage in one's own circle as a thing he knew all about; it had worked out splendidly for him. Aunt Hester was not only his kind, they were brought up inside the same wall at Springmount, and had married with the blessing of both families, which were one.

If anything, Aunt Hester had more of the stateliness of English gentry than he, or of that rarer American strain which survives in a few vanishing habitats of Boston, New York and Philadelphia. Compared with her English cognates she was more homespun, certainly less compromising. While she had welcomed refugees to the sixteen-foot long groaning board as a part of her Quaker duty, she expected they would show a Quaker energy in return.

She would come to breakfast with a small list of tasks to be apportioned for the day or the weekend, and it would run something like this: "Cultivate the orchard ready for sowing grass seed. Work on bricks between times and haul broken bricks to the gully in meadow. Rake the lawn and spread 1½ tons ground lime and 1½ tons superphosphate. Uncover the strawberries, leaving straw between the rows. Sprinkle a little nitrate on the asparagus and strawberries, without touching the strawberry leaves. Finish painting the yard furniture. Water the newly planted trees, especially hollies and pines. Get the honeysuckle off the wall. Make wren houses from the gourds. Manure around the big box bushes. Fill the roller and roll the lawn."

As for von Loewenstein, though he had dropped the von, he was an aristocratic Jew, of a family that had connections in the capitals of Europe, where they had another tradition, of writing, painting, composing, or just talking, as if talking indeed was a high calling. They had always been artists or philosophers or patrons of the arts or philosophy, and they hardly knew anything about any other kind of job. Loewenstein was like that city Jew who complained of expenses and how much his family ate: "Und eppels, dot boy of mine, he eats dem eppels like dey grew on trees." So how could he take to repairing fences or harvesting fruit?

He hung around the house as out of key as the battered upright piano on which he picked out rather harsh dissonances. He wondered how such wealthy people could have such a dismal piano, not knowing the real wonder was that they had one at all. A generation ago music was one of the arts of the devil for Friends, and though the Copes and Woodruffs used to get together on holidays and sing the old favorites in their clear voices, the only instruments they had to accompany them were the mouth organ and the jew-sharp, which perhaps the Overseers had found too small to frown on. But the younger Cope daughter, Gretel, had insisted on piano lessons, so this battered upright had been bought from a neighboring church.

Mostly Loewenstein would talk, dominating the dinner table with heavily accented discourses on music, the arts, and the philosophy of transcendence. When Aunt Hester began to suggest jobs, he was at a loss. He didn't know how to wash dishes, forgot about making his own bed, didn't care whether it was ever made or changed; and though he was one of the deepest wits in the West, and talked, at least in German, divinely, they got tired of his table-rambles, not on the ground of substance, but just because, as Daniel was later to observe, anybody who came without a clear official stamp and social seal on him, certifying; "This professor so-and-so is a recognized authority on such-and-such, and can now and then tell us a little something about it" — if anybody stood up on his hind legs like Lazarus from the grave and declared himself about religion, science, art or history, any of the things one should spend a lifetime getting to be prophetic on — the whole tribe would bridle up in that propriety of the herd, from which Lucy's father, long ago, to their common dismay, had quietly but unalterably withdrawn. So the profundity of what he spoke was little salve to Aunt Hester's feelings, when Loewenstein, with the German-Jewish abandon which fights out the issues of mind as if they were worth fighting for, threw himself into the exposition, pacing the room, or tugging his tattered shreds of paleoanthropus fur, and crying out in the guttural giant-speech of the Wessobrunner Gebet ("Dat gefregen ih mit firahim"): "But that's just what it *is*; the property of spirit *is* TRANSCENDENCE."

Max Loewenstein, on the other side, was no more comforted by the disciplined reserve and earthly vigilance of the place. It was a hive of doing, of what he could only call bustle. Daniel had thought of the Mill as a place of peace, though not so much so as Woodruff farm. But he did not mind cutting up a tree in the morning for the luxury of an afternoon by the mill dam. As for Loewenstein, he had never had an axe in his hand. The European tradition could not have turned out a more impractical man.

His bodily shape declared how far he lived out of physical connection. He had one of those Semitic frames whimsically suggestive of a bird. On long pipestem white legs was a spraddly mass of back, chest and belly, out of which the wise old head craned up on a quizzically twisted neck. At Appalachian they would go down the rocky trail to the waterfall in its fen-walled hollow. Max would scramble down, change clothes, swim, change and struggle out, only now and then interrupting talk about distant wise concerns with an echo of somebody's "fine water" or "beautiful place," transforming even such pleasantries by the oracular emphasis of his deep-mouthed speech. Sometimes, as he tripped or banged his shins or as his arthritis twinged him, he would boost the volume of whatever he was saying, turning the most indifferent phrases to an Oi weh of ululation; and if he happened to be at the bottom of one of the steep places trying to climb out, he would look up, still talking of profound matters, groan and flap his arms, like a fledgling aspiring to fly.

His ineffectuality was lovable, but you had to pay the price: At Appalachian they had been swimming in the hole under the falls. Max was on the shallow side, dipping and splashing, splendidly unaquatic. Daniel had swum across and climbed up the slippery rocks by the fall. Little Octavia was wading near Max in the shallows. She went in too deep and buoyancy took away her traction. In slow motion, daintily tripping, she drifted out on the shelving bottom. As her lips bubbled under, she gave a cry. Daniel looked around. "Catch her, Max," he yelled; "catch Octavia."

Splashing and blowing: "Wuaagh! Maarvelous! Aarrgh!" the great gutturals.

Daniel was so far away, he shouted again and waved his arms: "Hey, Max! Help Octavia!"

"How? Wundervoll, ahh?"

Daniel slithered down the rocks, knocking and skinning himself; he plunged and swam. When he got to Octavia, she was going down for what was at least the third time. He pulled her up and slapped the water out of her. Choking, coughing, she howled.

"Ach, Gott! I did not knaaw," said Loewenstein. "She might have draawned," roaring in what Octavia called his giant talk.

At the Mill it might have been predicted that Max would take on himself the rolling of the lawn. And anybody could have told that when the roller was filled with water, Max would let it go on the hill, or that the roller, having dragged Max halfway down, would let him go and pursue its course into the mill race, taking out a bed of flowers, part of a low wall, and a couple of young dogwoods.

Next morning Uncle Steward announced that a wing they had been building on the house was finished, and that all hands should appear on deck (the sea captain ancestry cropping out) to move books over to the new library. It was incredible, Max said. They moved the entire library, thousands of volumes, in a single day. "But you can't think about books or order them this way," he told Aunt Hester.

Of course Loewenstein would have piled up an armload of books and started over. But he was sure to drop them as he went in the door, and groping to pick them up, what should he hit on but an old tome on Quakerism, opened to the exact passage which seemed to illuminate the busy mystery of the Copes. He would sit hunched on the threshold reading while Uncle Steward and Aunt Hester and the rest trooped by heaped with countless volumes. Loewenstein couldn't possibly have dealt with books that way, even with dull books. Loading or unloading, he must be picking them up one by one, leafing through, asking questions, in short, as Aunt Hester saw it, getting in the way.

"I wish you wouldn't talk so much," she told him in a fury.

But the strangest institution was at the dinner table, where Aunt Hester, looking through her special gold-rimmed carving spectacles and regally wielding the long sharpened knife, apportioned the rewards to each according to his merit, focusing on a brawny visiting cousin or grown son: "Yes, George, thee has worked hard today. I think thee deserves a decent morsel." And she would hack him off a solid slab of the beef. "And what about thee, Arthur?" to a grandson. "Has thee cleaned the garage as thee planned?" (It was Hester Cope who had laid that plan.) "Well, a moderate morsel." For a week or two she gave the immigrant the benefit of the doubt. One did not starve a newcomer. But as time passed and he gave more of the day and night to that excruciating idleness he called working on his book, she stopped asking the hopeful question. Lowering her voice and eyes, she would shave off the thinnest sliver and spread it like gold leaf on the plate of the visiting drone.

So in time hunger would have driven him away. But it was not allowed to come to that. One morning Aunt Hester took him aside. He did not repeat what she said; no doubt it was regal and polite. But his summary of the result was that he had been thrown out of Berlin by Hitler, and again out of Austria, and that finally he had been thrown out of Quaker Mill by Hester Cope.

Daniel was not to get the details of this straight until after the wedding. So the supreme evidence of limitation (that wise old Jew having become for him a touchstone of range in others) was not on hand until it would have been too late had there been anything to be regretted. But even if it had burst on him that morning, as Aunt Betsy and Max von Loewenstein burst on Lucy, it would not have altered anything, because he already knew. He could hardly have missed seeing that the worth of this clan rested on something almost stuffy, the other aspect of their balanced calm. It was only that from the first, sensing this, he knew that Lucy, end-product of that line, had somehow been born to surpass it; and when the separation papers were signed and he was free, that Easter time, to go to Woodruff Farm and meet her father, he guessed, if not how, then through whom.

Considering from all sides the impossible fact of their alliance, they had both been asking and partly answering the question — as she had done once and for all the frightening forenoon of that wedding, when his aunt had appeared, and then Max, and then Daniel himself had confronted the relatives, and her uncle had drawn her aside for a last talk, reinforcing what every respectable preacher in the region had also told her; and she avoided Daniel and went to her room, shaking in her shoes, thinking she couldn't go ahead, she wouldn't, it was crazy; and actually started down to see her daddy and call the whole thing off, even on the wedding day, but met Daniel on the stairs coming up to look for her, stared at him, and laughed, he looked so disreputable and wild, yet not at all as she had envisaged him through her uncle and the preachers of Germantown — not dangerous, just grotesquely, egocentrically there. Present. So it was not pity. And it was not even passion, though her relatives would hardly have been convinced of that if they could have seen what followed the meeting on the stairs. No, it was an intuition, not rational perhaps, but also not of the passion, that by some trick of engineering a bridge could be erected at this point, and that it might bear a considerable bulk of trade.

She laughed and took him to her room and told him how scared she had been. He looked serious and said he didn't blame her, it was a long gamble; if what she felt was just pity or passion or anything that might wear off, she'd better say so, because another blowup would be too many. Then she embraced him and said she was sure; it wasn't pity or passion at all. He laced his arms around her and kissed her, and they fell back on the bed and made love. Passion — not just, but plenty — more perhaps than Uncle Steward would have found whole-some. So they got up smiling and went down to face the music.

Though that was only the preliminary music — talk and luncheon. A few hours later when she had put on the wedding dress and the preacher had arrived, she was still so weak, as she came from the house and down the steps to the lawn where everybody had fallen silent but the shaggy-headed best man, obliviously arguing how timid reactionary politics had dissociated itself from every people's move-ment and cut us off from the current of the world, how conservative caution offered nothing in an age requiring revolution — while all the conservatives and Republicans who made up the gathering fell back astonished — the great guttural voice booming on: "It's the poles of energy; you have your choice, to risk fire or be sealed in ice . . . " — walking into that great blaze, she felt her knees trembling so, that if her father had not been there to lean on, walking by her side, holding her arm, she would surely have fainted away. And then, when he left her, as instructed, and she had to go it alone, converging with Daniel on the redheaded country preacher, she might never have made it . . .

But twelve white ducks she had raised and fed, sensing her pres-ence, came around the comer of the house waddling and quacking, and fell in line behind her. So she took strength, and with that train of gabbling bridesmaids, she walked pale to the altar, which was a bank of lilies, and standing, white as a lily, a duck, a swan, she opened her trembling bill and spoke the fatal words.

While the gaudy peacock her Quaker father, for some reason or other, liked to keep around the place, that bird of luxurious male pride, spread out the iridescent fan of his tail, and violated the whole yard and farm with the raucous assault of his cry.

8 ~ The Delta Set

"Hell, B.J., I just got off the plane. You aren't taking me to a party?"

"I sure am. I'd never hear the last, if you stayed home the night of my aunt's barbecue. Everybody in the Delta is going to be there, and Lynn Wells is going to dance, when they've had enough drinks to appreciate her. As a matter of fact, she dances like an angel. But remember, you're old enough to be her father, so don't give her the tiger's eye."

"You can post a warning, B.J., to protect her from me. So it's the week of your aunt's barbecue, where everybody is going to be, and Lynn Wells is going to dance like an angel, and you pack your own wife off to Natchez, and then tell me not to mess around . . ."

The phone was ringing, and B.J. had grabbed it: "Who? Well I'm damned. What are you doin in Delta Landing? Well where are you then? In Florida? Sure, I know you live in Florida, but I didn't think you'd be phonin from way down there. Just want to talk? What you been drinkin? Naw, Jane's not here. She's down at Natchez. You know her mother couldn't manage a month without her. Me? I wouldn't be caught dead down there. Yeah, they struck oil, but it hasn't changed a thing. Same old antebellum. And the ticks are terrible. Jane asked her uncle what she could do about em, and he said wear a couple of greasy rags tied round your legs and they won't bother you. So I guess they're walkin the plantation bundled up in greasy rags. If I'd a been there they'd a got me down and tied em on me whether or no. No, I'm not complainin; I stay home. Nothin much. Makin a little music now, and then. I've organized a chamber orchestra. Hell, man, there's nobody from this town ever learned to play. These are Yankees, from the air base. I'm teachin two of em to play the cello, navy wives. Got em into fourth position. Not posture, position. It's music. Sure Jane's comin back; whatdya think? Give her your love? Well I will, as soon as I can get the greasy rags and ticks off of her. Same to you . . .

"Crazy guy. College roommate. Lives down at the bottom of Florida. Wanted to say hello."

B.J. had grown up on a plantation south of town. His father, Mr. Farnham, had bought it from Major Shields and then married the Major's daughter, so the Major never had to move. Which was lucky, because it would have taken a derrick. Daniel could remember him sitting on the porch filling the whole swing; singing throaty songs about "I fought with old Marse Robert . . ." I hates the Constitution, the Spangled Banner" and the rest. They said he was the fattest man in the Delta, and you'd have gone further than that to have found his equal. He used to say it was to pay him back for riding so hard and getting so little to eat through the War; but Mrs. Farnham would stand with her hands on her hips and say: "Daddy Major, it's because you've eaten so much and sat so still ever afterwards."

He got so big, they said he couldn't undo his own britches, so he had a colored boy named Penny Whistle, who went around with him all the time to unbutton the Major and get him ready for making water. Daniel had heard the story from his father and had assumed it was true, though later, at the University of Virginia, he heard the same thing about another fat Confederate. Anyway, according to the account, the Major was walking down the alley to the post office one winter day when he had to go. He hauled over to the bushes and the boy undid the buttons. But his fingers were cold; he fumbled and nothing came to hand. "Ah'm sorry Major," he stammered, "but Ah cain't find it; Ah jus cain't find it." Major Shields roared down at him:

"By God;" he said, "you better find it, you scoundrel. You had it last."

That was B.J.'s grandfather on his mother's side. But B.J.'s father had come from the North, and that grandfather had fought for emancipation. The son had grown up believing in the cause, so about 1900 he came, with his whole fortune, and bought the run-down Shields plantation. He put up brick Negro cabins with running water and plumbing. Like other idealists of the age he thought ideals would pay. After twenty years of fighting through floods, crop failures and depressions, not to mention stopped up drains (in those days, they'd have flushed a dead cat down the stool), and bailing his darkies out of jail after love-brawls and razor fights: "I have paid the price of all explorers," he told Judge Byrne. "I have spent my life and the heritage of my fathers running a free boardinghouse for Negroes."

When Mr. Farnham died only the land was left. B.J. held on to it, working in his aunt's department store, and writing for the paper at night. Then the town began to grow in his direction. He made a fortune in a few years, selling lots. At the right moment he cashed in on the whole plantation and bought the town newspaper, which was on its last legs. His father's ambition seemed to have revived in him in a practical way. With the paper, B.J. could not only fight the Citizens' Councils and push for reform, he could turn the fight into news; and however people disapproved, news was money. He fought the Memorial issue, to have a war monument with all the names; and when the Council wouldn't allow the Negro names, he forced them to have no names at all, a blank tablet, about which he wrote editorials that were reprinted all over the nation. He fought the voting issue and the school issue. One day he began to use Mr. and Mrs. in writing about Negroes. As always part of the town rose in rebellion. Old subscriptions were canceled, but new ones more than replaced them. The Mississippi legislature voted him an enemy to the state. He answered with articles in the *Saturday Evening Post*. What could anybody do? He was rich; he was famous; the place worshiped fame.

He built himself an air-conditioned house, bought a harpsichord and records of early music, started an orchestra. He lived in Delta Landing as if his library — Purcell sounding on the filtered air — was the town's center. . .

"How's the great cause of Integration in Delta Landing, B.J.?"

They were walking through the moonlit wood, a stand of the old oak forest B.J. and Daniel had explored in their youth, after the tornado had twisted down great limbs of the trees, a park-suburb now, with B.J.'s house at one end and the house of B.J.'s aunt at the other.

"Integration! The word's a farce. You know integration's gone backward. I used to think pressure from the North would help, but I swear to God, I don't know. Two years ago I wrote an article for *Harper's* on Negro establishments here that had always been patronized by white people. Do you know every one of them's had to close since? No threats, nothing; they just lose business, go broke. It's easy for me, I'm safe, and I made money off the article; but what about the Negroes I tried to encourage? Even the Nelson Street whore house is gone, though I didn't have anything to do with that. Besides, it was only integrated one way. They had white girls and black girls and white customers and black customers; but the white men came in the front and could take their pick; the black men had to come in the back and stick to their color."

"You mean Madam Bosoni's has that been closed?"

"Her name is Mrs. Jessie Queen. But that's the place. It was raided on last winter."

"Why that was an institution of the town."

"Sure. Jessie Queen was a good citizen. When I used to work in my aunt's store she would come in to buy Christmas presents for her girls who had married and gone away. She would send them lacy black underwear with notes like: 'To Fat Cat, for old times. Love, Jessie.' She saved her money and paid the police and never had any trouble until that old maid schoolteacher, Miss Cramer, moved into the corner house next door, You remember, she came to Junior High to teach while we were there; used to stand at the top of the stairs scratching herself in the wrong place? What can a woman expect when she moves into a white house on a colored street? But of course she called the police. 'There's something wrong in that house,' she said; 'There's men coming there all the time. There's white men coming there and there's Negroes coming there, and there's sailors coming there.' It was one of the sailors who touched her off, knocking at her door by mistake, saying he wanted a girl, and when she said there weren't any girls there, he must have been blind drunk, because he told the old bat: 'What the hell, honey, you'll do.' So she had the police clean it up. And can you imagine, it was the integration angle that raised the fuss —as if it hadn't been that way for fifty years. We published a paid announcement for Jessie when she left town. It said: 'Mrs. Jessie Queen regrets to disappoint her faithful customers, but discovers that because of discrimination, Delta Landing is no longer a decent place to bring up her children in.'"

The back yard was strung with lanterns; and the glow and babble of voices spilled over into the woods. The whole area had been sprayed with D.D.T., to polish off the mosquitoes, along with whatever other small life was in the air or on the earth or in the waters under the earth. There was a smell of poison dew on the leaves, but the cocktails were flowing, and to judge by the noise, care was half drowned. B.J.'s aunt, who had horrified the family long ago by marrying a Jew, and who now owned half the town, met them in the hall. She had some of the fat and some of the vigor of Major Shields. She bubbled over Daniel with the excited squeals of Southern ladies. Then she took him in to introduce him to some of the guests, or rather to remind him of people he had known but partly forgotten.

These were in the living room, close to the source of drink:

Emily — though in her case it was no doubt fear of the night air. No introduction needed.

Her husband — no introduction could possibly lend him interest.

These two were standing in front of the sofa. Seated in a large chair, a bit out of things, was Lawyer Hargreaves' wife, as gentle a white-haired little lady as the Old South could breed.

Drifting toward her, Mr. Wilson, with his blue skin and Presbyterian ways. He was drinking unspiked fruit punch, but plenty.

By the table, Herb Finlay, drinking as much of the spiked type as possible, though it produced little alleviation. He used to play electric trains with Daniel's brother.

B.J.'s cousin, who was putting all his money into building tugboats, stood in the middle of the rug. His wife Patsy was by him, of Daniel's age, Patricia Towne Dudley's charming daughter. More conspicuous were the cousin's associates, Mr. and Mrs. Pink Jones, looking like crawfish at a lobster broil. They were of the new river-rich, the barge crowd, and had made incredible money since World War II. They used to run the *Island Queen*, but now they were creeping into society.

The introductions were more than a naming of names. There were threshold recoveries, auras of gossip and memory released by the face, the touch of hands, conversations in the mind's receiver:

"Mr. Wilson? Looks like a zombie. Purply-blue. I never saw a man such a color."

"He can't help it. The doctor gave him some ointment for a skin rash years ago. Told him to see if it didn't clear it up. So he never went back, just kept on using that ointment all year. When he did go back it was about his complexion: 'Doc,' he says, 'what makes me so blue? My wife says I look like a corpse.' 'You do look like the devil,' says the doctor. 'You must be poisoned. What're you takin?' 'I'm not takin anything but that medicine you gave me to smear on the rash.' 'What rash? What medicine?' 'Don't you remember, last year I had a rash, and you told me to smear that stuff on it? Well, the rash spread everywhere, but I kept smearin it, and now it's under control.' 'Under control?' said the doctor. 'That medicine should only have been used a short time.' (It had gentian violet, or zinc, or something in it.) 'You mean you've been smearin it all over yourself for a year and never asked me? Man, you'll be blue till the day you die.'"

"And the day after, I should imagine."

Other voices entered, crisscross; confusing the play:

"I'm not talkin about his color. That's not what makes him a zombie. He won't look you in the eye. I had to go to the warehouse today, and he came up trying to be friendly, but it wouldn't work. I tell you, he's a moral fish."

"Mr. Wilson? What are you talkin about? Everybody knows he's the most Christian gentleman in town and a leader of the Y.M.C.A. and the Baptist Church."

"That's the devil of it. It shows religion and morality aren't enough. It makes me weep to look at him. 'See,' his face says: 'God wrecks you by good impulses.' "

"Good impulses! The man's a moral coward. Blakely works there, and when he told him the books were crooked, Mr. Wilson wouldn't do a thing. The whole place was crooked and he was afraid to open it up."

"What do you expect? His own cousin stole the money. And Mr. Wilson was as noble as a man could be. He sold his house and borrowed on his land and paid the whole thing out and saved the family from disgrace, though everybody knew."

"You bet he saved him. And he's still got him workin down there. He puts all his kinfolks on the payroll and gives them more money than Blakely gets, whether they loaf or steal. And that's what you call a Christian gentleman. Well I call him a moral zombie."

Even in imagination Daniel's voice would be breaking in, going way back in the talk, as if he had a reaction time like a dinosaur and something had just reached his nerve centers: "Sounds like Dr. Fisher. Guess he sent quite a bill for making the poor guy go blue."

That settled Mr. Wilson. And Herb Finlay? Who could forget Herb, idiot-savant with the big head? He had astonished his teachers in the second and third grades by doing long division instantly in that bubble pate. Then he began to memorize statistics about everything, all the phone numbers and car licenses in Delta Landing. He could tell how many spars were in the Brooklyn Bridge and all the other bridges. In his teens he used to interrupt a company saying: "Do you know?" It was always: Do you know — "that if a cat walked so many steps a minute across such and such suspension bridge and never broke the rhythm, it would go into resonant vibration and fall down?" Because he had figured it out, and claimed to have predicted the one that went to pieces out west when the soldiers marched across it.

Yes, and at the time when he and Little Gerald were so wrapped up in trains, Finlay had memorized the timetable of the Illinois Central, and suddenly it came to him that if they would make a few changes in routing, they could do the same business with two less trains. He wrote them a short letter. They checked, and sure enough, it was true; so they sent an agent to the town to offer Finlay a job. At his house all they could get from the maid was that Herb Finlay was at school. The fellow went along, thinking it must be the math teacher over there. As a matter of fact, Finlay was in math class, but as the door opened, out came this eleven-year-old skinny boy with the big bubble head. The fellow had to go away without hiring him; and Herbert never developed after that, though he kept on fetching up statistics whenever a conversation lagged.

It was hardly lagging as Daniel entered the room. Segregation was the issue. There had been warnings about mongrelizing and the fall of Rome, Mr. Wilson and Pink Jones holding forth, in different styles, but to the same effect; and some gorbellied men with chamber of commerce connections were drifting in at the doors, ready to have their say and maybe bait editor Farnham, when Mrs. Hargreaves, in the sweetest voice one ever heard and with the guaranteed aristocratic

Southern turn, spoke from her chair: "You great big men make me tired. You know this is a democracy and, integration has got to come. So you might just as well get used to it."

The room went as noiseless as if it had been evacuated. The influx at the doors reversed itself. Daniel was about to say: "I congratulate you, ma'am," but he thought: "Who am I, coming from the North?" People looked around and sipped their cocktails. It was Herb Finlay's chance, as always, to take up the slack.

"Do you know," he said, "what it is that women control sixty-five percent of in these United States?"

The sigh-was of relief: "What is it?" they said.

Finlay leaned forward in his prophetic way, as if he'd solved the problem of the ages: "Property," he said, "that's what it is. Women control sixty-five percent of all the property in the United States of America."

"And do you know what women control one hundred percent of in these United States of America?" It was Mrs. Pink Jones, leaning in like over the rail of her tugboat, her drink in one hand, the other on her hip, her shoulder slung forward and the wrinkled elbow advanced, and such a weathered grin on her face nobody could think at all.

"No. What?" they said, staring.

That outrageous tugboat grin opened: "What do women control one hundred percent of?" She laid the answer in front of them like showing her underwear, the drawled single word: "Puuhssy. "

The company fell apart. Finlay looked as if he had to get to the phone book fast to memorize a hundred new numbers. Mr. Wilson turned off smothering noises in his chest. And poor Emily, who took the brunt of it face to face, like an accusation against her, and maybe it was, went whiter than she had been before and sank onto the sofa; and if the sofa hadn't been there she would have hit the floor.

As Daniel looked around,' silly sweet Patsy, with whom he had meant to talk, had disappeared, but Mrs. Hargreaves was still sitting in her chair, undisturbed as ever. Daniel spoke to her and asked if her husband was at the party. Mr. Hargreaves, she thought, was watching the barbecue. Daniel and B.J. went into the yard and found the old lawyer by the pit where the steer was being carved.

"Mr. Hargreaves, I'd like to sue that hospital. They never told me they were keeping my aunt there and they never answered my letters; they've held her by force and driven her half crazy."

Mr. Hargreaves put his hand on Daniel's and lowered his voice, as if he didn't want the Lord God to overhear them. "Don't say things like that, Daniel. It won't do any good. The hospital would say they were following Dr. Fisher's orders. And Dr. Fisher meant it for the best, you know."

"Meant the devil! Why didn't they answer my letters? I hate the hospitals and the doctors and the stranglehold they've got on us. I don't care for the courts either, but at the moment I'd rather sue than pay."

"Daniel," he said, "I tell you as your lawyer and your friend, stop talking about it. You wouldn't have the chance of a snowball in hell. Somebody's got to pay those bills, and Miss Betsy's not in fit shape. I'll go with you in the morning and we'll let her sign power of attorney, so you can take charge of everything."

"Let her! Mr. Hargreaves, if you think Betsy Byrne is going to sign power of attorney to me or anybody else without being forced to, you've got another think coming."

"You're wrong, Daniel," said B.J. "When I went to see her she kept saying she wanted to turn it all over to you. So many worries, she said, and she was so tired."

"She's said that for years, and what's come of it? Trouble with you, B.J., you've never had to deal with an old maid Southern aunt and a Byrne to boot."

"Shucks," said BJ., "they're all alike. My wife's got three aunts in Natchez, just the same."

Patricia Towne Dudley rushed over, almost tumbling them into the barbecue pit. "Oh Daniel, I'm so relieved you've come. We've all been worried sick about poor Betsy, and those Colesons with her all the time, like vultures. She's out of her mind, you know. What ever are you going to do?"

"If I'd been tied down in the hospital, Mrs. Dudley, I'd be out of my mind too. I'm going to take her home, and find somebody to look after her, and if I can't find anybody else, I'll ask the Colesons. What would you suggest?"

"Why Daniel, none of us have the least idea what to do with her. She wouldn't stay in a nursing home. One night at the hospital she came tearing out of the room in the middle of the night dragging a couple of nurses with her, little as she is, and gave such a push on the elevator button, she drove it clear into the wall, and sprained her thumb too."

As if Daniel didn't know.

From the plane he had gone straight to the hospital. In the disinfected lounge where people in leather chairs waited news of birth or dying, he asked the room number; then he walked up the back stairs.

He had been younger the other time, when he leapt up the steps three at a stride.

It was Judge Byrne then who raised himself in the bed — "Suffering Mother of God, when will he come?" — and sank back as he had been doing for days, the heart pounding in the big chest: "Why did I give up? Why not keep on until I dropped?"

Daniel had stood in the door, instinct with force — as Gerald Byrne, forty years earlier, leaping up a steamship companionway and knocking at a certain cabin, had stood before Elspeth, married traveler, his first total love. In the boy's face the old man read the shock of his own change: the skin a parchment on the bones, the arms withered, the nose pointed, only the eyes under beetling brows impassioned as always, but more frustrated. And then the wasteful power of the young arms embraced him; he felt the smooth cheek hardly downed, an electric charged sphere against the flaccid roughness of his. He fell to the pillow, shaking his head: "Son, son, they've almost got the old man down."

Struggling to sitting again, he breathed in gasps, holding his white shins to balance himself against falling backward, his gaze on the shrunken calves, his voice ranging on, between a sigh and the old oratorical power; he recounted the mortal sufficiency of his fatal four disorders, and how the Lord could have spared artillery, but unfortunately a Byrne was tough to kill. He shook his head and slipped back, panting: "Ring, son . . . Have to have oxygen . . . Too much talk . . . "

Daniel pulled the cord. No one came. Gerald Byrne sat up with a force that made the former weakness like a sham, his voice surging a moment to the boom that had echoed through the auditoriums of the state: "A man had as lief pray for water in hell as for service in this beastly morgue. Go out there, son, and tell that nurse to come a runnin. Don't get that hatchet-faced one; I want little Miss Trigg."

But the hatchet-face had appeared in the door. "Woman!" the judge roared, "I've had trouble enough with you. Don't let me see your face again." She withdrew. The voice wilted to its whisper: "Get little Miss Trigg, son. Tell her I can't breathe."

"Ah, my love," he said as they returned, "I'm afraid I've got to have more air."

She slipped the tiny rubber tube up his nostril, stuck it in place with adhesive.

"Careful, sweetheart," he said, "my face is all over raw. Don't hit that scab. Find a new place."

She turned the valve. "And take this pill," she said; "you need a rest."

The water gauge hovered between three and four; oxygen bubbled from the tank into the dying assemblage of cells. The breathing eased. "Better," he sighed. Feeling strength, he rose to the grand manner: "It's amazing, in an age of science, with a thousand-dollar apparatus to supply oxygen, that the only link between the man and the machine is this barbarous adhesive. Look at my face. How could anybody invent such a system?"

The flow of bottled gas, protracting the voice, protracted whatever behind the voice rose up, vociferous. It was time to confront something, but Daniel was young. "You look strong," he said. "We'll take you home soon" — falling into the hospital false ways.

"We've got to talk straight," said his father. "But not now. I'm too tired." He dozed off on the word . . .

The same hospital. Daniel climbing the same back stair. The same floor, and through the smell of ether to what was almost the same room. The door was hardly ajar. Daniel pushed it back. Aunt Bets was sitting in the chair by the window, looking vacant yet tense. A raw-boned nurse hung over her, as if she had just pushed her down and would do it again if she got the chance. There is a family resemblance which appears only when the bone structure is revealed, and the more it is revealed, the larger the family. Hers was revealed: the perdurable mummy, the clan of the woeful skull.

Daniel did not know if she would recognize him, but she rose. The big nurse leaned forward, ready to grab her if she tried anything. "It's all right," he said. "Leave the room." For he saw his aunt's tears.

"Dannie," she said. "You've come at last. It's been so long. But I'm stronger now" — checking the sniffles. "I didn't want to be sick, but I couldn't help it. I'm ashamed of myself, but we all have to be sick sometime. But you've come, and it's time to go home. I'll get my pocketbook, and we'll run along." She staggered to the dresser and opened the drawer. "The house is just around the comer."

Whatever she was thinking of — the nursing home of her youth, or Dr. Fisher's house — this hospital was a mile and a half from her part of town.

"Aunt Bets," Daniel said, planting a kiss on the pasty cheek, "it's a long way home. You can't walk it today. Sit down and let's talk. I've got to find a key and get the house cleaned and hire somebody to look after us before we can go."

She shifted levels. As if he had joined in the conspiracy to hold her. "That's not your problem," she said. "Mother and I will attend to that."

He took her hand. "Aunt Bets," he said, "Grandmother died some years back."

Wide eyes. "No," she whispered, "Daddy's dead, but Mother didn't die. She'll have Nellie fix your room. Nellie's young, but she can clean."

(Nellie Bly, hunched on her shaky porch, rubbing creosote into a flea-bitten gray head. Daniel will go the next day: "Is that for looks or health?" he will ask. She gets up, shuffling and cackling before she recognizes him. Then she falls on his neck and asks for news of poor Miss Betsy. "Dey done hilt her too long, Misser Daniel. Ah's pinin to see her, but Ah couldn't go back to dat horse-spittal. Seem like dey must a give her a shock evry day, jus to holt her there.")

"I've got to get home," Aunt Betsy said. "Mother will be worried. Besides, there's a party at the Lakes'. Brother's taking me. And we have to pack for Europe."

She was a temple not in space but in time, enclave within enclave. From the vulgar yard of today she could retire, through successive sanctums, toward her holy of holies, the great year of 1903 (great in hope, at least) when she had come out, and Brother as a young legislator had introduced her to the society of Jackson, and then in the summer had taken her abroad.

Like him she had grown up in the dream. Standing at the center of the soul's landscape, one saw, in every direction, bright vistas: lovers in the glow of eternal vows sitting under the arching sympathy of trees, turtle doves paired on the branches; and of course there was the future, the Columbian exhibit of a world growing nobler and richer; but most of all TRAVEL as if the *exotic* had changed its spelling to beckon like Eros, like love. From coffee tins she had collected week to week colored souvenir cards, on one side a map, on the other the chromowonder of a faraway scene: Newport, a gingerbread mansion of a New York tycoon, waves breaking and a sail in the wind, and on the beach and veranda debutantes and eligible young men; or there was a shot of the Western Plains, a pair of braves on white horses against a plunging brown sea of buffalo; then the remoter callings — Hawaiian nights, palms, life warm and sweet as the always fruiting mango; or this one, reminding a prim age of covert joys — slaves and odalisques by a pool in a Persian harem; but always most treasured, most returned to, were the views of Europe: Warwick Castle, Anne Hathaway's cottage, a swan on the Avon, Swiss glaciers, ruins of a Roman villa among olives by an Italian lake, Florence from Oltr'Amo — culture, art — memories, my children!

Aunt Bets took the purse from the drawer and started for the door; but the white-robed woman who had been lurking outside popped in, taking her by the arm: "Now Miss Byrne, you can't go yet. Dr. Fisher's got to see you, and then it'll be bedtime." She pushed her down into the chair. "Give me that pocketbook; you won't be needin it awhile."

"It's good of Dr. Fisher to have me in his house this way," Aunt Bets murmured (a quixotic assurance he was not to send a bill), "but I won't impose on him any longer. It's fine to go visiting in the daytime; but I don't like to sleep in a strange bed. Ill just walk on now, and look after Mother." She got up, as no doubt she had been doing every fifteen minutes for these last fifteen days, as if the discussion of why she should stay had not even occurred.

The nurse caught her, and in another tone, like the keeper of a reform school, snarled: "Miss Byrne, you don't want to have trouble now, while your nephew's here." Then quietly: "He's goin to take you home, but you have to wait for Dr. Fisher. I can't have you leavin without Dr. Fisher's O.K. He'll be here soon. It's gettin dark. I'll pull the curtains."

Aunt Betsy resigned herself to the chair. "One thing I will say" — her voice rose to a pent-up fury — "Dr. Albert Fisher has certainly turned his house into a sanatorium. It beats all how he can want so many people around all the time."

The door opened. The balding Dr. Fisher entered with his prissy strut.

"Dr. Al," Aunt Betsy said, struggling for elevation in the deep chair, "Daniel's come to take me home. I want you to tell these nurses to leave me alone. You know I'm perfectly able to walk home."

"It's dark, Miss Betsy; you can't walk home now. It's a long way to your house."

"Why it's hardly a block. We're right on Bolivar."

"No ma'am," he drawled, "this hospital is on Belmont."

"Al Fisher," she said, gathering herself together. "I want you to stop all this talk and confusion. You call this a hospital, but it's not a hospital, it's a home. You call this Belmont Avenue, but it's not Belmont, it's Bolivar. This whole town is in a dreadful state of turmoil because of people calling things by names they aren't supposed to have. There are too many people hired on the taxpayers' money to change the names of streets; but you know better, and I know better, so don't talk nonsense."

"Well, Miss Betsy," he said, "let's see how you are." He took out the stethoscope. She yielded to its authority. "You're fine," he said, "doin fine."

"Good," she answered, heaving up from the chair. "I'll be going." But she saw the nurse at the door. She took a step toward the curtained window, then turned to Dr. Fisher. "I'd better not go down that way. I don't need any broken bones from any dark stairs."

It was a clean drop to the ground.

"No ma'am," said Dr. Fisher, "I wouldn't go down that way. It's dangerous. You spend the night where you are, and Daniel will come for you in the morning."

"I hate to admit it," she nodded, "but I'm tired. So tired. I'll stay one night with you, Dr. Fisher; and we'll get to everything tomorrow . . .".

Daniel had left the hospital in the dusk and walked south on streets that had not existed twenty years before. He cut across yards as if they were still the goldenrod fields where he had played with Ginny and circuses had come in the fall. He climbed a fence, stopped to eat figs off somebody's tree, then jumped a canal ditch, where his father had got lost once in a pathless canebrake. Skirting the cemetery, he came to the woods along what was left of Rattlesnake Bayou. When he was a boy it was a virgin forest, cleared of underbrush at one end to make a city park, where oaks towered over grass, shading a whirligig fountain and a children's merry-go-round.

It had been a genuine town in that day, with some sense of decor. From the cotton-bale and steamboat-lively river landing stretched three or four blocks of the local whiteway. There were stores and office buildings rising to the four-story central one where Judge Byrne in the top comer suite could look out over the roofs and the levee to the river in flood stage sweeping brown above the town. There was an opera house with second rate concerts and plays; there were brick churches, a big stone Elks Club with a ball room, a library, a courthouse, the elegant hotel with seafoods brought fresh from New Orleans and iced fountains where a boy in the summer could drink until he foundered. Oak-lined avenues ran from the business center, with Victorian houses of the old town, and the more ostentatious ones of the new; these also rose to the monstrous antebellum imitation with its yard-thick walls and tem-ple pillars, which Judge Byrne had built to compensate for something or impress somebody. Pockets of Colored town were tucked away in handy places, as under the armpits or between flanks of the structure. Down the greenways of the avenues streetcars ran past schools and the military academy which clung to a precarious existence, out through goldenrod fields along Fairview to the town park with its great oaks, and the fountain and merry-go-round spinning in the grateful shade.

Where the town now had spread into B.J.'s cotton fields for miles around, and shopping centers had sprung up (on treeless concrete highways, sizzling under the summer sun, with acres on acres of picture-windowed, jerry-built boxes of housing developments, planted, of all trees, with scrubby Chinese elms — no center, no articulation, no sign of a park or civic life, no opera, the old centers falling into squalor behind advancing waves of unplanned growth, filling fields wastefully cleared and as wastefully converted into town. It was not just the Delta, the South; it was Boston, New York, Baltimore — Glen Bumie; say — an image of booming America.

One lovely place, the former park, which could no longer be maintained by the shrinking power of the expanding city, had come by some finagling into private hands. The forest along the shores of the bayou had been turned into a place of fashion, where large houses of Queen Anne, Tudor and ranch design were scattered in a broken grove. The nymphs had departed. Though at B.J.'s aunt's, the Delta matrons were almost nymphs again, a Bacchic rout, with their heavily domesticated fauns, washing down barbecued beef with drinks of all kinds, milling in a lighted yard where folding chairs were being placed around an improvised stage . . .

Lynn Wells began to dance. Daniel lost all interest in the mastication of beef tenderloin. The music was from records, and she had chosen the slow movement from Beethoven's Seventh, which offered little enough, at the surface, for her motions; but she plunged through that — as devastatingly abandoned as the original archangel dancing in the void the night before the Fall.

What Daniel gave her was no ordinary tiger's eye, but it was some kind of burning assent. Their gaze was linked as she danced, and she performed, as if she were the knight and he the mistress, more splendidly for that grafting. When she had finished, a group gathered around her, toasting the dance, talking of art. She stood, a shade taller than Daniel, slim, in the pose of artful rest which only a dancer can get away with, the feet and legs conscious of themselves, the head tilted to the left, with the studied grace of a goldenrod. Stirred by the drinks, by Lynn Wells' glances, by questions about his work, Daniel warmed to his destiny, let the arrogant claims he mostly suppressed slip out of the bag.

"Pure art, that's the trend, The only purity I want is commitment. I'd rather load my art with all they say it can't carry — symbol, message — than risk its being as anemic as I find theirs.

"I took some of my landscapes to a dealer in New York. 'Oh no,' he said, 'those are too academic for us.' I looked around, and by God, he didn't have a thing but imitations of Dufy, imitations of Klee, little Braques, little Pollocks. The fool didn't know where the academy was.

"When I had my show of prints up there: 'You may be a genius,' an artist told me, 'but you aren't a painter.' That was because I had talked about a theory of art as symbolic language. 'Nobody can be a painter and think for a minute about what paint means.' That was one of the biggest Abstract Expressionists in New York. 'All right,' I said, 'what about Leonardo?' Leonardo, it turned out, wasn't a painter. 'And what about Michelangelo?' Of course Michelangelo wasn't a painter either; he wasn't even a sculptor; Lord knows what he was. 'And what about Blake?' Because Blake is my example of what I aim at. But any fool would have known the answer: Blake was less a painter than the other two. 'You damned purists,' I said, 'you split the categories until you strain out everybody but your own shrimp size. By the same rule Dante's not a poet, nor Milton, nor Goethe. Thank God I'm a genius. I'd rather be a genius than what you call a painter any day.' So I go ahead with my work, and when anybody wants to drop the categories and look, he'll see something, that's all."

"But if you work in a secret language," said B.J., "how's anybody going to decode it?"

"Either I'm crazy, or I'm sane," said Daniel. "If I'm crazy it doesn't matter. If I'm sane, it'll be like any other language, it'll carry its key. People will have to keep at it."

"How do you know anybody will give it that much time?"

"I know the time given to works of art is commensurate with their power; if I don't know that, I assume it; it's an article of faith."

"All right," said B.J., "how do you know you've got that much power?"

"For Christ's sake, you're a writer yourself."

"I'm a journalist. If they don't read mine today, nobody's going to look at it tomorrow."

"O.K. Forget you're a writer. You've fought for a cause; you've been in love. When a Gandhi sits there in prison and might die tomorrow from a hunger strike, what knowledge has he got whether it's going to do good or harm? Or Christ on the cross? There are things a man's got no right to pry into. If he's a genius or a dud, he's the last one entitled to know. Anybody who wills a thing has to will it as if he was the son of God. And that kind of faith gives power. If you love a girl long enough and hard enough, it's mighty seldom you don't get her."

"You mean it's mighty seldom you don't get her," B.J. said.

Lynn Wells had watched Daniel, standing in a caricature of her own pose, one foot on top of another, the hipshot pose, his hands conducting; she had watched him talking, as he had watched her in the grip of the dance. "Ask Lynn Wells," Daniel said; "she can tell you plenty about the passion of art."

But one of the local literati, a small descendant of some old LeFlore, who had sold his birthright of the Huck Finn river for a veneer of smart Quarterlies, broke the pause with a touch of hauteur, to ask Daniel if he had read such-and-such in the Swalee Review or The Pakistan, and wasn't it great. As a matter of fact, Daniel had, and he gave way to another tirade.

"Look at me, man! I have two legs, arms, eyes, one nose, one mouth, the usual organs, like you, like all these others, like people for thousands of years. I have a wife and children, a home, some decent friends. That's what our life is. Sure, I know about the bomb and transvaluation of values and that junk. No doubt, there's a history of spirit; things get out of date and new things are discovered. But it's not as if everything got so altered you couldn't feel and write like a man. 'Will-o'-the-wisp frail shawms under depressed air pumps of worse declension clip the castrate fruit of their brows in heaven's amnesty' — exhausted stuff...

"It's a fad, I tell you, it's a fad. It was hatched up in Paris a hundred years ago by unkenneled romantics who spun it from their bowels, and for them it was real. But because you're caught in it, don't think it's you. It's *à la mode*. Go back to nature. That's why Lynn Wells danced to Beethoven. It's like the human pulse, like breathing."

Daniel, from visiting celebrity, was assuming his old role of traveling nuisance. His reputation was a kind of bank account, which would allow him reasonable credit as practicing artist. But to talk like Blake, Michelangelo and Plato joined into one upset these Delta folk as it upset the Quakers. Persona non grata.

Except that Lynn Wells was strangely pleased. Whatever that crazy soil had planted in these two, they knew it for the same. His talk opened roads of destiny. She looked at him, her head on the slim neck inclined, a gesture in which the glory of dance was comprised. He groaned to the bottom of his soul that we do not have innumerable lives, to take our fortune again and again. He pulled B.J. aside, funneling his violence into a whisper.

"For God's sake, let's clear out. Delta parties aren't in my line. My father never went, and my grandfather didn't and I see why. There's one person I want to be with and it wouldn't do us any good. But Christ, she's beautiful."

They were hunting for the hostess, when dear chuckleheaded Patsy came up waving. Daniel grabbed her with the desperate sense of how safe she was. He gave her a hug and a kiss, while she giggled: "Daniel Byrne! What's got into you? Such affection. And in front of all these people."

"Dear love, Patsy," he said. She had won his heart once from Emily, when she let down her long hair on a moonlit hayride on the ferry. He had praised and stroked it in his shy way, and had wondered afterwards when he would drop by her house some morning or afternoon how she would keep him waiting a few minutes and then come downstairs with that glorious hair combed to her waist, saying he had interrupted her fixing or drying it. Since then he had gambled too much on long hair, and besides Patsy had cut hers off and become so much the mother, she began asking about his children and telling of hers, how little Pati was five and in the Junior Cotillion Club, going to dances in long dresses and with a date — would you believe it, she was already talking of loving little Teddy LeFlore. But Patsy's sparkling eyes betrayed her. Reliving it Daniel thought — pushing their kids from the cradle into courtship, trying to bring back some abysmal *Gone With the Wind.*

Patsy rattled on, her mother's child in that, though with the sweetness of her father, Betsy's old beau, Fran Dudley, making those appalling breaks she always slipped into and never recognized — about her house and how the painters had dropped the mantle of the ceiling light in the kitchen, and it had to be ordered from New York, and she was "so tired of working in that kitchen with those bare bu'bs"; and if Daniel had wanted to tell her that her Mississippi accent could be compromised with, at least to the extent of putting an "l" in that word, he wouldn't have had time, because she had charged on, talking about how hot it was, and whether Daniel wasn't just knocked out coming from the East that way, that her sister had come home from the West Coast and said it was terrible: "Poor Sis hasn't been in heat like this since I don't know when."

They found the hostess.

"Lovely party . . . So glad."

"Remember, now; come to see us."

"Yes, yes. Goodnight."

"Night-night."

A gibbous moon.

The poison-sprayed woods received them.

9 ~ The Meeting

It was midnight. Lucy would have been asleep for hours. Daniel had missed an appointment she would have kept, though she would not blame him, women at their best being more devoted than men. At ten in the East, which would have been nine here, they were to have joined in thoughtful contemplation of the moon.

She would have slipped from Aunt Hester's house out through the orchard to the Mill Creek, where the moon through hemlocks made a rippled road spilling in troughs and planes on the swifter water. Leaving the father her aunts or cousins had been talking of in the room, she would have sought the other father, of the silence and night: the one she always carried in her heart —

How they canoed up Racket Lake and made the portage over to Forked Lake and up Forked Lake to the island at its head, where they pitched camp; and he, cutting a balsam, showed them how to stick twigs in the ground to make a fragrant bed. —'Until evening, when they paddled in the mist, past a swamp of flooded tamaracks, up the stream that feeds the lake, the banks closing in as they approached the ford. Three deer resolved themselves out of the haze, a stag and two does, drinking. They lifted their heads and stood quiet, the paddle hanging in the air, dripping. The silence distilled itself around the three deer looking at the father and children, the children and father looking at the deer. Then the current gained; the canoe drifted backward. The deer, lowering their heads, faded in the mist, drinking ,as before. In the white stillness the father paddled back to camp. They stretched on the balsam beds. Fog condensed in the fir trees. Above it the stars went milky on their courses . . .

So remembering, she had come to the creek by the mill dam, where the water spread pale in the moon; and on the other shore, indistinct, deer or man, a lighted bush or stone, a form congealed out of the night and became the genius of the place, the power she had come to meet. She stood for the tryst, waiting — as when the deer were revealed — until the darkness asked: "To meet? With whom?" And the answer came, like a resonance of the moon and water: "With both. They join in me .. I am making them one." . . .

Leaving the hushed house, Daniel stole into the Delta night —

Since all action in the end is at a distance, the particles which act being fields in the void, consciousness could not stretch out to gather the imprints of its sensuous awareness, not pass them over synapses from cell to cell, unless the things it touches and the things on which it rides floated like itself in awareness, moonlight, a consonance of water.

That was what he needed, water, the element of all mating - earth the Orphic egg, permeable . . .

With loping strides he moved through the luminous grove; and reached the edge, where oaks gave way to cypress, gray feathers on craggy limbs, and the bayou, beyond tapering trunks and knees, spread itself, waveless, currentless, a sepia reflecting sheen.

And there too was the presence, a dim whiteness on the other shore, to which one did not call or gesture, since only thought could apply. Daniel was farsighted; at any moment he could look, as he would say, beyond infinity. He blurred his eyes.

And saw this return to the dark and fluid a fit rallying point for the meeting which would be theirs again and again — a likely clairvoyance, for this vapor-world to crystallize into memories of ordered form. It had been in England, ten years ago, in front of the Druid Cave in the Malvern Hills, a meeting that reached back to another, thirty years earlier still, at the same place, when Meryl Grafton had closed with Adam Woodruff, to rove west, the old poem in her mind:

Away is huere wynter woe
When woderove springeth.

In the same place and after the crisis of another war, Lucy had met Daniel, her lawless frontier, the farthest southward and westward reach of her nature — he then at the nadir of his own disruption, and she in pursuit of the opposite quarter.

She had gone to stay with her mother's relations. Daniel, after Appalachian and a second fellowship abroad, had stopped briefly in England; though he had not come to terms with it. He had only prepared the way by meeting Lucy. It was years later, and together, as they repeated her pilgrimage to family shrines now his by marriage, that he experienced that phase of her, the heritage — shades of Austen and Trollope — which she had gone first to assimilate, and which he, by some law of dowry, had come to possess, possessing her.

Lucy alone, then both together, their ocean crossings merged into one —

The chalk cliffs broke tree-crowned out of the blue and white of the sea. The coast nearing magnified above the Channel — a walled garden. Lights flashed through the night. The next morning they went ashore. Books, history and romance, her mother's talk, had made it her own: the wholesome quaint people with the folk-rooted speech, preserving humor and humanity through rigors of war and postwar.

She rode (they both rode) through always more beautiful country, that island in an island, old pastoral England — hawthorn-powdered April, or August say, like Keats's Autumn, or Blake's, laden with apples, plums, pears — and arrived, under the blue line of the Malvern Hills, at the yew-bordered village, the cousin's house, their center.

Queen Anne brickwork rose over lawns and pastures; hedge-row elms soared into the mist. The family gathered on the terrace for their laughing meals, the six children cramming down loads of brown bread and butter, bees swarming to the jam pot or clinging to the children's treacle-smeared mouths. The groomed master of the house drove home from the city in his funereally polished 1920 black Rolls; he stalked into the cellar, a sly humor just betraying itself on the masklike face, and came up with one of those literary quotations they bandied back and forth like tennis balls: "O, for a draught of vintage!" or "To be drowned in a butt of Malmsey," or "Is't not fine to swim in wine, and turn upon the toe," and of course with the mildewed bottle, one of those great Burgundies or clarets he could still produce because he and his father had laid them down.

From there the trips were made: to the cathedrals, Worcester, Gloucester, Lichfield, to Stratford for the plays; to some of the sights all tourists see: Warwick, Oxford, Hardwick Hall to the north, and southward Compton Wynyates, the Tudor mansion sending woodsmoke from its chimneys as they drove at sunset through the gilded grove; but mostly it was a personal pursuit, to harvest the family past. From the city factory where Lucy's great-grandfather had repaired the family fortune, to the workers' schools his son had founded (one of the philanthropies on a younger son's road to the baronetcy), through the art museum, where the Grafton collection filled a memorial room, the search led out to villages her mother had told her of, the church where the favorite uncle had been vicar — the saintly Clarence, lurching over the long route of his parish, a lean figure in black with a scholar's hunch and kind eyes, his red nose beaked over a shy smile, a Knight of the Woeful Countenance, mounted on a stranger beast than Rocinante, the outmoded tricycle with the thin front wheel of huge circumference and the tiny rear ones, creaking up the hills and rushing with terrible speed into the valleys — and then to the country house where Meryl Grafton had grown up, and at last to the Druid Cave over Great Malvern.

But it was the cream-colored stone manor house among gardens and tall trees that Lucy seemed to know before she saw it — as if she had walked the paths of the walled kitchen garden, and heard the incessant cawing from the elms over the rookery, and smelled the sour smell of the dropping-splotched drive, or withdrawn for tea to the wicker chairs on the cloistered side, where the velvet lawn sloped from the Lebanon Cedar to the oak wood, and the mansion took the sun behind them. When she read the inscription over the Tudor porch, the motto of decorum:

> Plenti and grase
> Be in this plase
> While every man is pleased in his degre
> There is both pease and unite
> Salaman saith there is non accorde
> Where every man would be a lorde —

she remembered it, as if she had been the child who had lived there fifty years before —

It was near Christmas. The weather was rainy and cold. Meryl's day began in the day nursery on the third floor. If it was sunny, Nanny would be sitting by the window at her work. But today the wind was moaning in the larch tree and rattling sleet and rain against the windows; they were gathered at the nursery fire. The coal was piled high in the grate; and Nanny was telling them stories while she decorated their petticoats and nightgowns with fairy tucks and featherstitchings.

She had come to them three years before, and by now she was their mainstay. The afternoon she arrived a temporary nurse had been dismissed. It had been a tiresome long day for the two children high in the big house — such a day as this — with the wind sighing in the larch at the window. When the nursery maid, who was also partly a kitchen girl, had served tea and lit the lamps, she packed up the dishes and left the children for the life of the kitchen. Meryl was with her little sister Meg. The other children had outgrown the nursery. Before six o'clock somebody would come up to dress them and take them down for the drawing room hour with their parents. It was five now, dark and lonely. They did not think of going down before they were sent for. Apart from the fear of the long black stairs, it did not occur to them as a possible course. They sat by the fire, while Meg imagined terrors, and then demanded a visit to the night nursery down the back corridor. It could not be postponed. Meryl led her. What an array of difficult little buttons held up the frilly cotton drawers and the white flannel ones she wore beneath for warmth; what a trial to undo them in the dark cold and tell her there was nothing to be afraid of, when Meryl herself could not know what the shadows of the farther room or of the steep stairs might contain.

As a matter of fact, they contained only Nanny. There were steps, a door opened, and the wholesome girl, strong, mature, quiet, came in and held out her arms: "Here I be, my beauties; I'm to be your Nanny now, who's to look after you from this time on."

That was years ago. It was morning now. Nanny sat by the fire stitching and telling of her life in the village, while the children told of theirs. Christmas was coming, but there was something else in the air.. They kept running to the window to see if the rain had let up. Soon, a cold bit of blue sky was breaking through clouds.

Then they heard the sound, far off, the stirring sound, the music coming sweet through the winter air. It was the brass band from the village. Every holiday they tramped over the country with their horns to play carols for the gentry, drink free ale, and take a subscription for local charities. There was a rush for the window, and there they were, filing up the drive. Soon sixteen men were standing in a circle on the rain-sparkled lawn. "Tarump, tarump," went the great drum, and the shiny trumpets took up the peal: "The Mistletoe Bough."

But it was not Christmas yet. Why had the band come early? Yes. It was election day. Their father was to be elected for Parliament again.

So they would have two celebrations this year. They struggled into coats and boots and ran downstairs and out onto the gravel walk to sing and applaud. And there was their father, tall, with his sideburns and his noble head, nodding to the villagers with the easy condescension that becomes the great.

The Victorian Age . . . Though the whole time was pregnant with turn-of-the-century, and thinkers had written transforming words, and poets foreseeing the upheaval had celebrated or lamented it; though Cezanne and Van Gogh had painted and Debussy composed and Rimbaud had written, and Joyce was growing up in Ireland, and Yeats and Shaw were snuffing the air for "the great change"; though communism had been born and the revolt of the masses, and even the rise of the backward races, yellow and black, was getting under way; though Meryl's own father read the coming war in the rising power of Germany and used his parliamentary eloquence to urge preparedness, hardly anticipating what war would mean — for all this, England was still the old England, the most prosperous green island of the former world, in which almost nothing could remind a child how fatefully the centuries were revolving.

If forests were laid waste, it was not in England; England was maintained by remoter devastations. It is true, derelict workers would migrate in the fall from the slag-heap Black Country to the north, to pick fruit or harvest grain; but they were not as ominous as the wagon caravans of dusky gypsies with children one could not play with for fear "one might catch something," or the tramps swinging along with sacks over their shoulders and looks so outcast as to approve their reputation for stealing children and taking them "the Lord knows where"; but tramps and gypsies had been in England time out of mind.

The only roads were country lanes between walls and hedge-rows. They were made of rocks crushed with hammers by hale old County Men; and the only modem behemoth to frighten the horses as they drew carriages and dogcarts there, was the steam roller which packed the rocks to a level bed.

("Steer as near the roller as you can," Meryl's mother urged, as the shying horses approached the monster. "Nearer, nearer; they have to have room to spring or they'll carry you into the hedgerow." It seemed impossible to draw on the right rein, but one had to: "Nearer, nearer!" And they shot up even, almost grazing the great cylinder. Now a piston let out a roar and hiss of steam, and the right horse, black 'Sultan, reared, his ears laid flat and his sleek haunches gathered under him, quivering like springs. He leaped forward and to the side, Sahib catching the alarm, surging with him. But they were past. And the mother: "So, that's all there is to it. Slow Sultan, slow! Draw the rein. Remember, steer close to the danger; it is like the rock Scylla.")

Then it was calm again, the peaceful green countryside, with cottages and the Georgian houses of the gentry, no developments yet, no hedgerow elms cut down for lumber, no signs of crisis or want of capital, only "plenty and grace, and each one pleased in his degree." Why even the little boys by the roadside took off their caps as they came along and the girls dropped a curtsy, even to Meryl, a child, if she walked out alone, distinguished by some mystery of dress, face, or bearing as one of those to whom respects are due. It was a small sweet island, floating over a world of violence, buoyed up by the violence it used and deplored.

This was election day. The children wanted to walk with Nanny to the village. They took the lane between bare lime trees, past the Gothic church where their ancestors lay in Purbeck and alabaster, past the parish school, where groans of the commoners were heard, reciting something in unison, and then along the row of pollarded willows by the dammed brook. The current turned scythe mills established long ago. Meryl peered into firelighted smithies. Men bent over glowing steel amidst the thump of hammers and the droning of whetstones. Bandy-legged smiths, gnarled Vulcans. Would one never find Apollo at the forge?

Farther along, John, the cabinetmaker, stood at the whirring lathe. His cottage was beside the shop. It was cozy and bright, very different from the stone manor with its lonely great rooms. A little garden went down to the stream which sparkled in the sun. John's mother was a godmother of Nanny's, so they often stopped there. "John," Meryl had said one day when the young man joined them in the garden, "when I grow up we must marry and go to Canada and have a cottage like this in the new country."

John stepped to the shop door, smoothing a table leg with long fingers. Bending to the herb borders of the path, he picked a sprig of rosemary, carelessly, and put it in his mouth. Meryl could not imagine any of her father's friends chewing a sprig of rosemary while they talked, though her saintly Uncle Clarence might have been willing to try.

The village was a row of thatched cottages, with a few statelier houses and shops of brick novelties: the Christmas toys had been set up in the window. Mr. Noel wound them up and set them going. The small train chugged round, the toy carpenter jerked his saw across a log, while the dancing bear danced so wildly that he fell over on his back, his four legs whirling in the air. And plump Mr. Noel stood in the door bowing and scraping like a wind-up toy himself.

The working people were gathered from all around for the voting. There was talk of the Liberal Party and how much better off the country would be with the new lot than with the old. Meryl's mouth dropped open. Here was their yardman, Sumner, of the weird shape, whose legs, through some fault of clothes or structure, never fitted his body, so he stumped around like a rag doll with a voluminous stuffy rear. It was he who would come from the garden house some time in May with the swing and ladder, walk across the lawn to the summer nursery under the beech tree. He would lean the ladder against the chosen limb, climb precariously and tie the rope. When everything was ready, he would sit in the swing, draw himself to the top of the slope, and giving a huge push and a pump, go soaring out; that portentous rear billowing in the sky like a captive balloon.

"There now, young laidies," he would say, "if it'll 'euld me; Oi reckon as 'ow it'll 'euld you."

Here he was, their staunchest retainer, standing on election day talking in a big voice about throwing out the Conservatives, the party of Church and decency, by virtue of which her father, this man's own master, held a position of power. Meryl stepped up and tugged at Sumner's coat. "Sumner," she said, "tell me: you're not a Liberal, are you?"

He looked down at the stem slight form; he gave a sheepish grin: "Yes, miss, Oi am."

"But you don't wish my father to be defeated, do you, Sumner?"

"Eu, neu, miss, Oi'd never wish 'arm to the Marster."

Her father was re-elected with the old majority. Otherwise the Liberals swept the country. Meryl knew now that the people she watched and admired, the scythe makers and John at the lathe with crafty hands, the gardeners, perhaps Nanny herself, were of the new persuasion. She began to understand about that time how far she was on their side.

Saturday had come. They were sitting at teatime by the great west window, the sun setting in winter glory over the Malvern Hills. Her father was reading poetry aloud, while her mother practiced painting, as she loved to do. Meryl took notice. It was Shelley her father was reading, he was delivering it with fire, and it was not conservative, it was the reverse. Then she observed her mother's hands. The left hand held the watercolors, while the right ran the brush with quick strokes along the paper. They were large hands, but deft and fine. Meryl thought of the cabinetmaker sliding his fingers over the turned wood. She raised her own hands to the orange light and curved her slim fingers. "Yes," she thought, "they are the hands of a craftsman."

That evening, for the first time, the weekly paying of the servants became a torment to her. About six o'clock the parlor-maid came into the lamplit drawing room and murmured gently: "The men are here, sir."

"Oh very good, Storer," said her father; "send them in when I ring."

He was playing solitaire and mulling over the elections, his victory, the party's loss. He went on with the game, as if it was fit that gardeners and coachmen who had worked all week and wanted to get home to their wives and suppers should cool their heels, attending his leisure. But Meryl came to his chair. "Father," she said, "the men are waiting."

He widened his eyes. She was already tall and slim for her age, with a long shapely neck above the lace ruffle. Her face had something of Sienese art: the long nose, the olive-smooth complexion, the oval brown eyes that would work such havoc on later admirers. He played another card, almost stubbornly, then shrugged and said: "Very well, Meryl, ring the bell."

The men trooped in, one by one, caps in hand, while Meryl, sinking into the leather chair, leafed her favorite picture book: Indians in the wilds of America . . .

Like morning and evening of one revealing day — to be pieced together at thousands of miles distance by Meryl, a mother, telling her children the filtered memories, not in order, but as they arose; to be reclaimed by a daughter; and finally, at a third remove, the mother dead and the daughter married, to arch themselves in the warm night of a son-in-law's brooding, shapes across a sluggish bayou.

All action being at a distance, it is not that there is anything impossible about telepathy or clairvoyance or the rest; it is not a question of possibility, but of the realized modes of the actual. If sitting and thinking of the dice can make them fall one way, it is no stranger in itself than that wishing them so I should reach out my hand and turn them over. It is only that we are accustomed to one mode; we know it exists. Nature has pursued certain paths into the wilderness, has hung these and not other webs across the void. These are the means to revive the akashic record, to summon spirits from the dead and voices out of absence: language, intuition, memory, spells of speech, calligraphs on a page.

Lucy had turned back from the mill dam to the house, cradling the father-memory that had come to her as quietly as mist in the moonlight. But before she reached the porch the other recollection had struck, widening daylight doors with a flash that was almost terror: the sun-webbed distance of roaring white water. It was the Susquehanna. Even when they were children their father had taken them down appalling rapids. Suddenly, with the catlike crouch that never rocked the canoe, he stood up in the stem, scanning the broken wide spread of dangerous water, weighed it, chose a path, and fell to his knees paddling and issuing clipped orders: "Lucy! Adam! On your right now, hard." In a gust of spray and foam they swept past loud rocks, lurching. "Now hold." He stemmed, and threaded a green channel to the next shoot. "Both of you now, on the left. Harder." And again the thrill of danger, as the boat, like a wild horse, leapt under them, the clawed black rocks churning by . . .

Dear One:

A short note before sleep. Coleman Thorndyk was here tonight. He was doing consultations in Philadelphia and stayed for supper. Over the carcase of a fine young duckling, I told him about Aunt Betsy, and he said if you would write the details he would give you his medical opinion. He wants to help if he can. We also talked about your lectures, which he says are splendid, and are making an impact, though no-body half understands them. He is fond of you, though one couldn't have guessed it at first. But that was through Uncle Steward, poor dear, and even he is coming round. He asked about you at the hospital today. They say he is better, though of course anything can happen . . .

(Vectors of force, lancings over the distance the moon also bridged, quickening in Daniel's thought, as perhaps in Lucy's dream, not moments, but the texture, his life and hers and the life of their kin, stretching back east and south before they were born, not warp or woof, but the fabric of their weaving.)

"You see," Thorndyk had said, when he asked them out to lunch the year before they were married, "there are psychological affinities. If a man has schizophrenic leanings, he's drawn to other schizophrenics. So he chooses a woman to marry. It may be the worst thing for him. But if you let him inspect a roomful of people, he'll hit on his type every time."

It was in a seafood restaurant in Philadelphia, and they were eating piles of steamed long-neck clams, which Daniel, not to the actual benefit of the conversation, kept calling the uncircumcised. "But it can't be true," he said, picking one up by the prong and dropping it in his mouth. "We can learn something. We don't have to go through our lives sitting down again and again on the same old hot stove."

"You can't change your affinity," said the psychoanalyst.

"What it amounts to is that you suppress it. Instead of being drawn, you're repelled. So you make your next choice. If a schizophrenic was drawn to a paranoiac before, maybe he takes a manic-depressive now, or a hysteric . . . "

It had not been clear whether he was speaking theoretically or of Daniel and Lucy, but he leaned forward and drove it home: "Daniel, for example, inclines to the schizophrenic. These are general terms; they don't mean he's crazy. He can take it as a compliment. Puts him in the type with Blake and Nijinsky, Melville, Ryder, maybe Picasso. Now for his first wife — as far as I can tell — he chose another schizophrenic with a persecution paranoia."

No doubt, at Uncle Steward's request, Dr. Thorndyk had looked into the case. "A persecution paranoia" — he may even have tried to talk with Sibyl.

"That neurotic suffering must have moved him. I say it still does. But he fights it now because he got burned. When he feels drawn to such a woman, he begins to compensate. What does he turn to instead? To Lucy. And what is Lucy? — My dear, you mustn't be troubled by the names: they only refer to types. She is what we call the hysterical, or as some would say, the epileptic type."

Lucy was looking at him with puzzled eyes; but Daniel broke into a laugh, a shade on the nervous side, and began. to twist his body into knots, saying: "Come on, Lucy, let's throw a fit." Dr. Thorndyk went on without noticing.

"She has that temperament from her father. It has to do with the mystical. She'd like to withdraw from the world. At this stage Daniel is captured by that retiring. But it may still be wrong for him. Maybe what he needs is the last thing he'd be drawn to, a solid, average woman. Meanwhile, Lucy is endangered. "

"If Lucy is endangered," Daniel said, "so am I; and I'm not schizophrenic enough to be a hog for punishment. If you were an oracle, we might break it off. But who wants to run from bugaboos? What you psychiatrists ignore is chance. If we meet a certain person at a certain time, good; if it's somebody else, we're in a fix. A man has to hope he won't throw snake-eyes twice in a row."

"Psychology makes a science of what you call chance," said Thorndyk. "Do you think any chance in the world could have brought you, of all possible women, two so related to your own character?"

"Shucks," said Daniel, "there are ten women I might have married if it had happened that way; and they were as different from each other as Sibyl and Lucy. The ones I got were thrust upon me."

"People used to say the same thing about dreams," said the analyst, "but the psyche has its reasons. Look back at the time when you and Lucy first met. How did it come about? Surely you recognize what I'm talking about?"

The scene opened for them both: the patchwork quilt of England spread below, dappled with sun and cloud, a landscape so gentle and gay it seemed a realm of fairy queens and good magic — though Daniel, staring at his easel and scowling through his brows, had not been painting it that way.

Lucy spoke: "I went up to the Druid Cave over Malvern. I wanted to see the spot where my father and mother decided to get married. And there was Daniel, standing in front of an easel, painting the craziest picture."

"All right," said Thorndyk, "he was there. But what drew you together?"

"Nothing," said Daniel. "We weren't drawn together. We hardly spoke a word. It was weeks later, after I had been back to France and was on a boat going to the United States, that we docked in Southampton and Lucy came aboard. 'That girl looks familiar,' I thought; but I didn't recognize her. Then I walked around the deck and met her three or four times. She was striding the other way and stopping to look back at England. She was sorry to leave her cousins, but I didn't know that. She had a mean look. 'There's a vixen,' I said, 'will make some man unhappy; or maybe she's doing it already, and that's her trouble.' I didn't want to single her out, because I had tried one termagant already."

"How did it happen then?" asked Thorndyk. "Don't tell me she chased you down."

"The way I've been telling you," said Daniel. *(As if nobody knew when anything happened, much less planned it, but after varying lengths of time situations were discovered to be.)* "I went to dinner and sat where I was assigned, and there she was across the table, looking me over. 'Didn't I see you painting a picture up on the Malvern Hills?' she said. That mean look had gone off her face, so you didn't know how it got there. After dinner we walked on the deck. We talked a while and then we sat quiet. Like at Meeting. I tell you it was a quiet crossing." Daniel cried out, another person interrupting himself: "My

Lord, do you think I don't know there are causes in things, that what happens looks as predictable as the course of the stars? I only say if there's a law, it's not ours. Fate, history, the gods, there's something that conspires. It conspires in the cells to make us, and in what you call the psyche, and maybe the best we can do is to go along."

"If you're going to be mystical," said the analyst, "1 can't argue with you; but as far as science goes, the psychological types play the role."

Daniel subsided, thinking.

Maybe so. Maybe all explanation is circumlocution, and the psychological no worse than another. Though if the causes were psychological, it was deeper than the psychologist knew. Who could finger every fiber of the joining beings, feel it out before- hand and make predictions on the chances of a harmonious blend? One thing in particular Thorndyk had not set in the equation —

That where Daniel, without knowing it, by some creative commitment to himself or god, had beat down all former associates, made them feel threatened or neglected, or both in one, overshadowed by an eruption beyond the usual range (they called him domineering, a claim he hardly understood, since whatever domineered was spontaneous, merely his nature), that where this force more than anything else had first lured and then unstrung Sibyl, who had nothing to buttress against it — Lucy not only brought the foil it needed, she could use its thrust. Compared to the passionate Sibyl she appeared gentle and bland, but she was not as easily endangered, because her very mildness was an inherited strength, as her strength was a kind of yielding. Her soul, it seemed, had been possessed by one Asmodeus already — her father — who for all his retiring ways must have been some kind of original world energy. So what normal man of their Quaker moderate circles could have faced up, through her, to that image, have looked into the now disembodied eyes and not been cowed — like Sibyl earlier, reduced to the instability all force awakens where it is not counterposed with force? Who could have foreseen that the violence which was Daniel's handicap before, and which had alarmed his own friends and advocates, was to work in his favor? Uncle Steward had wanted Lucy to marry someone of a kindred balance. But could anything but a daemonic power have moved into that farm — the land made in the father's mold, like a stubborn flesh stamped and transformed by his spirit, the pastures he had brought back from gullies, the pine wood he planted, the furniture he made, the iron-work he wrought, the rugs and blankets he had woven, the pond he dammed and canoes he fashioned, the pictures he painted, the or-chard he grafted, the library he read and annotated, the plant collec-tion he pressed and catalogued, the journals known and unknown he had written — it was incredible, but there was nothing in the house or on the land into which he had not infused some shaping force of his being; so how could anything but an equally world-bestriding soul have climbed into that saddle and actually have ridden there?

It was a question of the limits of tolerance. Sometimes it seemed to Lucy that she was only a meeting ground where her father and hus-band, shoulder to shoulder and eye to eye, could confront each other and be resolved. And if she was content with this situation and Daniel unsuspectingly at home in it, what should the ghost of the dead, those dead who are always thrusting through the living for a seat of contin-uance, to sway and be swayed, what should the ghost of the dead do but bless them?

Daniel, looking over Rattlesnake Bayou, his eyes blurred beyond infinity, shook himself, as if to put off the spell of moon and water, of the motionless white form, cypress, bush or shrub, light or ghostly shade, that faced him from across the stream. He did not know if he was communing with the living or the dead. At any rate, he had kept his appointment. There had been a meeting, if late. He walked back among the white-trunked oaks, while frogs and katydids clamored in the night.

10 ~ The Search

Now Daniel was living in Aunt Betsy's house. . .

The morning after the party he had gone with Mr. Hargreaves to the hospital. Aunt Betsy had sat up with a cagey look, as if they had come to commit her.

"Good morning, Mr. Hargreaves."

"Good morning, Miss Betsy. Glad to see you looking so well."

She was on her guard. Too suddenly Mr. Hargreaves broached the matter: "Here's your nephew come down to look after things, and there's bills to be paid; so he'd better have power of attorney. I've got the papers, Miss Betsy . . . "

"No need for that, Mr. Hargreaves. I'll go to the bank in the morning and borrow the money."

"You can't go in the morning, Miss Betsy; tomorrow is Sunday."

"Tomorrow, Mr. Hargreaves, is Monday."

"Well, Miss Betsy, whichever it is, here's all the bills for months and months. You haven't paid them, and somebody's got to pay them."

"Sha! Mr. Hargreaves, don't you fret your head about my bills."

"There's six hundred dollars owing right here at the hospital. How much do you have in that bank?"

"It's none of your business, Mr. Hargreaves, what I've got in the bank. Besides" (as if it was a point in her favor) "there's almost nothing there."

"Miss Betsy, if Daniel's going to help you, he'll have to have authority to use that account."

"If you've got to know," she cried, "there's just about two-bits there."

They gave it up. She put her scrawl on a few items she could not see to read, keeping the power and the glory in her own hands. Daniel went to the bank and found twenty-five hundred dollars sitting in the checking account. She had sold a shack in the spring without saying anything about it. Then he went to see about getting her house ready for them . . .

"Maybe you don't know it," B.J. had said, "but there's a cat been shut up there for a month and nobody caring how the chips fell. You heard about that colored school the superintendent visited? He walked in while they were conjugating verbs. 'Conjugate creep,' said the teacher. 'Creep?' The boy studied. 'De cat crep in the house, she crap: she crope out.' You know how it goes on," B.J. said. "Well, Miss Betsy's cat has been shut up, she done shat, she has shitten; she never crope out and she never stole in, she just crapped around here and stooled around there; and that house ought to be fumigated before anybody tries to stay there. I told Coleson to get the blamed cat out; but he said Miss Betsy gave him strict orders not to let it get away, she's afraid it'd be lost. I even went to see that wife of his — used to be Little Lilly Harp, Big Lilly's child" . . .

"You mean Mrs. Coleson is Big Lilly Harp's daughter?"

"Sure. Didn't you know that? The lean one, that had the accident years back and broke her forehead, so she keeps that big black spit curl trained down to cover the hole."

"I don't know," said Daniel. "I remember Big Lilly well enough. She had the jazz band. She'd sit down on the bench and pull the piano up to her."

"Sure, and there was the time she went to the country club tanked up with gin and aspirin, and stepped on the cover of the cesspool. It broke, and she wedged herself in the mouth like a stopper. Everybody pulled, but they couldn't get her out. So somebody tied a rope under her arms, took it over a limb to the back of the car, and they hoisted her into the air. Then they turned on the hose and sprayed the cess-pool off of her. She walked in wet and sober, and played with the band.

"Think how that woman must have smelled when she came from the cesspool. Well, it wasn't anything to the way your aunt's house smells now."

"That's nothing." Daniel told him. "You should have smelled it last winter when the heaters were going."

But he had forgotten the difference between a memory and a fact. When the skeleton key turned in the hole and the door creaked open, that smell was a fact — a volcano, a hurricane; it blew him out of there; he crashed the glass door back and gasped for the sultry Delta air as if it was the nectar of paradise.

Then he went to the shacks. It was not just to pile Pelion on Ossa to see what defiance he could rise to; he had to look for somebody to help him clean. First old Nellie, hearing he was going to bring "po Miss Betsy" home, put her rickety bones, and her porch as well, through the paces of a jig. In the glory of the moment she called her great-niece from around the comer, a voluptuous yellow girl, with whom she contracted to work that afternoon. They came and puttered around, but got nowhere. The yellow girl was supposed to come again the next day, but when Daniel went to open the house, it was not the voluptuous Sue who was waiting in the swing. The measure of his need had gone down into the grapevine of the Colored town, and Savannah had answered the call. She sat on the porch, rough-hewn, coal black, staring at him with eyes of dogged endurance. She had just finished steering the last old maid of the town into the port of healing, and was ready for another charge.

"I guess you know what you're up against," Daniel told her. "She's been acting queer."

"I nursed Miss Willie. If I hadn't of knowed about Miss Betsy, I wouldn't of come. It's like a business you got to finish up." She gave him a look of grim conspiracy and went to work . . .

Now he and Aunt Betsy and Savannah were in the house. Daniel was living toward the morning of that waking in the leak-stained room where he waked every morning, the day of that going, as he went every day, to the market for groceries, his thoughts climbing north and east in search of Lucy, and slipping back, as on a hill of dust, into these dens; he was living toward a climax day when he would return along the oak-lined avenue and push the cleaning into the front bedroom he had not yet explored.

And Lucy was waking in the white room at the Mill, walking onto the balcony, going down to breakfast with Aunt Hester, driving with her to Philadelphia to see Uncle Steward, to read to him in the hospital, then out to Springmount to eat lunch with Aunt Chris in the original Woodruff house, or to help entertain visiting cousins. She was sitting on the Cope lawn listening to the tea talk, through chance narrations groping for a lost father or an absent love; and she too was moving toward a climax day when Uncle Steward would say to her: "Lucy, it's been on my conscience, the secretary at the Mill. It belonged to thy grandmother, and perhaps it should have gone to thy father. Thee should clean it out and store the papers, because it is thine."

He had a way of appropriating family treasures, journals, old pictures, and it was not often that his conscience drove him to restore the property. Having done it now, he would change his tone, drop the Quaker "thee", his eyes sparkling with mischief as he told something on Cousin Nathaniel Pendle: how the pious old coot passed a signaling cop at an intersection, and was waved to the side of the road, protesting: "Friend, I did not see thee waving thy little red wand, and if I had, I would not have known what thee meant." Or how he got up in Meeting lately (Uncle Steward's plant must have been working on Sundays) and told a long tale about some Friends who started out with unslaked lime in a barge on the canal one first-day, how they hit a rock and water poured in; the lime began to cook like the brimstone of the Lord; they had to jump ashore, and all they saved from the wreck was their shovel. He sat down, leaving everybody wondering: "A shovel? So what? Was it to leave those chastened sinners at least the means of honest labor?" But only the Lord, who had inspired Cousin Nathaniel, could have made it clear.

Lucy would leave the hospital as usual and go to Springmount; she would sit listening to the talk, every phrase stirring resonances of memory —

"Thee can be sure," Aunt Chris had said, "thy parents had a hard time those early years . . . "

A hard time. A joyful time. It is the hardness you make joy of:

There was spring with new lambs, summer with sheep-shearing and fruit gathering, fall with apple butter boiling in the cauldron in the yard, and in winter there was the hog to be killed. (Of course Lucy had kept journals too, even as a child, so that recall could be documented:

> We butchered early in the day. Great fun. Did not watch the
> killing part, but Elder said Dad rammed a pitchfork handle
> down the hog's throat. Hogs are bothersome to butcher.)

Once the block and tackle was tied to the apple tree and the scalded carcass had been hoisted onto the trestle over the saw- horses, the family joined in. Adam Woodruff stood scraping off the hair Lucy had climbed onto the trestle and was hauling away at the pig's tail. Her sister Evan leaned over the head end, laughing and showing her teeth, pretending to take a bite of souse.

Or there were turkeys to dress for Thanksgiving market. The birds were hung from a pine beam laid slanting against the barn. Lucy's mother stood in an artful curve, plucking the highest bird with grace and speed like playing the harp. Evan was next; her bird hung somewhat lower. Lucy was at work on the breast of a third turkey, the head of which just dragged the ground. Her little brother, under the angle of the beam, was plucking the rear end of her bird.

They had tried everything, sheep, pigs, bees, truck, dairy; but the only thing that made money was those turkeys, her mother's venture, and they required almost a money-mill grind. The pasture between the house and pond, where daffodils and crocus made a display now in the spring, had been divided by mesh fences hung with burlap bags. The stupid gobblers would fight to the death, even through wire; so each had to have a curtained corridor for himself and his hens, where he could not even see the others. And when the little turkeys cracked the shells, they would cluster in piles and smother unless somebody was watching. At hatching time Lucy's mother had to take her blankets down to the brooder houses and sleep where she could shine a flashlight now and then to make sure the chicks were in order.

Lucy's father had helped too, but he had the rest of the farm to look after, the unprofitable part. Profit was not in his line. (That time he sold the pony, the little buggy, saddle; bridle and all— "What are you asking for it, Mr. Woodruff?" — "I don't know what it's worth; what do you want to give?" And the yokel, banking on Mr. Woodruff's reputation: "How about forty dollars?" Lucy was a child, but she sensed the swindle, and ran to her mother crying: "Come quickly, Mother. Daddy is selling the pony and buggy and all for forty dollars." Her mother's quiet tones restrained her: "Don't think about it, my dear. That's Dad's business. Let him take care of that.")

Even the turkeys he had used for whimsical purposes. He was preoccupied with hypnosis, the fourth dimension and immersion of the animal soul in nature; and he had experimented with putting the turkeys into a trance state. He used to tie a cloth bag, or sometimes a dirty handkerchief over their heads and rub them some special way, and they would keel over with their legs up and lie in the field, hypnotized, or as he put it, with a smile that never told how far he was serious: "gone out into the fourth dimension." . . .

Lucy listened, every phrase stirring resonances . . .

But the search, the fugal chase, was common. Or perhaps it was Daniel's even more than Lucy's. She would have been content to revive the father she remembered. But for Daniel something new had to be found. Whenever he reached out for Lucy, there was the image and mystery of Adam Woodruff, withdrawing under the gesture and smile, hinting: "If you want to know anything about Lucy and how you come to have her, you had better find me."

Yet what was to be found? That he had broken from Quaker limitation? That had been going on in every generation. There was the younger son of Sea Captain Cope, who died in a Baltimore pub, and of whom merchant Cope wrote his sister: "I have seen death throes not to be recounted. Inscrutable are the ways of God. Some he uses to advance his purpose by a life of goodly example; others manifest the fruits of iniquity in the terror of their punishment. Such was Gideon Cope, our poor departed brother." There was even a renegade Pendle, years later, who became a Trappist monk, broke his vows, lived in sin, wrote atheistic tracts, and on his deathbed left his bones to a science foundation, though they were found so riddled with pox as to be of doubtful value.

The achievement was not to escape under strain, or even to stay in the clan, letting off steam with quaint devices, as chasing butterflies or peddling souvenirs at football games, the mock Indian arrow shot through your skull; it was more Promethean than that: to carry away the life of the sect in a flaming mutant.

So much was clear: that the traits of Uncle Steward, end-fruit of the Quaker clock man, and of Nathaniel Pendle, mystical eccentric, each bearing some trace of the other, as in cross breeds, had been grafted somehow onto the gentle Woodruff stem to produce Lucy's father. Clear and in order —

Except that Adam Woodruff, the result of these minglings, remained a mystery, even in the frame built to receive him, incommensurate with the analysis, supremely so by want of evidence. The remembered shy unveilings of his youth, with now and then a diffident but startled question: "Do you think the aura could be modified by a magnetic field?" or "Do you suppose it flows outward in the case of telepathy?" — and if one voiced incipient surprise: "Aura? What aura?" he might answer: "The psychic emanation. It appears as a blue-green glow around the body in the dark" — until, sensing how weak communication was, he would retire; such evidence was inadequate to frame the question, much less to give it an answer.

And where was anything else to be uncovered? It was Woodruff Farm which ghosts or records might be expected to haunt, and whatever had been left there Daniel had gone through long before, beginning after the burial; in fact, he began during it.

He and Lucy had been living in Chicago at the time. It was one of those years when the girl-named hurricanes fell in love with our coasts and came raging up east and north. (In the Caribbean they used to say as long as the hurricanes were named for saints they gave us a wide berth.) Lucy's parents had been camping in the Blue Ridge. The storm advanced that way; and they raced the southern violence, trying to reach the farm before it struck.

They had left the winding chain of the Skyline Drive behind, leaves and small branches flying in the air or falling on the road around them, trees torn and tossing like clouds; hour by hour they sped down the coastal hills; until finally, on the last slope, where the main highway plunged to Broad Creek before the sideroad, the village, the lane to the farm — on their own threshold — they met the force of the storm, or something solider, its agent: a huge black oak that had held out stubbornly, one of those remnant giants among scrub growth, undermined by the embankment, blew over in front of the car.

Was his compunction for Meryl — even as he flung out an arm to protect her from the shattering — tempered by the rightness of their being together? What could be known was the effect: the ineffectual braking swerve, the car telescoped against splintered wood, bodies crushed on steel and glass.

In the face of that, it was hard to voice the other conviction, that it was fit for the tree and the man, two patriarchs, to have met and been spared worse. For the tree it would have been blight, one of those plagues that attend the clearing of the world, dead limbs appearing at the top and spreading down, the tree a center of corruption threatening the rest — as the chestnuts had been threatened and had died out, as the elms were dying.

For the man too then; was a deliverance. Although one could not think of him as old, he had been warned the last years of rising blood pressure, hardening of the arteries and weakening of the heart over driven in the Copean labors the farm log recorded:

> Today rented a mixer, mixed, carried and poured 400 square feet of cement for the floor of the milking stable . . .
> Today with the help of Elder and his son, got up the walls and roof of the milk house . . .
> Today planted 1000 New Deal pine trees on the gullied hills above the back stream . . .

He had been warned, but he had not slacked the pace. Suppose he had reached home the day of the storm. He would have found a shambles which Daniel and the rest took a week to get clear: the lane a maze of fallen limbs, the silver maple shattered in the side yard, the light wires down and the dam half eroded. He would have sailed in with the power saw he had bought after an earlier storm, had taught himself to use, and in one day had cleared off a comparable wreckage; he would have done it again, have come in exhausted and thrown himself down in his study, after recording in the log: so many hours spent cleaning such and such Augean stables; he would have spread a dark cloth over his face as he did now in his psychic pursuits (using a sock if he found nothing handier — as Lucy and her mother would giggle, enough to swoon him into a vision right there), or if it was night, have stretched out with his eyes wide on darkness, waiting for the shapes he was learning to see: a shifting beauty of colors that dilated into a blue iris, through which he could glimpse the higher-dimensional reality: the face at the waterfall, the white Spitz dog, a guardian spirit, staring into time — he would have been lying so, invoking his presences, and surely, then or some such day, the vessel would have burst, on the retina of those visions, or in the brain, and left him blind or paralyzed. He was too tough to have died right off; it would have been a long suffering, with all the protraction doctors could devise — perhaps the fibrous heart and panting struggle through which Judge Byrne had lived and could not reach the end of. A Woodruff might have managed with more patience and decorum; but for him as for the oak there were mitigations.

And even for Meryl, though she was younger and had more life to look forward to (life hardly to be relished once he was dead), there were hints of danger. She had gone to Philadelphia ten years before for the removal of a small growth of doubtful benignity. Perhaps in her, as in her English mother and sister, the tentacles had begun to spread which would first give warning when they had reached too far; she would have slipped into that whirlpool of operations and radiation experiments circling to a funnel of such pain that even a spirit most competent to turn martyrdom into grace would have chosen the other meeting, the body arrested, the soul rushing on.

Adam had wished to be cremated, and Meryl long ago had acquiesced; so their ashes were prepared, mingled in a small container. Uncle Steward had arranged for an undertaker, and would have paid him too; but to bury a tin box without coffin or any costly service vexed the mortician. He ventured to grumble, and the children let him go with alacrity. The service had to be public, but the burying, they thought, could be a family matter; and by family they meant of themselves, an affair for three.

The son had dug a hole in the field under the tabletop pine. With his sisters he slipped off before breakfast the day of the Quaker service, one of those glorious fall mornings when the dogwood and sumac begin to turn and the gum is spotted with red; they stole out with a quiet request that their spouses not join them.

Like a conspiracy of the unconscious, to keep father and mother a property of the true blood — an infantile regression, to grip the remnants of a family whose ingrown claspings would have been pathological if they had not rooted in something benign. What were the daughters doing but protecting against time, the world, and their own marriages, the father of their childhood and the earliest tender love of a brother? So they would have wished anything but that the brother's wife should stand with him while the ashes went into the ground; and the brother must have felt the same about those raiders from outerness who had ravished off his sisters.

They gathered to reconstitute the fair field, Eden and Enna — et in Arcadia ego. The turning woods ringed the pasture. They stood, a curious triangle, aspiring to an impossible consummation. At their center was the small round hole the brother had spaded, lined like a bird's nest with green pine boughs. In the circle rested the square tin box, the mother-and-father-holding containment in the containing earth-hole. The three stood dry-eyed around that vessel of two made one, while the wheel of the pine spread above them — stood, squaring the circle of past in the fall flowing away of present — until the brother lifted the spade and the dirt fell, sealing in the earth and the unconscious what had been evoked and was now held.

Yet not in the unconscious only of Oedipus relations, or if so, not simply destructive: it was Oedipus the healer. Even the in-laws at home, exploring the momentary fellowship of exclusion, must have guessed at a subtle play between that regression and returning love.

Daniel, meanwhile, had withdrawn from the rejected others. He had left the two of them talking, and going into the study, had opened the farm log, which during Adam Woodruff's life it would have been awkward to tackle:

> Being interested at present in Time Regression, I am recording my dreams:
>
> We were walking in the second story of an old museum with a figure robed in white. I noticed a dried-up mummy lying on a table. "That is Steward Cope," said the guide. Soon we came to a black-arched marble fireplace with a Maltese cat and five kittens lying before it. I stroked the cat with my foot and thought of young Adam . . .
>
> Riding with Meryl in the Jersey Pine Barrens. Went up a little sandy road to show her a particularly choice piece of woods. These had all been cut down and a sordid town built there. A mounted policeman stood quietly under a tree. I cursed the system and woke in despair . . .
>
> Was sitting on a dais in a large hall near the front door, I think at Springmount. Guests were entering as for a funeral. I had a heavy fishing pole in my hands, on which a live possum was suspended. As each guest entered, he was accompanied by this possum swung through the air, curling and wiggling along at the level of his face. Woke up refreshed.
>
> In Meryl's room eating. Had jelly on my elbow. Two men came to the front door to see me. We went walking around the farm, business unspecified, for some time, when they mentioned that their credit was good, but hard to get supplies. "We sell ether," they said, "and represent the S.P.CA." I told them I was not interested, as I shot all my animals, and leading them behind the barn, took aim at an old crippled cow, killing her instantly. They were horrified at my brutality and left, wiping the dust from their shoes . . .
>
> I climbed down the sloping side of a sailing ship, holding to the teak railings. Went down a stairway and was in an empty barn, the inside covered with soft cardboard. I

went to sleep. Waked in an upper bunk, my face near the ceiling. Noticed how dust and dirt had stuck to the damp beams on which I had breathed. Leaving the ship we found ourselves in a green amphitheater, as at Three Fountains in France.' I was told a tropical rite was to be celebrated. Walking to the middle of the bowl, Meryl and I found a pit with a deep hole in the center in which a steel rod like a piston was working. A native approached smiling, and giving me an oil can, asked if I would keep the machine going for the festival . . .

Was out in a large open grove of walnuts at night. Chris threw a flashlight beam up in the tops of the trees and I shot with a .22 rifle at different birds flying about. Shot a large horned owl, but he went off. Tried to catch two tree toads but failed, so biding my time, I saw them sitting on a twig and shot them with my gun . . .

On the way to Canada. Continued by boat. We went down the swift current cleverly dodging rocks. Finally we landed near a railway terminal and I went to see the far-famed beech tree that grew there. It and its mother tree grew together in a green hollow. They spread out above me, enormous. A spring bubbled up among roots that gripped into the dark like hands. As I bent to drink, I shed tears . . .

A log of sleeping and waking. Among daily notes of jobs begun or accomplished, cows bulling, cows serviced (he gave them names from the family, so it was like mythology: "Lucy mounted by McNutt's bull"), or calves dropped, there were other imperative assignments for the mind, hardly to be carried out to his satisfaction:

Solve this! If the greatest of these was love, how would we advance? Love has a softening effect; it is the selfish man who gets things done. But perhaps progress is at fault and love should rule.

Large trees are storehouses of electrical energy transmissible
to human beings. Prove it!

Think this out: As natural beauty is destroyed, man turns
into himself to cultivate the spirit. This may be right for
man, but what of nature?

Daniel was sitting on the long bench sofa in the study which was
already hushed and somber. Over the wide fireplace hung one of the
dead man's paintings. He had been dissatisfied with it, as with all his
work, but Lucy had got it framed for him and he had hung it here.
It depicted a wood from the inside, almost lost in trees. Through a
mystery of grays and greens, shifting yellow lights and receding white
trunks drew the eye in and in, without rest, without answer.

Daniel dropped his eyes and saw the old man's moccasins, worn
to the individual shape of the foot, waiting on the hearth, asserting a
form not to be filled. It was as near as one could get. Everything led to
the same terminus, the shape to be filled, a hint of the force that must
have filled it. There they had stuck, on the elusive track, the vortex
whirling in the air where a power had acted.

Meryl's history circled in the same field, pointing toward the same
center, unexplored. Something had altered her. No doubt what drew
her to Woodruff Farm was already latent in the girl, as she wandered
the orchard where linnets were singing and chaffinches building their
lichen nests in the crotches; as she climbed those trees and sang like
a lark or linnet in the English spring; or played in the haycocks all a
haymaking day, while maids and menservants turned out to rake and
giggle and make eyes; or as she rode home with the rest on the fragrant hay wain, or sat at the harvest festival in the stillroom, watching
with aloof wonder that workers' kermess of dance and laughter: "Up
with my heels and down with my head, and this is the way to make
cocklebread." It had led her to the firelighted smithies and the shop of
the cabinetmaker with the strong hands, to whom she had said: "We

must marry when I am grown, John, and go to America."

The last family photograph set her off from the rest. It was made halfway through the war. The sideburned father looked old and tired; the heroic optimism was gone down the drain:

> We planned to bring the world under a rule,
> Who are but weasels fighting in a hole.

The mother retained some youthful charm, but saddened; the son and heir was not present; he had been killed in the battle of the Somme just before; only his loss was reflected in the parents' eyes. The other sisters were subdued, their sweethearts too killed in France. But Meryl was the center, their favorite, their love — such an oval English face, so clear in complexion and with such a curious blend of dreaming sweetness and of freshness almost bold. That bold dream was sending her to France, a volunteer in the Friends' Service. Still, it would have come to nothing; it was a feminine yearning that would have sighed and set into the norm. What it required was a force. And how had Adam Woodruff, product of a tradition as staid as hers and provincial besides, become the locus for the incursion of such potency into time?

That was the hiatus in their lives. It was strange that among all the documents and accounts of a family saving such things, the critical years remained untouched. There were journals from Adam's childhood, small nature books, records of animals seen, with precise drawings of specimens collected; there was one which bridged adolescence and attested (though it contained only bird-sightings) to some transformation: from 1905 to 1906, between one entry and another, the handwriting tightened and launched itself from a round feminine base, child-variant of the ancestral Woodruff, to an angular, intense, even Germanic script, slanting, bold, related to the Copes', but more impulsive, the character he was to use from then on. That was all. And these records stopped before the first war, while the farm log and the test did not pick up until years after; so the time when the chemistry occurred when the elements danced into shape, engendering a union, farm and future in the sanction of which they all lived, was without evidence.

This was the search in which Daniel, willy-nilly, was involved, by every act of reaching out toward Lucy. But it was a search beset with difficulty. Even the leads she gave him were too often false starts. As when Daniel was drinking wine from a bottle on a picnic in the hemlock wood. She looked at him pensively and said: "Daddy used always . . . "And he paused, waiting for the story, the clue: "Daddy used to give cows an enema with a wine bottle."

A queer opening; but the Woodruffs were like that. "Yes?" Daniel said as with her father, in the dark which way her fancy might lead: a comic tale, a poignant revival? But nothing came forth. Until a little gurgling sound began, liquid as bubbles in a pool, began and increased, a giggling laughter.

"Only when you opened your lips," she said, "it reminded me of a cow's ass." And she rippled away with delight.

The father lurked in the joke, somewhere, but inaccessible. For all his search, Daniel had scarcely advanced beyond where he had stuck that day of the funeral: the jottings of-the farm log, the empty moccasins waiting by the hearth. Meanwhile he was in the South. And days were passing.

He was seeing Coleson about the property, the rents that had been collected or should have been collected; he was asking him about moving in to look after Aunt Betsy, and getting no answer. And Mrs. Coleson (sure enough, Little Lilly, as lean as her mother had been fat, and with the black spit curl on her forehead) was haunting around sitting and talking, getting upset about what Daniel thought was one of the few blessings of the place, that it had no radio, nothing but a broken-down old set from the thirties; so here she came, out of pure kindness, lugging in a rattling little portable for Aunt Betsy to listen to. Once it was there the cursed thing would have to be turned on — if nothing else to give the old music box a breathing spell. Now Sunday had come round again. The radio was squawking local programs, and the Colesons coming in to call — Daniel fighting inch by inch to clean the place — when all of a sudden there it would be, one of those polarities Lucy used to tease him about: "Not polar bears, girl," he said, "polarities."

She, of course would have gone to Quaker Meeting in the clean white repose of the half-cube room — the square white ceiling raised a demi-side from the square maple floor — everything milky cool and clean, but for the amber blinds, which subdued the sunlight to a warmer glow. People would come in sedate groups and quietly take their seats. Except for one Negro family and a few other evident converts, the Friends had the look of relatives: the same Quaker gray eyes, the blond hair of the children darkening in adults to mouse or tan, then verging back with age to a soft gray. A few younger women branched out in varieties of hairdo, but the old ladies, if they had strayed that way, returned to the tight bun gathering straight strands combed back. The room filled in silence. The young mothers kept watch over their children, touching them now and then, a stroke that induced quiet; the old people sat abstracted, their wrinkled faces calm.

The first speaker was sure to be a Price or another of the lesser weights. He would ramble through something dull about bridges: how a bridge had to be made from shore to shore strong enough to take the traffic and high enough to let floods go under and founded on a rock to endure, and how we should erect on the rock of God's love bridges so engineered from nation to nation and people to people.

A conscientious teacher would get up next and hold forth at even greater length about the education of the young and old, and how much it meant to the world. As you thought you couldn't take it any more, he would sit down, and a distant-looking old lady would rise and say in a musing voice: "Love silence, even in the mind; for thoughts are to that as words to the body, troublesome; much speaking, as much thinking, spends, and in many thoughts, as in words, there is sin."

After that, not even the younger Pendle would venture to speak, though he was in love with the B Minor Mass, and used to trouble the Meeting with Catholic meditations on "Oh Lamb of God who takest away the sins of the world." The hush must continue unbroken, until the most aged gentleman on the Facing Bench turns and shakes hands with his neighbor, bringing that session to a close.

But for Daniel, hunched at the desk in the dark hall, it would be the radio blaring back from his youth remembered revivals, white or colored — the two could almost merge — the vapory sagging tent, the crowd milling, more and more drawn into the frenzy, rolling on the earth by the board platform where the lean evangelist flanked by moaning angels leaned out, yielding to the rhythm; in the dark room it was all there, carried on the throbbing voice —

"Here we are gathered in this tent and out there at the radios; we gonna praise God-a-mighty. Now I want you, if you hope to please Him, do what Christ says. What I put here on the altar, you put out there on the radio. Put sugar on the radio. Because sugar is the sweet of the world. Then put ashes on the radio. Any old ashes you have, it don't matter which. Put ashes on the radio. 'Cause Moses when he went into Egypt land for to talk to the Pharaoh, before he give the sign he had to give, threw ashes into the wind to cut off the evil vibrations and bring peace to the world. Give us peace, O Lord. Cut off those evil vibrations. Put ashes on the radio. Then put a glass of water, cause Jesus baptized us in the rivers of the waters. Then put two books on the radio. Let one be the Bible and the other the telephone book or any old book you have, it don't matter which. Because the blessin of the books will payoff all your old bills, all the bills for you and your family. Then put a light on the radio, a lamp or a candle or any old light. It don't have to be plugged into the electricity. Cause Jesus

Christ is the light of the world. Now we're going to sing: 'Jesus, Jesus, I'm a-callin you to come.'"

The singers broke into a howl as the vibrato of an electronic guitar, the most decayed product of this age, joined with the prehistory of the Zulus in a beat of spiritual jazz, from the tumult of which the voice shook itself: "O Lord, we're havin a hot time here today. The Lord is in His holy place. We are really enjoyin our Saviour. Take it away, Baby." The soprano over the rest rose in an obbligato soar, under which the chorus ebbed in moans and ejaculations: "Amen. O Lord," until speech formed again through the abandon, the preacher shouting the singers down in the Christian black magic of his final prayer —

"Now Lord, I'm a-callin you. Come down here and bless all the people in this tent. Bless all the people standin outside this tent. Bless all the people listenin on the radio. O God, I'm a tellin you. Bless everybody, Lord. Bless em in the ashes of peace. Bless em in the waters on the radio. Bless em in the books on the radio. And God, God, if you love me, pay all the bills of everybody through the books. Don't make em have to pay any more. Everybody listen to me: you don't have to pay anything any more. Bless my sister, Lord; bless my brother. Bless em in the sugar. Let em have the sweet of the world. Bless everybody, Lord; you got to bless us all. And bless Mister Johnson, Lord, wherever he is, bless his wax, bless him in the light on the radio, bless him with the light, cause he done kept this program on the radio for a long long time."

Sometimes one is caught in a destiny as if it possessed a satanic power. If one could be calm and wait, perhaps the crisis would pass; as in an undertow, one might circle and come to shore. But something prevents that. When Dante met the three beasts, he had no choice but, as in a dream, to sound the pit to the center. What was holding Daniel from Lucy was nothing but the fact of being in the Delta a thousand miles away from her, and whether he groped toward her or not, in time they would come together. But the power of what he faced made the quest unavoidable. The real separation became symbolic, the symbolic separation real. In the world of mind, which is where we live, the road of his marriage had to be discovered, and he searched for it as frantically as if in fact there was no other way to reach Lucy again.

Yet where was the search to begin? The only thread he could follow did not lead toward her but away. It was a depth analysis he had undertaken or was caught in. His aunt would oppose; her ghost when she was dead would oppose, standing in front of the desk, the bedroom door, with outstretched warning hands. But he had no alternative. He went down into the Byrne labyrinth, groping toward a nucleus of dark in which the minotaur would turn, baring its horn in an almost expected flash of pearl and steel.

11 ~ Speak Comfortably

EVEN AUNT BETSY had wanted Daniel to explore something. In that house where everything else was a jumble, there was the one display window of the past to which she had led him –like all solicitous kinsmen of the North and South, exhorting: "Hymn the columned facade . . . Speak ye comfortably unto Jerusalem" — though what she said was: "Not this room, Dannie, not that desk. If you're bound to go through something, here; these are the photographs of your father."

She laid the parchment-bound album in his hand. Had the grandmother brought it together in the happier time it recorded; or had both of them pasted it with their venom through the long estrangement; or was it the one thing Aunt Betsy had put to rights while the rest fell apart around her?

"And turn on the music box, Brother. What is the name of that waltz? I used to play it on the piano, but I don't think I could now. Turn on the music box, Brother."

She called him that sometimes, forgetting . . . Or remembering the young man she wanted him to revive . . . To celebrate . . . And why not?

You could tell from the pictures he grew up alone — a Yankee father with no pretensions, a mother with plenty, but without station. And the house reverberating with the indignity, that in a town doubling every ten years, where everybody was making money hand-over-fist and spending it like crazy, Daniel Byrne should putter on with his photography, his chickens and his bees, and be the one man not only making nothing but not interested in making anything.

Alone. A bookish solitude. And around him a gambler's rush of the gilded South and West. Cotton itself was a gamble. Torrential rains might fall on a white crop laid by, beat it down, flood it, and the seeds would sprout in the bolls. So it was borrow again, risk again, and next year, maybe, a fortune. That yearly snatching at wealth from a land prone to be whored but whorishly evasive, was the clue — to night-lighted steamboats floating down the boils and whirls, to the booming river towns" with unpaved streets, dust in summer and a sea of mud in winter, and plush saloons with gamblers in the card rooms behind the bar, painted girls upstairs, and levee-building Irishmen below, drinking, waiting their turns. Young Gerald was aloof from it all; but like the yearly pulse of the river, rise and fall, boom and bust, systole, diastole, it beat in his blood.

You could visualize the photographed, wide-eyed boy crouched behind a bench in the one-room school that day the new teacher, a West Point cadet who had been crippled by hazing and had left the Academy, established discipline. The grown-up boys had provoked punishment by a calculated offence, and then, as the master took his rod and called out the leader, they went for him in a concerted rush. Seeing them coming, he dropped the rod, wheeled, and wading in with his fists (only the leg was crippled), he felled half a dozen, cowed the rest, whipping them by turns, while the frightened pale face looked out from behind the bench, watching with remote wonder, and suddenly, cheered.

It was law and order, heroism, the right mastery of darkness. This was the parable that went to work in the boy's heart, some Horatio Alger image of success — not financial only, but total, a moral victory approved by wealth and fame.

With the deepening of voice and the growth of body hair, Gerald Byrne put the badge of that ambition on his face and went to college.

He may not have worn it too conspicuously the first day — hardly fifteen and small for his age — traveling alone to Memphis to wait in the strange city, and catch the afternoon train east and again south for Oxford. He sat at the car window in the fall twilight weeping.

And there as always, the guardian angel of virtue, the tall man with aquiline features and piercing eyes, the magnetic personality of the 'eighties and 'nineties, inquiring:

"Where are you going?"

Sobs. "To Oxford.. . sir."

"You don't mean you're entering the University?"

Sobs. "Yes sir."

"Where do you come from?"

"From Delta Landing, sir."

"Do you know anybody at Oxford?"

"No, sir."

"Well, go to sleep. I'll wake you when we get there. You can spend the rest of the night at my house. Tomorrow I'll show you around."

It was George K. George, the keenest lawyer in the state, later a senator. He found the boy a room, found him friends, enrolled him in his own fraternity, told them to protect this prodigy and he would win them honors. And he did: debating, declamation, composition, top grades. At the lawyer's request, they did not drink, curse or gamble in the boy's presence. He went through four years of college and did not know there was a whorehouse in the town.

Better if they could have shielded George K. George. How could the sharpest mind in Mississippi go without some devil's lease to pay for that eminence? What moved Gerald Byrne most about the relationship, and what he was to tell his children over Sunday dinners, an example of principle in action, happened years later, when the senator was a broken man, and Judge Byrne, now the promising figure, was put in charge of the fraternity celebration at Oxford. Speakers had been asked: the governor, the state bishop, the supreme justice; to these Judge Byrne added George; he made him the feature of the day.

"Judge," he was told, "Senator George will come drunk; he's always drunk; and he'll knock the program into a cocked hat." "After what he's done for this chapter," said Gerald Byrne, with the fighting set of his jaw, not clenched but swung forward, asserting a prominence scarcely attested by the bone: "Senator George can dance the can-can on the banqueting table. He has that right. I do not think he will exercise the right. But as long as I am chairman, he will be principal speaker, whether he comes drunk or sober."

As Judge Byrne was to tell the story years after, not for amusement, but "to edification and comfort," the melodramatic close would ring out in clarion tones: "So the senator came. And he was as sober as a judge. He didn't touch a drop at the banquet. And he made the finest speech I have ever heard. He sat down with tears in his eyes. Our loyalty, he said to a friend, had done more for his faith in man than all the preachings of the preachers. So the boy of the twilight twenty years before had managed to help the man who had helped him."

The great tear-jerker close. But it was all true. It was Gerald Byrne at the ideal focus of his age.

The portraits of that time rose with an assertive gesture, from the wide-eyed frightened boy, through the smooth-cheeked college youth — an energy wistfully poised, at the romantic moment when it might almost have gone any way: writer, scholar, statesman. Then it formulated itself, stepped forth on the next page in full regalia, the finished power. Under bristling proud mustaches appeared the man in his prime, intensified, narrowed, the poetic poignance ironed out under the conscious thrust of the jaw. This was the lawyer and politician, the form that could undergo calamity and be weathered to a dark wisdom, but could not change its course. The destiny was set on which Gerald Byrne was already approaching his height.

Not that you could have told him that. He thought he had just

begun. Was not nature constituted to reward virtue and honest ambition? And was there anybody in the state who wore these qualities as
visibly stamped upon him as the young Delta lawyer with shoulders
thrown back and chin raised?

He had no clients yet, but he had studied nights and got admitted
to the bar; he had set up his shingle on an office, to which he walked
every morning, pacing the business blocks of the town, shaking hands
with everybody, letting them know who he was and what ideas he
had, above all, feel the firmness of his grip. Then he would storm
into the office as if he had business, close the door, and bone away
all morning at law. At noon he would spread out his sandwiches, the
main contents of the briefcase, eat deliberately, dust the crumbs from
his lap, and after another turn on the street, sit, with more delight,
reading Shakespeare or history. At four he would walk home, shaking
hands and swelling out his chest, compensating for the shortness of
his stature.

The first client seemed an intruder, breaking in with the impeach-
ing question: "Are you a lawyer?" It was a painter whose landlady had
grabbed his effects for a five-dollar debt and now claimed seven-fifty.
He was mad enough to sue her.

"Give up the two-fifty and keep out of court," said Gerald.

The man had run upstairs. He stood panting, looking down
at Gerald Byrne with surprise that was almost disgust. "Well, I'm
damned," he said. "You're a hell of a lawyer." But as he left, "Thanks
anyway," he said. "I'll take your advice."

Next week a carpenter came in. He wanted to sue the saloonkeeper
for a twenty-five dollar debt. The stakes were rising. "It's hardly worth
a suit," said Gerald, "but I tell you what you do. Go down there and
call Bennie out of the saloon. Tell him unless he pays, you're going to
make his face look like a squashed bug."

"You mean that?" said the client. He was a big man.

"Of course I mean it. And if you have to hit him, I'll defend you free of charge. But it won't come to that."

The man came back with a roll of bills. "It worked," he said, "and I'm going to pay you."

"I can't charge for that kind of advice," said Gerald. "Come back when you've got something worthwhile."

They came.

Garrulous letters, those summers, to his mother and Betsy, when they would travel from the heat to Kentucky:

> Dear "Folkses": There is not much to tell about Cashan and Tot. She has been looking more radiant all the time, but he worries about his clothes and the wedding trip, says he wishes he never had got in this mess. Yesterday he came to the office. Betsy's dog Chee Wee, "that cussed little creetur," has been camping out there, and has filled the place with the first fruits of his fleas. Cashan sat picking them off and saying again and again: "But I can't be married with all these fleas."
>
> If this practice keeps up, I will be rich or crazy. I never saw anything to touch it. In two weeks I have done a cash business of $226, which in a year would amount to five or six thousand. Let that "sorter soak in". I am simply paralyzed and wonder if it is a streak of luck. But it keeps coming. "Took it easy" as the pickpocket said.
>
> Business at the gallery, I fear, has been dull. Besides, Father afflicts himself about your new house, Mother, though under Mr. Bates' charge it goes up nicely, and should rent well. No amount of persuasion will keep Father from rolling up his sleeves like a yard man and going around every evening in FRONT of the house to pick up scraps, so anybody coming by to see the building can admire his industry.
>
> I am as disheartened as you, Betsy, at the idea of a tin bucket in our ancestral well. Tell Grandmother we have heard of the old oaken bucket all our lives, and when we

come to the log cabin where we were born, we cannot accept "the old rusty bucket, the battered tin bucket that hangs
by the well."

The Farnhams, I discover, have supper about nine o'clock,
an unholy practice; but there is no telling what people will
do if you let them alone. Also, Jake Wyrin came in today
with a little piece of paper on the back of which he wanted a
sample of my penmanship. He was grieved when I told him
I had no sympathy with the autograph craze anyway.

Father says he has been too busy to write, that there is
nothing to say, and he never did like to write besides. When I
press him, he mumbles: "Tell them all is well." Then he sighs,
as if he had done a huge work, and settles back to recover.

I depose there is no more news in me. Write when you
can. The names are Daniel and Gerald Byrne, and our address is Delta Landing. Your respective brother & son.

GERALD

In a few years the young man was sent without opposition to the
state legislature. He did not have to run. It went by a sort of local appointment in that day.

Youth on its climb into power. And all aboveboard. There was politics, of course, one might say intrigue — but not slimy. It was honor
in action. How had it miscarried? Where had the divine machinery
gone wrong? Or how had a shifty-eyed creep from the hills slipped in
before him, shunted him off on a siding, played double with the governor —? "Twas a dirty little coward by the name of Mister Howard
that laid Gerald Byrne in his grave." And Governor Vandamar, that
more lurid figure of the betrayed democratic dream, a man with all
the entangled greatness of a tragic hero — how had the two-faced
Howard Gyves sold them both down the river and advanced himself
on the gains of the sale, climbing into the buggy of state under the
cheering acclaim of all the rednecks of the hills, as they gave the reins
of power into those moist and flaccid hands?

That handshake was a horror. Something spawned of the primal snake, belonging to the nightmare of original sin and sulphurous damnation, a ghost out of place in the sunshine of Jeffersonian enlightenment in which Gerald Byrne's American landscape was bathed. Yet there he was, the governor's false friend, advanced into the inner council of their strategies, he of the pasty face and slippery hand, with a name that already hinted at his role, the ball and chain, the clog and very bilboes of the state — Gyves.

The election for United States Senator had been thrown by a draw into the Mississippi legislature, and there was ballot after ballot, with weeks of scheming and horse-trading, while the aristocratic forces of LeFlore and the populist forces of Vandamar jockied. LeFlore was the lawyer son of a silver-spooned line of Delta planters going back to Virginia cavaliers and New Orleans French favorites of the crown. Vandamar, then governor, was the issue of pioneers whose name itself was obscure, corrupted Dutch, riding a mixture of Scotch-Irish, with a dash of Indian thrown in. He had grown up in the Reconstruction hills, splitting rails like Lincoln and reading what books he could find, mostly the Bible and Bobby Bums. He had absorbed literally and passionately the pioneers' creed of equality — except that he wore the curse of its po-white Southern branch like a hairy birthmark or cloven heel — the nigger-hating stubborn conviction that blacks were not men but peeled-off cotton-picking apes.

This was Vandamar, an equivocal figure, with his love of pageantry and display, riding over the state in a buggy drawn by four coal-black chargers, his own hair shoulder long, black and straight as the horses' manes, framing a beaked face over broad-shouldered tall strength — the whole getup boasting that small diversion of Indian blood he claimed with such pride (a fighting business to have asked him why Indian rather than African?) — he had courted the people with truth and quackery and been lifted from sharecropping into a colonial mansion he had bought and restored — the romantic Vandamar, in whom the democratic will, by the nature of the shabby demos in which he shared, became a satanic fall, archangel into snake, democrat imperceptibly shading over into demagogue.

And there was the young Delta lawyer, fired with ambition, searching his conscience for a directive — which was the right side? The components of his parentage split apart, as on every issue. The mother spoke in him, shrewd: "LeFlore is of the first family in your town, a connection to which we have aspired; it is the entree for you and for Betsy;" and the father's voice, blunt: "Are you of the party of the LeFlores? Have you played their cards or drunk their liquor? Have you been waited on by their Negroes?" And then, as whenever the abstract antithesis confronts the real, the voices would change sides, under-cutting what they had said — hers shrewder still: "Of course, Vandamar is governor. If you can override the LeFlores, it is better than fawning;" the father's voice less practical, the bearded image turning away with a shrug: "A plague on both their houses. Be true to yourself."

It was not the debate of forebears that could have decided, or if it was, it had been decided in his blood — the childhood leaning by which he admired Lincoln more than all leaders of the aristocratic Old South. And did not Vandamar, except for the cloven hoof, have enough of Lincoln in him to turn the scale?

The judgment, however, was still seeking a side when the governor called the thirty-year-old legislator to the executive mansion.

A crucial time. The circuit judge of the Delta district had resigned a few days before, and the young lawyer had already roused his friends to his candidacy. The appointment was in Vandamar's hands.

Gerald Byrne was introduced into the study. He advanced the levers of chest and jaw. "Governor Vandamar," he said, "I want you to understand that I am petitioning to be Chancellor. I am a young man with just seven years experience at the law. If I am appointed, I will do my best. But I am an idealist, and I think the best qualified man should have the place. If you find a candidate more richly endowed, you should appoint him, and I won't admire you the less."

The governor towered in well-cut black over the plumpening small potency before him. He said nothing at first, only looked, and then in his cavernous voice. "Tell me about the men who oppose you."

The lawyer raised his face a notch higher, as in the photographs of the parchment album, uplifted to the gleam: "There is Judge Thorpe of Greenwood," he said. "He has been judge of the lower court for almost twenty years. That is a valuable experience." He did not add that Judge Thorpe had sometimes been drunk on the bench, because one did not sling mud, and besides Thorpe was said to have reformed. "And there is Phelps, a distinguished member of my own bar." He pulled out the stops of praise.

The governor nodded: "You have splendid opponents. The court will be fortunate, however I choose. But will you stay to dinner at the mansion? We may talk further."

Gerald Byrne squared his shoulders, the setting-up exercises of the noble spirit: "Governor, I would like to accept. But on condition that we say no more of my petition."

It was a night he would remember, would perpetuate in the memory of his children. The veils of privacy were withdrawn, the governor stood amiably exhibited, with his handsome wife (he had not found her among the sharecroppers of the hills) and three children — the dear girl Ruth, who sat in the young lawyer's lap and asked for a story and kissed him goodnight as she went to bed. Then Gerald Byrne and the governor stood on the bearskin rug before the fire, smoking cigars and talking of literature. Over all conflicts of background and opinion, worst of all their difference about the Negro, this taste they shared, They sensed the rifts and avoided them, while the governor paced the floor reciting poem after poem in his great circus voice, Markham and Bobby Bums and the radical Shelley, prophets of his loyalty.

His enemies used to accuse him of a pretended love for the people, since no Delta aristocrat could credit that fondness for rednecks from the hills. But it was no pose. He would pick them up on the streets when he was walking with a visiting senator or a federal judge, greet them by name and take them to the mansion for lunch, talk of home doings and crops, or lend them money; the very men who called Vandamar insincere objected because he had no sense of class.

"Is there for honest poverty . . ." and "A man's a man for a' that . . ." he grandly recited. Gerald Byrne filled the silences with his own favorites, the swelling soliloquies from *Hamlet*, or "All the world's a stage," or "Man, proud man drest in a little brief authority . . ." And there was the passage from Milton, the rhetoric of the liberal hope: "All is best, though oft we doubt ... And ever best found in the close."

That evening not a word of politics was spoken.

The governor called each petitioner for such an interview. Thorpe came last, the most experienced man. Did the governor tell him as much? He took the train for Vicksburg full of confidence, began to celebrate with a few drinks, and wound up on a binge which shattered the peace of a bawdy house. Next day the phones were ringing.

"Gerald," said a supporter, "Thorpe was drunk last night, in Vicksburg. You ought to let the governor know."

"What do you take me for?" said Byrne. "Keep it quiet."

But somebody told. When the phone rang again (did Gerald Byrne have to stumble through that shuttered room, as Daniel did now, to answer it?), Vandamar was announcing his appointment. "But why the devil didn't you warn me about Thorpe? I almost appointed the man."

"It was hardly my place," said Judge Byrne.

"I suppose you would see it that way. Your scruples could have hurt the state."

Could have . . . But did not. Everything had come round — "the inscrutable dispose." High-mindedness had not only shown its mettle, it had paid.

Now Gerald Byrne went from town to town hearing and decreeing. It was not all clear sailing. There were situations: which almost defied the operation of virtue. As on the first day of court in the swampiest and most backward county, where the middle-aged couple stood up in a proceeding for divorce. They had been married thirty years and had a family. When the Judge heard this, he raised his voice, and with Biblical and Shakespearean quotations: "Love suffereth long and is kind,'" and "O, no! it is an ever-fixed mark," lectured them on the sanctity of marriage, saying he would continue the case for six months, in hopes they would reconsider. As his eloquence died, the lawyer at whose house he was staying in that district, a college chum, leaned over and whispered: "You're full of pee and high purposes, Judge, and it's a pleasure to hear such a speech; but I doubt if it hit the mark. That old man was convicted last week of having a child by his own daughter."

Days there were when the ideal floated down an appalling darkness. But mostly virtue in action vindicated the divine . . .

The pinch-nose glasses perched on a bristling profile over a collar so high and stiff it grazed the plump chin — that was the aspect he presented to the feuders in Yazoo County, when the lanky sheriff did not appear to open court, and it was learned by phone that he was ten miles up the railroad in his native village, battling a hostile gang. An enemy had pulled a gun in a close election; the sheriff had shot him. The dead man's friends were gathering in the saloon, the sheriff's friends in the hardware store.

Criminal cases were not under Judge Byrne's jurisdiction; but it was his sheriff. He called for a horse to catch the local train. "Don't go down there, Judge," they told him. "You'll get killed. Let the fools fight it out."

"I can't have open war in my district," he announced.

He got off the train and walked down the middle of the street between rival guns. He did not look to the right hand or to the left until he came to the saloon. The guns, through the shutter, pursued that willful profile as it wheeled full face against them. The Judge was let in. He arrested the leader, Quincy, bonded him over, made him swear to hold his fire. Then he walked to the hardware store and told the sheriff to come to court and do his duty, or be jailed.

"How we goin to git to court?" said the sheriff.

"Down that street, the way I come," said the Judge. "The train is waiting."

"They'll shoot us," said the sheriff.

"Quincy gave me his word. But I'll walk to the right of you, to make sure."

"Damn it," said the sheriff, "it's suicide. But I've got as much guts as you have."

So the five-foot-four judge and the six-foot-three sheriff paced the street past the saloon windows bristling with guns. As they reached the train, a Quincy man broke from the saloon and ran after them, yelling: "Hold on there; I'm going to town." He climbed aboard laughing. "Judge," he said, "you're the demdest. That man Quincy is a sharpshooter from way back. He looked out of the saloon and saw the sheriff's head bobbin along way up over yours. 'I could kill the sheriff,' he said, 'and never touch a hair of the Judge's head. But I give the little devil my word, and I'll stick to it.'"

That was the summit of the climb, though Gerald Byrne did not know it. He would have thought the stars were the limit.

He was in the legislature and appellate Chancellor too, and a friend of the governor's — riding along like a bold knight errant with his visor raised, and disorder falling into shape around him; why even the woman he had determined to marry, for all his mother's objections and her own misgivings, was yielding, with every turn he made through her district, to his impetuous demands.

And here came the sneaking Gyves, already state senator, with his limp hand and fishy smile, and his eyes flitting like bats; he appeared in the Judge's hotel room in Jackson at a meeting of the governor's privy council, when the election for United States Senator had been thrown into the Mississippi House; and Judge Byrne, despite his Delta loyalties, was leading Vandamar's fight against the aristocrat LeFlore.

"Who will be at the meeting, tonight?" Gerald Byrne had asked.

The governor had named them off. "Yes, and there's Gyves."

"Not Senator Gyves?"

"Yes," said Vandamar, "Gyves. He's loyal."

But what loyalty could subsist with that wilting hand? Judge Byrne would wake sometimes in the night, crumpling the fingers of that slimy loyalty, which had squirmed and ditched them all and come out sole winner. How had the upright shoulders served no purpose but to jostle worthy men from their places and boost little Gyves into the world-saddle? Was the villain; the serpent, to blame, or was there some flaw in the cult of the proud shoulders? How could Judge Byrne in the torment of those nights do anything but arraign the snake?

Though if the snake was the cause, he was coming to life everywhere. The first World War was hatching from the liberal shell. Old and sick, Vandamar opposed our intervention. Had he been the demagogue he was called, he might have judged better. After four years of crusading against "a war of money and oil," he was voted down by his own hillbillies.

War and postwar. Byrne's friends were falling out of power. But he would not admit that the enlightened dream had always been cradled in the snake's coils. He prepared a base for eruption. Already before the war he had married, and been disowned by his mother; he had taken Octavia for an extravagant whirl abroad, and had built her a mansion beyond her needs or desires. Now he was in debt; the boom years were approaching; the volcano began to fume. Renouncing all political ties, he ran on his own for governor, against Gyves.

It put him $40,000 in the hole.

That was half of the outbreak, the political phase — to serve his state. At the same time some aristocratic notion of being a landowner and planter crested with the other folly in a single spendthrift wave. The year of the great bubble, when everything went wild, he took on twenty-five hundred acres of run-down farm, woods and swamp, though he knew nothing of farming, bought it at peak; loaded with mortgages, and swung on through the ensuing bust, down to the bottom of the Great Depression, abandoning it finally for taxes after he had sunk another $40,000 there.

The mother, who had suckled his ambition, might have cautioned against hopes so patently mad, but he and she were not on speaking terms. Gerald Byrne came back from the campaign in debt for life, his practice shaken, his trust embittered. The mother's grudging reconciliation came too late to change anything. It could only afford a base for lacerating reminders and insidious attacks on Octavia.

("I will not presume to say what happened," Cousin Lura had written Daniel, having read his name in connection with an art show somewhere, "but evidently the skeins of life's pattern became woefully tangled, and it seems they were not able to adjust to the situation. The last time I saw your father, he had sustained great losses, especially his mother's death and the death of your brother; but I was shocked by his attitude — bitter and inconsolable, as if he had been placed under curse by an evil God. I told him that was blasphemy, and that he should take Christ for his Redeemer. I am not sure he followed my advice; but I hope you, in a life so given to fame and the world, will remember now your Creator in the days of your youth . . .")

Whatever had occurred, it was a descent that was to end on the hospital bed. If one had called it a betrayal of the dreamer by the dream, that would not have been simply metaphorical, but night after night, the fact —

A night train was crawling over lurching rails, the hanging gas lamps swinging. It let Judge Byrne off somewhere in the dregs of all Mississippi towns. He staggered in the dark along a street of dust or mud, stumbling over sleeping cows, pigs, and through their drop-pings, until he reached a frame house like a barn with a dim light and the weathered sign: "Hotel." He knocked. A sleepy landlord opened to a cornshuck bed, moldy, rustling, the cobs sharp under the ticking. He waked, if he had slept at all, to bad coffee, biscuits of fallen dough, chips of liver fried hard as the heels of shoes. He slopped through mud and rain to a courthouse packed with stinking, tobacco-chew-ing strangers, empty faces with no wish to be filled. It did not come sequence by sequence in the dream, but all at once, the impact of the moment in that texture: he opened his mouth to speak, his tongue already forming noble words, and was met on all sides by a jeering insane laughter, the re-echoed fierce hootings of an owl.

He would wake now indeed, in a clammy sweat, thinking he had fallen into that trap of politics again. He would lie shaken, until the quiet of his own brick house, his own bed on the sleeping porch under the great oaks of his own yard, flowed back around him — a comfort. But then, like the ticking of a dock, the tally of his debts and losses began to sound. He had waked from nightmare into failure. Sitting up, he would smoke a pipe, and rolling over with a groan, try to find his way back into sleep. But it was one or the other: the conscious toll of his blunders, or in some haunted fastness of the dream, the ribald hall, where a mob jeered at the great ideals.

That was nowhere recorded in the album. Among its portraits was no face folded in sorrow, smoking a pipe through the midnight watches. The man of grief had been discarded by the official man-agement. Nothing remained but the parchment-bound souvenirs of a Chancellor, who had gone forth like an emissary of light, and re-turned to gratify a mother's pride and a sister's love.

If the last glowing photograph hinted at the catastrophe, it was by something as small as the shadow of a man at noon, a negligible re-minder that there is a complement to light. Like all the plump faces on cigar boxes and razor tins, it bore the mark of some sickness: ego ipse sum — the conscious chin raised — ambition, self-betrayed.

Daniel groped through the Byrne labyrinth, living toward a flash in which the face would be consumed . . .

Also: *one box of age-yellowed Sunshine Blotters,* each adorned with a happy small verse, as: "God's in his heaven — All's right with the world;" and another: "Sunrise never failed us yet," and a third: "Life is good, life is fair, and love awaits thee everywhere."

— And in the lower compartment of the same desk, hundreds of beautiful photographs made by the dreamy skilled artist-photographer, her father, of the plumply luscious, too self-conscious girl in all attitudes of posed romantic longing — subjects conceived as subjects, the young thing who had never loved anybody but father and mother and more still her ten years older brother, or been loved by anybody but these, standing in mellow and year-lending light, holding a letter and looking with nineteenth-century walled-up eyes into the camera, the letter a bill of lading or receipt for photos delivered or reckoning for others to be returned, but simulating what she had not and in fact never would receive, a love note, a billet-doux, And the increasingly adolescent and romantically sentimental girl in beautiful print after print, decked out in costumes of lace and finery that might have been found in the studio of a Rembrandt, a veritable display over the same model, the same plumply lush and subtly repellent young girl with the same over-anxious and yearning eyes.

"Life is good, life is fair, and love awaits thee everywhere."

She who had come out as was the custom in the better circles of those pretentious southern towns with a party for which the preparations of dress and attitudinizing were even more elaborate than for the artful photos at which her father had practiced his skill, a party on a Saturday night, to which all the boys were invited, and where she had rushed in that nervous way from one to another, trying to engage them all, to assure herself beaus and admirers for years to come, talking a stream of impulsive nonsense and playing the piano for that gang of yokel aristocrats who would have been just as bored had she played it better; and then the next day, Sunday afternoon, when the youth who had accepted the coming-out at face value were entitled to call and make their return engagements with the fair addition to the local set, she sat in her laciest costume and most buxom palpitant heaving of the never-to-be maternal breasts, sat all afternoon waiting for the bell, the step on the porch, a shy rap at the glass, and nobody came; and she spoiled her lace and ruffles by running to the attic, throwing herself down on her brother's bed, and drowning the place with such paroxysms of tears as not even he, coming home from a business trip, with all his ambitious young charm — like hers, self-conscious, egoistic, but, as recorded in the parchment album, victoriously so — not even he, the most loved, could allay.

— The legend precipitated itself, coagulating around the picture, while Daniel wrestled with it: "What? Nobody came? Nobody at all? How do you know?"

He had heard it. Not from anyone he could name. Certainly not from Aunt Betsy, talking as she rocked, spilling all the town's beans but her own; not even from his father, though his father must have been the carrier; nor was it likely his mother would have come that close to gossiping, though she would have had it from the father — she, with a classical Greek calm on her face, telling the boy whenever he reported anything damaging: "If you can't say something good about a person, son, don't say anything at all" — an admonition that would polish off most of the world's literature; still, he had not made it up, however natural that might seem; it had come from somewhere; so it must have been through his sister, to whom the father, under circumstances equally trying, might have revealed it — a set of facts, indisputable.

Though even now, as he took from the photograph some instinctive male panic, to get the hell out of there, the question launched itself:, "Why nobody? What could operate on an entire township of assumed gentry to make them simultaneously renege on such a function?" And every time, the backwash of the question exposed the same answer: It must have been something deeper, something in the house, in the mother's thrust into town, the promotion of little Betsy, a goal her brother would have treated like any other, to be conquered by the dynamics of virtue; it was some sense of the future in the past. One felt it in the picture, the impulsive girl turning up moist eyes (note the Greuze maidens on the wall, those Greuze prints proper old ladies of the South loved, poor dears, never catching the phallic sense: the prissy hot babe longing to revive a spent (bird — "Sweet, would I were thy bird" — or the one who has cracked her pitcher on the big spouting lion and looks as if she'd as lief crack it again); under the walled-up hopeful eyes — as the Revolution lurks under Greuze — lurked a foreboding the image focused and proclaimed.

— She, who that morning, old and dying, had stretched her withered unloved body on the bed that the breakdown of her controls always befouled, the scrawny' legs raised, thinking of struggling up for another day, while the ugly little kitten jumping up walked on her belly, she playing aimlessly with it; while even through a crack of the blinded room a ray of the rising sun miraculously spilled through motes it gilded onto the bed, spilled onto the sheets where she also in the loosening and uncontrol of sickness and age had and did spill — played, the summer sun, while the cat played too, and the woman petting it, vacant as a child, "It's a nice Kitty, and Aunt Betsy loves her," smiled.

"For love awaits thee everywhere."

— She who ten days before in her hospital delusion told of attending a party at the Lake estate and of the shocking and worse goings on, and how she was disheartened and would not go back again

— there having indeed been a ball at that antebellum and still ruinously preserved mansion of a spendthrift and self-ruined family, a ball to which, more than fifty years ago, she had not been invited: it was a week after her own coming-out party, and after the whole ostentatiously invited establishment of Lake aristocrats had eaten her refreshments and given themselves airs in her parlor and invited her brother as a handy stag, without mentioning or alluding to her, as if her social launching were hardly their concern . . .

And indeed from that moment the road of society and marriage open to her had shifted from one of columned houses, along which her mother would have given victorious assent, to the other, where hard-working people of small background lived in unpretentious flats — in the end only to Fran Dudley, who came down from the hills, rawboned, lean and slow, with his Adam's apple going like an elevator in the ostrich neck, who struggled out an awkward proposal, to be half accepted by the starry-eyed Betsy, and then, the next day, categorically refused at the mother's vexed insistence, her Kentucky aspirations balked and rebelling at the shape and origin of that ungraced wooer — refused with the ivory-tipped pen lying in the drawer, the note blotted, no doubt, with one of these Sunshine Blotters which Fran had brought as a souvenir offering from the hardware store, perhaps with this loose and somewhat ink-smeared one Daniel now held, inscribed: "For love awaits thee . . ."

And what would he do with those blotters when the final point of inescapable sorting came? — what but stand before them in a vacillation as deep as the swamp he labored in, read them, leaf them, catch scenes and odors rising like dust off the yellowed pages, put them in a pile of things to keep, souvenirs for posterity, then pick them up again in rage and hurl them in to the discard which is all lives, deeds, past, the trash of being, shouting: "Go to hell, go to hell; you've had your time . . ."

"For love awaits . . ."

Also—

Black shining gummy-when-squashed eggs of hundreds of crawling black shiny roaches, interspersed with the small brown-black droppings of living and dead generations of mice, mixed in the tattered nest-shreds of mouse-chewed ends of old letters and newspapers and photographs, converted with the roaches, silverfish, and other nameless disgusting six- (or six-hundred-) legged crawling and slinking things, into their traditional and sociable home . . .

And like the drawer but of a different vintage, a different month or year's deposit, the box under the inlaid desk and indeed under any table and every desk, bed and chair and in every comer and heaping every surface — for she had gone six years without cleaning, throwing unsorted correspondence down as it fell ("I'll get to that tomorrow"): magazines, Christmas cards, insurance policies, advertisements, bills, deeds, receipts, into these nauseously to-mouse-and-roach-abandoned boxes — heaped and piled — as she moved from room to room, taking another workspace when the last was filled . . .

And then inevitably these papers and boxes to be appropriated by the ratty stray mottled brown and gray and black cat with the sprung tail curled in/reverse over its back exposing the too frequently used cloacal orifice which had now for the ugly creature's two years existence (her baby she called it, her love, it's a nice kitty) gushed brown effluence into those same boxes and papers, as into comers, unswept dusky nooks of the curtain . . . blinded rooms of the closed-up stuffy house reeking in winter with gas space heaters burning their fumes without benefit of chimney directly into the air (the cheapest form of heating) and warming from even the oldest and most summer-dried and time-dusted of those smeary brown leavings their innate and hideous foetor . . .

But this was summer; and he would walk along the street under the willow-leaved oak trees, the image of the spring on the Maryland farm clear in his mind, he and Lucy bending to drink at the earth basin — a sequence his being must imitate, to draw from the serpentine hold of the southern ground some filtered clarity, a field of validating antinomies, or abstract shift of light and shade down the oak avenue, or a song, nothing but the stress and release of an improvised song.

Singing (in triumph or desperation?) he walks through the mounting heat, coming from the grocery now, carrying the brown paper bag to the house, that web of the dead mother and of the dying child, his aunt, returning to childhood, playing with the cat, lonely in the befouled bed —

"Not this desk . . . Not that room . . ."

Speak comfortably . . .

While the whirlwind — Jehovah-Behemoth — roars in his ears: "Have you searched into the foundations of the deep? Gird up your loins, and declare . . ."

12 ~ Letters

Letters now were making the trek Lucy and Daniel had made, by surface or air, from Delta Landing to Memphis, over the Appalachians to Washington, Baltimore, Philadelphia, and out to the maple-shadowed banks of Quaker Mill, tides of the life between them — north and again south — corpuscles of what their souls were reaching out to accomplish.

As when Daniel's father had left Octavia the third summer of their marriage and gone east on business (she was nursing little Hilda and could not travel): one afternoon he took a train to the ocean, the blue and white undulation of force, to remain their common love when other ties had weakened. He stood on the dunes in lonely elation, tearing his heart to have her beside him — while she, in the upstairs bedroom of the house in Delta Landing, noticing the time, got up to feed the baby and received the vision: the house walls opened on what Leonardo saw once and spread to the ends of the earth, writing cryptic words, "The sea at Piompino, all foaming water." But this, unwritten, stirred its answer; at least the parents had thought so, and Daniel had not doubted it, assuming — in the total mystery of thought— there might be such accords, quantum transmissions, of which the investigation would not be how or why, but the statistics of occurrence.

His parents too, in that happier time, had reached out toward incomparable soul-union, though they had not achieved it in the commerce of every day . . .

"But I told you to let me know, Octavia. Suffering Mother of God!"

The best thing I can do for your mother, son, is to send her abroad for a time with you. I had thought your brother's death might bring us together, but somehow I have failed. She is withal the loftiest character I have known.

Letters from God dropped in the street, undelivered. God perhaps can afford the prodigality, but can we?

Burrowing in the drawers, burrowing in the pantry: comic interludes, tragedies, now and then a saving ray. As behind jars of rancid grits and peas and bottles of the grandfather's homemade wines (older in two generations than the amphora of Etruscan kings), the seals broken and wines thick with mold, or if not so visibly spoiled, of a taste, if you ventured, like those imported Burgundies Daniel's father brought home during prohibition, loaded with mothballs by a Baptist revenuer, old vintages that would tempt you to try, until the camphor smell or taste took you like a fist in the snout or a clutch on the windpipe — among such, one bottle appeared, a Yiddish sacramental brandy, made in 1890 from grapes grown on the hills of Palestine, its cork also half rotted away, but saved by a margin, the brandy strong, clear, an amphiole of sacred fire in a hell of damped flames. God bless the Jews.

When I feel thrown down by the job and drowned under the stale air, so that waving my arms in desperate breast-stroke I reach no surface, I raise the Yiddish brandy, and saying "To Loewenstein," or "to my Grandfather" (the old man, with the big nose and white rabbi beard, like one of Rembrandt's prophets — why shouldn't he have had Hebrew blood mixed in with the rest? — my namesake, who died before I was born, but has been a presence in my life from the first, as in the picture that hung by my bed: my father holding baby Hilda

before a full length mirror; it was the last year of Grandfather's
life, when he kept up the commerce with our family, though
Grandmother forbade it, while she and Betsy hounded him
so, that sitting with my mother once, telling her of his troubles, he broke into tears; that was the time of the picture, and
as he squeezed the bulb he leaned in, wasted, with his gossa-
mer beard and hair, and caught himself in the mirror, a pitiful
smiling ghost, as he has materialized again and again in my
life); so I drink, toasting him or Loewenstein, or sometimes,
murmuring with Romeo: "Here's to my love," I take the tiniest
sip; for that's all I can afford. And then I seize on the other
relief and write you a letter, Lucy, my *flower delyce* . . .

Letters were making the trek, carriers . . .

Daniel had set up shop on the creaking veneered table in the apartment side of the house. Here he brought bills, statements, papers by
the armload, by the carton, to sort through, file, discard —

Souvenirs of solitary journeys, journeys so confused, one could
hold up any of ten duplicate garish cards and say: "Aunt Bets, what
is it?" and she would shake her head: "I don't know, I'm ashamed of
myself, but I can't remember."

There she was, photographed with the gang, laughing over a Mexican
meal in a garden in Acapulco, or with a famous church or Indian ruin
as the background and the Greyhound bus standing alongside. "I don't
know. I ought to know; but I've forgotten." On the back:

Dear Miss B.: You wanted me to send you the photos. Not
that we need them to remember such a time. Take care of
your sweet self. Your Mexican traveling friend — remember,
with the frizzled hair and the boy in the army? Write me. . .

Now and then a card or trinket, something, would trigger the
memory; she would smile sentimentally: "Yes, I remember that," and
then would come the story —

"That's the cigarette case your father brought me from Chicago. It's tortoise shell. Of course I didn't smoke, but he said I could keep cards in it. He got it for the Chinese dragon. You see how the tail winds in three loops? He said they were like our three river bends. And the dragon means something. Red on tortoise shell. So handsome. Patricia Towne was here when your father came home with Fran Dudley. Such admiration. But he brought her nothing. And she turned to Fran. I had rather your father . . ."

Imagine it — Patricia Towne Dudley, who had come to Judge Byrne's office later when she was thinking of a divorce, though he dissuaded her. "Now Gerald," she began, "I want to tell you everything in order, right from the start. I'm a Southern lady, but I have a weak back . . ." And maybe he did betray her in deepest consequence, revealing this non sequitur, as it seems he revealed more . . . A tight packet of letters, a small town farce, a satyr play:

> Dear Betsy: What did a *certain person* tell you of my affairs? You know whom I mean and what I mean. Upon my return from a *certain place,* I sought his assistance against such. I went in confidence and offered to pay. "'There is nothing to pay for friendship," he said. But he has passed something on to you. Was that in keeping with the ethics of his profession? *Ask him for me.*
>
> What you have told others you should follow up and undo. It is mere gossip without the foundation of truth. *Be sure you do.*
>
> You have boasted of your loyalty to your friends. Here is one you have failed. Everybody who knows you knows you can ask more impertinent questions about everybody's private affairs than anybody one knows. Heretofore I have passed this up as trivial, and so it was, too trivial on your part for a person to have stooped to.
>
> In the gossip that goes round, be assured *you and yours* have not escaped and will not. Though I do not gossip.

Things have come to me years ago which I have not repeated. I am perfect in my walk of life. If you did as well,
you could thank your lucky stars, if there were such things.
"Thou art inexcusable . . . that judgest . . . for thou doest the
same things" (Romans 2: 1). It is out of love I tell you your
faults and risk your displeasure.

Yours,
Patricia Towne Dudley

Daniel sat at the warped table, the bottle of Jewish brandy before
him. "The sea at Piompino all foaming water." He felt within himself
the presence of another. It was Lucy, seated at the tall mahogany secretary which should have been Adam Woodruff's, but which Uncle
Steward had latched onto. They sat, emanation and spectre, each
reaching for the other.

> My Love: I seem gay and the visit is going well, though I re-
> alize how completely my life is with you. Even the thoughts
> of Daddy and the old days pale beside our happiness. When
> I think that only half the time has passed, I hardly know
> how I can last it out. Then I go into Aunt Hester's garden
> and pull weeds furiously. How is it possible that ten years
> ago my life seemed full, though I had no experience of all
> you mean to me?

She had come from Philadelphia and Springmount with Uncle
Steward's instructions in her mind: "Clean out the secretary at the
Mill and store the papers." Entering the drive she had stopped for the
mail. The letter from Daniel would have set a new term into the equation, affording parallel solutions. She would sit at the desk, looking
at the envelope, exploring the cubby holes, opening, reading, filing,
answering; all those threads would knit to a simultaneity.

From the first cubbyhole:

> My dear husband: I am beginning to put a few of my thoughts
> into shape, hardly knowing whether they are for thee or
> merely a communing with myself. But it has been a relief to
> my spirit so to express myself; and leisure and privacy are sel-
> dom to be found nowadays when we could talk with each
> other. Make allowances for me in my anxiety, and do not let
> this opening of my heart turn thee from me, for I know that
> in thy spiritual journey thee has left me far behind.
>
> Do not doubt my thankfulness to the Author of all good
> for the blessing of thee and our almost twenty years to-
> gether. But spiritual gifts manifest themselves diversely in
> diverse temperaments, and it is not unnatural that I should
> sometimes differ with thee in some detail . . .

Lucy had seen the letter before. Her father had copied it long
ago. It was from Patience Comfort Cope, Lucy's great-great-aunt by
Woodruff and her great-great-grandmother by Cope. It had been
written to the pious Moneygrubber, though whether he had received
it nobody knew, Ezra Cope, Biblical old skinflint, with all the money
of the Pennsylvania Railroad. Come, a clue to his character —

Once he had discovered some chunks of moldy dried bread crust
on the crossbar under the table, where his son, Albert, had put them
years before to get out of eating them; so he called the boy in, now a
big fellow in his teens, gave him a moral lecture against deceit, and
made *him* eat the moldy bread.

> With regard to the exercise of our duty to our children,
> I acknowledge that thee far surpasses me in vigilance and
> faithfulness; but I have their welfare also at heart, and would
> not wish them to forsake the paths of virtue or forget the
> fear of the Lord. Believe this of me, and do not doubt the
> wakeful hours and tearful conflicts I have passed through
> on this account, if I tell thee that perhaps we should trust

more to gentleness and less to enforced obedience. No one
could have been with thee through these latter years without feeling that thee lives up to a higher standard than most
men; but there are some enjoyments natural to the young,
which may be admissible within bounds, though now distasteful to thee. I do not counsel leniency, my dear, but there
are times when we must trust and hope for the best, and let
discipline come from a more powerful Hand than ours.

Patience. One had only to raise one's eyes to see her on the wall; for
she was Uncle Steward's grandmother. She had been photographed at
the end of her life at a window in Springmount. The heavy curtains,
pulled back, lighted her serene face, wrinkled, the Quaker bonnet, a
shawl white on gray, the knitting. She had died before Lucy was born,
but Lucy seemed to remember her much the same, though older; so
great was the family resemblance; what Lucy remembered was the
daughter, Aunt Hannah, whom Adam Woodruff had photographed
at the same window on her hundredth birthday.

And in the final cubby hole, to which Lucy would come before
opening the central compartment, bided the memorials of Aunt
Hannah, written for her nieces and nephews in her last years:

> When the Prices came from Church Lane, they brought
> their precious Willy to play with us. We were wicked snobs
> and didn't care for outside children. Well, we had our donkey
> cart, I think Albert always drove, and we would put Willy at
> the back; we would all be standing, and would drive swiftly
> down the gravel road, and when we got to the turn someone
> would push Willy off and then we'd call him cry-baby. We
> never could bear him, poor little pale-faced boy. Strange he
> should grow up to marry my sister Elsie.

And to generate those present Prices — "Not phlegm, Abe. Mucus."
Yet even that, Patience and Hannah would have endured quietly, spite

tamed under reserves of the photographed exterior. They were like Whistler's mother, all of them, that reliable and rooted in Yankee sense — none of the flaring confessionals under which Daniel had lived, of an infinite pride and broken bitterness.

> Dear Betsy Byrne: I have had no word from you, but I wish to illustrate by reminding you of what happened in your car. You know I once witnessed a car strike yours at that comer. So how could you rise up so *pompously* and proclaim to *let you alone*, that you were driving that car, when one of us (I) warned you of a danger you did not see?
>
> And whatever else you may be holding over me, so *pompously* also, it is without justification. You are one of those "intruding into things he hath not seen, vainly puffed up by his fleshly mind." And verily "you will have your reward."
>
> The one who planted the seed of this mischief, your friend, passed on to me everybody's affairs in town practically. I stayed by that one *until I could know whereof I say these things*. All such are works of darkness. I have no part but to uncover them. I count as my friends those who know themselves to be good. If you cover your faults so pompously in this, I shall count you out. There is nothing lower than a *scandalmonger*. Yours, P. T. D.

Thoughts on the carriers of letters, Lucy's serenely formed, bearing the Apollonian of Quaker Mill into the terror of his Dionysian; and now his fiercely scratched messages of outcry, sowing dragons' teeth in her landscape of calm:

> Honeyloins: Working all day and sleeping in the muddle, the stopped-up toilet stinking, mosquitoes buzzing in the heat and biting, one day blurs with the next. There is no sense how long I have been down here or what I have written about.
>
> Except there have been cycles of weather: a spell of Gulf air like the tropics in rainy season, gray rivers from a sky

blotched sun and cloud, then steaming light and more dark floods of rain.

Getting out of the house takes me to the heart of worse gloom, the shacks, the Negro problem (or should one say the White problem?) brewing like a storm; the South dumber and blinder; I have never been here when it lay on me in such a pall. The only relief between houses is walking down the alleys and picking everywhere my fill of heat-ripened glorious figs — how could I have survived without them?

Though already, thinking of her as he wrote, and sipping the sacramental brandy, he smiled, chaos that far admitting first light, if only to heighten its testimony of bane:

For I can't eat hearty around the house. Savannah is a poor cook anyway, but what if she were good, what would she have to work with? This morning, for the third time, Aunt Bets trailed lumps of puttysoft dung on rugs and floors as she staggered to the bathroom. The first time, Savannah remonstrated with her as with a child: "Now looky heah. Look what you done on the flo. And on the sheets. Thas doo-doo, Why'n ch'you go to the bathroom and be better?"

But today she shook her grim old head and went to scrubbing. She never comes, though, until ten or so in the morning, and meanwhile I've had to get the breakfast and answer the phone, which rang like everything in her bedroom (one of her cronies, Patricia Towne Dudley, asking if Betsy was still out of her head), and if you don't watch out in this blinded house, you'll step in it, and anyhow it smells; so by the time Savannah comes I feel like I'd been a week rolling in shit. If only Aunt Betsy's legs weren't so slow and her guts so swift. I'm getting a close-stool to put by her bed.

Even the envelope, as Lucy had drawn it from the box, attested to the depth of that immersion. It was of shoddy paper, resurrected from some dusty bin; to the stains of age it added a smeary corner of cat dung or a squashed roach egg. Aunt Betsy would have saved it, and Daniel, with the crazy parsimony he had inherited not only from her but from his mother's impoverished youth, was not one to throw it away. No doubt he would bring a pack of them home in his suitcase, with Lord knows what other treasured mementos:

> Betsy Byrne: You passed me in the bank today without speaking, though I tried to speak. Also at the D.A.R. meeting I tried to speak from across the room, but you turned away. I have not run down your apartments as you say, though I may have admitted they were *not very modern* in their furnishings. And if I remarked that I did not care for your part of town, that did not reflect on your home or your mother. Some nice people still live there.
>
> I am told you had nothing to do with leaving my name out of the D.A.R. report. I am glad, because I had laid it right at your door. It seemed characteristic. But I apologize for thinking so. Yours sincerely, P. T. D.

Detritus . . .

And in the well-kept Germantown house, where everything was decorous and properly managed, the maids and the man-servant like something trained long ago in the old world, Patience and Hannah sat at the window, the same wrinkled face, looking at the evening, reserved:

> I hardly know how to express to thee what I wish to say, and I would speak cautiously, lest thee should think me an advocate of deviations; but I have lately feared that we were getting to pass rather too much time on first-days with reading of scriptures. Of course it is desirable to occupy the children's time on first-day properly and to give them suitable Bible instruction; but perhaps so much during the day and in the evening too makes them a little indifferent and restive. I desire thee not to think me unmindful of the

importance of right instruction, or ungrateful for the advantage of listening to thee read; but are there not some sociable family enjoyments (I do not mean enjoyments of a vain or pernicious kind) which might be allowed?

The child of that union, Aunt Hannah, had loved art in her youth, but it had been suppressed in her. She had not been allowed paints of any kind, even colors, except for a box of bright ribbons her more worldly grandfather, merchant Cope, had given her. These she could take out only on certain occasions and weave into little fabrics, but never for long and never on first-days. The deepest love of her life had been music. She had wanted to play the violin, but that too had been denied.

In the end music took its revenges.

"Adam," she said on a visit to the farm from Swallowfield, "I want thee to make my coffin and keep it ready for me. I won't have any money spent on it."

"But Aunt Hannah," he said, "it would be melancholy to have thy coffin hanging around waiting for thee to die."

"Nonsense, dear, thee can keep wood in it."

"But I don't like the idea of making thy coffin."

"Well, Adam, thee must do it anyway."

Before she left she gave instructions for her funeral. She wanted Handel's Largo sung for the occasion. Uncle Steward might have told her Quaker funerals did not go with music, but all Adam said was: "Aunt Hannah, I don't think there are any words to Handel's Largo."

"Then you will all have to hum it. I want Handel's Largo, and there won't be any instrument to play it on."

When the funeral came, it was held at Springmount. Gretel Cope's practice piano was moved into the hall, and an in-law from Virginia, who was not even a Friend, walked through the assemblage in solemn black (Quakers never wore mourning), sat under the chestnut archway, and played the Largo so that everybody wept. They had not experienced music as a part of ritual, and the solemn harmonies, played by a stranger who had come among them to give Aunt Hannah what she could only get by dying, broke them down.

> It's a funny fancy, but when I look at my old daguerreo-types, I feel I would have loved that little child and under-stood her. I would love to have been her mother, to hug and kiss her and make her laugh, and to educate her in the love of all the things I loved. (I am not mad, most noble Festus, but it is a great thing to have imagination and pretend.)

Hannah Cope's memorials, waiting in the last cubbyhole …

If Lucy had lifted Daniel from the prison of blind force, there was the other incarceration from which his being had battered her. She wrote:

> It is almost ten years, dear one. You may have forgotten, so I remind you, that by the time you get this, our anniver-sary will be near, and you may toast me in a glass of wine or a sip of your Yiddish brandy.
>
> When I remember that day, the thing I like best of all was when our red-haired preacher pronounced us man and wife, you kissed me on the forehead. I knew then that every-thing was all right, and I have known it ever since. Think of me on the 13th and throw a kiss across all those plains and mountains.

Daniel's letter lay beside her. It was Coleman Thorndyk, psychia-trist, who had looked at that handwriting in those days, the inconstant sprawl, some letters held in and restrained with a cramped almost pretty rondure, others flaring out in slanting eruptive haste, the writh-ing tail of a dragon — and the size, angle, the whole character chang-ing from word to word and from line to line; "Insanely unstable," he had said in his pontifical way, "a violence obviously at war with itself."

No doubt. But as Lucy had learned, the warfare was not entirely destructive. There were dangers a person could learn to avoid, if not absolutely, then to skirt — even benign Quakers taking a hellish excitement in playing with fire. Though once she had been frightened.

That was years ago. Daniel had been away for almost a month at an art colony, working all day, and to judge from his letters, thinking of her. For he needed a woman. Obviously some men could be bachelors. Many of her family friends were, and even the married ones had waited until they were thirty-five or more, as her father had done, for all his impulsiveness. But Daniel was of the cleft-egg kind. It was not just a physical matter, though that was the fiercest necessity; his soul too was unfulfilled, an atom of hydrogen or sodium. He would drive himself off in the summers to work, but he couldn't stand it more than a month. Then he began to go like a motor without a load, working all day and finally through the night, until the flywheel, he said, was ready to go to pieces. From day to day he wrote more passionate letters, and he came back in a frenzy not only to be with Lucy, but to be at her. Lucy's lack may have been as strong, but it was of the sentiment. She would be lonely and weep, then throw herself into housework or the garden, to pass the time. When he came home she was satisfied; his mere presence gave her peace.

That summer he had returned as usual. She met the plane with the children, who were tiny then; but she hardly recognized him. He had not only grown his hair, which she had been after him months earlier to cut, and which he had promised to take care of, but had cultivated a beard, a sly-looking goatee with devilish slim mustaches and scrubby patches up the cheeks mingling with downy hair tumbling around his ears; even worse, to keep the front locks from falling in his eyes, he had accepted from some woman — she must have meant it as a joke — a plastic coronet such as girls wear, and had set it on his head as if it was the normal thing. (It was weird how coming from Mississippi and that family of his, he had cut off from the world, as if not recognizing its modes was the only way not to be enslaved by them.)

He stepped off the plane with his beard and long hair and his dirty clothes, carrying his bags and trailing a raincoat, and running over to her dropped everything to fling out his arms for the embrace he had been counting on — and she had too, but in a way these circumstances reversed. As he loped up, she felt she didn't want any part of him. Her proper phase took over, saying this was egocentric, exhibitionism and disease.

("Well," he said later, "the band is the most practical thing in the world. You never have to go to the barber; your hair is out of your eyes; you hardly have to comb or brush it, and it's always in place. Why can't a man get the same use out of it a girl can?")

Her face suffered a change, as if she had smelled something. Involuntarily she turned away. He saw that and stopped. He was sensitive too, shockingly proud; he never offered himself or his art on any market where promotion was required.

The children didn't care how long his hair was, or if he had a goat's beard or a fox's tail growing at his rump. They ran chanting a chorus of da-da-das to hang on his waist like leeches. So the encounter was temporarily averted. He rode home inquiring politely how she was and the farm was, while she asked about his painting and the rest, as if they had been formal friends.

They got home too late for him to have driven to the barber, even if he had been willing to do so. Actually it would have been impossible for him now. She felt this and suspected that in a rather subtle game of chess she had perhaps moved wrong; but it wasn't worth bothering about. He had only to subside into her orbit, to accept a certain remoteness until the impediment was removed, and they could come round gently; the weather would swing back to fair and warmer without the need of a hurricane. What she refused to recognize was that he could not wait.

Through the first part of the evening the children constituted a damper, and that operated on her side, which was of family and balance, in short the woman's side. When they were put to bed, Lucy said she was tired; she went to her room and lay down with her Jane Austen — *Mansfield Park* it was bound to be, a favorite. She began to read as if this was any other night in the routine of civilized existence, while Daniel in the study fumed, hunting a means of attack.

"The snake Moses raised in the desert healed the sickly Hebrews" — hardly an effective opening; nor Blake: "The Messiah or Satan . . . one of the antediluvians who are our energies." He might have begun with a lecture on Austen; but he had done that years ago and would not repeat it.

"Of course I like her, in her place. What the poor dear couldn't understand is that life is no one-way street, that she's not the whole of it but one of the poles. Take Fanny Price — delicate sweet thing, gets knocked up by noise, excitement, vulgarity, exercise. The way Austen treats it, you'd think such incapacity was a virtue. And there's Crawford, a peppy guy, would make a nifty little mate for her. But he can't hang around months while Fanny soulfully refuses him; has to exercise the codpiece. So he consoles himself with the married cousin. Chuck him out the window. And who gets the poor dear? Nobody but her gentle cousin Edmund, who's lived with her since childhood and never suffered a single glance, thought or word that savored of the flesh. Besides he's a proper preacher. It's like you Springmount Quakers marrying your kin. No danger they'll hatch a loud family, like Fanny's unfortunate mother, who has reproduced herself into vulgarity. No, everything in that quarter is going to be quiet and peaceful, a triumph of the vegetative art.

"Isn't it pretty plain that the fundamental virtue of all these Austen heroines and the men who get them is that they don't like to SCREW very much?

"Now I try to write and paint; and it's simply a fact that nobody can wiggle the pen while the other is wiggling. So I don't condemn restraint. But it needs transfusions to keep it alive.

"Here you are, you and all you come from, as sweet as Fanny Price. And here I stand like the Devil himself, the injection prepared. What was it the Delta preacher said? 'As the eagle stirreth up his nest, so the Lawd gonna stirreth up his people. And brethren and sistern, when the Lawd stirreth up his people, I tell you, he gonna use me for the spoon!'"

Several times Daniel came from the piled-up correspondence of his study, appeared in the bedroom, groping for a meeting. But the only possibility would have been a thaw from Lucy, while she saw no way but to take time out for cooling.

"I can't think," he said; "I can't work and I can't read, much less sleep." He was forcibly calm, standing by the bed with his shaggy beard and hair.

"You promised to get your hair cut," she said softly. "I don't like it that way. And I hate a beard. It's not as if it was you at all. But we don't have to talk about it tonight. We're both tired. I've come to bed with a book and I'm going to read and go to sleep. You do the same, and everything will work out. Just be calm."

"Calm?" he said, waving his arms to break from that context. "Is that the only value you see in life? Is it better than passion and love and righteous anger and all? I've been working for a month and I haven't thought about barbers or beards or any of that trash, and not a soul in the colony mentioned my hair or beard or the hairband, because they were working too and didn't give a damn.

"I married you as a woman, not as a propriety, and to let some nonsense about hair get in the way of greeting a man who's been wanting you for weeks — why it's criminal, that's what. Did you see the children draw back and talk about my hair? No, they came and hugged me. Because love has nothing to do with such pussyfooting.

When you turned aside at the airport, that hurt me, and now there's no bridge left from me to you. You'll have to come over here, that's all. And you'd better do it. I'll get the hair off tomorrow, but not as a price for favors. You find a way to accommodate this quarrel, because we can't spend the night in the deep-freeze."

He stalked to his study again, expecting her to follow, or at least to call after him. But she was as proud as he; he could wait until tomorrow. She turned out the light and rolled to the wall. She would have gone to sleep too, without any trouble, and waked up calm, gentle, a bit distant, a mildly offended Platonic friend.

In fact, she had almost dozed off when he flung the door back with a crash that shook the room, and banging in, slammed it behind him. He struck the light switch, putting on the overhead glare. And now she sat up vexed, but still controlled. "I have to get up tomorrow at the regular time, and I need sleep." But he had sprung at her and was heaving her up by the shoulders, half in rage, half supplication, growling: "I told you there was a problem. What are you going to do? What are you going to do?"

"Do?" she said. "I'm not doing anything. I'm just trying to go to sleep."

"Well do something quick." And he ran amuck.

They had called it that for a joke, though she had never been the object of it before. Only the children. He was almost too yielding with them, except he cultivated a breaking point at which he claimed to lose all notion of what he was about, leaping after the offender like an orangutang (he told them his great-great-great-grandfather was an ape), shaking the child, sometimes hurling it half across the room, though by chance it always seemed to light on a bed or sofa, not hurt, but awed, as if it had been in the grip of a tornadic power. Then he would come to himself, apologize, inquire what he had done, make up, saying he couldn't help himself when he ran amuck; they would have to be careful, because they knew how he was. When ultimate authority was needed, he had only to say: "You better look out now Mardie (or Hester); it'd be too bad if I'd run amuck," for them to go like walking on eggs. He used to justify his attacks by saying they inculcated a tragic sense, that the world human and divine is formed in love and terror; but they might have been justified empirically as well.

Lucy should have been aware of this as she felt herself dragged and shaken. Maybe he knew what he was about. Maybe he had sensed there was one way to reach her, not next week, but now, and that was violence. But how violent would he be? He hadn't touched the scissors that lay on the dresser or the hammer she had left by the bed when she put up the curtain rod that afternoon; he was only wrenching her with his hands, so she should have been reassured, even amused, but she wasn't. He was too strong and she had been timid from childhood; her very nightmares were of being violently pursued, and this was one of those nightmares come true.

He was shaking her and she was calling out: "What are you doing? Let me go. What's the matter with you? You aren't yourself." And he, having plummeted out of the stage diction he mostly spoke, down into the dialect of the South, not what he had been taught by mother, father, the schools, all monitors, not to mention a life abroad and in the North and East, but what as a boy he had spoken with boys, white and colored, when they ran and fought together ("What, what, chicken butt, come around the house and lick it up"), he was shaking her, mouthing: "You bet I'm not myself; or maybe this is *me*, the natchel Dan Byrne. Whadjew think I was? Have you taken this long to find out I don't ride the Main Line from the Bank and Trust to read the paper of an evening? Or that love is a goddam daemonic force; you can't turn it off and on like a hydrant? Or what it can't flow through it drowns?"

"Listen to yourself," said Lucy in the clear crisp speech which was all she knew or wanted to know. "You don't even sound like you used to. I don't know what's come over you. Nobody acts like that but people who are low."

"Low, by God! That's just what I pretend to be, low-down flesh and blood. You better learn from the low. They talk straight and they screw straight and they fight straight, and where they can't go they creep. Did you want me to be gentle? What way did you leave for me to be gentle? What way did you leave for me to touch you but to fight you? And I had to touch you. I love you, don't you understand? I'm amazed how different we are." (Shaking her.) "What has a man's hair got to do with his lovin a woman or her lovin him? And me four weeks thinkin about you, and I got to come home and *fight* you in order to *fuck* you."

Now she was sobbing:' "I wish my mommie and daddy were here –" sobbing but clinging to him, hugging him and at the same time sobbing great hysterical sobs — as the psychiatrist had warned, the epileptic type.

While Daniel petted her: "Don't sob that way. Gulping all that air you'll give yourself the fantods. I wish they were here too, but they're not, they're dead, and you've only got me, whatever I'm worth, and the question is, what are we going to do about it?"

She laced him round, all that calm inundated, asking through delirious weeping: "But do you love me? Do you love me?"

"Do you have to ask that?" he said. "What do you think I've been showing you all this time?"

A mischievous smile floated up through tears: "It was a crazy way to show it."

"Don't start me on that again," said Daniel. "Did you want me to sleep in another room for a week so you could keep calm? Now stop talking. We've talked enough." He shut her mouth. "Do you want me now, or not? Because if you don't, I figure I can shake you some more."

She allowed she did. In time her hysterical sobbing was succeeded by another, different, though it sounded much the same. As her uncle had feared, it was passion, the link between South and East, their divergent shores. But they met well on it, they slept afterwards and waked in good spirits. She never tackled him quite so head-on again.

> Little Hester keeps saying she misses you because you are so joky. I agree with her; but I miss you for other reasons as well. I confess, Ducky, I have had a number of revealing dreams about that . . .

There was one dream, though, which she did not mention, did not even remember, having lost touch with it almost in the act of waking. And if she had remembered, she might not have told, since relationship is based on privacies. They used to describe their dreams, but not entirely.

As when Daniel dreamed he was sitting in a tree writing with a vacuum point pen and it began to squeak. A dainty gray bird (Daniel used to call Lucy his woodbird) came flitting from branch to branch, getting closer to the pen, its head cocked. Daniel raised the pen, but the shrill cheeping, which was from air being drawn into the point, went on. The bird took the pen in its bill and tried to flyaway. "No," Daniel said, "it's only a pen." The bird tugged, beating her wings. He put the cap on, muffling the sound. She cocked her head, heard the difference, she understood. Flying to his shoulder she nestled against his cheek.

Having just waked from the dream, he was telling it to Lucy. At this point she gave a murmur of delight: "But what a lovely dream." . . . He could not go on — could not tell her that the bird, flitting to a branch and rakishly raising its tail, had dropped a turd and turned into a girl, not Lucy, but some nude stranger, that the dream had become sex.

So, years earlier, when Lucy had waked crying wordless cries and wringing the sheet in her hands, and Daniel had sprung up thinking of Sibyl, she had not explained the dream nor he his fears, though in effect they were the same: that in some weird participation she had been changed into the other. She had waked before waking — waked into nightmare, alone, in a padded cell, caught in the madness which had once fallen on Sibyl, and which was nothing but the walled perversion of a love which is hate. She waked crying, to be met by Daniel's cry.

So now at the Mill. This time Daniel could not hear, or if the alarm penetrated some fastness of his Delta sleep, it did not rouse him. But Lucy waked and walked to the balcony, where slowly the moonlight, the murmur of the mill creek flowing, restored her to peace. She did not write of the dream; it had faded. One could not even call it suppressed; but dispelled, as darkness by the day.

> My posterior, by the way, has enlarged to such an extent that I can't squeeze into my jeans. Yesterday I had to buy a new pair for gardening. I hope you will still love me, though I am overblown. I am marking the time. Your hairy heiress
>   LUCY

And his from the cave:

> Aunt Bets fell again this morning; in fact she does almost every day, just topples over, so far without hurting herself, mainly while she's hunting that ugly cat (that crapping-companion); then she lies down to recover, petting the nuisance and murmuring: "Yes, she loves Aunt Bets; she's a good kitty."
> I'm trying to get the po-whites to move in and take over the housekeeping, rent free and for something besides. Lord knows I don't envy them the job . . .

The sheep calmly feeding out the window in the upper pasture under the woods affirmed the continuum the dragon had invaded. Lucy smiled. It was a controlled violence, his, and she its proper ambiance. She read:

> My love for you is great, but this writing must be short. I have to get groceries in time for Savannah to cook.
> Since our anniversary is near, I'll tell you that my window

in this hell is not only the little Palestine brandy from Grandfather, but our first Valentine, the one you painted for me ten years ago. I brought it along by chance, in my sketch case. You remember the gay little scenes in the heart: us drinking from the broken wine bottle in the park, and huddled on the ship's deck under the blanket, and over the farm at sunset, rather pensive, waiting for the train? It was a godsend through that snowy spring, and now again in this Delta heat.

I am alarmed about your tail being so plump, but know an exercise that will help when we are together

— Affuctionate husband, Daniel

It had been so gentle and dreamlike, that valentine, with its tints and brushstrokes suggesting a tender innocence, illustrations for a children's story: *The Tale of Lucy Love*. No wonder Lucy's father had taken Daniel aside and cautioned him. Anybody might have doubted the "outcome when this airy bubble fell into the fiery furnace and the lions' den. "Lucy's never been strong. She's not a dynamo. Take it easy. You've got too much energy. It would make a person tired just to watch you. Don't wear her out."

But she surprised them. She gave herself to housekeeping, cooking, all the skills of a wife, to be tackled and learned with winsome efficiency. She must have surprised even her small Quaker self. The nights were warm. She had been brought up with no prudery of any kind. Her father preferred four-letter words for things in the course of nature, and on their camping trips the family would run out naked for morning and evening swims; so it didn't trouble her that the muslin gown rode above her hips, a cluster of dark in the moonlight accentuating her divided whiteness. They would wake together far in the night, she looking at him, her eyes bright with the moon. He would run his fingers over her flank, his hand brushing her lightly, and she would turn to him.

We must restrain anything we believe is wrong, yet we should allow in part for the animal spirits of the young. Don't think me wanting in reverence for the best, my dear husband; but sometimes Albert and Elsie and sometimes even Hannah, though not in a faultfinding way, are disspirited and depressed. I do not wish life to be tedious or gloomy for them if it can be avoided. Let me not seem to urge my view of the subject upon thee, or to give the impression that I am right, but it seems best we should sometimes look at these things together. And please forgive me for anything, I have said of which thee cannot approve. Let us try to keep near and be long-suffering with one another. Thy loving wife.

PATIENCE

The letter was in the first cubbyhole. And in the last, Aunt Hannah, a hundred years old, told of her childhood:

Sometimes we would sleep at Uncle Adam Woodruff's. They had high bedsteads with feather beds piled on them and at the side were steps covered with carpet to climb into bed. Uncle Adam, ignoring the steps, would start running from the end of the room and take a leap into the feather bed. One time he gave such a leap that he landed on the hard floor on the other side. But I'm sure he laughed long afterwards. He was thin with blue eyes and rosy cheeks.

Later he and Aunt Evie had their legs cut off short (not their own legs, but those of the high post bed). There I am giggling too, just as Uncle Adam and Aunt Evie and even mother would do. I don't recall Father laughing heartily. I'm glad I can laugh at a hundred years, but then, as my teeth are all coming out I don't dare to; for a poor old wrinkled woman with a blind eye and lacking teeth needs to treasure what good looks she has and not be a scarecrow.

But I often laugh aloud in the middle of the night when I

recall some funny thing and no one can see me. That's better than nightmares or snoring . . .

On the other table:

> Betsy: You have not replied to my message. You were never a friend of mine, or you couldn't have acted so. Whatever ill you are holding over me is your own evil. Remember, it belongs to you and not to me. *I am perfect in all my dealings.*
> P. T. D.

A farce, a satyr play. The curtain fell, while the voice of the narrator wandered on: "Patricia Towne… A coiled dragon of fire . . . The tail like the bends in the river … So pretty."

Lucy knew theirs was not that ideal blending of souls, without stress or tension, which she had seen or imagined in her parents. Yet picturing Daniel, his hair tumbling to his devil-soaring eye-brows, over the intense passion of close-set eyes, she affirmed.

Loving him, even his flaws seemed dear. It was like his theory of art — to turn defects into advantages — as he used to quote Blake: "If the fool would persist in his folly, he would become wise." Sitting together over the void, they persisted, flinging webs and girders of the impossible span — a strange inversion of fact and idea, as if the actual could become such only by being known, contemplated in its intricacies of response and cause . . .

But it was not like Lucy to muse when there were jobs to be done. She filed the letter from Patience Cope and the memorials of Aunt Hannah. Then she opened the central hinged compartment of the secretary —

And found —

13 ~ Let There Be Light

Daniel, repeating the opening of the Book: "And darkness was upon the face of the deep . . . And God said, Let there be light: and there was light," weighed it: "Yes; but when light crept into the secrets of dark, did God draw back from the act, unwishing the words, saying: Let the things of darkness root in the dark unrevealed!" —

Bringing that little bag of groceries to the house, he had followed a course almost as circuitous as the river's to the sea. Yet there it was before him, peeled to a drab earth color, the porch sagging, his aunt in a house-dress that hung on her like an old window curtain, wrinkled and coffee-stained, the gray hair stringy down her back (those full auburn curls that once combed out to her knees, and of which she and her mother had been inordinately proud), staggering from the door, looking for the cat, her wailful voice raised: "Here kitty, here kitty; kitty, kitty, kitty" —

Savannah was lumbering after her like a big black bulldog: "Miss Betsy, Miss Betsy, come on back now and let me finish yo hair. That cat's all right. Don't you worry bout that cat."

Savannah turned on him as he climbed the steps: "Misser Daniel, I don't hardly know what to do nex. She done bus loose in the night again, and I tried to clean it up, but she start hollerin, want me to comb her hair. 'I's cleanin now, Miss Betsy,' I tol her, 'can't you wait till I bees finished?' 'Don't you bother longer nothin but what I tell you,' she said. 'I want you to come here now and comb my hair.' So I come, and there she was settin in the darkest cawnuh of the hall. 'Miss Betsy,'

I say, 'why don't you go out on the porch where we have some light? I can't see nothin in here.' 'You come where I tell you,' she said. 'Here's where I always comb my hair, and it's plenty light for me.' So I start combin her in the dark. But I hain't no mo'n got the tangles combed out down her back when she jump up traipsin over the house looking for that kitty. Said she worried less it's loss. And me prayin to God it'd never be found. What I goan do nex, Misser Daniel?"

"Well," he said, "you've got her on the porch; fix her hair. I'll get the cat. Then you clean out that front room. We've got to get that room cleaned before I leave. And my wife phoned last night blubbering for me to come home."

"Aunt Betsy," he said, "you sit down here and get your hair finished. I'll go find that kitty." She sat down, minding like a child.

The cat was under the porch. By the time Daniel had recovered it the hair was combed. So he sent Savannah into the front room, while he went next door to see if the carpenters were on the job. When he got back Savannah was on the porch, swinging. "Misser Daniel," she said, "what I goan do bout that room? She won't let me touch it. 'You leave it be,' she says, 'I'll get to that tomorrow.'"

"We've got to touch it," he said. "Come on. I'll tell her it's bound to be touched."

Not that touching would do it any good. Not that anything would do it good but the touch of fire. It was the front bedroom where Daniel's grandmother and grandfather had slept long ago. Paneled bay windows at the porch reached to the floor. It was not a badly shaped room in a Victorian way, and had been furnished once in the same style. Now it could not be called either furnished or shaped. All shape had been obscured, all furnishing inundated. It was a terminal moraine, that room, a deposit of all that had constituted their lives.

One could still sense some lowest layer, the bedrock of what the grandmother had left there: the heavy great furniture, the walnut-framed photographs on the wall . . .

— The old photographer, her husband, had framed them, and what an exercise in penitence that must have been; but he had not made them. One saw at a glance they were of a sterner era, different from the whimsically lighted records of his skill. No, she had brought them with her down the river from that Kentucky center of her false pride: There was her Boone mother, grave as a corpse and steely gray, with the Civil War tight-lipped, hard-jawed severity that fills the portraits of the 'fifties and 'sixties, that makes one ask of the women, and never get an answer, how they could have courted and kissed, nightly offered themselves to the cohabital embrace, sighed and panted and gotten children, held them to those stony faces for a cooing motherly caress; and there was her Baine father, a match, and more than a match, for those fierce women, a Frankenstein monster of bony-cheeked, mad-eyed command, the overswing of the power pendulum that had rushed back in the next generation changing the sex; so it was no wonder Hilda (the name the beat-down but still steely mother had chosen, as if to vindicate in the daughter her undefeated sex, Hilda, the Battle Maiden) had run away at fifteen with the gentle fatherly photographer — one had thought of him, being twenty years older and experienced already by one marriage, as seducing the innocent thing, but it may have been different; no doubt in that beautiful slight figure the photographer had caught in his seduction picture, the only picture in the room by his hand — and breaking into the grimness of those others like a birth of romantic love — no doubt even in that winsome smiling girl there was a secret instinct, as of the ichnemon for its prey, that this man was the vehicle on whom she, a child of fifteen, sent to his studio tent to be festively portrayed, could avenge the domineering swing of her own father's excess, tightening the world in those flexions of spirit by which ambition (and did ever woman more aspire to have greatness arrow from her loins?) gathers its force and is launched from the bow . . .

That was the bedrock of the room. Over it, unconsolidated, lay the Cenozoic gravels —

Big pine cones of ponderosa and sugar pine brought from California and set up on tables or hung around the walls —

And rocks: since little Betsy, coming from an alluvial land, had always been crazy about rocks, and had brought them home from all her trips — the attic in fact was a repository of baggage broken open by the weight of rocks shipped freight or express or checked on tickets, from that trunk which as a girl the first summer in the Ozarks she had insisted on loading with little else, though the mother warned: "Daughter, it'll break, as sure as sin," while the father and brother spoiled her: "Oh let her have them," but break it did, sin being infallible, and about half the rocks arrived in a wreck of a trunk tied together somehow with express office cords — it was in the attic now, with the other trunks and valises she had filled time after time; thinking some time they would get there, even down to the small leather traveling case sprung two years ago with gleaming quartz from Mexico — and all those rocks had found their way into this room on the mantel or hearth or heaped on the floor around the walls —

Then bottles: bottles of every color, shape and size manufactured over the last hundred years, tied to the wall on nails, or set up in front of the windows on rough board shelves crazily attached there — for a decoration, she said, but actually to avoid throwing them away, to put off the painful moment of separation from anything — also inevitably to prevent cleaning, since no wall or window so pine-cone- and bottle-bedizened could ever be scrubbed, swept or dusted . . .

No, the case was hopeless, but he set Savannah to work. Then he turned from the dresser, the window, the light, that head-on encounter (had he caught it already, a glint of sun on pearl and steel?), he turned, avoiding the worst, yet starting a process that would lead him there — some Oedipus whose encounter with fact is to see actualized what he is in potentiality, and at the same time to learn the cost of that actualization — he sat down in front of the cedar chest, under the faded influence of the portraits on the wall, and went ahead with what he had been days at already, sorting pictures, papers, deeds, throwing most away, putting a few in a smaller box of things to be kept, God knows why kept, but kept for later sortings, and still the waste moment of decision as the paper hovered in air, the eye scanning it, the life of some irrecoverable past to be laid maybe in the saved pile, and then with violence, as if he had not only to conquer himself but to beat back the outraged ancestral manes, caught up and hurled into the hell-mouth of oblivion: "No, by God, you've been around long enough."

Bank statements of years unsorted, with the checks never tallied, went down in dusty cascades. Daniel opened an envelope as it fell: slips of canceled money. Then he jumped. Payments to Coleson, payments to Coleson, work and materials, total, a hundred and fifty dollars, in a month. He took another envelope at random, another month, another year: to Coleson, a hundred and ten. If he gave up the Colesons, where was he to turn? He pulled out the statements for the past two years, put them in a box for later reference; the rest he threw away;

Like all the work in the house it was excavation, geological excavation, back and back in time. Now it was from the strata of the last war when all the apartments were rented and the yearly income was staggering, but Betsy was fighting for more, which by her method would have meant less — she was always trying to raise the rents, though she was getting more than the chopped-up warrens were worth, and almost more than the traffic would bear. The whole file was full of altercations with the regulating power: "Order Denying Petition — insofar as painting and papering is just ordinary maintenance and not an increase in service . . ." — and there stapled to the denial and crying the folly of having asked to raise the rent anyway, was the petition itself, showing why she had repapered and painted — in the hope of getting what the higher rent would have forbidden, a tenant — she had scrawled in the blank labeled Occupant: "Vacant since March 1." As if in some book of sound business practice she had read, or her mother had read to her and she had memorized: "When property stands empty, raise the rent." And here were sheaves of them: orders denying petition, orders decreasing rent. They had saved her from her own madness; so that if the despised controls had only been continued, she would be as rich as she had crazily aimed at being . . .

Now the war years were dug through, and he came out in the 'thirties, a long troubled time of depression and struggle, when his grandmother also was alive and they were borrowing money to buy more land, and slowly, by miserly sparing and scraping, paying it out, until the quitclaim was clipped to the little hill of receipts and stored away with the other fossils in the chest; and here and there were revealing small signs of a sharper way to amass properties, those loans made to impoverished owners with their land as security, and then deeds of conveyance: "Whereas we James Chase and Harriet Abbot Chase, husband and wife, are indebted . . . we do hereby convey and warrant unto Hilda Byrne the following lot or parcel of land, to-wit" . . .

And now they were back where the streets of the town were being paved, and there were certificates of assignment and special assessments for every curb and gutter, with interest on the city loans at 7 per cent per annum . . . And now scores of account books from 1880 to the present, with day-by-day expenses on apartments against rents collected, first in the meticulous hand of the grandmother and then in the loosening scrawl of the aunt . . .

And then letters. Letters upon letters from that nuclear cluster of the family's best years — as the photographs and pictures of Europe in the reception hall attested, along with the ramblings of the aunt in her diabetic descent toward imbecility, or the glowing stories Daniel's father used to tell over Sunday dinners, especially, with all the enlargements of Southern rhetoric, when lecturers or cultured guests would share the meal — the early century years of their glory, down to the marriage and subsequent furies of war, depression and failure which had torn them limb from limb. Daniel scanned the letters one by one, each hovering between heaven and hell, while, through the closed door, a plaintive sound announced his aunt's entry into the hall of their past.

It was her sitting room now. Once it had opened between decorative columns into the music room — where the abortive parties had been staged — had opened and received light; but she had shut it off since, had sealed up all that far side of the house with false walls so she could rent it during the war, though now, except for Daniel, it was vacant. The hall remained windowless, book cases of black mahogany all around, and above them, pictures one could hardly make out in the gloom, scarcely distinguish the temple of Paestum from the Castle of San Angelo —

That sound came from the hall; it was the Swiss music box Daniel's father had bought her on the grand tour, the trip of their lives, before he broke away and married against their imperious will — the inane bright tinkling sifted through the shuttered house, while Daniel sorted through letters, and now trinkets and photos, all leading back to that time, the gay tinkling: "Listen to the mockingbird, listen to the mockingbird; the mockingbird sits singing all the day."

He raised the photo from the chest. In his childhood it had hung on the wall, but the glass had been broken and never repaired. There they were, caught by the subtle art of the bearded photographer, caught, posed and framed, each in his oval window, framed together behind one mat, in one molding, the four who formed that configuration (for the older son never appeared, the half-son bearing the photographer's name, therefore preventing the child-wife's still loving wish to name her firstborn Daniel, preventing, it seemed, causelessly, until the steamer arrived with the existent Dannie and revealed the wanderer's past, his reluctance causeless before: "No, Hilda, I don't want a son named with my name. I've always liked the name Gerald. I want to call him that." And she: "But why not Daniel, like you? Aren't you proud to have a son carry on your name?" And he, avoiding the confession time would obviate: "No, I've never liked having two of the same name in the same house. Let it skip a generation. I want him to be Gerald"); there they were, behind one mat in the single gold molding, the four of them, and the question, how shall four be grouped to make a dramatic interplay, the old man had answered as he did all problems of his art with a subtlety almost too telling: for he stood alone, in his oval to the left, equivocally smiling his bearded smile, while the other three were tied by all the links of family, if not love exactly, then interest, passion, in a word, of power, they were linked and bound, those three: the son was between mother and daughter, that son brought up by her to a life of ambition; he was in his high white collar, his chin and face raised to the light; he was already judge and thinking toward senate, governorship — there was no limit to his thoughts, as the smooth-cheeked, proud, mustached face declared them; and his mother on the far right, opposite the old man, in her separate window, was looking in toward the son; there was no light or shade on her at all, she was etched in outline, the shapely cut of her eye intense under the crisp brow beside the crisp sharp nose and over the crisp tight lips, separated from the sharp ear by a flat whiteness of cheek, everything flat, precise and shrewd, even the hair hastily caught from the brow and coiled in a forceful bun, and the little lace collar and embroidered black dress, the black she always wore and that people later assumed was mourning for her husband, forgetting that if she mourned she started earlier, the day that namesake son, young Daniel (for her always the illegitimate) came down on the steamboat with the telltale letter; she was looking in the direction of her own son, Gerald, while beyond him, and beyond the daughter, in smiling estrangement at the other end of the frame, the father ,hovered, out of their world, untouched by the etched forcefulness of the wife's gaze, which by a kind of hypnosis seemed to be focused on and driving the son, the son bathed in a different light, a glow of the dream she could not in the least understand, could only hope shrewdly would succeed, would prove to the world the mettle he came from; and there, to the left of the son, between father and son, her back actually turned to the father, on whom she should have gazed, was the daughter; she was wrapped in the most golden light of all — it was in catching youth that the old man seemed to hit on his miracles of lighting; her face was glowing like ivory or porcelain against a glowing ground, their darling Betsy, to whom older visitors from all parts of the country (though never beaux) would write back as the sweetest girl in old Miss, and so obedient to her mother; and she had the dreamiest eyes; she was gazing with rapt admiration away from the father at the proud face of the brother, she and the mother, both concentrating on him; together the three of them made an altarpiece as it were, focused and self-contained, except that the young man's look was to the left (his right), as if towards the sister, but beyond her quite, perhaps beyond the whole frame and constellation, perhaps to the capitol in Jackson or more likely in Washington; yet still, within the grouping of the picture, undeniably toward the old man, the bearded gentle father with the detached smile of art; it was as if that son had been formed by the mother; his being was caught in the web of power she ruled; Lord knows, he did not consciously wish to be like the father, the amiably ineffectual old father, whose only victories were his smile, his detachment, and his unprofitable art; he wanted to be laureled victor in the world; growing up under the tutelage of the mother had assured that he would never imitate the father; no, but he worshiped the father. He was a dutiful mother's son and he reverberated with the siren music she had sung him from the cradle, and he was a devoted older brother and spoiled little Bess unmercifully, but the dreaming impractical father was the only thing he truly loved.

So there they were, exhibited, four photographs on a single board, the three and the one, all wrong, quite out of order. For the central pillar of the three should not have been the son but the father; such driving ambition and pride is the function of the generative; and the isolated single oval should have been the mother, evasive, ungraspable, with something of the phantom; and it should not have been the mother to the right gazing at the son, but the daughter gazing at the father; and where the daughter was should have been the son, between father and mother, held in the field of masculine power, but looking the other way, drawn outward to the mystery of the mother's dream. It was all inverted, twisted world without end, and in that twisting lay the germ of everything to follow.

For there had been something wrong with that engendering, and Daniel, looking at the picture while the music box tinkled from the hall, the aunt sitting by it humming the tunes: "Listen to the Mockingbird," Daniel knew what it was — the reversal of the male and female symbolic roles. As if there was a kind of propriety in the sexes, a fit relation for benign birth, as if the daemonic and placid should be so dealt out to man and woman, husband and wife — the male earth, and also fire, volcanic builders and subverters, type of the Carnivore and Promethean, shaping in violence or shattering in the wildness of the lunge; and the female water, more water than air, earth-mirroring, yielding, but persistent, balancing through aeons as the plant balances against fire — dissolving too, but with a subtle labiance, of which the gray harmonious exposed shelves and ledges of slowly laid limestone suggest the mystery, the undulant blue depths from which they come, though compressed and thrust up by the daemonic other. (or if the flame has made a closer sally, more fiercely constricting the stone embryo, the layered gray leaves of limestone set into marble, crystal masses, blending in their artful mottlings the petrifaction of waves and tongues of fire).

But in that family it had all been backward; the rock and fire were the fierce mother, the father was the yielding, in every way, misplacedly, the water-spirit. So it was right (or fit in its wrongness) that he was a photographer, one who like the watery surface images all objects, even the infinite sky, that he would lend or give, impractically surrendering possessions, ambition, wishing only to relax into the mystical mood he was denied, being always harried by the grim assault of that Female Faustian energy and jealous daemonic tongue. While she, grasping for houses, land, power, the things he scorned, drove him out to collect the rents, evict delinquents, he moaning and grieving, never rebelling, only imploring under his breath the deity ineffectual as he: "Dear Lord, deliver me."

Ineffectual, except once the dear Lord, or the old man's patron element, Water, took his part. It was during the spring rise, one of those yearly reversals when the fluid nature assumed for a time the volcanic role. And the wife came home with the news, furious, against what she hardly knew, the river, gods, whatever destinies and rank persuaders of the cheating lying world had swayed her to invest in just those ill-omened messages, those particular parcels of house and land situate on the always friable bank (though she had got them for a song and already paid them out in exorbitant rents), raging most against him, the husband — sensing by his vague smile a complicity with the liquid betrayer: "The most useless hulk of a man God ever sent to cumber the earth. While you sit here rocking and dreaming, our houses have gone in the river, that whole Poplar Street row of houses. And the miserable sheriff who was there on the spot watching it had the effrontery to tell me there was nothing he could do. Will you get up and go down there and act like a man, and make him take some action? Do you understand me? The houses have caved off, gone in the river."

But the old man sat smiling and rocking, intoning to himself — though she managed to hear and be nudged into explosion — "Thank the merciful Lord, thank the blessed merciful Lord."

Then, as she came against him, he changed it, a skillful parry (knowing the doctrinal hard piety of her Calvinist upbringing), sanctified his unworldliness from the Book, saying: "The Lord gave and the Lord hath taken away, blessed be the name of the Lord." . . .

Daniel put the photograph aside. And there under it, as if chance had brought them together, lay a pompous roll of paper and a home-made valentine, the roll a Phrenological Delineation of Judge Gerald Byrne, certifiably undertaken by Professor J. Q. Fitzgerald of Chicago, stating:

> You have a head measuring 22 -1/2 inches in circumfer-ence. This is approaching the very largest sized head, and it goes with a body weight of 175 to 185 pounds, that is, in or-der to have adequate physical support for such a brain mass.
>
> Your temperament is mental-vital, this means thought-feeling, The mental element predominates; this relates to the convexed condition of the upper forehead, the seat of causality; the vital relates to the back of the head, the seat of the social faculties, with alimentiveness and vitativeness: hence your temperament gives great capacity for intellectual thought and also social magnetism.
>
> The will element corresponding to bones, ligaments, muscles, is not as positive a function, though you have de-veloped organs of destructiveness, that is, of energy.
>
> Your lungs and heart are certainly powerful organs, and as a consequence, you have a splendid circulation and your blood is well oxygenated. I would advise ten minutes of exercise with the shoulder and arm muscles each morn-ing, punching a bag or swinging Indian clubs, bringing into play all the muscles of chest, back, shoulders, arms. Combativeness relates to this portion of the body, that is courage, which gives coolness of will, as in the lion, prize-fighter and warrior.

(Daniel remembering those daily mysterious applications of his always overweight father to the Indian clubs and punching bag — so alien to his nature that if one had not grown up with it one would have demanded: "But why do you do it, and how did it begin?" — the strain of those exercises, then a plunge summer or winter into a cold tub, and the shaved emergence from the bathroom of the hero, chest filled, chin upraised.)

You have a large faculty of ideality, a hopeful attitude of mind: the future must hold great things in store, not only for you but for mankind. This makes you a man of strong convictions, what might be termed a hustler.

You must complement these energy functions with agreeableness and social magnetism. Be conciliatory, sugar coat the pill, so to speak. Put all the feeling you are capable of into your handshake. You will find in a few years you will have power over those with whom you come into contact.

(Though he had practiced that from the first: the young lawyer happily reading law and Shakespeare in the empty office, yet forcing himself twice a day to put on the dynamic mask, to go down and walk the streets, greet the townspeople as if he was already running for office, though at the moment he was only whistling for a wind.)

Your strong affectional nature you undoubtedly have from your mother, that is, love of children, home and friends; your destructiveness and acquisitiveness from your father, these being the masculine faculties. It is the mother's side you must cultivate. This will best be done by marrying and assuming the responsibilities of family life.

The temperament of the lady you marry should be mental and motive; she should be dark, at least bordering on the brunette type, and should be relatively taller than yourself and more willowy. This will give a proper balance for the inheritance of your children. She should have a head measuring about 21-1/4 inches in circumference with a rounded upper forehead and better development of the faculty of music than you possess. If these conditions are fulfilled, differences of origin, age or fortune will not prevent a perfect harmony.

For final advice I would tell you to rely on the faculties of magnetism, agreeableness and ideality. To understand one's temperament is of great value. You are not the will element by nature, and therefore if you try to dominate the situation through the faculty of will, your progress must be slow and a constant fight; it will be, so to speak, uphill work; but if you unite feeling and amativeness with your already magnificent intellectual qualities, you will find the world working for you, and will succeed even beyond your present hopes.

It was incredible how right the phrenologist was, how right and wrong — right in enough things to make the wrong more disastrous, perverting what insights there were. The measurements of the head had not revealed to him that the whole family was set up in reverse. Under the disguise of the Celtic name he was no doubt a clever German Jew who had grown up on Goethe, and who thought that the polarity of male and female must always be as in the Dichtung und Wahrheit, acquisitiveness and destructiveness from the father and affectional nature from the mother, and that the way to flow out in creativity is to return to the mother, taming the mother in a wife, the tall willowy dark and motive amativeness, through whose love one would blossom forth, adding agreeableness to ideality and heightening the magnetism of the handshake, until effortless and will-less power would pour from the dynamo of the perfected being as light and radiance from the sun. But there was no chance of a peaceful issue of the mother-quest in this case, since the mother was in fact the acquisitive, ambitious and destructive energy, and the father the quiet and affectional, which the son inevitably desired yet could not grasp, for it was before him not in the mother but the father, the amiable, always failing father.

So the search for the willowy dark woman (that description already like a jargon account of the one he would choose) was simply the pursuit of a will-o'-the-wisp he must always pursue out could never hold; and maybe he should have reconciled himself to his fate the other way and married as vixenish a shrew as his own mother and at least been prodded on the hard road toward eminence; but the phrenologist spoke and the desire followed, and the willowy dark water-spirit was prepared (would he actually measure her head before the commitment?), that mystical quiet and heaven-reflecting pool, of which, after twenty years by the tantalizing and elusive rim, he could only say again and again: "Your mother is the noblest spirit I have known," and grit the teeth of his soul because he had not understood or possessed her, had rather in the vexation of his love and repudiation of what she represented, heightened his impatience almost into violence against her (the frustrating liquid retirement), had broken her love, in effect cast her off, while seizing at, lamenting her.

So the relaxation of the will was also an impossibility. The phrenologist had advised another man. It is true the power of will was weak, though he strained it to seem strong; but the substitute was unavailable. His parentage had prepared for that, and the recommended marriage only gave it effect. He could never yield to the flow of instinctive vitality; it was planning, reaching, willing — how truly the man had spoken — an uphill grind all the way, but there was no choice; he was destined to labor and will, will and labor, and the labor and will to break and the whole project fail.

And here beside the phrenological recommendation was the unused alternate, the valentine, dating itself by the snappy new model of a Packard roadster with high buggy seats and a long low hood, spoked wheels and carriage lamps, a picture pasted in the middle of a big red cardboard heart, with phrases all round it patched from odd words and sentences of print, the lighter side of Judge Byrne: under the car, "Get in and go ahead," and around it here and there: "TRAVEL," "Out there where the air is pure," "absolutely freed from germs, vermin, moth eggs, everything unclean or injurious," "unerring principles," "simple, direct," "*courtly ways*," "THE MAINE WOODS," "Fine Tobacco," "Quite a jolly party as they climbed into the big car," and at the bottom: "Success and pleasure too."

That was the lighter side; but there were two hearts. The other was more earnest, the character the mother had formed. Here the domed

Washington capitol was at the center, an airy little image from a cartoon somewhere, the steps leading up and up, and around it like a halo were the key-words of his worship: "honor," "knowledge," "power," "success," and retreating from the center a swirl of words and phrases: "Strikingly superior," "Gentleman from Mississippi," "Maker of Millions," "Dreams of Congress," "Language and Literature," "Rule men and charm women," "The Man who knows," and at the base in wistful patchwork: "Clings to" (in small letters, and then larger) "Reveries of a Bachelor."

On the back, where the two hearts were tied, was written in the affected hand of the mother-favored and hopeful Patricia Towne: "Preeminently! The Heart's Desire of Judge Byrne." So maybe the mother knew best. At least a tongue turned sharp after the gush of courtship (and if ever a tongue was sure to turn it was Patricia Towne's, as poor old Fran could have testified) might have spurred him on to the goals for which the Battle Maiden had bred him; and he would have had this much in common with Patricia, that she would have appreciated the pomp and circumstance he would aim at for a wife's reward, the mansion, executive if possible, the silver and fine linen, the visiting celebrities in the leather-backed library — everything the hazel-wand water-spirit to whom he was irresistibly and phrenologically drawn turned distant eyes upon, or not upon — away from — a gaze wide and detached as that of Christ at the magistrates of this world: "You have spoken" — such a gaze as He turned even on the loving Mary that Easter morning when she knelt in the garden and He looked and then gazed away: "Do not touch me, for I am not yet ascended . . ."

Maybe the fierce mother was right, knowing how far her son bore her nature or the features she had stamped on his, feeling prophetically in him because she felt it so furiously in herself, the rage of the time-and-earth force before the mystery of those eyes, the timeless withdrawal of that woman who had also the effrontery to come from the broken Mississippi hills. Or was it only an interference, a vixenish spoiling of what might have been a love, even a happiness, by her own jealous spite perverting it to the laceration it became?

Daniel threw the valentine aside and burrowed into the lowest depth of the chest as if it contained the answer to that question — while the tinkle of the music box shimmered through the house, his aunt rewinding it when it died, so it would perk up and rehearse the series of Blue Danube and the Crowing Hen and the rest, back to the jaunty refrain of the Mockingbird — he burrowed, but found only, tied in a single packet and constituting the last exposed heart of the deposit, his grandmother's little personal book of memoranda and clippings, from 1871 when the just married couple came on the steamboat to Delta Landing, down almost to the end of the century: random jottings of things to buy and the young housewife's precise record of recipes for the husband of her still girlish infatuation, pecan sticks and blackberry cordial —

When suddenly, under the year 1880 of the great discovery, the descent of a full-grown and rowdy son bearing the name of her .husband, and testifying to a marriage, propagation and divorce of which she had until that moment not even heard, these ironically juxtaposed treasurings:

A slip of paper like a certified bank check from the Bank of Delta Landing to Daniel Byrne, on New Year's day of 1880, that leap year of which the old man would wish the extra day and Lord knows how many more had been left out, as Job, thereafter his model, would have said, "Let it not be numbered in the count of the year," a check made out in the name of the "BANK OF PROSPERITY (With Surplus Stock and Boundless Capital): On Demand, Please bestow upon Daniel Byrne, *Three Hundred and Sixty-six HAPPY DAYS*, Value received in friendship, and charge same to account of THE GODDESS OF FORTUNE, State of Felicity, courtesy Bank of Delta Landing" (the bank also to fail that year, taking the pitiful small savings of Daniel Byrne with it into Fortune's inaccessible kingdom).

And second, this newspaper clipping dated July 1880, as if she had been searching the papers and magazines feverishly for it since April when the steamboat docked with the adolescent Dannie — not tearstained, but yellowed and browned as if passion-scorched and hate-burned — treasured in the innermost sanctum of the then twenty-four-year-old wife's journal:

> TREACHERY: : Injury may wound and be forgiven, insult may sting and be forgotten; but treachery bewilders and chills us; and we know even while we struggle to pardon, that for it there is no oblivion. A brightness and a melody has gone from our lives when once we learn that we have been betrayed; an asp has sprung from amidst the flowers of our paradise, and we can never walk there as fearlessly as before. Trust, that blessed portion of youth and inexperience, has been driven from its stronghold in our hearts, and a few moments have sufficed to change us forever.

The clipping might have been there by chance, though the date underlined its meaning; but that was not the only underlining. As if to proclaim and hold it up to the avenging gods in unmistakable accusation, she had scored with a firm black-inked stroke under the first clause of the last sentence: *"Trust, that blessed portion of youth and inexperience, has been driven from its stronghold in our hearts."*

And had she not been changed? She sat in the central hand-colored photo over the mantel on the wall, the seduction picture, contrasting so strangely with the others in the room (and whatever the old man's faults, he was an artist, a photographer of the most painterly power); there she sat in her Sunday dress, as she had been sent by her parents to his studio tent in the small river town in Kentucky; it was the Lippi story again, the sitter won and possessed in the act of eternizing her beauty, as if for that tinted record of her girlhood she was ready to sacrifice everything — or was it the artist. who, for that image partly of his own devising, sacrificed and was destroyed? At any rate, against the parents' knowledge, certainly against their will; and by what maturer charms who could say, he had won her, at a single sitting, the beauty of the countryside, and only fifteen years of age.

She sat, the hand gently folded against the cheek under the sloping fold of the bonnet, the lace and black-velvet collar tied under the chin, the curve of the body caressed by the oval frame at whose center was the tenderer smooth oval of face, with the almost playful gaiety of the eyes, and at the base, a masterstroke, the left hand in the lap held carelessly — as if to say see what I have plucked without thinking, what thoughtlessly I hold — the tinted, always significant rose.

Had she not been changed? Her later image brooded like a presence in the shadowed room, driving her son for victories he could not achieve, possessing and closing her daughter in the bitter pride in which she lived: the wasted, pale face, still sharply beautiful, the hand groping the surface of the clock, ascertaining the passage of minutes, hours and the fruitless years, first of estrangement, and then of reconciliation —

The almost blind orbs probing as the delicate white hand fastened on one's shoulder: "Tell me, Dannie, who are your school friends, and what families do they come from? " And to little Gerald: "Does your mother still complain of her heart? If you ask me, it's not her heart at all." Then to Daniel's father: "And did you know, Gerald, the Bolsheviks cut off the fingers of the Russian nobles to take their rings?" Or to his sister: "What kind of a person is Nancy's mother? Is she a good talker?" To Daniel's father again: "Had you heard, son, that Mrs. Walters is a dope fiend?" —

Had she not been changed?

But her book of jottings had not delivered itself of all it had to say. There was a letter, folded with the yellowed clipping on treachery, though from a few years later and another world, the western golden hills of success in California, that ultimate mecca of the pioneer spirit

— from the Hon. J. G. McClain, on engraved letterhead, Attorney-at-Law, San Francisco, a flowingly penned treasure folded in the record book like another barb of self-tormenting memory:

> Dear Mrs. Byrne:
>
> By mere accident I glanced today at a copy of the *Kentucky Star* lying on my desk, and read: "Mrs. Hilda Baine Byrne, of Delta Landing, Mississippi, is visiting in Paducah," and at once, strong as the flash of a great meteor, memory brought back that bright and vibrant girl I esteemed more than twenty years ago, esteemed and lost sight of and moved here in some bitterness — a memory rather forced back from me by the not unrewarding cares of a prosperous business life — and I could not refrain from offering her my congratulations that her life has been spared up to these maturer years, or expressing my sincere wishes for her happiness now and in the time to come.
>
> And I feel sure she will accept kindly the statement that I am still respectfully and devotedly,
>
> > hers,
> > J. G. MCCLAIN

This almost smug letter of the successful barrister, her old beau, proud he had made much of himself, though she had scorned his offer, or rather in the midst of what he had hoped were deliberations on that account, had eloped with an itinerant photographer — smug, but more touched with regret, still yearning for the image, the hand lightly folded in the lap holding the rose, the oval soft image the photographer had recorded.

The letter and clipping had been creased together, as if what had been thrown away should be linked in perpetual bond with the treachery she had espoused, reminder of how resentful she could afford to be.

As for the craftsman, who had struck that beauty in silver, and been so heavily struck by reason of it, if ever he wished for his rival's success, there was no record of it in the coffer. True, he sometimes asserted his independence to the extent of going off on photographing tours up and down the river. He would set up his tent in some sleepy village, displaying on a board in the blistering sun his exquisite wares; and always (the complexion of hope in the breast of the son having been inherited from the father) he expected the miracle, the year of wonder, when his art would be appreciated, when some horse-riding patrician or walking immigrant shopkeeper would see the display, break out in the raptures of genius recognized, and lead the town in a rush of orders, commissions, success. But the orders never came, or came so slowly and so badly paid (as he got older he had less power to collect on a bill) that he would hardly make expenses. Then he would think of his Kentucky Belle wife, tinted perhaps with the colors in which he had first invested her, and of the family he loved, the sweet-nutted pecan tree, the dream of a home. He would write disheartened letters, while she in her bedroom snapped the whip of her temper: Daniel as always a failure, expedition after expedition and never a profit, and all this projected against the lost alternate of California gold. And the fact that Daniel, whatever else, was an artist, an astonishing artist, did not sway her in the least; she was hardly aware what the word meant, and whether he was or was not she never knew, nor did anybody else but the old man himself. He bore the burden of that knowledge alone — or was it a reward, mirrored in the secret patience of his smile? She, at any rate, could only add up the account books and reckon as clearly as night from day that Daniel was a failure, and that if it were not for weekly small rents on shacks colored and white which she had fought for and acquired, they would not go on living from year to year …

It was the third Daniel who stood among the disembowelings of the chest, as the door from the hall or reception room (whatever you called it would not make it less dark) was flung back. He looked up, startled, as if caught in a trespass, though he was only doing what had to be done. There stood his aunt, the run-down music box dying away on an odd bar of the Crowing Hen. The sunken eyes, beaked nose and mummy skin struck a resonance of corpses; it was one face, her mother's, his father's, her own as it would stare from the coffin.

She stood, weak and pitiful, swaying as if she might fall to the floor, yet determined to save the house from the fate of being cleaned; so that Savannah looked up from the trash-heaped dresser to which she had just gone, after a futile attempt at the table — curious who would win the encounter. But Aunt Betsy's voice was too weak to be more than pleading: "Don't fiddle with that stuff, Dannie, I'll get to it tomorrow." He took her by the arm and led her back to the swing on the porch, and finding the cat again, put it in her lap, saying: "Why don't you pet the kitty, Aunt Bets? It's a nice kitty."

When a cry of alarm broke from the bedroom: "Lord God amighty, 'Misser Daniel, Misser Daniel!" And he hurried in and saw Savannah catching back her hand, as before when she found the snake rattles in the hall drawer, with more violence now and from something deadlier than' the rattler, a glint of light on pearl and steel — Daniel must even have been looking for it, though he was not sure his aunt had brought it home — the square-built Colt automatic (a present from the grandmother to Judge Byrne, on his going abroad— $14.30 plus $2.00 for the pearl grip), the feel of which, before he was conscious what it was, came threateningly to his hand: that ray of sun down the mote-laden air on the metallic blue barrel opening, of all memories, the one he was least tempted to disturb, the last skeleton-closet in the house of Byrne —

He had known it was coming, but it had not come. The time was far into the darkest watch of the morning. He was tossing on a mattress thrown down on the library floor. That was fifteen years ago in the other house, the columned brick one of his own childhood and his father's pride. The upper floor was torn up to be made into apartments. Daniel himself had begun it, worn out with talking over plans that led nowhere, had taken the axe to the first regretted partition, brought it down in a cloud of plaster, like crossing a Rubicon of no return.

Rolling on the mattress, struggling through long hours of the night with adversaries of fear and desire, against which the father too must be struggling, the powerful old man stretched out with digitalis and oxygen for an interminable and costly dying, not to mention the pain — the son had met with him as never before, though they had fished and talked together and grown closer as the years passed —

Those collection trips in the Depression when he had driven the old man over the baking flat Delta, until a water tank would appear in the distance and one of the crummy towns at which the Judge did business would materialize around them — the gravel road rutted with traffic, bumping over the railroad tracks by the little station behind the cotton gin; and now they, would park in front of the general store, dogs in the road, pigs rooting, the slow drawling men spitting and talking as they had done for generations, preserved in the shimmering heat as in alcohol, and the father would pick up the grief case, as he called it, and with shoulders squared, the fighting chin raised — assuming the pose of power for a work he abhorred — would launch himself against the town, while Daniel waited in the steaming car, washed over by the languid drawl of loungers under the tin awning — a beefy man yawning: "Lawd, man ahm so tiaahud, so tiaahud."

And his neighbor: "Whuhz zu mattuh wi you Coennul?"

The first, a planter who lived by the river landing: "Ah ain had no sleep fuh days."

"Whatchabeen doin, man?"

"Man, Ah been out wid tawches evy niaaght down at the bauhuh piut, triauyin tu keep the niuggus fum clubbin the whiaht peaurch" —

Until the Judge returned, shoulders slumped, the chin slack, as if the punching bag had hit back; but the pocketbook loaded with the stuff that kept such collectors from his own door.

They had grown closer through the years, but now they had joined in love and pain, fear, even desire; their wills had merged in a single act, a double decision, yet they had lain awake more than half the night and the act had not come, the old man facing alone the incalculable resolution his soul hated and his fate required —

He had always despised the cowardice of self-destruction. Through that long agony of Depression, when the world of his activity dried up around him, and merchants, lawyers, bankers, his friends, fearfully involved, had gone home and blown out their brains, he had shaken his head — that Stoicism of escape too easy — had gone back to the office, to the dogged fight each day to earn enough to meet the interest on debts which would otherwise have had their house and perhaps more in fee simple — sweating for money to pay for money already lived through before it was made, and the children to go to college and the establishment to be maintained in the style to which they were accustomed —

Not that anybody drove him to that style, least of all his wife; she would have been content like Hamlet in a walnut shell, queen of infinite space and not even have had bad dreams; no, it was his own, or his inherited values — as though, if he could not hold the love he shattered daily with possessive outbreaks, he could at least justify himself before the eternal gods by keeping her in a templed mansion with servants and a garden and food, such as nobles of old enjoyed, at least show her and the state and nation his stature by living as if he were what he had failed to become, governor of Mississippi, or something higher — Let the blame, thought Daniel, fall where it was due —

Yet mention also the tragic magnitude, the glinting of light in darkness — and who but the misguided are ultimately of tragic concern? —how despising bankruptcy or other escape, he carried that load like his private portion of the world-betrayal through which he lived: the liberal Europe of hope and natural good, to which he had taken his sister for the accumulation of things recording the dream, to which in age he had wished to return, that Europe crushed under tyrannies of the left and right, slipping through the first war and depression, the rise of Mussolini, Stalin, Hitler, toward a second and more apocalyptic conflict of which he saw only the downhill half — for they were almost at the solsticial bottom that night of tossing and waiting for a phone call announcing what the boy would have canceled and in canceling willed again, struggling with himself as the old man was struggling, deciding, renouncing, counterwilling and again sealing himself in the act by the confirmation of its inevitability, making the choice again and again, and as soon wishing it had not been made or that the destroying fields of public and private calamity had not made it be made, or made his the critical role in its making.

For he had taken his father the gun.

And he could only lie there wishing he had not, yet knowing if it were still to do he would do it — tormented in fact, not merely with pity and dread, but with surprise that the call had not already come — thinking how much surer the Romans even of the gloom-filled decline had been, when wife, son, or true servant was on hand to open the veins, to witness for playwrights unborn the steadfastness of a dying resolve —

Daniel had fallen in with the evasive ways of the place and age. In the maudlin falseness of the hospital ("be out of here soon"), it was the father who had enforced honesty — he would never be out of there; the practice was finished, the bills unpayable, and without seventy-five round iron dollars rolling into the office every blessed day, the obligations could not be met — Why, there was that life insurance, almost the only thing left, borrowed on to the hilt, and if the next payment, which fell in two weeks, wasn't found, the whole investment, into which he had poured a lifetime of money better put elsewhere, would go down the drain — and who was he to hang around for no purpose but to make a pauper of his wife?

While always, behind the scenes, unmentionably hinted at, the father not knowing how much the son knew, the son unable — though a week of going to the office and trying to straighten accounts and answer incoming mail, sorting through files so voluminous and without all system and scratchings so illegible that it seemed the father had carried all that staggering trade on the burdened shelves of memory alone, had made this much clear — the son unable or unwilling for the father to know how far he was privy to the worst — always, behind the silence, lurked the last terror, like a loaded pack of cards a player has once in his life stowed in his cuff, or had stowed on him: that shortage in the legal account (no worse in cold cash than the other now impossible borrowings, but another thing in name) which he had lived with for twenty years, since the day he returned from electioneering in the bust and found his partner (leaving him, like a sinking ship, for California and fuller fortunes) had taken as a closing settlement the thousand stipulated in the boom, but at a grim juncture and under changed values, taken them from the only source of money land and politics had left undrained, from the commercial account, on which they could both draw, but which was not in fact theirs; so from that time on, harmless as it looked, there had always been a gap between the collection and remitting of monies; the general flow was large enough to obscure the hiatus; everything that came in was of course going out again and satisfying creditors for whom the Judge conducted the largest such business in the state; but if at any moment the wheels stopped turning, there it was, that troublesome deficit, a month's appropriation from the fiduciary flow; so that if collections did not go on from day to day and week to week, there was nothing left to pay back what had already been received.

And he had been sick too long. It was just the daily arrival of letters tending from doubtful inquiry to the first rumbling of threatened storm: "Had such and such claim been collected on as the debtor averred, and if so why had the remittance been so long delayed?" that had apprised the son, that week of wrestling with the office files, what the situation was. So it was no wonder his father had lived for years under what physically was called high blood pressure, the nagging sense that sickness was impossible and rest absurd —

Daniel recalling how, when the leg cramps would wake him, the old man would sit up in bed, hammering at his own knotted and contracted calves, with the abstract frustration of someone beating at a broken down machine, which he would get rid of if he had a handy substitute. The boy would go over and knead the muscles clenched like bone, until slowly they would relax, and the father would lie back between thanks and a moan. That was the medical aspect; but not only the bodily seizures waked him. There were cramps of spirit that would rouse him with deeper groans to light his stinking corncob, the feeble flame catching and dying like the blaze of his hope, revealing a face so stricken it was indelibly seared on the consciousness of the son, though he had not known the mystery of that grief.

Two months the father had lain in the hospital, and if money was not found it was more than the life insurance and welfare of his wife that was at stake, it was the name he had cared for above the titles he had run after: those newspaper clippings which graced even the laceration of a losing race for governor: "Gerald Byrne, State Senator and Judge, upright and true to every trust confided in him, public or private; an able lawyer, successful business man, deep thinker and high-toned Christian gentleman, one of the big men of the state, fearless in the advocacy of high purpose" —

More than bankruptcy was the issue, though the father never spoke of that to the son, nor the son to the father, not clearly, hinting only, half aware each knew what the other implied; they talked rather of the mother, the insurance, the payment that had to be met and could not be met, of his health, the hospital bills, and that something would have to be done.

Something. They did not say what. And then the father with clumsy subterfuge, not even trying to fool the boy, or if trying, doing it so badly they both knew it was a failure, and knew the other knew, in all the repeating mirrors of confronting countenances — the father began to talk of going home — home — soon — and of how he had prophetic dreams of thieves breaking into the house, trying to steal from Octavia; so he wanted his little pistol, which he had lent Betsy after her mother's death; he wanted it loaded and got ready for him to take home.

Or maybe that was the honest way in the long run, each knowing but accepting the device. For the old man had not been a lawyer for nothing, and the counterfeit was a hint what colors the son should sail under, not a command only, but an alibi, invented for a boy so hot-headed the father knew he would never invent one for himself, might, even with this one ready-made, insist on blurting out the truth; so he assumed the mask: this was all he wanted the gun for; Daniel should get it from Betsy, be sure it was loaded, bring it to the hospital and put it in his suitcase, so that when he went home he would have it with him.

Against which the son remonstrated as if speaking to another point: Very well, the gun. But as for the insurance, they could let it go, sell out, pay the debts that had to be paid, take bankruptcy on the rest, and come live with him. "As for life," he said, "we didn't choose it, and as far as I'm concerned, we don't unchoose it, at least not for money or pride."

The father answered in the same vein, as if the whole thing were a school debate: "Maybe. Every man has a right to his opinion. But not to force it on others. Maybe you and I and the Christian Church disapprove of suicide; but there may be circumstances where it's the right thing. And who wants to play God almighty and tell other people what to do? Leave that to the doctors."

The boy could only repeat that the best thing would be to take what came, sell out and move away, though even as he said it, he knew his father — living on bottled oxygen and pride — neither would nor could.

Then he went to his aunt. Between them too the same rigmarole had to be acted out, but more in the dark, more doubtful — she was afraid for brother to have the gun. He had spoken to her about it some weeks ago. She had considered taking it to him, but she was so worried. She had emptied the cartridges. They were old anyway and might be useless. She would give it to Daniel, but he must be cautious. Brother was not himself; he had been depressed. It was all so hopeless for him. Death would be a deliverance.

She handed over the empty pistol. The compact cold square of pearl on metal had learned the feel of his hand, and his hand, taking the feel of it, had stamped it on his brain, so that now, seeing only the glint of morning sun, fifteen years after, on that blue and pearl, he had felt the joyless square impressure —

Not as he felt it that day going to the hardware store holding the gun in his pocket, the hardware store where he walked as always into the back office den of his father's friend and Betsy's old beau, Fran Dudley, owner now (Patricia Towne had pushed him to that), but still dull and slow; Fran raised his far-sighted weary eyes behind enlarging lenses and fixed on Daniel a look of dubious understanding, heard the story about the father's planning to come home and wanting protection, the gun put in order and loaded: "Well, let's see," he said, taking it and shaking his head. "I went to see old Ger'ld the other day. I hate to see him so. This here is a thirty-two. A nice little pistol. Ger'ld's had that a long time. You just fill this clip. Now for God's sake hold it careful; it's no toy. And tell your Dad it's loaded. Don't let him go fiddlin with it. But I guess he knows what he's doing" —

It was not the feel as he carried it in his pocket to the hardware store that flashed with the glint across him now, sinister as that was — nor even the more sinister feel of the thing loaded as he took it into the hospital and met his father's almost disinterested: "You've got it, have you? Is it loaded? Put it down in my suitcase in the cabinet over there. It'll be all right. I couldn't get out of bed to get over there anyway; but when I get ready to go home, I'll have it with me. Remember that: I couldn't get over to get it if I tried, but when I go home, it'll be there."

They sat a while, neither of them talking much, until the father: "You'd better go to supper now. You've been a good son, though I never favored you among the children. You were the stubbornest and hardest of all, but maybe that was better for you in the end. You went your own way; but I've lost the others and somehow I've kept you. God bless you boy. And take care of your mother. We've drifted apart, but she's the noblest spirit I've ever known." He gripped the boy in an embrace of the old desperate power, then lay back exhausted and panting, his heart racing and his breath coming in painful gasps: "Go get the nurse, son, I'll have to have some air. And for God's sake, get little Miss Trigg. Not that horse-faced woman. If she was on the infernal shore, I'd turn back from the stream."

No, what came to him now was not the grip of the gun as he took it to the hardware store, or as he held it loaded in his pocket climbing the hospital stair, nor the last touch of it as he left it in the wardrobe. It was more real and deadly than that, hallucination being always the indelible reality. It was not the feel of the gun as he, Daniel, had held it, but as his father had, as they held it together the long hours of that night in weird communion, the barrel pointed at the great chest where the enlarged heart surged — both holding it through the slow dark, waiting for what? Silence? The right time? A mood of prayer? A terminal resolve? The two of them waiting in lonely togetherness, tossing on separate beds.

Until finally one must have dozed, a fitful doze of nightmarish imagining more real than attested fact, the dream-invading sense of holding the rectangular grip, the metal round mouth at the skin just left of the chest's center, felt out and carefully placed, under the rib cage, pointing upward, motionless, motionless — and then a moment like all others undifferentiated by anything except that it tore itself from time and became roaringly eternal, the round cold metal mouth spouting its jet of flame, searing the whole soul a split instant of changeless change (the old man had been lying weeks in a torment he thought near to that of dying, but it was peripheral only; there is a moment and intensity beyond all that trifling pain when one can still pronounce: "I suffer"), that instant, the crash, the meteor tearing into the sky of the heart, setting the family features in a satanic grimace — "I have always been a churchman," he had said the last day, "and once I wrote a treatise on God, which sometime you may read, and almost persuaded myself of immortality; but as I come nearer to what they call the door, I think there is nothing beyond; and I ask nothing but peace." Yet what peace could coexist with the stamp of that final seizure and gasping for air? — the grimace, like the feel of the gun, and tied with it, branded on the boy's memory, the expression his own face must have assumed the instant of waking from the hallucination in which the gun spoke and the flame tore not only the father but the son, the son too waking, into life as the father out of it, waking with a cry, which congealed on his lips, caught up and silenced by a dawning sense — regret poised in fierce contention with relief, praise, even gratulation . . .

For the phone was ringing. Ringing. Daniel running to answer, and his mother too awake, knowing that the moment waited for with fear, and more fearful than fear, with longing, had come. And he to tell her the means and soothe her cries hysterical with self-accusation, that what had once seemed an ineradicable love had worn down to this lonely dying.

Then he went to the hospital to witness the grimace, while the doctor, his tenderly preserved prey so rudely forced, pulled back the sheet and showed, as a criminal is shown his handiwork, the accusation of the powder-burned chest, the clenched hand on the gun, that heaven-denying countenance; and the police stood by and required a statement, and he gave them, like a last submission to the dead, the evasive account the dead had suggested, staring meanwhile at the finally mother-conquered face . . .

Though it was hard to reconstruct it later, the unaltered record of that night, hard even to think of it as the same man as the powdered witness of heaven's beatitude the funeral parlor made of the remains — cutting from within to the horror-clenched nexus of the muscles, massaging and soothing, if not from the mind, that testament of the gall's breaking on the heart, and nothing, nothing beyond; it was hard to reconstruct from what was exposed next day to the community in a casket of ebony and bronze (the style the Byrnes were accustomed to), over which admirers and old ladies sighed and spoke comfort — false, disgusting. Yes. But pyramids, mortuary busts, grave stele, Etruscan tombs, harps and lutes, the shepherd, the vine and well? As if moral space were round. As if ultimate baseness should prove vindicable, negation of negation, a falseness of divine myth summoning out of complicity with the lie an image truer than fact — whatever had beckoned beyond the leer.

Now his aunt had the gun. He must have known it all along. Had he not approached the house in that foreknowledge, ignored the glinting, as he circled in the vortex, exploring the lair? She would hardly have let it be thrown away, least of all because it had sanctified itself by a family mission — or should one say, prepared itself for missions to come? Of which Savannah mouthed the danger: "Don't touch it Misser Daniel; it'll go off for sure."

But strangely enough, the clip had been removed, as if to check or refill it, and one drawer was open in which a box of old cartridges lay, one among the rest that had been fired long ago. The clip, indeed, was half filled, but it had not been fitted into the pistol, and the whole thing, drawer, cartridges, clip and gun, had been left carelessly in the mess of the dresser, to glint in the probing lost ray of the sun, opening that past — and what future?

He had chosen once; he chose again; though he must have known the choice was idle, was perhaps only the fruit of a dubious desire —

"Don't bother, Savannah," he said. "This gun's not loaded. The bullets are out and the clip's broken. It used to be my father's. She's had it for years. Don't fiddle with it. It can't do any harm."

"No suh," she said. "Ah ain't fiddlin with it. An if it ain't loaded, it's all right. But if that's Judge Byrne's gun, you better look out."

She gave him one of her looks of sinister knowledge, and went on with the cleaning that could never clean, that could never remove the first layer in a shambles nothing could help, nothing at all but the touch of fire . . .

Once more the door would open and his aunt would appear — like one of the crawling things first light uncovered in the dark — repeating: "Leave this room alone, Dannie. I'll get to it tomorrow." And Daniel would answer — not her but himself, the original question: Did God unwisb the words? "No. When light crept into the pockets of the un-formed, and God looked and saw the obscene squirming and knew He would come to assume flesh there — poised on the brink of the brown river from which He might have withdrawn, He not only let the first word stand: Let there be light, He blessed the revealing light, He blessed it and called it Good.

14 ~ The Once Born

Lucy had opened the secretary and found what Daniel also, in the depths of his immersion, was finding:

The bulky envelope came plastered with stamps, her note at the top: "Save for me" — as if he could have thrown it away. He spread out twenty closely written pages, her transcripts from what the compartment had contained — for him the missing pieces in a puzzle almost despaired of.

Homecoming no doubt should be such a descent, to commune and reascend (though hard and rare) with the saving word. But if the word in this case was the actual bridge, to be built again by being explored, the discovery had begun at the wrong end. From the bog of Byrne clear across to Cope's Mill there could have been no span without the piers and pylons of some middle terms. And if middle terms were in question, it was not Daniel's father who made one, however much he had aspired to the East. Nor was it Lucy's mother, though she had reached as far west and south as from the Grafton base she could. No, the terms were to exhibit themselves in the form of a cross, the male from the female and female from the male receiving an essential fitness.

Lucy had found the packet, tied and inscribed: "Adam Woodruff, 1916-20"; she had opened and read. Disrupting her usual hours, she had sat up late several nights copying sections for Daniel. Now he was the one who was lunging ahead, dragging Lucy in his wake; or perhaps both of them were being swept along, while the resurrected ghost leapt forth, stronger than either.

How far Lucy had been possessed, the calligraphy declared. She had begun in her brave neat hand, akin to her father's but round and feminine. But from page to page hers had become the script of Adam Woodruff. As if the pencil-smudged yellowed notebooks from the first World War had contained a spirit that could fling back the leaves like linen clothes and step forth, a puzzling ubiquity, one of the fierce innocents, beyond the human, with the almost frightening impact of every life- force.

Surely he had frightened the family. He must even have frightened himself, the family propriety being part of him. What else was the source of the retiring in which he cloaked himself? But in these journals he flamed out, a phenomenon of stripped vitality. Even Lucy, glad to penetrate her origins, had been startled. This was not the father she had meant to revive.

— A cold winter. They were snowbound at the farm. The white trees closed in the house like an igloo. Roaring logs made a warm mystery. But the children were recovering from measles and had to be amused. For Christmas a blackboard appeared with chalks of all colors. They took turns, each drawing a picture for the others. After a couple of days the mother joined in, and finally the father. He took the chalk, playful, like a raccoon toying with a bait, made a mark and jumped back in surprise. As they watched, an attic scene emerged, a snowbound little dormer, a picture on the wall crooked, a tiny fire, a tousled bed, the chamber pot under it, and tucked up in the bed a poor rat gentleman, ill and forlorn, waiting for spring. That ended the game. Nobody would erase Mr. Rat. He remained until the spring breeze melted the chalk like snow —

That was the father Lucy would have liked to discover. But this one? She read, copied, gave thanks for the evidence, but passed it on to Daniel. The leaf, which lives by combustion, avoids the flame.

Crimes are the natural outbreak against the falseness of civilization, and are as much to be encouraged as condemned.
Can a man kill without sin? Why not? Bhagavadgita. Screw
all the women you please if you do it with a pure heart.

She had not included that passage in her transcript, though Daniel
would note it later, when the originals would come to his hand —
when he would sit as she had done far into the night, recalling the
empty slippers, the painting of the woods and the shadowy man he
had hardly known, but whose comings and goings had given hints
of some elusive godhead under the skin — when he would read, and
murmur: "The birth of Ore, the burning babe. Of such is the kingdom
of heaven."

No wonder Uncle Steward, the literal steward of the clan, had in-
carcerated the journals. No wonder Adam's mother, when they were
sent from Camp Heath and from France, had turned them over to
him — not to be destroyed, but like the Shakespeare in the lock-vault
at Springmount, to be kept safe, from readers. Whatever sent Adam
Woodruff across the Susquehanna to seclude himself in pine woods
had operated on his records, swallowing them with hardly a gurgling
noise, until years later, in the sickness of the guardian spirit, Adam's
daughter would sit in the dead of night copying what had been sealed
against anybody's recognizing what was obviously there: "I come not
to bring peace but a sword."

The account began before the war when Adam left Uncle Steward's
factory, and fled, a boy playing hooky, though he was thirty years old
— to any available wilderness:

No more trade in the sweat mill. Uncle Steward offered me
a third share, "Take the reamer," I said; "I was a fool to have
invented it." He groaned about the waste of mechanical talent.

"I'll use it to pitch my tent." So I left, FREE. The money mills defied, undeified. Next, the war-mills in Washington.

Caught the 10: 29 west, my house on my back. Got off in second-growth wilderness and walked up the creek. Found a buzzard's nest behind a big log. The old bird watched from a tree — bald head, drooping wings. I took the eggs. Shot a Prothonotary Warbler and skinned it for my collection. Caught a big king snake, chasing him over the rocks. Took the skin for my room. Repented, too late for the snake.

This country seems to have been settled long ago. Now it's going, as some would say, downhill — the natural way. Cabins fall into ruins; woods creep back over fields. Man, the excrescence on nature, wanes. Birds on the increase, quail tame. I pitched camp under a cliff across from an island. Ate, then sketched —

Thinking I would like to be able to paint, to get down in color and line something of my self, simple and clean. Then I thought: it would be external, canvas, worthless as an end, as a means, something to supersede. Better put my ideals into the proportionate development of my own being, to create something always changing, which by service to others will endure forever. True living is the highest art.

Tried to cross on a big log to the island, Sank to the armpits. Stripped and swam. Under the cliff saw a phoebe's nest with four eggs. Left it. Hauled out and ran over the island. Caught a jumping mouse. Killed it and had to swim to the mainland holding it by the back of the neck in my teeth . . (Have mounted it, #369.)

Spent only one night because I wanted to get my specimens home. Told Mother I had left Uncle Steward and was going to camp in the Pine Barrens until the army took me.

If he had been a German follower of Nietzsche, he might not have been so stretched on the rack of the moral problem. But he was a naive American Friend. The Ben Franklin optimism of the trading Copes, and the gentle Woodruff belief in a good and loving God had reached him almost unchallenged. So he had to wrestle with the old dilemmas as if for the first time: "Whence this root of evil in the world? If honesty is the best policy, why such prospering of the wicked in their ways? How should a maniac have more strength than a man who is sane? Can drink and dope inspire poetry and art? Explain the fascination of the mind and heart with fire! Vindicate the love of nature which makes me a head-hunter and collector of skins!"

And there was the first World War, an involvement of such kind, romantic idealism run wild, mammocking the real. He would have no truck with it. So he went to Camp Heath, drafted but rebelling. The Friends were with him in that. That was how he survived. But his journals lacked the proper tone. Even the style was a revolt, broken sentences jotted down on a pocket pad, stripped of pronouns and peripheral words — like the thoughts and acts recorded — an attestation of force:

> A big bare place eight miles by eight square, the size of Philadelphia, but city of brotherly hate; rows of barracks, 200 men each stretch as far as you can see in every direction. Am thrown with the rest, same routine: drill all morning, dinner at noon, rest until one, then back at it, a seven-mile trot and more drill, eight hours a day, to get worn out and sleep like dead until called by a cussing sergeant: "Drop this and pick up that, you low-down sons-of-bitches." So back to drill.
>
> I resist all the way, make no bones about it, tell them all, boys, corporals; captain, I'm not for them, will wear no uniform, carry no gun. The uniforms haven't come yet; they bide their time. The men play craps every night on the floor of the bedroom. I read or write. Impossible to mix with the gang, though I beat them at broad jump, boxing, Indian wrestling, talking is something else, oil and water.
>
> Tried to come to terms with a country fellow who bunks by me. Ideas wouldn't wash. In desperation asked when

they stuck hogs in his neighborhood. He opened his mouth wide: "Huh?" Gave him up.

Glad when the uniforms come and I can bring this to a head, fling mine down and get transferred to a barrack with others of my ilk. The crap game fast and furious. Would like most of all a skiddoo via Gunpowder Creek to camp in the woods, not this camp, or be out in the pine barrens, hear an owl call and another one way off answer: Who-whoooo.

Volunteered in a call for carpenters — to be doing something. Was told to build a stand, I thought for a privy, so I did it; but it turned out some kind of trench to practice throwing bombs from. I stepped up and told them Quakers didn't throw bombs or build stands to throw them out of. Sailed in with the hammer to wreck what I had made. They lugged me off to the guard-house. "You have no authority," I shouted. "I'm not a soldier; I'm a civilian."

Next day ordered to take all my stuff and march two miles under guard. Landed in the CO barrack near the outskirts of the camp. Like coming home — Harry Stambler and others I have known . . .

It's a madhouse here. A big barrack, upstairs Mennonites, Assembly of God Dunkards, Saints in Christ, Seventh-Day Adventists, Holy Rollers, Church of the Apostolic Faith, Brotherhood of Mystics, Vegetarians, Quakers, Orthodox and Hicksite, .all claiming religious objection under form 174; below, a boiling moiling gang of socialists and others not recognized by the law. But at present everybody upstairs and downstairs is making his own law, fighting it out with the military what he'll do and not do and who has the say-so.

The government will never make anything of some of these fellows. There's no evidence of a normal mind to work on. The six-foot-six officer we call our nurse went around questioning everybody what their stand was. "I refuse to do anything but eat," one of the Mystics sang out. Curious mysticism. The Apostles answer everything with a scriptural quotation. One refused to chop kindling. When the nurse asked why, he said: "What God hath joined together, let not man put asunder."

This is what the army is up against: a Russian Jew named Klein, a little man up to my shoulder, has been a teacher, translates into various languages and writes Hebrew poems; has long black hair, a strange old face but with pink-and-white baby cheeks. He didn't answer the draft; walked down on his own, then refused to take orders, wouldn't even eat. A strict vegetarian, he won't touch anything cooked in animal fat. When he wouldn't drill, they locked him up on bread and water. That did no good, so they transferred him to the C.O.'s. Here it's the same problem. He won't go on the hikes, says it breaks his train of thought. He won't help in the kitchen; he won't eat. "No dinner tonight," he says in the evenings, shrugs, and goes back to his writing. The officers nag him, but it's like talking to the air. When they threaten him with court martial and five years prison: "Go ahead," he says, "give me fifty years." . . . Today, after a hunger strike of a week, he's been carted off in an ambulance to be tube fed. When he gets his strength back, his family will send down special foods for him to cook on his own oil stove.

Such victories necessarily seem ridiculous. We are, struggling for an ideal which is out of place, which can't be explained, and which leads us to waste our lives talking or doing trivial things: washing dishes, picking up cigarette butts, chopping kindling.

"Yes, Mr. Woodruff," a visitor said, "but remember, you are an American citizen." What could I answer? I almost envy the deserter from the Blue Ridge, a bearded blond giant, who is brought to our mess under guard, a conquered savage, eats without a word and is taken away. For us, we hang around, argue on religious points, get nowhere. If this is standing up for one's rights, what do you call sitting down? I'd like to see more fur in the air.

In the afternoon we troop out for our walk, like little kids behind our six-and-a-half foot nurse, each sect clustering together, the sheepish Amish Mennonites, in black suits, large collars, floppy black hats, trailing at the rear. We pass bayonet practice fields where men lunge at gunny sacks stuffed with straw, or stab straw bodies on the ground, twisting the bayonet with a cutting motion, and snarling all the time as if that was part of the game. They straighten up as we go by: "Jesus Christ," they jeer, "look at God's anointed."

Maybe that's our role, to be ridiculous, to let them know there are more ways of being crazy, that the devil isn't the only god. As I told the doctor when he tried to examine me and I caught him up: "No you don't. Not with that spatula. If you haven't learned your business, I'll teach you. That thing has to be sterilized before it goes into my mouth." . . .

Sleeping in a heap this way, it's hard to keep fit. A cold morning shower helps, in the open air, an icicle on the spigot. Then push-ups and chinning. The farm Mystics and Dunkards look at me open-mouthed. Not having their chores to do, they lie around, put on weight. The one who wouldn't do anything but eat looks like a prize Hereford now.

In the afternoon I lug water from the spring. The camp water is so messed up with chlorinated lime it's not fit to drink. I walk two miles a day for a bucketful. I asked the nurse, but he said no, so I go without asking, and nobody cares.

Evenings we argue, or I play the mouth organ or write. Our colored Adventist, Collier, who refuses to take life or to work on Saturdays (he could almost say any day), yells out: "Goin to de sto. Who wants cake from de sto?" He buys it for ten cents and sells it for fifteen and does a flourishing business. The socialists discuss the advantages of free love — an academic issue here.

It's the primitive Bible believers who get on your nerves, arguing about Joshua and the sun, and whether Jonah could have lived in the whale. "Why not," I say, "if a hundred of us keep alive, cooped up in this barrack?" One of the Apostles has a speech impediment so when he talks he blows air bubbles and looks as if he was adjusting a quid. He peers

through thick glasses under his felt hat to argue with a socialist about how much air there was for Jonah to breathe.
"The whale had wind on his belly," I say. If this is religion,
let me out.

That Apostle is the one who wouldn't play games on
Thanksgiving, afraid it might be idolatrous. He has never
been to Philadelphia, though he comes from Lancaster. I
told him it was a nice little town about twice "the size of
New York. "Yes," he said, "I hearn tell on it." I rib him for
entertainment. He's down on smoking. "Can you imagine
Jesus Christ on the street comer," he says, "smoking a cigarette?" So when I happen to see him: "Mac," I say, "have you
got a cigarette on you?" "Woodruff," he says, "ye're at enmity
with God." or "Woodruff, ye're a blighted fig."

My opposition to war grows all the time, but it grows less
religious. The Quaker stand rests on the teachings of Christ.
But I don't need Christ to tell me war is insane. There's no
room left in the army to be a man, not even the kind of man
civilization needs. The socialists, who free their objection
from religious grounds, make better sense. All these petti-
fogging nations with their patriotism and jealousy have no
more place in a world that requires brotherhood.

The socialists are right also about the money-mill: "My
greenbacks lie over the ocean." (Go tell Aunt Rhody, and
Uncle Steward too.) But their atheism is a bore. As I told Rose,
a bright communist Jew with whom I mostly agree: "You
should look at the sunrise." He couldn't see the connection.

The Mennonites are at the other extreme; they run religion into the ground. Today we had one of those great winter sun-sets. The Mennonites didn't see it, any more than the
socialists. They were both cooped up in the dark hall, the
socialists ranting about a classless society (a little Irish mick
with his Derby hat, no color, black whiskers and a pipe,
haranguing them from a table top), the Mennonites, with
elders and ladies from a local congregation, wailing dole-
ful ditties — something about "Lord give us light" — while

outside the whole world was flooded and drowned with nothing else but.

Even the Mennonites, though, or the slab-sided Mystics beat the religions of the world. What's happened out there would make anybody down on God. A preacher came to the Y.M.C.A. to talk to the soldiers. We sent an Irish Brother over to report. "There's many a way of getting to heaven around here," he told us when he came back, "but that Y preaches the worst. A slippery old divil with white hair got up and said: 'Boys, take yer Bibles into the trenches with ye and read em, and the Lord Jesus Christ will help ye catch the Kaiser.' "

Through it all, the Quakers clan together. We have our beds in a corner of the dorm; we eat together; we buy special foods to pep up our meals; we even walk together and talk together, as if we were the people and wisdom would die with us. But the socialists are democratic. They mix with the soldiers, talking all the time, spreading the word. They risk more, too, because they aren't covered by the law. I've given up saying I'm a Quaker. I don't want to hide behind the Quaker name, any more than behind the army . . .

A blow by blow account:

To make us less inde-goddam-pendent, forty or fifty soldiers were sent in to mess with us. They cursed and ordered us around, and when they heard anybody saying grace, they would yell out, "Jesus Christ, hand me my wings." So we said we wouldn't wait on any soldiers at all. Then we decided not to prepare any food which would go to soldiers. When they tried to force us, our Kitchen Police walked out.

So we were summoned to General Bond, a gaunt man, with hair and skin the same iron-gray. He paced around in leather puttees and cursed, and said if we didn't have a yellow streak a yard wide, why didn't we do something for the country, we couldn't just lie around like a bunch of chestnut worms. He asked how many would object to doing work around the camp. We rose almost to a man. Stambler said he would do no work that might replace a soldier or help the military machine, either in camp or at the front, or that might seem to recognize their authority.

The General looked as if he was going to throw a fit, but he got a grip on himself and went on down the list. "Would anybody cook?"

"Nobody, if it was for soldiers."

"Who in hell would it be for? They're soldiers of your country."

"The country we claim doesn't need soldiers."

"Will anybody work for the Y.W.C.A.? — Help make your mothers and sisters more comfortable?"

It's a civilian organization, so I said I would try. Others cautioned: it might help the military. A Mennonite said: "Don't give the benefit of the doubt to the army, give it to God." I said I would see for myself. "You're no Friend," he said, "you're a friend to the World." And another: "Brother, you have to be born again."

I went to the Y.W. and was errand boy: fetch a soldier for his visiting wife, wash dishes with the colored maids, sit at a desk and look wise, take such-and-such to Corporal So-and-so. "I didn't come here to serve soldiers," I said.

"Well I'm damned," said the manager. "What kind of a son-of-a-bitch are you?"

So I quit. The God-lovers had been right by instinct.

Then I was called back to the General's office and Captain Warfield asked why I left the Y. I said I didn't want to serve the military or the Y; or any other organization of mon-ey-mill American society. "What are you," said the Captain, "a Quaker or a socialist?"

I gave him both barrels: "I'm an objector because war is wrong, not because I happen to be a Quaker. We're not here to hide under our sects, but to stand for peace. You can't separate the socialists from the Quakers just because we happen to know some big-wigs in Washington."

"If that's the case," he said, "I order you to move down with the socialists."

"I'd been thinking of requesting it," I said, "but I don't take military orders."

"You get your stuff downstairs before night, anyway," he yelled after me.

Next day, about three-thirty, I was reading when they called me to the small office downstairs. Captain Warfield and the Lieutenant had come over. "I told you yesterday to move," Warfield said. "I give you until five o'clock to get your bed downstairs."

"I won't do it," I said.

He flew off the handle and kicked the chair across the room. "Do you defy me?"

I sung out: "I defy all military authority."

"I'll court-martial you," he screamed.

"You can't," I said, "I'm a civilian."

(That's the possible good we do — in a fight one can feel it — to keep the walls from closing, hold a little sea-room and latitude, in the end for everybody, just by knocking the wind from their stuffy dignity, saying every day what we will do and what we won't do — to keep them always unsure, and mad.)

The soldiers moved me down by force. "Fine," I said. "I wanted to go anyway. But when you ordered me, what could I do?"

Now I bunk with the long-hairs, as lively as a circus. Except that stuff about Rockefeller and a war for oil gets tiresome. As if there weren't other causes.

The army's next move was to soften us up with a picture of war horrors. We were all marched to the Y. without knowing what for, and then this atrocity stuff went on the screen. But in the middle of it our Negro saint went wild (his wife has run off with another man and sold out everything he owned, so he's unstrung); he stood up in the path of the light, waving his arms and shouting: "He's a-comin, he's a-comin, O Lord, Jesus Christ is a-comin." Two guards grabbed him, but the Mennonites and others broke out singing hymns, and the Commies yelled "Down with Capitalist War, Down with Capitalist War," until the show broke up. The officers were fit to be tied. They've got the notion Stambler and I are ringleaders in this, which suits me fine.

We struck the next blow in mess hall, or rather received it, in Quaker fashion. They have put their share of soldiers on K.P. now, so we can't say we are doing their work, but Stambler and I decided against mixing as such, and since it was his time for duty, he refused. The mess lieutenant told him: "If you don't work, you won't eat; and don't come back to dinner with the rest or I'll break your goddamned neck." Of course Harry appeared as usual.

The Lieutenant was waiting by the counter. He motioned to a soldier eating his dinner, a blacksmith, and told him to take Harry out and lick him. They went out the side door and the blacksmith said: "Put up your fists," but Harry wouldn't. The soldier hit him in the eye and knocked him down. Harry got up with blood on his cheekbone and walked toward the door. The Lieutenant, at the top of the steps, said "Hit him again." The soldier caught Harry on the chin, and down he went. But he got up as before and stumbled for the door. "Again," said the Lieutenant. But the blacksmith just stood there, as if he hadn't heard the order. So Harry walked past the Lieutenant and into mess.

There was a lot of excitement, soldiers making way for him and asking questions. "My Lord," one said to me, "I didn't know you had consciences like that." Harry sat down and began to eat.

If the Lieutenant had any sense, he'd have left it that way, but he was bound to make a fool of himself; so when the meal was over and the K.P.'s were starting to clear the dishes, he came in with three soldiers. They grabbed Stambler and delivered him to the kitchen. I went along, though I wasn't on duty. The mess sergeant had them tear off Stambler's coat and sweater. Then they pushed him up to one of the sinks. "Get to work now," cursed the Sergeant, "or you'll take a trip to the hospital."

Stambler was calm. "Sergeant," he said, "you know I refused to work before, and I was knocked down, and I believe conditions have not changed." He was standing with his back to the sink while they faced him: "Work, you yellow bastard, or we'll cave your face in." Stambler lectured them very coolly about the way of non-violence. Our K.P.'s and some soldiers were looking on with their mouths open; it was thunder out of the blue.

When taunts and curses didn't affect Harry's sermon (he was standing with his face raised, bearing witness), the Sergeant lost his head and swatted him in the face, screaming: "Shut up, you son-of-a-bitch, shut up."

I walked over and stood by Harry. "Maybe you think you're men," I said, "but I say you're a pack of bullies. If you want to hit somebody, hit me too, because I'll never work in this kitchen again. I'll back Harry Stambler to the limit." The Sergeant took me a crack in the face, and one of his bullies grabbed Stambler by the throat.

By this time the Kitchen Police had seen all they could take. Rose was one of them, my new bunk neighbor, a bright little Jew who goes to sleep puffing a big black cigar; he was sick the other night and I took off his shoes and got him comfortable. He came over and stood by me. "I'm a Socialist," he said; "we don't subscribe to non-violence; but I don't subscribe to you either, Mister Sergeant. I stand with the Quakers." And one of our rawboned Irish farm hands, Pat Doherty, slammed his big hand down on the table, so worked up he was almost in tears, and said: "I could lick all four of ye, but I stand with the Quakers. Go ahead. Hit me. Ye got divils in ye as big as pigs. And what's more, I'll never lift hide on another potato in this kitchen, so help me God."

We had them on the run; but the mess lieutenant charged back in with twelve or fifteen soldiers; they picked Harry up and took him through to the cook's bedroom, threatening something about "a third degree and no mistake."

I ran top speed to headquarters and told General Bond

he better stop that Lieutenant if he didn't want him in trouble, because I was going to report the whole thing to Washington. My last complaint was forwarded by the Civil Liberties Bureau straight to the Secretary of War, and he came right back on our officers. So we have them fairly hypnotized. He sent Captain Warfield down, and Stambler was taken to the infirmary for a checkup and treatment. Now all our men, socialists and the rest, have agreed not to lift a finger until the situation is cleared up. We initiated a strike with a Quaker Meeting, hymn singing from the Mennonites, a wild demonstration from the Workers of the World. Finally sleep ended the excitement.

As I opened the window for the night, I saw Orion in a black sky, and thought: "The world still revolves; tomorrow the sun will laugh at our petty struggles, which some day will seem a dream." But what can we do? Dream it out . . .

Though the dream gets threadbare. After these orgies of protest and discussion, a reaction sets in. We want to get away, not from camp only, but from ourselves. Our experiences and opinions grow stale, everything is petty, and the place is tired of us.

There was a sham court-martial; the lieutenant and mess sergeant were reprimanded. We are assured there will be no more brutality, and we have been moved to a new barrack further out, among the colored troops. A Negro captain shot himself here, and after that the soldiers wouldn't stay, broke the place up, saying it was haunted. We've fixed it and discover no ghost. We have our own mess, arrange our own service. So we are working and eating again.

On the whole we're better off. Though there is a campaign of small annoyances. We have colored guards armed around the house; they keep us jailed up and we are not allowed visitors or packages. One day soldiers Came in and ripped out all our new bookshelves. No more food or easy chairs in the rooms. Then the windows were nailed open a foot in the big freeze. Six feet from the red-hot stove, the temperature was 36 degrees and at the end of the room it was 28. That was second-day evening. We stayed in bed most of the day; but still we got sore throats and colds, and I had fever for several days.

Still no decision from Washington about us. The army ha begun clearing us out with mental tests. In some cases the test is hardly needed. Our Apostle with the speech impediment, MacGrady, came out bubbling and laughing: "They got nothing out of me; I told them nothing." As if they'd been pumping him for secrets. Among other things they laid three little blocks of wood on the desk, which he was to arrange in the order of weight. He wouldn't touch them. "I see them, they are all right," he said, "let them lie." When they told him they weren't dice, he said they could be made into dice, and he wasn't going to fiddle with them.

Some of the boys are glad to be sent home that way. Pat, who has gone to pieces since the big kitchen row, has made a good case for himself. To establish evidence among the cooks, he weighed out twenty pounds of sugar for a pudding and put it through the meat grinder. At the test, they asked him how many legs a Zulu has. He said "Eight." He sat rubbing one leg until the examiner told him to cut it and hold out his hands. He presented a finger at a time, again and again, until they gave him up. He came out whirling his arms round his head. Said he didn't mind being crazy, but how long would he have to act the part?

I think they would have liked to get rid of Stambler that way, but we had determined not to accept such a verdict, and he kept his head and made the grade. "Well, if you aren't crazy now," the doctor told him, "you will be. Just go on the way you are, and you'll be a raving maniac in a few years."

When I went in, a colonel happened to be there, and we got into an argument. "I've got a mind to give you an order now, and if you don't obey it, see that you are locked up for twenty years."

"Give me your order," I said. But he walked out.

I got on better with the doctor. I told him I wouldn't accept a verdict of crazy. "As long as there's a peace movement alive in this country, I'll be sane, and you can't deny it. Of course, if the army once gets the country under its heel and makes it impossible for a man to stand up and say what he'll do and what he won't, then you can call me a maniac or a criminal, whichever you please, and act accordingly. But you'll have to wait a while, because the country's not that ripe yet. And it's our job to hold it back."

It sounds great. But when we kill time in the barrack, we lose confidence. If we achieve anything it's remote; while the living is from day to day, and that's deadly. We are restless, full of rumors about the war and what's to be done with us.

The socialists seem bitter and profane. They scrap like dogs. But underneath they are clever and kindhearted. They call themselves atheists, but in substance their views are not unlike mine. The style, though, is different, fierce and obscene. The other night they did a take-off on the Catholic Church. I went along at first, but it got rawer and rawer, mocking saints and Christ, until everything holy was stripped to the bone. "I don't like hypocrisy any more than you do," I told Rose, "but some things should be sacred."

"Sacred dogshit," he said.

The colored guards are warming up to us. Sometimes they join the sport, and we have a regular minstrel show. But underneath we're fed up. Spring only makes us more blue. We sit in the windows with our legs hanging out, longing for freedom. A sergeant below yells: "All youse guys line up," and those who feel like it march off to get wood. Our horsing around is to kill time; everything is to kill time. We go to bed often at nine, just to sleep it out. When can we call our lives our own?

It's the socialists who keep up hope. They say the Russian and German workers are combining, and that they'll break Germany wide open. Then there'll be big doings, a great shuffle, a new deal. Anyhow, our world is sick.

The officers count on a long war. They say the government is planning for five years. Yesterday we heard a roaring in the air. A big biplane flew over the field. It was a cold day, blowing great guns, but he soared along banking and stunting. I had never seen an airplane so close before. We will have the power to destroy the world.

Five thousand new men came in this week, with shipping tags in their buttonholes, tramping along, some solemn, some singing and whistling, others under liquor, all driven like sheep to a goal not of their choosing. And other men are leaving for the front. I watched about a thousand march to the siding. I was thinking how they were going to the front to give their lives, and I felt almost like a shirker, when a sergeant in the barrack yelled out: "What the hell are they, whites or boogies?"

Men or cattle? It was all one to him . . .

Now, after an episode of jail, Adam Woodruff was yanked out, uncarcerated, by pulls he did not appeal to; he came to the surface running loose over the fields of France:

The valley of the Meuse. The lovely rolling country pitted and scarred.

Along the roads you can pick up abandoned uniforms, rifle belts, cartridges, helmets, hand grenades. There are lean-tos full of gas masks and huge dumps of howitzer shells. The waste is appalling.

The little towns blown up, deserted. Nobody. But rooks croaking and of course the rats, and maybe a solitary gaunt hare jumping from the bushes by a ruined wall and dodging over cratered fields. And no roads or railroads to get anything there, no way to reach them but by tramping — how is the Mission going to get these places going again? We are patching roof holes and laying tiles in one village where the whole thing should be torn down and built afresh — or given back to the wild . . .

It was the journal still, the laconic phrases of the daily account:

> We have been living in abandoned German shacks and dugouts, tearing them down around us and hauling off the materials. When we started taking the roof off the rest drove down to sleep at the Equippe, but I stayed under the open sky. Thursday I slept under a haystack and leaned a piece of the wrecked roof across me to keep off the dew. A big rat kept coming out and running over my blankets, until I kicked at the right moment and he sailed up against the roof with a crash and a squeal. That discouraged him for the night.
>
> I ate some meat the next day that poisoned me, so Saturday I lay around sick. By Sunday I felt better and went boar hunting. About two miles in the forest I saw large fresh boar tracks crossing the road. Came where the boar had been digging for mast under the beech trees; the ground was ripped up like earth-works, eighteen inches deep. Then I heard them worrying each other in the next valley, growling and yelping more like dogs than pigs. Before I caught sight of them I got the smell. A billy goat is perfume to a boar. Then I saw some woodchoppers circling through the forest. As I came over the ridge, they let go with a pack of dogs. The boar turned to run, but I shot the biggest tusker in the neck. He wheeled round and round and fell. The dogs and the Frogs lit out after the others, but got nothing. By the time they came back I had the skin almost ripped off. They sat around grouching and admiring, but when I gave them the carcass they left content. I'm going to keep the hide for a trophy.

It was what Lucy had copied and Daniel was reading; the pages were before him, but superseded. They lay like a husk, over which the blue-eyed stranger strode, at large — Adam, the Once Born.

He was liberated from the dry rot of prison camp to the wet mold of that shell-torn land: pocked farms, splintered woods, craters full of water, the water green with scum, trenches rotten with flesh, the earth a slime of decay.

He was still in the army, in name, but released to the Red Cross, to rebuild — and inevitably, since it confirmed what he thought of civilization, to take a grim delight in that waste:

Walked through the wood of the Crows, splintered logs, stumps buried in the ground. Reached the center of the front. Shell craters overlap: the four and five foot holes of the 75s, the ten-foot ones of the 105s, the 20-foot gouges of mortar shells. In the white chalk rock the craters have filled with water, clear, with green plants growing in it and water spiders throwing shadows on the floor. The trenches follow the contours. In the machine gun nests are unexploded shells stacked along the wall and hand grenades like condensed milk cans with handles about a foot long out the bottoms.

As I walked along, climbing over craters and trenches and worming through barbed wire tangles everywhere, I meditated on the power of man. Then I saw a Frenchman lying in a pool of water, one leg on shore. I got a knife and watch from among the bones. Further on were the Germans, a number in one crater — as little Chris used to say, eaten by cannonballs. I picked up leg bones and vertebrae and threw them away when I found better ones, as you do picking flowers. The battle was almost three years ago, back in 1916, but still the ground is upside down. "It was a famous victory."

I took away a shinbone on which I have written: "German shinbone, Mort Hommes, 11-3-' 18." Showed it to one of the Fort Meade coons from the barrack. He wouldn't touch it, but marveled at the writing. "Well now, suh, how do dat come? Do all dese Germen got writin on dey bones?"

I had opened a hand grenade and cleaned out the charge under water, and refitted it with a fuse. "Looky here," I said, "what is this thing?" — taking it out of my knapsack and yanking at the firing pin. His eyes bugged out and he started backing off as fast as he could: "Thow it fum you suh; thow it fum you!" But I tagged after him. "How's that?" I said. "What is the thing, anyway?"

— As if they had had their war, and wrecked what they could, piled up their dumps, thrown down guns in trenches and tanks in exploded towns, and gone away, left everything a shambles; and he, whose conscience had removed him from the event, had somehow become its heir. So what could he do but assume his heritage, pry into everything, and with a kind of archangelic health, sport with the relics of their murderous rage?

He would stand on the lip of a trench or crater, open the shutter, and it would all be recorded: skulls lying around like toothy rocks with the holes of eyes, limbs with shreds of meat or boots hanging to the bones, helmets, guns, canteens, scattered among the dismembered dead. Then he would sail in to gather souvenirs:

> Salvaged a rusty machine gun from a pillbox under the apple trees above the village. Took it up in the hills after work and shot it off. Have fixed it up O.K., but owing to faulty cartridges it misses about every fifth explosion.

Salvaging, that was the word. He salvaged whole towns and villages as nonchalantly as he picked up a German shinbone:

> After supper tonight crawled into a tomb that had a hole blown in it by a shell, and found a coffin and body, a titled fellow who died in 1849. Salvaged two mother-of-pearl handles from the coffin.

The Frogs might have called it grave-robbing. But Adam Woodruff seems to have grasped the inescapable fact, that life is nothing else. So he salvaged the casket handles, and two years later attached them to a crib of Susquehanna walnut he made for his first child. Because it was not only France he was salvaging, but a future. He was practicing the skills which (in the gullied half-South of exploded fortunes, families, lives) were to build Woodruff Farm.

Now he had an armory of salvaged and reactivated guns, not to mention grenades, shells and the rest, and he went like an angel of death and mercy, killing off a riot of things gone wild: cats, rats and weasels that ran through everything and fought together at night — though if he had left them alone they might have taken care of one another:

> Shot an old tiger tom prowling behind the barracks. Hit him in the head and blew his brains out. The Frogs say, "Pooquah? Pooquah?"

(Even Lucy at this point had waived the scribe's role to the extent of bracketing an exclamation after the entry (!) and that was enough to trigger in Daniel's mind her implied bafflement: "But he was so fond of cats; he liked them better than dogs. He would make a noise between, a purr and a meow, and strange cats would sidle up and rub his legs; he would pick them up and scrub them under his chin; but they better not hang around. Let him see them after rabbits or birds, here he came, with a pistol in his hand and doom on his face. When I was a girl he paced through the bedroom once about dawn, making for the balcony, cocking the gun as he went. I got there just as it cracked off, and saw my big yellow tabby way down by the martin box jump up in the air and fall back dead. I ran up to Daddy beating his stomach with my fists and yelling: 'That's *my* cat, you old fool.' It didn't make any difference to him whose cat it was.")

Pooquah? There was plenty of that:

> Thirsty on my walk. Milked somebody's cow into a German helmet. A French woman yelled over the field: "Pooquah?"
>
> The river is swift and full of fish. Threw a grenade into the pool below the bridge. Big explosion and water fountained up. "Pooquah?" said the Frogs. I swam in and caught five fish as they floated up stunned. We fried them for supper.

He was not drawn to the Frogs, tight-fisted petit-bourgeois; and they must have shuddered as this apparition from the West confronted their broken-down old-world, determined to put it back together and to explore the vulcanism that had torn it apart. No doubt the outward aspect was disturbing. Their shrewd opinion of the young man must have been "sick." But the sickness was theirs; it lay on their age; he walked through that hell untouched by its fumes; like a primitive smiling Apollo come down to the fields of Troy, he whistled among the corpses.

All day he worked at carpentry, plumbing, wiring, ditch digging, road laying, sawing wrecked trees, repairing tractors and machines, rehabilitating something for returning refugees who took it often without thanks, sometimes complaining that it was not as it was before (those unadorned serviceable cottages of Neuilly, a foretaste of the prefab, set up in drab Quaker rows along patched streets in the still pitted fields):

> Thirty families want to return at once, so we have put up thirty portable houses . . .
>
> Unloading freight cars all day . . .
>
> Sawing wood with the circular saw. Trouble keeping the engine going: battery almost worthless and water in the gas. Every now and then hit shrapnel embedded in the logs,

> taking the edge off the teeth. Time out to regrind. Kept at it
> all day, two German prisoners feeding me the logs. Finished
> up by the barracks and moved the saw . . .

He worked like a jinni, and when the work was done, sported with macabre lustiness . . .

And now it was the dead of winter. A deep snow fell, and Adam Woodruff took to chasing rabbits as he had done at Camp Heath. There, he had gone out with a yellow-haired socialist of German birth, who had worked up to be a manager in Bethlehem Steel. They were fond of each other and had discussed postwar plans, even studying Spanish for a while, talking about "developing South America" (they were ready for anything, however incongruous). With the dull diet and deep snow they had tried running down rabbits, chasing them for miles, yelping like dogs, until they could knock them over with a stick, for they had no guns. Then they would boil them until they were tender and fry them smothered in gravy. Now such a snow fell on the rolling plains of France.

Five miles from the Equippe was La Grange, a manor run by the Mission, where livestock was raised for cost distribution to returning farmers. Six months before, Meryl Grafton had come over as a volunteer. With an American girl, she was looking after everything from rabbits and chickens to goats and cows. Crouched on the back porch of the building, a blue bow in her dark English hair accenting the slim oval of her English face, she was holding a Belgian hare as big as a dog.

It was a tame rabbit, which she was tending, though in time it would go to some French farmer, and after breeding more of its kind, would be skinned and eaten — in short, it was not being raised for its own good; but Meryl, for the moment, was cherishing it, crouched as in a painting by Gainsborough, the rabbit held against the high and shapely Sarah Siddons breasts.

While her husband-to-be favored her with the first sight of his person as he loped over the snowfields, baying like a hound, in pursuit of another rabbit, a wild one, with which he intended to supplement his too starchy ration. The chase had gone on for more than a mile and the rabbit was winded. Adam caught it as it dodged around a bush behind the Grange, crashed down on its back with a stick, paralyzing it instantly. He then snatched it up, and drawing his knife, peeled the skin off on the spot, burying the guts under the snow, except for the liver and heart, which he wrapped, with the rest of the carcass, in the pelt and tucked into his knapsack.

Putting the tame hare in its cage, Meryl came up, astonished. The coyote man, standing in a circle of, bloodstained snow, looked at her, his fine slim lips and clear blue eyes opening to the angel smile of the entirely unfallen. "I'm Adam Woodruff," he said, "with the Red Cross at Varennes."

"And I'm Meryl Grafton, at the Grange. Why did you kill the rabbit?"

"Why do you raise the rabbits?" he asked, and showed her the white teeth of his smile.

They may already have been in love. But they would not have known it without Adam's cousin.

That was Samuel Cope Aldrich, who had grown up with Adam at Springmount, and who was now in charge of a neighboring unit. Being married, he was quartered with his wife in a house sixteen miles away, beyond the Grange, a stone and thatch cottage left from before the war. They lived comfortably, getting vegetables and poultry from local farmers, exploring the French language and cooking, and of course asking Adam over from time to time to eat and spend the night. It was several weeks after the rabbit hunt when he was invited and found Miss Grafton and her American friend whom Cousin Kathy had wanted him to meet.

They feasted on rice omelet with apple pie and cheese, and afterwards sat around the fire, roasting chestnuts and telling stories of an America to which Meryl had always been drawn —

"You remember when Uncle Alf first came to see us at Springmount, how lean and long he was? When we met him in the box-bordered walk little Mary said: 'Thee great thin thing thee, how old is thee?' 'I'm half a century old.' 'O-o-o-o-h,' said Mary. 'O-o-o-o-h.'"

"And the stories he told about the Maine Woods and waking up under the bear?"

"He had hung his knapsack over him in the lean-to and it had chocolate in it; so along in the night a noise waked him and he sat up and buried his face in the groin of a bear. It was standing astride him going for the chocolate. He let out such a yell that the bear ran off, but Uncle Alf sat there the rest of the night beating a tin plate with a spoon, afraid to go back to sleep."

It was late when they went to bed, Adam in the loft, the girls in the spare room.

They got up to one of those bright days that occasionally bless the north European winter, as if the Gulf Stream had lavished all its resources to produce a single Mediterranean morning, sunny, almost warm, though with a wind brisk enough to keep back the prevailing cloud. They walked through the forest on the russet floor, under oaks bunchy with mistletoe, and Adam swarmed up a gnarled tree to cut bunches of berries for the girls. They returned to the cottage, threw themselves down in the sun by the mottled wall, sheltered on both sides by yews, and talked away the morning, laughing, soaking up the sun.

Next week they were invited again. This time Adam rode the sixteen miles through a cold drizzle, cycling at top speed and singing the whole way, as if the winter night were a spring morning.

The journal took on a sprinkling of Miss G.'s and M. G.'s, and finally plain Meryl's. Adam trapped a magpie and took it to her to train. Then Meryl came over to see the work he was doing. He seemed to be all over the place, turning his hand from one job to another. From the houses they were building, he would be called to repair the dynamo in the electric plant; sometimes he took a turn at the forge, or suddenly he was asked to look at an old Mogul tractor nobody could get to go. It was hardly telepathy; machines aren't equipped that way; but he had some mysterious power over them. He would fiddle around a bit, hardly knowing what he did; and suddenly the old wreck of a Mogul would begin to roar like twenty thousand demons, and charge off over the field, Adam Woodruff sitting there pulling levers and working pedals as if he'd grown up with the thing, though he had never operated one before. The Frogs didn't know whether to admire him or suspect he was in cahoots with the devil. Meryl, who had grown up loving such crafts, must have felt, as she watched him, that the whole thing had been raised to a level of capricious wizardry.

Next he went to the Grange to watch her operations:

> Friday there was a sale of chickens and rabbits brought up in trucks from Southern France for the refugees here. There is a château with a barrack behind, once occupied by soldiers, now filled with animals. The whole thing is managed by two girls, Miss Grafton, from England, and Miss Hancock of Philadelphia. I went up to see what was going on.
>
> I rigged up the scales, and the girls got a table and then kept guard at one door. The other door was the entrance. Six or eight people were let in at one time. They were almost all women, got excited and began to scream. Chickens were dragged out of the crates and the dust and squawking was fierce. Often a woman would have three chickens, one by the leg, another by a wing, and the third by its tail feathers maybe, each struggling and flopping, while she kneeled on the floor by Miss Grafton's table to get out her purse. One short little woman came up holding three large hares by their ears, while they danced along like companions at her side. All the animals were dumped in a sack together and sold by the kilo. Sometimes a threshing rabbit upset the

> scales; and platform, weights and all fell with a crash. Then the sack would come open and chickens and rabbits would get loose and scamper around like crazy. Once an old hag tapped me on the shoulder and said, "parti," pointing to a huge rabbit disappearing across the field.
>
> In half an hour the show was over and I went to Varennes. The sales are run at a loss, but it is a wonderful work.

He could hardly have admired the efficiency; yet it was not simply Meryl's suave beauty. As he saw her managing the tumultuous market, he pictured her as mistress of a farm that he foresaw he was going to found.

The delicious European spring began, and even those fierce explorations of the front took on hints of blessing, honey out of the dead:

> Found a caved-in dugout with the remains of legs kicking from under the dirt. It was a warm day, and in a crevice of the broken roof bees were coming and going. I rolled down my sleeves, and pulling an old sack I found in the dugout over my head, went to it, scooping the honey out with my right hand, getting only four stings. I ate it like a bear, with grubs and pollen, sweet, meat, vegetable. The best pieces I wrapped in paper and took to give Meryl.

There were things he tried to learn from her: the French language, even to like the Frogs. An uphill job. He took to German, but neither his mouth nor his ears would curl around the subtler French sounds. As for the people, he hated the pursy little ways they had before the war and seemed to be continuing toward the next. The underfed German prisoners appealed to him more. He would invite them over and feed them until they rubbed their bellies and said "Genug." Then they would sit around and talk in a medley of English and German about the League of Nations, socialism, the new world.

Meryl was afraid of Germans and fond of the French. She wanted to show Adam how pleasant they were. "Bon jour ma belle," the neighboring farmer would bow to her, the meerschaum pipe curled from his ironic mouth, as much a fixture of the face as the floppy ears or handlebar mustache, "Bon jour," and he would trundle his wheelbarrow up to get free manure or whatever they happened to be giving him. The next time he invited her for dinner en famille, she got Adam included. Bon Jour killed one of his precious fowl; but while Meryl and the family received this or that piece, what faced Adam as he looked at his plate was the comby old rooster's head, staring through a gravy like brown blood.

When Adam saw Meryl giving little French girls bread and jam, and the girls running off buried to the eyes in it, and coming back with turnips and dandelion greens which they presented her with curtsies and compliments, he was all admiration; but he went on writing in his journal:

> The refugee house has been delayed for a week while one old Frenchman decides whether to lease the land or plant potatoes there . . .
>
> We are staying up later than ever to keep the power plant we built going. The Frogs got together and asked that the lights be kept on an hour longer. Before the war they used wax drips. Some people have no talent for virtue. Give me the Eskimos every time . . .

The long sweet spring continued. April led through May and into June. The interminable cold rains seemed to terminate at last. Orchards were white and pink and the woods powder-green. Fields were covered with daisies, and the roads bordered with spikes of blue flowers sprinkled with the white dust of the road; and a pollen smell was heavy on you as you walked down the lanes; so that you forgot in the fragrance the odor of the dead. There were cool clear nights when the nightingales sang in the thickets along the streams; and it was time, after the war and work and loneliness, for hearts, like the earth, to venture into bloom.

Adam had ridden over various times with the intention of popping the question, but there were interruptions, visitors and more sales. He was still hanging fire on the eve of Meryl's departure. Desperate, he asked her to go on a picnic at the Abbaye Trois Fontaines.

They had been living for months among ruins, but these were different, like the English abbeys, matured through centuries. The fountains came from the limestone under a hill of oaks; they flowed in ducts and sluices beneath the lawn and garden among ivy-covered ruins; then they broke out on the west side of the grounds and fell to a green pool.

The two ate in that secret valley. The air was moist and full of the twitterings of strange birds. The ivy and moss were bright with water. Adam knew almost nothing about Meryl, but he said he loved her, and asked her to go away with him to America or Canada, to get a farm where they could live with nature, in the wild — while that tame nature of ruins and a garden murmured around them.

It was what Meryl had dreamed of since childhood; and she must have been in love. But this young man with the pale blue eyes, lying so peacefully in the grass, quoting from "Kubla Khan" about the fountains of their pleasure ground, seemed as unfathomable as the poem. She did not know how he lived or if he was mad or sane. The other image, of a yelping hunter snatching at a rabbit over fields of snow, arched itself like a question above the soft-voiced Quaker; and while that appearance stirred her more than this, it was with a longing that had the feel of fear. In the best parlor manner of Sir Thomas Grafton's daughter, she said that she treasured his esteem, but that they were almost strangers. Then she fled, to the Grange, her room, the train, to England. Neither of them could know how this proposal would work underground.

Nothing to write; a feast on wind. There is a six-foot-six giant named Marsh in the group. He has the proportions of a well- groomed knitting needle, and when indoors goes about on hands and knees. We sallied out for the harmless pleasures of first-day, inspecting the Crown Prince's Dugout City. You can wander hours under ground through tunnels, and sometimes see Germans sitting at a table where the gas killed them. I was going along in the lead, but stepped on a fuse, and part of the room ahead of me exploded. We gave that up in favor of the open air.

Ran more than a mile to a hilltop which the Germans held for a long time, a fine eminence, from which we threw grenades, watching them explode in the valley. As we were eating cherries and discussing the relative value of the works left us by Thomas a Kempis and Martin Luther (concluding neither had caught the true vibration of spirit), I spied a leg sticking out of the dirt.

I seized a battered shovel, and with a rush of holy zeal, soon unearthed the lovely gentleman. His skull lay between his feet. I scooped it up and threw it on the shovel at Marsh. The brains were sagging out a hole in the rear, and in the rear it took Marsh, without an introduction. The skull was silent, but Marsh roared.

Far off in the village, the French were making an unholy racket blowing off bombs, warming up for Bastille Day tomorrow. Sad a Christian nation would profane the Sabbath.

There was a new bitterness in the style. A day or so later he went out alone:

Walking back from the front in the evening, a horrible musty smell over everything, the graves dug up and the American bodies being removed. This work is left to the niggers. A truckload was just finishing. They had unearthed a body, put wires around him, and were dragging him out.

One big buck was laughing and yelling: "Come on out here now and stand up, you son of a bitch." They loaded him on and rode off through the dead-smelling mist, the live bodies upright, looking over the tailgate, the rest stacked prone — a ghastly crew.

It was an experience that would bear fruit at a masquerade party on Halloween, his birthday, just before he left France. His old friend Stambler had arrived from Leavenworth, and came into the hall, with a couple of others, blacked up as Negro soldiers, carrying picks and shovels. They began prizing off floorboards, until they lifted up the whitened corpse of Marsh — at which instant, with a vast flash of gunpowder, Adam surged from below, dressed as a devil in his half-cured boar's skin, and with a toasting fork pursued the sheeted carrion as it fled wailing.

Though by that time his resurrection from the dead and exorcising of his own demon was about to get under way. For Meryl and he had been writing. She had returned to the somehow stuffy quiet of Grafton Hall. There were occasional parties at the Squire's, mannered exchanges with formal young men, her peers, and then the ride home after dark, the horses' hooves clopping in the night, the small side lamps of the carriage casting a flitting gleam on the hedgerows. That had seemed magical when she was a child; it was tiresome now. Into this pastoral ennui, letters, running the gamut of exploding dugouts, exhumed corpses, memories of youth, philosophy and the keen observations of a naturalist, appeared as startlingly as had the author when he first came bounding over the snow. Her fear had been of the thing desired; with time and distance, the perspectives of correspondence, desire began to transform even fear into its likeness. Before long, she was not only in love, she knew it. She wrote a tentative acceptance. Adam answered that he would come to England in the fall and let her make sure. It was then that

Meryl enrolled in a cooking school and was taught how to make bag pudding.

Naturally there were ups and downs. Having almost over-reached the cautions of her nature in committing herself, Meryl backed off, her doubts reinforced by her father's amazement: "But a man you hardly know! What is his position? You surely will not marry an adventurer?" For three weeks she did not write, half repenting.

Adam, fed up with the work, fed up with the French, waited for a letter. He had to talk to somebody. He lit on a compatriot of hers, a British socialist objector, a small rugged man who spoke dialect and had grown up around the mines. He had met Meryl once or twice at the Grange, but his conviction was independent of that. Adam got an earful:

> Very blue, not having heard from M. This P.M. Rawell told me a lot of stuff that did not please me at all — "Ye've bit off more than ye can chew. Are ye daft, man? Don't stick it." Social parasites, he said, rotten as a class. One a lord in Parliament and one a soldier of the empire in India, and that she came over here for the game. Had talked of going to New Zealand to buy a farm just for adventure. "A sick bunch, the aristocracy." As soon marry into the money mill.
>
> Tonight a drunken French guard beat a German prisoner, the man I invited over and gave chocolate to. I almost decided to quit work in France. Why should I sweat like sin without pay for swine who keep prisoners and treat them like slaves? The French I have had anything to do with won't work, they are half-drunk at least once a day, their morals are filthy and they steal the clothes almost off your back. In this village we had 1500 pounds of nails stolen out of houses we were building free of charge for them.
>
> The French paper keeps writing about "blond beasts." The beasts I see around here tend to be brunette. And now the peace is spoiled and another war in the making because of

their pettiness and Wilson's not having the guts to stick to his points. I'm about ready to give it up and go home. I had thought by England, but I'm not even sure of that.

Some of this must have crept through to Meryl. In the panic of loss she veered to the other side, wrote her best letter, about nature, childhood, her indifference to money and rank, and that he should come as soon as possible. So he chose, acted on impulse, as if what the socialist Rawell had said might be true enough, and he would live by it if he couldn't have Meryl; but if he could, he'd put up with the contradiction. He broke the news to his mother:

Dear Mother: I would have written thee long ago about this little matter, but it was unsure. In July I asked Meryl Grafton, a girl from England, to marry me, but received the reply she didn't know me well enough. Later she wrote from England that she missed me and wanted to know if I could marry a girl as changeable as she. I love her more than I ever thought possible, but told her I would come to England to give her another chance, as she might not like me as well.

She lives in a place called Grafton Hall and is the daughter of Lord and Lady Grafton, or something to that effect. One of the family is a member of parliament and one a soldier in India. I pity her on that score. But she is an adventurous kind of girl, a walker and climber, as different from most English girls as day from night. She doesn't care a rap for money, hates towns, is keen to come to America and have plenty of dogs and kids. She wants to grow morally and spir-itually. She likes poetry, has been studying Italian painters, and takes cooking lessons. She is 24 years old and ought to know her own mind. No plan is too wild for her. We may go up to the Canadian Northwest and get a homestead, who can tell? Thee would love her dearly. She is the only girl I ever heard of who was expelled from school, or practically so.

She is too good a' sport to care about money, and we are going to live for something better. When you grind away all day at the old money mill, you have nothing left when the day is over. We are going to live a very particular, ideal life, exactly as we please, and if we can't do it in Germantown, we will go to British Columbia, or somewhere where we can. Compree? I think we might start up a farm and raise bees or chickens or rabbits. She could do that, and I could do hunting and truck farming. Oh it will be a great life. Love to you all, and keep this little matter dark till you hear otherwise.

By the way, when thee cleaned out my drawer for the guests, where did thee put the eagle and the turkey buzzard? Can't thee find a tight drawer and sprinkle them with camphor, because I can't pick that kind of fruit on every tree? And if they are shoved on some shelf up in the south garret, they will be nothing but food for moths. Love. ADAM

(From that copied letter, lines of force radiated backward, re-creating the vision on which Lucy and Daniel had been borne, as from the original, power had streamed forward, generating a farm and future, their past now, in which they groped for understanding.)

Adam came to Grafton Hall in his class-protesting baggy clothes, his pockets loaded with German vertebrae and a dead jumping mouse, a tattered trench coat over one arm, trailing in the dirt (the coat was a godsend; if he'd lost that, there was always the half-cured boar skin he was looking for some way to use) ; he appeared, and confronted Sir Thomas with an enigma. That polished gentleman could hardly get it out of his head that this shabby young man was a fortune hunter of some kind, though the blue eyes seemed to declaim against fortune: "Your money is corrupting and your rank out of date, but Meryl is something else; she surpasses her origins."

The family gathered in the evening, to be entertained by tales of the prison and Adam's hunger strike, or of the front, or perhaps of curing insanity by hypnosis, or of spiritualism and telepathy. Adam would feel it had been a good discussion, but the Baronet would go upstairs shaking his head: "What an extraordinary man! Whatever can he be aiming at?" Until Meryl and Adam picnicked at the Druid cave in the mists of Malvern and determined to marry at once in spite of opposition. So they left for America, disowned.

In time the mother and sisters brought things round. At that stage it took a woman perhaps to appreciate Adam. But the reconciliation only presented him with a fresh dilemma: the Maryland farm which he was slowly bringing back from erosion, was being kept afloat (his own inheritance not having come in yet) by dividends from England, Meryl's share of what Rawell had called the blood money of imperialist war and extortion.

The once-born do not justify, they live. But nobody is completely once-born. There remained the battleground of the journal, questions unanswered, contradictions of a radical innocence operating in time. Why could the free spirit not build its Utopia without the devil's aid?

In the sweltering Mississippi room, Daniel took the measure of the cleavage: the retiring Adam Woodruff he had known — the stripped force of this apparition. He could analyze the tension, as in the empty study that morning of the funeral he had failed in doing. Call it active and passive: that such an energy should be devoted to Quietism, to the mystical surrender of self; or conversely, that a Quietist should be drawn at every moment to the life and act of flame.

In the end it became a grief to him even to mow a pasture; and he kept some neglected corners of fields, as by the entrance lane along the stream. As you drove in you saw the house over head-high weeds — those weeds with names like flowers: boneset, ironweed, snakeroot, ageratum, pride of the meadow — and you wondered what kind of desuetude you were driving to. He liked these to fight it out with green tooth and claw. Though even there he was not consistent; he could never control himself when thistles appeared, but would charge down with the spade and a grim look, as for coon hunters, a cat, a sheep-killing dog.

But for a man who had mowed the whole farm in a day with the rough old tractor and rattling bar mower, a man of such Quaker order that you could never leave anything, hammer, book, pencil anywhere in the house for a minute and go away, without the chance of his passing through, picking it up and returning it where it belonged, while you went in desperation wondering what the devil you could have done with it — for that tidiness and force of the land-nature to be so given to the oceanic surrender, that all the interventions which were the texture of living seemed desecrations — that must have been the source of his hypertension, not as the doctor thought, a strenuous exercise of his natural powers. There was a spasm of will blocking itself from act; it was what had suppressed the sensuous arts in him, painting and the rest, had called them trivial, though he was inescapably driven to paint, carve and weave, to stamp his image on matter.

The killing and shooting of his youth gave him worse pangs. It was a battle he not only fought out waking, but even in his dreams. If he polished off a few cats still, that was because they were interlopers, like men, old-world sycophants, meddling in the balance of nature. But wild beasts he gave up killing altogether. Even the bird and mammal collections of his youth were pushed out of sight, into the attic and then out under the eaves, the eagle and the turkey buzzard, exorcised reminders. The farm was deeded over to the life of the wild.

The last few years he would not keep a dog. They annoyed their betters. So the vegetable garden became a playground and cafeteria for anything certifiably to the wilderness born. That final summer the family harvested scarcely a raspberry or an ear of com; the lush stands of Golden Bantam and long double row of berry bushes were so diligently tended by raccoons — the little black hands reaching up all night, conveying the paradisical fruits to the busy jaws. The most Adam Woodruff would do to oppose them was to rig up rows of electric lights to burn over the garden, to startle the invaders with brightness. It may even have worked the first night or so (floodlighting the bedrooms also, and making sleep less rewarding), but the coons adjusted faster than the sleepers; soon they came in greater droves than before. The old man was delighted; you would have thought he had planned it that way. Of course he would raise his hands and shake his head — a gesture of surprised surrender — but too obviously chuckling about his coon carnival, acting out the pantomime in which the lively hands reaching for the berries were his, the bright eyes rejoicing in the light. "Tell all those other coons to come along to Mister Woodruff's," he would say: "he's got the garden lighted up for us." And then he would mimic the other raccoons out in the hills, looking across at the night glow, relaying the message: "Come on now, children, we're going over to the coon carnival at Mister Woodruff's tonight."

If he was some kind of Faust man, it was a whimsical one. Still, the devil-struggle was there. It was what raised him above the Copes, or flung him beneath them, what saved him, in any case, from their perfection, what gave him a tragic point of meeting, even with Judge Byrne. Lucy might have wondered how far this was reshaping Adam Woodruff in the Byrne image. But the records were there. It was recognizing the affinity that she had sent them to Daniel in the first place. The smiling gentleness her father matured to was a tide pool under whose blue surface there were hints of red claws working.

Did he know how many must be sacrificed to hold a zone of relative calm? Consult the journal:

> Aug. 13, 1919, Varennes Equippe: Discharged from the army at last, "Character poor." Letter from Meryl. A red-letter day.
>
> Spring these thoughts in the discussion tonight: There is no unselfish act; selfishness damns and saves.
>
> Love your enemies, advance the evil; hate your enemies, destroy yourself. Where is the line? Forget it, and be.

Since all paradises are fool's paradises, why not inhabit them?

"It ain't no sin to take off your skin and dance around in your bones."

— But your *own* bones.

15 ~ The Visit

With regard to the symmetry of the bridge, Where is the pylon in the South?

It was not that the question needed to be asked, or had not been asked before, or that any lost documents were required for its answer. It was only that the cleaning of the house had raised it more urgently than before, at the same time attaching Daniel there — while the answer lay thirty miles to the south. For he had a mother who lived in the Delta, though no longer in town.

He had phoned her twice since coming, but she could not hear over the phone — could not, or would not; it broke into her world. There was nothing Daniel could do but wait, and mean- while patch up the car. He ripped off the smashed door, tied down the seat carriage with wire, soldered the radiator, and there it was, an airy jalopy, ventilated in thunderstorms, easy to get into and out of, easy to represent as a wreck when Aunt Betsy would stagger out determined to drive.

At last the Colesons had agreed. It had come to an end, the blind bargaining where you feel your way, like trying different baits fishing: "This apartment, of course, free — it's bigger than what you have — and ten percent for collecting rents, and by the hour for fixing the property; and if Mrs. Coleson should prepare meals, how much would that be?" — "Meals? I dunno." "But would you do it, and when could you move in?" No answer. And days passing, a week, days, two weeks, and more days. "Thirty.. . Forty.. . What about fifty a month,

with the free apartment and the rest? Would that cover it?" "I dunno."
Then as if it had been understood right along — or you'd spat on the
bait and that was all it needed: "Why surely, Daniel, we're glad to help
any way we kin."

Today they were moving. Like breaking out of jail, Daniel started
south for the visit.

He took the old road by choice. It left town behind the columned
house where he grew up as a boy, apartments now, under enormous
trees. They were water oaks, quick to grow. Planted when his father
was a boy, they had been in their prime in his youth; now the trunks
were eight feet through, but the low spreading limbs he had climbed
and run on were gone, and the crowns were thinning out. In a few
years the whole planting would be dead, trees coeval with the men,
that have like death that we have. The road passed the cemetery, then
it bore south, following the bends of the river, mostly in sight of the
levee, through fields that had been wooded swamps, where he had
explored and hunted and caught malaria as a boy.

To the left, at the end of its double cedar lane, was the plantation
house B.J. had grownup in, where Daniel had cycled for visits — one
of those slave-built, thick-walled, wide-windowed houses Southern
writers are always seizing on or cooking up, with its genuine ineradicable bloodstain on the hall floor . . .

Then right, the side road leading to Lake Lamar, outside the levee.
They had gone there to fish, his mother too in the old days. She used
to catch more than the rest, but then she had given it up — "no longer
a pleasure to take life," she said, though there may have been more
reasons. While the car continued on the main road, Daniel sent his
thoughts down the side lane seeking the connection, a wraith of her
haunting the place: "The noblest spirit . . . "

— As if search for the mother would inevitably raise the father's
voice —

Daniel was thirteen. He was the only one who went on getting up at three in the morning so they could be on the water by sunrise. He liked the endurance of it, and had schooled himself to sleep flat on his back, so when his father came to wake him, he would spring up, yanked by the presence, before the voice had spoken. They would get a bite of breakfast and drive in the dark. It was fine to walk in the first light past the cypress down to the fluted water. If the old Negro who kept the boats and eked out a living fishing was still asleep, they would untie a skiff and row out to the arbor, and when he came from his shack he would sing out: "Mawnin Judge, is de carviivous element stirrin dis mawnin?" Or if he had got there before them, they would hail him: "What luck, Uncle?" If he had been out any time, he was sure to have a string, but he would shake his head, as if no fish in the lake was worth his trouble except maybe a five pound bass: "Poly, Judge, poly. Nothin bitin but de crappie." How he knew they were crappie was a question; everybody else said white perch; but he would haul up a heavy string, what Judge Byrne called "those big saddle-blanket perch," and slough them back into the water, groaning: "Mighty poly."

The outing was the thing. And if the fishing turned out dull, Daniel would swim. At first he was only practicing; but one day, when the far shore looked almost as near as this, he decided he could make it, and went on without saying anything. He had got to the other side, paused for breath on the mud flat, and was starting back, when his father came from his brooding and looked around. Nothing. Only the wide water curving between green curving shores. "So it comes to this, the risk of getting and the torment of raising them. Where could he have gone but down?"

Judge Byrne set up a shout for the Negro: "Have you seen my son swimming around here, Uncle?"

The Negro stared, scratching his head: "No suh. Ah mean Ah done seed him, but Ah doan see him no mo."

And then far out over the water, like the answering descent of the angel messenger, both men saw at the same time, and cried out, the fleeting white exposure of one hooked arm, a pause, and another, then the first again, the regular slow beat of the distance crawl.

"My son, how could I have gone home and faced your mother?"

The road lay long and straight across the swamp-streaked cotton-rowed flatness of the land. There had been more woods then, virgin stands of oak, pecan, gum, to be girdled and burned by shiftless settlers — straggly swamp-cotton showing in new fields among fire-blackened boles; but still in the distance were the trees, residual dumps merging to a dark horizon endlessly retreating as you moved; so the white concrete strip became a circular belt on which the car went round and round, returning time after time to the same unpainted cabin, to be approached and passed, to dwindle in the unchanging spoked wheels of cotton, hubbed by the unchanging woods.

In the same way he had driven his father in the Depression, moving at fifty-five miles an hour over the recurrent expanse. There was no traffic, no crossings, few curves. Why steer at all? One could rig up a photoelectric device, two sensitive spots behind an image-forming lens, automatically controlling the wheel. But the road must be white and the shoulders dark. In passing, the driver would take over.

As the mind wandered, the foot followed the instinct of its gravity, bore down on the accelerator. Judge Byrne came from his pipe cloud, "My God, son, you're doing sixty." The foot was raised, the speed fell to fifty-seven; the Judge subsided, smoking. For years they had been raising the family speed limit, beginning at twenty-five in the old Willys Knight convertible. Sixty remained the mile-a-minute ultimate not to be contemplated without alarm. Let a vicious motorist shoot by, swerving on the curves, the Judge was sure to cry: "That crazy fool. He must be doing sixty" — a remark which never seemed to lose its edge, even when their car was moving at fifty-nine.

But it was the mother Daniel was driving to see — the wind blowing in the ripped-off door of his aunt's wrecked car, the great clouds going by, dark below, thickening toward rain, soaring white pillars above, massively recurrent in a giant sky, the sun between clouds drawing water up long rays; it was the mother, his essential source - not just in the stupid sense that she had borne him (did he call it stupid because the wonder of birth lay under the burden of his father's oratory, those perorations of Southern speeches on public sacrifice or the destiny of man, where courageous American woman went down into the valley of the shadow and emerged victorious, cradling the guerdon of an infant life, while the golden wings of freedom burned, and the very bowels of God growled after truth and righteousness?), not simply that, but that he had drawn from her something stronger than his father's drive, the ground on which it rested, or as in old myths of the world, the sea that buoyed it up — an opening at the center of the soul into which everything could withdraw — his mother was the clue, yet it was almost impossible to say how: it did not submit to words, the very route to visit her was a chain of associations and acts that were of the father and aunt, the aunt's car, the remembered father sitting by his side . . .

As if in the ambivalence of land and water one would choose to worship water and make a pilgrimage to the clearest and most light-suffused spring, yet spend the whole day in the land- attached vicissitudes of going, uphill and down dale, through field and forest, to come at evening by the round orifice of liquid silence, and look, the gaze melting into the water, then turn and go back, having found nothing to say.

For she lived in the connections of the land, the Byrne ambition and despair, The house to which Daniel was driving, Avon, her apartment in a ruin over Lake Austramere, was all that remained of half a county of field, swamp and wood murderously borrowed on, which Judge Byrne had bought and called a good investment.

(What else did he mean by investing, but to snatch at something that would set them all up like Croesus — and be left holding the bag? That farm, talked up for a sure fortune; which in the boom fever he had and then bubbles of oil, as fly-by-night drillers or pretend-drillers would say they could strike it rich under that land, and the father would pour in money and get letters from Chicago. "Desperately need drilling equipment. Soil samples leave no doubt. Send five hundred more dollars" — a day or two of throwing out the great chest and the chin raised, everybody half-infected with that confidence, and then no letters, no address, names not traceable, and Gerald Byrne cursing all investments, most of all speculation in oil, saying: "Suffering Mother of God, why try to make investments? Now there was Major Evremond only today telling me I should put something into Standard Oil, a stock bound to grow. You'd think he was a wise man to look at him, and had experience of the world; but he's a babe in arms. If ever you catch me investing in oil again — I've had my fling — there's nothing in oil but a swindle. If you can't trust the men you have personal contact with, how can you trust some company up in New Jersey that pretends to be selling you something on a Wall Street stock exchange? No, I've had my fill of investments" . . . Until the next time, when maybe it would not be oil, but a couple of educated Negroes who had moved to St. Louis and invented a device for straightening kinked hair, and all they needed was a little capital to make a killing, and then, as if he had waited all that time for just such a scheme, he would invest again — and wind up cursing all investments.)

There is always a burnt-out mansion in the landscape of the old South; the Byrne's had Avon, though the fire had been long before, some tragedy of a wife and children, in which the estranged husband was involved. When Judge Byrne had owned the debt-ridden land behind it, he had thought of the house, rebuilt, as a patrician seat for one of his children, probably Daniel, who at that stage was so worthless in school, it would be a miracle if they could make anything of him but a planter.

But the mother had settled there instead. It was one of those chances dependent on so many things, that no one could have guessed it would happen that way. It was the impractical wife who had settled the office files after her husband's death. She had lived in three rooms of the town house, and rented the rest, paying off debts and investing her insurance (actually investing it, in a mutual fund which in fact grew), until, with Daniel's help, and in a time of physical recovery, her arthritis seeming to yield to cortisone, she had put the town house in an agent's hands, and had built herself a convenient apartment in the brick walls of Avon, on the cypress-fronted lake lot she had always loved. There was a portico of limestone columns. They had been floated down on barges from the north, through the chute and into the lake, before the levees closed the lake from the river, when those higher banks were a cultivated clearing in end- less woods. Behind the portico were her rooms, looking over the water. The rest of the ruin she had made into a walled garden and greenhouse. There she lived like a recluse, scarcely going out.

Sometimes friends came to visit. And her old servant Lethe, who had been with her almost since her marriage — born a slave — moved into the former slave quarters. Being ninety years old and at least as feeble as her mistress, she called a granddaughter down from the north to live with her, do the shopping, see to her, and as far as possible, to the white lady. Though the white lady was so used to doing for herself that to go to the village store, to help a bit in the garden, and simply to be around in case of sickness or a fall, was all that was required.

At the landmark tree ("Water, water," they had cried as children, driving down to the plantation or to swim and fish, "I see it. I saw it first."), the road turned at right angles and followed the mile-wide curving lake, one of those placid oxbows cast off by the river before white men came here. A few miles, almost to the village of Refuge, and the vast green tent of live oaks, with the dark magnolia and holly, came into view. Then the mellowed brickwork of the ruin appeared and the four gray pillars carrying a weathered architrave.

Daniel had passed the town house, his father's display piece and the shelter of his own boyhood, with a casual look, a sadness mainly for its dying trees; he was stirred as he approached this other house, not simply because his mother was there, but be- cause she belonged there; it was the ideal temporal retreat of her timelessness . . .

And there she was — Lord — what a crazy woman, at her age, half down with arthritis and always' giddy and subject to falls; she had climbed up on the old stone porch wall under the columns to poke into the architrave with a long fishing pole. A washbucket, mop and broom lay on the floor beneath her. Daniel knew what she was doing. He had argued with her about it before. She was poking the messy sparrow nests out of the ledges of the capitals and architrave, standing there on the edge of the parapet, her neck craned upward, in a position she could never manage except for the martyrdom of some such useless undertaking, the dirt and straw falling in her hair and eyes, while she lunged with the awkward heavy bamboo — why even if she didn't fall, she would have to go to bed and suffer with sore shoulders and a cricked neck for days maybe to pay for this self-righteousness.

And it was all a display. She had probably timed it unconsciously to coincide with his coming, to show him that while he was looking after Aunt Betsy, she was struggling along against grim odds and with the Lord knows what. It was that stubborn orneriness she brought from the hills. And she was not going to step aside, either, certainly not for the pain, and not even for him. Because she wouldn't be beholden. It would do no good to tell her the birds might as well stay up there, or if they had to come out, how easy it would be to hire somebody for the job. She preferred to be doing it herself, so she could struggle down, teetering on the chair she had pulled to the rail, lean the pole against the wall and come forward to greet him, wiping the gray hair back from her perspiring face, and kissing him with that dutiful look he might have known she would wear, implying: "Well, son, I'm glad to see you; but you've come at a busy time."

"Ah, Mother, why will you work yourself to death with this kind of nonsense. Let me help you, anyway."

The wrong thing to say, emphasizing how much his help had been given elsewhere. In her conscious mind she was above jealousy. Although the aunt had not spoken to her since Judge Byrne's death, Octavia had always presented herself to be snubbed when they met in public. After the accident, she had even got a friend to drive her into town to the hospital, and had sat in Aunt Betsy's room, inquiring if there was anything she could do. But Miss Betsy had turned her face to the wall and held it that way until the upstart had left, discomfited.

Still, nobody escapes being human, and what is defeated in the open field breaks out in secret skirmishes. As Betsy Byrne, imprisoned in the hospital, went more and more out of her head, how could Daniel's mother deny the appropriateness of such a termination? She thought Daniel's coming south would present him with the sad duty of committing poor Betsy. When he phoned that he had taken her home, was living in that filth, cooking her meals and cleaning up after her, and with no solution in sight, she had been speechless because she would not condemn. But had she borne him to the futile evasion of such housekeeping?

She picked up the pole and was craning her neck again at the architrave. "Give me the pole, Mother," he said, "I can climb up on the base and reach it better."

"I can do it well enough myself," she said; "I've been doing it for years now." And then, no less stubborn, for all the humor: "Teach your granny to suck eggs."

"I'll sweep up the trash, then," he said, taking the broom.

"Leave it alone," she told him. "I'd rather do it myself. You'll only be here part of a day, and I'll have to go on managing as I have before. Your bothering with it upsets me. I'll be through in a minute."

As in his college days, when his sister graduated and went home, smoking, and driving out late with boys, and little Gerald was so quirkish and erratic in school that there were stem punishments from the father and resentment and asthma in the son — the family strain almost intolerable — his mother had scarcely written for weeks, except to say that Lethe was in the hospital and that with all the cooking and housework to do there was no time, until Daniel remonstrated, and received this answer:

> You may be right about the futility of my doing work a servant could do; but the more I can justify my existence now, the easier for me. I can't go into my reasons; you will simply have to trust me, and believe I am trying as well as I can to keep the semblance of a home for your brother. Matters are unfortunate for Hilda too, but I'm afraid it's too late to help her. More time for reading or writing would be useless to me at present. I've been glad to have my hands so full that there is no time for thought, and to be so tired at night that I sleep in spite of worry.

He had been on her side then, as the father had intended, raising the mother's image even in his own frustration. But as Daniel watched her, mount the ramparts again to attack those nests, he was seeing with his father's eyes: What a woman to have to break down into a loving and submissive bedmate! Better for Judge Byrne if he'd had a couple of wenches on the side, or been like Dr. Paul, whose wife complained to the ladies' club (for they had a cotton plantation and it was a weedy summer): "Dr. Paul hasn't been home for days; when he's not at the hospital, he's running around the countryside picking up hoers."

Martyrdom does not solve the human situation, does not intend to; it shatters it, and plants other hopes in the pieces. Daniel put down the broom and stood leaning against the wall, assuming a grim smile, while she strained and poked at the last goddamned precious tatters of straw — and once, almost losing what balance she had, staggered toward the five-foot drop at the outer edge.

Then he sprang up beside her, grabbed her and the pole together as he would if she'd been his wife and he'd had enough of her cursed stubbornness, pulled her back with actual force, saying: "Mother, I can't stand it. If you won't let me do it, you'll have to do it when I'm gone. I can't stop you then. But I'm hanged if I'll wait around while you wobble up there on the edge of nowhere, and for no purpose, because if that straw has to come down, you know I can knock it out in no time."

It was not surprising that she bridled up like an unruly horse, startled that he was pulling her back with physical force. It must have been what Judge Byrne never did — what she would have thought the last thing possible, to settle anything by brute power. When she had got complicated and ornery, Gerald Byrne had retired with gentlemanly fulminations, giving violence no vent; it was a battle of wills, and nobody could fight a will like hers, at least not with the will. The surprising thing was how briefly she bridled and how quickly she gave in. As if Daniel's grabbing her put the argument on a different plane.

"All right," she said, "get that last nest out, and we'll go in the house. Ethel can clean it up."

He sprang onto the base of the column. A single jab of the pole and the nest billowed out and came floating in shreds to the fern bed, while a couple of small eggs broke on the porch. He threw water over the eggs and gave them a perfunctory scrub. "Now show me your garden," he said, and he took her arm.

For that letter closed with a reassurance, though he had forgotten it:

> Don't be worried or unhappy about me. The moments are rare when we are worthy of ourselves. But if we are diverted from it, what we are remains. I have in me such a well of happiness. Often it seems that it is gone and nothing has savor, but when the tumult subsides, I find, miraculously, that it is still there. It is the abiding life of the soul.

So when he had leaned back against the wall and watched her stubbornly sweating it out with the pole, that penitential look warning him off: "It's my mortification; leave me alone;" he had asked in desperation, having come for a certain phenomenon of calm in the ruins: "Where is the reflecting spring, the pool?" and had questioned: "Choked? Muddied?" — until the answer came: "Wait; wait; it will clear."

Though what was clearing remained indefinable, a fountain into which one looked and saw mysteries.

It was as if she had never had a birth at all, not come as others do from parents known, but over the hills, like morning, like a spring out of that clay. Her mother had died almost before she could remember, and her father, sick and impoverished by the Civil War, had gone through her girlhood a silent wraith. Among so many children, Octavia had received his only treasure, the rusting cavalry saber he had fought with through the war. And his one emergence for her had been in that connection, when she had drawn the sword (she was eight or nine) and asked if that sword had killed many men. Yes, he said, but he did not like to talk about it; it was a bad time. She had been reading Uncle Tom's Cabin and was full of the horrors of slavery; she demanded how he could have fought in such a cause. He told her he didn't believe in slavery, he fought for state's rights, but that it was a time he would rather forget. The sword remained with her; it hung on the wall in the Byrne library; but the man who wielded it had melted almost without a trace.

No doubt she was always the darling of the litter. The last of ten, of whom two were dead, she was called Octavia. She was christened, in fact, Octavia Omega; for the father, along with his dog-eared library, had a curious taste in names. There was Luke Tupper, the oldest son, called Tup for short, his middle name certainly influenced by Shakespeare, as Octavia discovered later, to her embarrassment; and there was Ola Anna Dot, the oldest daughter, who answered to plain Bob; and of course there were the Pearls and Stellas and Eulas who crop up all over the hills. As for the Omega, it was corrupted into Old Nigger and abandoned.

In any case, she walked that war-cropped land like the alpha and omega both. It was not just fineness of feature, nor the instinct with which she drew poetry, music, ideas, from a dearth of resources; it was already a secret presence, as if she was communing with something. Even in those years when her body sprang like a weed to what was not yet its willowy, or rather its cypress, height — the ugly duckling stage through which loveliness seems to pass — you could not focus on the awkwardness or incompletion, because she was out of that context; like a pool reflecting ferns under a lichened rock, the long oval face and dark gray olive eyes were at peace. Not only that, they flowed peace, as if the pool was a source, a spring of what it contained.

In the Great Flood, when their fertile delta lay under the covering brown terror of the river and they had come for refuge back to the exhausted clay hills and the patient poor town of Jobes —like going backward or forward in time, down one of the cycles of rise and fall, to some primitive stem condition, when the treacherous bottomland of our temporal holdings is drowned, and we struggle by barge and creepy railroad and buggy, maybe at last by foot, to the Stoic ancestral hill, the run- down house that was never a mansion, civilization falling from us piece by piece — no cars now, almost no roads, coal oil lamps and candles replacing electric bulbs, plumbing unheard of — the smelly morning visits to the weathered outhouse, the lime-dusted offal below crawling with worms, and near, too near, the well with the rope and wooden bucket, typhoid in the summer (though the Byrnes were vaccinated), few books, and the language dropped back from the cultivated speech of the Delta library and visiting lecturers who would come in the Chautauqua series and stay a day or so with Judge Byrne, sit in that room as large as one of these hill houses, under the glass-enclosed rows of leatherbound volumes, and smoke Between-The-Acts cigars and talk of opera or Shakespeare or of Europe, nostalgically remembered — the language fallen back from that to the corny slow nasal drawl between tobacco juice spittings from the house porch or the Jackknife-carved wooden bench under the tin-roofed front of the village store: "Waal, I reckon one more day o sun and we'll git a mess ocawn off that there row" – and always the village idiot, some remote cousin, with his heavy tongue and lips drooling, and the dope-dipping old lout with the deformed ear, whom one of the sisters had married and clung to with the dogged endurance of the hills ("Sure," they said of him, "Lon went to work oncet and sweat, and he ain't never been to work sincet"); and there were aunts, uncles, cousins and in-laws — my Lord, the hills were crawling with them; at the family reunion under the cattle-scrubbed trees on the bare sloping yard of the patched-up house of their origin, there would be sixty or more, picnicking on fried chicken and biscuits arid buttermilk and home-smoked ham, and joking with each other: "Whyncha tell me you was comin? I'd a gone and wrung the neck o one o them neighbor's roosters" — and then sidling up to talk with Octavia, who had walked their hills like dawn and gone to a fuller life, of which she wore the traces like a gown — such a yard full of cognate and affiliated rednecks, that even a boy took the brunt of the strangeness, asking: "How did it come about? How did she spring up here?" And it was not simply the wonder that somebody could come from such a place and make good and return to be admired, but that wherever you pictured her, here as a child, or in the Delta library, or in a honeymoon gondola on the Grand Canal, she remained ungraspable, eliciting the same question: How did she arise — not here or there — but in time?

Her brothers must have felt it from the first. It was they who had scraped and borrowed to put her through college. Tup had gone to work on the railroad when he was a boy, had become a passenger conductor, saving his earnings and staying unmarried, to give Octavia her chance. Next was Spurge, the redheaded one — though you could never have said that in the hills; they had the Norman-English scorn of a freckled, redheaded churl. Octavia had chased a neighbor boy over the fields once pelting him with clods, because he had insisted Spurge had red hair. It was Spurge who had inherited something of what distinguished Octavia (though not in looks); he also read everything he could lay his hands on. He even wrote verse, or tried to, and talked of making a living by his pen — though he never met anybody who was ready to pay for that kind of fiddling around; anyway he gave it up for Octavia, planted his hopes in her, in the end nourished them with his blood.

He had been teaching country school and struggling to write in his spare time; but when Tup disclosed his plan of sending Octavia to college, Spurge wanted to contribute. And what was there through that entire stretch of farmed-out country that could actually offer a salary but the railroad? It kept running year after year, rain or shine, booms (if there were any) and busts (there were plenty), from Ohio to Mobile and back again, generating like vortices in its wake, towns that were already the stay of East Mississippi: Corinth and Tupelo, West Point and Meridian, not to mention Jobes.

Teaching was for room and board, but the railroad could pay money. But Tup would have done better to have stepped down and let Spurge have his easy place in the passenger car, and have begun again himself at the bottom (or top); for it was as a brakeman on the freights that Spurgeon had to start, and that meant climbing over the speeding cars, cranking the wheels that set the iron shoes, then leaping across the gap to crank the wheel on the next car, and Spurge had lost himself in poetry too long, also he had the weakness Octavia carried through life: motion made him dizzy and he was afraid of heights. It was a wonder he lived as long as he did and laid by as much as later appeared, designated by a makeshift will, and marked on the strongbox in his room: "My savings, to Octavia, for college."

It was a rainy night. Climbing from car to car as the long train went onto a siding and slowed for switching, Spurge, whose hair and mind the muse had touched with her fire, felt her vortex whirling in his brain, his penalty perhaps for having scorned her call; he fell, striking the iron coupling with his fiery head, and was hurled with a thud and cry between the wheels. He was cut precisely in two. Octavia never recovered, and never, of course, forgot; but it did not seem to prey on her any more than the death of a savior haunts the communicant who receives the sacrificial blood. As always until the end of her life, tragedy (she would have her share of it) only gave a richness of shadow to the strange peace in her eyes . . .

Wait, it will clear . . .

But how to fasten on what was revealed? For memory is built of traces, streaks in a cloud chamber, action, always action, implying: something passed here. Suppose the greatest mystery, human or subatomic, to lurk unmanifest — the infinite that opens at the heart of every flower. Who would comprehend it? It is not a problem peculiar to mystics. The words we traffic in hunt ghosts of substance down spoors of occurrence. And in what occurrence had Octavia been manifest — not this querulous ornery Octavia, but the true one she wanted to be worthy of? Memory, like the fields of Persepolis, bore witness to deeds.

Let any scene rise, spontaneously present itself: that library, say, where the sword was — come, the earliest memories: the old horn phonograph is going. And who will be winding it? Only the father — playing the records of Caruso and Galli-Curci. They are Octavia's records, but he has bought them for her, on those winter trips when he rushes her East to the theater and opera. And then he will set on the children's favorite, Sousa's Grand March. And they will all prance around together, grotesquely led by the goose-stepping father. Where is she? Who can tell? She is not in the picture. The whole house is full of her, but she is not marching; there is not that trace in the cloud-chamber. And now it is hide-the-handkerchief, Sunday afternoon, and the father rushes across the room, snuffing like a dog. "Cold, cold

. . . warm . . . warmer . . . hot, hot, hot." And he draws it out of the phonograph horn. "Ah ha!" And where is the mother again? You would
think she had no sense of game, though everything is pervaded with
her smile. It is the smile of mystery.

What Daniel faced in the fountain did not grow less disturbing.
As if nature held her goods in one or the other hand, and choosing
was always losing, building destroying, to raise one wall by the ruin
of another. As Daniel's art teacher had told him when he neglected
appointments: "I envy you this detachment, but you will always be a
vexation to the world." The nobleness that had made her soul a tem-
plate for his had made her a frustration to his father. Both must have
sensed it beforehand; seven years they had been in love and had put off
marriage, each given to another pursuit, he of power and she of quiet.
Slowly, they had lost the will to resist — he vibrantly compelling, she
— but what call was there for mystical ladies in that Mississippi?

Daniel took his mother's arm and led her into the house. They were
in harmony now. But he knew that the mother he walked by was not
the mystery he was in search of, any more than what she was saying
could effect its disclosure. When Lethe would come hobbling up to
embrace him, invoking the Lord to tell her how long it had been since
Daniel was there and how long he would stay, and then squinting at
his shoes, demand in her shrewd way: "Misser Dan, when you goan
give me dem old shoes to cut de toes out of fuh mah po feet?" — that
would not constitute an interruption — or when his mother told
her the flowers in the Chinese bowl should be thrown out, and she
insisted: "No ma'am. They a'nt wizzled yet. Ah keeps pullin off the
wizzled ones." Whatever was being communicated was on another
plane, not to be encompassed in either's bodily decrepitude or the
sounds of its utterance.

They walked through the small, light apartment, and out the French
doors into the garden. What made it most like a dream — or analogue
— "My love is a garden enclosed" — was the pool. The site had been

chosen because at this point on the high banks of Lake Austramere, one of the few fresh springs in the Delta broke out. It had been secured long ago by digging and piping, and was now an artesian well, of which the overflow fed a basin in the garden, and spilled down through a fern bed, along an artificial channel to the lake. There was nothing grand about it; it was as simple as possible, but rich with the colors of brick and foliage; and she had set up a plain old kitchen table among the wildflowers, with a view through the broken wall, out over the lake.

It was only this that revealed her. Because, of course, she would do nothing. At most she would bustle around for some coffee or tea. Then they would sit. Maybe she would tell him something of her youth, smiling in her distant way, inconsequential: how Twenty-Mile-Bottom went through their land, and how they would go down in the summer to the hole under the clay bank; or she would say what trouble she had sleeping lately — it must be the blood pressure — but that she had found a solution: if she recited Gray's "Elegy" slowly to herself: "The curfew tolls the knell of parting day . . . " by the time she came to "drowsy tinklings lull the distant fold," she would almost always doze off . . .

At last she would ask him to go to the cemetery and measure, and he would take out a great wad of pocket papers to make a note of it, or better two or three, so that if one was overlooked he would hit on the other; he would unfold a page, and be startled by what he had scribbled in the first dawn of that morning and already forgotten:

> What gave my father Judge Byrne a tragic and broken life
> I see as the crossover of the elements of fire and water, his
> father appearing as water and his mother as fire.
>   However, this inversion produced that result only as it operated within the western phase of the whole field, the lunge
> of pioneer progress and earthly aspiring.

For Adam Woodruff similarly received from his father the water gentleness and from his mother the Cope energy, though the same effects did not appear.

Because the earthly phase of that energy was efficient (of the dock) and the fire phase was mystical, and both were contained in the balance of the East.

Though Adam Woodruff reveals himself as having some Promethean features in common with my father, some of the frustrations and disillusions, in general he is more like my mother, both being nature lovers and transcendental mystics.

But where such mysticism (of nature) appears in the Woodruff line on the shore of order and constitutes a revolutionary buttress of the present bridge, manifesting itself under the image of fire; it presents itself in the Delta under a water affinity, as spiritual calm in the regional storm.

Adam Woodruff and Octavia Clayborne Byrne are therefore alike in so far as they validate and sustain the bridge; they are unlike in so far as they confront each other across the gulf from opposite shores.

16 ~ The Last Night

Under the caving clay embankment of a river somewhere up east, though the brown glimpsed dread of water could be nothing but the Mississippi — to slip and crawl under the belly of it, and arrive at a place so far overhung and gaping, it pays to slough it off; so the hand and whole arm inserted in the moist earth-fold, to heave and then duck, as small chunks clobber the neck and shoulders; but ahead there, to watch the main mass come rumping down, and be reminded: the voices smothered now — the children — and nothing, not a cry or finger, but absence to mock the buried struggle. Clawing through amorphous thudding dark, he tears sleep, treading the muck, crying: "Mardie, Hester, Octavia!" . . .

And lies panting, in sweat, on an even knottier mattress and in a dry-rot mustier space than he had suffered through for the last weeks — in the dim light from the street, the glued-wood embossed scrolls of the bed head towering above him like the jaws of hell. Yes. This would be the attic. He is lying on his father's bed. The Colesons are downstairs. They have moved in today. And on the wall, its outlines hardly showing in the street light filtered through moving trees, must be the picture his father bought at college, a black fire horse silhouetted against a city in flame, rearing and lashing with its hooves, the mane flying, the eyes glassy.

It was for this that Daniel had forgone the air-conditioned comfort of B.J.'s. B.J.'s wife, Jane, back from Natchez, and with all the ticks and greasy rags removed, had come twice to urge him: "Come on out and get a meal and a night's rest. B.J. wants to talk to you while you're here. You're driving yourself crazy. I swear to God, Daniel, you're like your Aunt Betsy. I don't know how your wife puts up with you." He had stopped for dinner on his way back from his mother's. But there had been too much to finish at Aunt Betsy's if he was going to leave the next day; besides, there was this attic, his father's bed, the fire horse . . . . He had returned like plunging into a bog to hunt for treasure — and found only nightmare.

He rolled over in the bed and got the flashlight off the floor. Click. The glare struck the wall, bounced back like the wild whinny of that curvetting Satan. Lord, what a picture. He swung the light. It fell on his suitcase half packed by the bed, and lying loose on it, letters. Lucy's sad one from two days ago: "Old family times love and sharing . . . because of this I have fallen down I am sorry;" and these from the children, mailed last week, but by surface, arrived today. The first was dictated, it reminded Daniel of a birthday he had forgotten, for which Lucy had supplied a present, in his name:

> Thank you for the night lantern. I hope you enjoy it. We brang Corny. He didn't make fuss in the car. I am, sorry you didn't come. I am five years old. We had a lovely cake, but you would not love the cake. We got some new dress-up hats and they are dinner hats. Corny is fine. The cake was too sweet for you. We don't have rain here. The grass is dried up. The cows are gone. I had my birthday two days ago.   MARDIE

Hester, the older, had written in her own sprawling hand:

> Corny is getting puppies now. She can't run or jump very well. We went to Aunt Chris. I picked beetles off her roses. We looked for presents in the yard. I got a word game, Mardie got crayons. Corny ate birthday cake. We got a broken down

nest out of the tree. The squirrels must have broken it down. Aunt Hester's flowers are getting dried up. We went back in the woods and saw a trail leading into somebody's com yard. We pretended we were coons eating the com. Uncle Steward is not here. He is still sick. Amen.

Whatever was to happen with his own impossible aims, this at least was some traffic the bridge had been built for — in the absence of sons to burden with what must remain unfulfilled — daughters growing in harmony. He read, like resurrecting them from the clay nightmare, brushing them off and setting them down neat and gentle under the maples at the Mill. Then he turned off the light.

On the way back from his mother's, pursuing the inclination of the branch road to Lake Lamar, he had gone ahead, and to the right again, on top of the old levee, to the breaking-off place where the 1927 flood had gone through, then around behind Lake Lamar, along a willow-arched chute, past the blue-hole gouged a hundred feet deep in the buckshot mud by that break, and then along a spur dike built after the river bends were cut off in the thirties (part of a forlorn scheme to keep the thing from coiling again, though it was going to coil, since, that river, sped up in time, as on the film of a growing plant, was simply alive and physically equipped, it was no mystical matter, with muscles of incalculable strength and a will to flex themselves), until he had come out of the woods where concrete aprons and revetments, underwashed and ripped out by the rooting of the archetypal wart hog, trailed down a clay bluff to the summer-shrunken water, low but still swirling, brown as Adonis' blood and a mile wide — the river — the quickening in his own veins attesting how far its force had formed him. One can go to the Methodist Sunday school all one pleases and learn science through the week, there remain savage gods, and this was one — this, and the night sky into which its violence flowed — the poles already in water, as by storm they were in the sky .

He got out of the car and went down the bank to where a dead cottonwood was snagged in the mud, the current swirling around it.

At such a place he had drunk after the flood, when he took the long river hikes and drank any water that was moving, bent down where it eddied around the snag and gulped his fill, but broke off, sniffing, something rotten as hell, stood up, and saw lying in the water the month-old corpse of a mule, the current swirling in the belly and gurgling around and under the snag to the exact place he had been drinking, while he straightened up in a revulsion that slowly calmed into pride: "I have drunk at the bowels of death and remain whole."

So now, he started to walk out on the snag, but drew back. There was a moccasin as thick as his arm coiled there, gray, the color of the wood, not moving, staring at him, the tongue flickering . . .

"And how the hell are you going to protect yourself," B.J. asked him, "if you leave your aunt and her house and money and everything in charge of Bud Coleson, and Little Lilly Coleson, who stole money once, your aunt said, out of her purse, as companion and keeper; how are you going to avoid being sold clear down the river?" (It was what Lucy had asked him, too, when he had first written about the Colesons, how loving and helpful, and that he would try to get them to move in: "Well, that would be kind indeed, but what do they plan to get out of it?"— Quaker shrewdness, for all the Quaker idealism, stripping off the rosy wrappings.) "Is there a will," B.J. asked, "and can you have it witnessed?"

"There's supposed to be a will," said Daniel, "but I haven't found it, and I can't ask her because it would look as if I cared about her leavings. Besides she doesn't know where anything is."

"So what makes you think there is one?"

The confidential voice of Mattie Crump, bosomy friend, had apprised him of that. She had billowed up the other day, seeing Daniel on the porch, wouldn't come in, didn't want Betsy to see her — the cat smell had just about polished that relation off — but she wanted to inquire in her bustling way: "Have you found Betsy's will, Daniel?" — "No ma'am; I don't know whether she's got a will." — "Well, I can tell you she had one because the last time she went east to see you, she came by our house with an old tin box and asked me to look after it for her. 'What's in it, Betsy?' I said. 'Nothin but some deeds and government bonds and family jewelry and a will,' she says; 'my will's in there, and I wouldn't like anything to happen to it.' 'But Betsy,' I told her, 'how can I be responsible for that stuff? We don't have a safe place. Why don't you take it to the bank?' — 'Sha!' she says, 'Mr. Jordan used to take anything for me that way and keep it, but these new people say I have to have a safety deposit box and a key and it costs five dollars. You put it under your bed; that's safe enough for me.' 'Well,' I said, 'I'll do it, but I don't like to do it.' Now if you're going to leave her with the Colesons" (that news had made the rounds fast) "you better be sure of that will. I don't like to say anything against the Colesons" ("Mrs. Coleson is in the front hall right now," Daniel whispered), "but Mr. Coleson —", she leaned forward over the obstruction of her bust, to utter a sibilance that pierced the house and yard — "Mr. Coleson drinks."

Daniel had gone on looking, but had found no such document to save him from the fanged potentialities.

As he stepped back off the cottonwood snag to where the jimson-weed weed was growing, he almost put his foot on another moccasin, a small one coiled by a thistle. It hissed, uncoiled, and slid off into the weeds.

That was the allegorical landscape of the Delta, a mud flat crossed with sloughs and bayous, snags and towheads, all alive with snakes, and in the center their great cold lair, the gaunt brownstone court-house, where his father had fought it out time after time, where Daniel had gone the day before to settle Aunt Betsy's taxes, and found the place burdened as never before with upstart men pretending to be rich on borrowed money, lawyers engrossing mortgaged possessions, elected officials lounging and spitting, records confused, tax bills rendered on houses long since sold or not hers in the first place, and some up for sale because she had never received notices — it was a den of cottonmouths in a fire-scorched plain, the old mud snake of the river having spawned a million fat sons and grandsons.

Once when he was a boy he had swum in a barrow pit outside the levee, had stroked off from the sandy bank to the willowed dark one. He had been thinking of hauling out over there and maybe taking a mud bath, when he had seen them, peppering the whole slope, and the tongues going. By God, it was not worth while setting foot on that shore, to pick your way slowly up the cracked sill, wondering when you would step wrong, and the cottonmouths assault you, and you fall flat, as in Dante's hell, your legs glued, and be a snake yourself, while the snake, his tail cleaving, would rise on legs pretending to be a man. For it was all pretending. Some had done it a generation or two and got used to it; they could act almost human; the rest were down on their bellies, coiled in the courts and porches of the baked land — racketeer doctors, nurses, undertakers, that shyster lawyer who had come to the house trying to get Aunt Betsy into court about the wreck, the insurance adjuster, ready to slip out of the damages, saying she didn't have a license, though she'd been paying insurance for generations — until Mr. Hargreaves, who had the fortune of birth and breeding to be walking upright, pulled some strings and the cottonmouths withdrew.

In half sleep things boiled up and subsided like spuds in a soup . . .

The whole bank peppered with them. Swim back. Better the open water, the devouring river. To float out under the Milky Way, stars bunched like grapes. Antares, red, and below it, Mars, in the tail of the Scorpion, sluicing the waves with blood. To dive down and down, water rustling in his ears.

And come up in a bright cove, red rocks, the ocean violet, a floor of white sand. A retreat of land by the sea. And Lucy, dark-haired, by his side, the combers breaking in foam. He thought: no menace. And then, as if the word had summoned an avenging sinusoid of tide, to see the wall of water coming in, cresting to a blue broken claw that hangs above, a moment of live suspension, everywhere shattering in spires and drops, the sunlight refracted orange through green; and falls. Choked. Fighting the backwash, to glimpse Lucy there, drifting out, crying. And dive. Breaststroke through the sand-settling water, eyes and hands groping . . . Found . . . But he cannot swim her to the surface. Planting his feet on the firm sand and her feet on his shoulders, he takes the traction of the weight and walks, as children play at doing, step by step, to walk her out. Until with a gurgling wail, the lips go under. On the roll of the wave he has lost his bearings; he is not walking back to land but deeper into the ocean. The want of air at the same instant and with the same dread stabbing his chest with pain, he springs up, thrusting her with him, kicking in the frenzy of suffocation. Air!

And again surfaces out of sleep, this time in the torment of having actually held his breath; he gasps, his heart racing . . . The attic room smelling of dust and dry rot, the towering headpiece of the bed, the black horse in the dim shifting light silhouetted against fire. Dreams.

Tomorrow he will be with Lucy. As in Isaiah: "Thou shalt no more be termed Forsaken." It would be Beulah, Blake's third state of the soul, the married land:

> a little moony night and silence
> With spaces of sweet gardens and a tent of elegant beauty . . .

There were not only the children's letters that afternoon, but a long one from Lucy sent days later, but airmail. She had put off her sad mood, hearing of his coming. And Uncle Steward had rallied. He had been improving from the first, slowly, but with no setbacks. Some kind of renewal of the lease must have been arranged. But what had yanked him out of the hospital and put him partly on his feet, and the rest of the time pushing around in a wheel chair, giving orders and managing a dozen workmen trucked out to the Mill from the city, was just the challenge of nature, thrilling as Lucy described it: after the long drought there had come great thunderstorms and a flash flood.

Like a proof of what impelled him to the Mill from the first. He had been looking for a country place when they heard of that one, and he and Hester drove out. It was desperately run down, the big house, the mill, the dam and race, even the tenant miller's cottage by the stream; and as they stopped the car, a decrepit widow woman, the owner, was leaning on a stick, laboring up an eroded stone path (where the granite stairs with the wrought iron railing swept up so confidently now); she was climbing the steep bank from the mill to the house. Even Aunt Hester, for all her love of tackling new tasks, (seeing that old woman as herself, widowed some day, laboring up that hill) was almost praying: "not this house, Lord, not this one." But Uncle Steward took one look and recognized his adversaries: ruin, neglect, most of all water, the implacable enemy, a genie to be tamed and chained, bound for their comfort and ease.

That was back in the twenties, but Uncle Steward was ahead of his time: hydroelectric. One look around and he caught the picture: the mill a generator, the bus bars humming with power, the great switch to be thrown, and current to course through copper conduits to the house, the barn, the greenhouse, the seedbed, to electric steam radiators in every room with enameled rheostat controls: Low, Medium, Hot; all winter the house to be warmed by the falling of the stream, downward nature diverted to its own praise; to wait for them weekends, holidays, whenever they wanted to slip away for the peace and refreshment of the country.

Rest, peace, quiet . . . He and Aunt Hester kept saying it to each other. Though they must have known they were talking double. It was scarcely the promise of quiet that brought that first flash to Uncle Steward's eyes, but of battle — with the earth and vegetation of course, but most of all, and with the mill as his *agent provocateur*, against that stream. He was engineer enough to know the mill was not going to run itself year in and year out — the dam and long race and race gates, not to mention the dynamo, through ice and spring thaw — to run itself and repair itself, and why would his eyes have gleamed that way if he had thought it would? Some problems were to arise which even he might not have calculated on, things too queer to have predicted: as that water snakes, when the gates were closed for cleaning, would crawl into the turbine, and get chopped up when it started again, denting the blades and jamming the works — but in general he must have known.

Certainly there was no sense of surprise or betrayal to the entries in the leatherbound log, as they came out, week after week and year after year to tackle their jobs:

> Twelve inch ice blocked the flume, putting the generator off; heat died; house pipes froze, several burst. A busy weekend, getting everything going again.
>
> Overhauling power plant, two days work; revamped generator, taking commutator to Philadelphia to turn it smooth. Undercut the mica, a tedious job.
>
> Belt off the generator, oil run out of one bearing. A morning's work.

Or the current would be undermining the dam, and the pool would have to be filled with rock and reinforced concrete poured in to take the spill. Or after irrigation was installed in the garden, the pump would be turned on in the summer and burn out. Some animal would have eaten the insulation off the wires, and two dead mice and part of a bird nest would be found in the motor. Once or twice in five years, when it happened that they drove out and found nothing haywire, the log attested the wonder: "Found everything for once in working order, no repairs necessary."

These occasions might almost have been letdowns, but for an endless list of projects they could turn their energies to. And every job, big or little, left the record of its joy: "Snow storm. Shoveling out. To my mind there is nothing more satisfying than making a clean straight-edged path through the snow!" That would be Aunt Hester; and then Uncle Steward: "Typical weekend. Hester and I drove down to get a rest. She planted 200 daffodils and 300 narcissus. I boxed the new trusses under the mill roof and smashed a finger. Bully time."

Best of all, there were floods. They had been coming at intervals right along, one every five to ten years. There had been the slow flood of 1933, when an Atlantic northeaster joined forces with a Bermuda hurricane, or the dab end of one, and it rained Monday, Tuesday, Wednesday, rising to a downpour that was blown horizontal on the wind, the creek at the same pace rising, overflowing its banks the first day, the garden and drive the second, and by the third surging down, almost to the roof of the mill, tearing trees from the race, the porch from the tenant house, in the end sweeping the bridges clean above and below, the old covered bridge from Sutter's mill going past their astonished windows like a wrecked scow. So the whole place had to be replanted, the ferns that had been brought in from the woods sought out again, the race dug free of sand, the abutments rebuilt, the under-mined stones cemented back in place. As in the beginning darkness had received its command: "so far and no farther" — "Be contained," said Uncle Steward, and it was contained.

There had been the small flash flood of '37 and the larger one of '44. Now it had happened again; this would not be the last and was surely not the worst, but it was enough; it had roused Uncle Steward: "Take up thy bed" (or thy wheelchair) "and walk." Thursday, Lucy wrote, the creek was peaceful and normal. That night and Friday, with astonishing thunderstorms over the whole valley, it rose almost twenty-five feet. From the dam down to the mill, trees were uprooted; furniture on the second floor of the tenant house was floating around. The porch took off again and the shutters were swung on the electric wires. The mill itself was a shambles, choked with mud, the machinery beginning to rust.

For several days Uncle Steward had been threatening to leave the hospital. Now he phoned the ambulance and was taken to the Mill. When the door was flung back and he stared into the soaked and tumbled interior — six inches of mud on the floor and a smell of mildew and sediment, the canoe washed from its hangings and crashed over the generator — his blue eyes beamed into the darkness. He gave one fierce snort, like a war-horse; it could have expressed anger, but it was more like keen delight.

If he had laid out the whole plan beforehand, invented the flood and practiced what he was going to do about it, he could not have wasted less motion. In half an hour he had the volunteer fire department from Quaker Crossing. They pumped from the stream and played the hoses on the floor, turned them into the penstock and turbine, washed out the sand and mud, using the element to work against itself. An hour more and he had trucked scores of workmen with tools and power saws from the Philadelphia plant, while he was wheeled everywhere, or getting up walked, leaning on his Scotch blackthorn, or joking waved it around, giving direction, and the men jumped to it: "Yes sir, Mr. Cope." And everything fell into place.

You could almost think the first founder of the Cope fortune, the sea captain, had come back to get the place shipshape after a pirate raid, that he was issuing the orders and the men answering: "Aye aye, Cap'n Cope; aye aye, sir."

Daniel had been three weeks in Mississippi puttering around his aunt's and messing with her real estate, and had accomplished virtually nothing, while Uncle Steward had got up from a stroke and in one day had contravened the damage of a destructive flood.

All right. Let him come down, Daniel thought, and apply his talents in the Delta, with Aunt Betsy's warrens for material and Bud Coleson as agent to build his toilets and set on his screen doors, and not that creek, but this river, trying to discharge two and a half million cubic feet a second, and no one day flash flood, but the '27 overflow, one break alone spilling a thousand times more than that Mill creek ever rose to — the Great Flood, in the shadow of which Daniel's boyhood had been passed.

They had looked out as children from the windows of his father's fourth story office towards the wharf; they had seen the steamboats booming south in the spring, lifted by that astonishing pressure-head over the roofs of the town; and Daniel, like all the youth, had been on the river's side. He had watched the big letters of the gauge on the wharf as the Negro changed them: 40 feet and rising, 50 feet and rising — the rain falling from ragged low clouds — 60 feet. He had heard talk of danger spots: Miller's Bend, Mound Landing, Lakeport, which could be held and which might go; of how the levee had been dynamited in Arkansas to ease the crest here. Until the climactic night arrived under a steady rumble of rain. His father had been out with the other men, helping guard convicts brought to pile sandbags and dike boils. He had come in after midnight, and some time before dawn the long howl of sirens, for which one had been waiting months, years even, roused them, the shrill treble sliding into bass and up again, then the other siren crossing the first. Everybody sprang from bed wondering, where? where? The phone rang, and his father got the news: Rowdy Bend, behind Lake Lamar.

They drove south in the dawn to the protection levee. There was a gap where the road came through. Segeen Wright, city engineer, was blocking it up with sandbags. He told Judge Byrne he could hold the flood out of town; so Judge Byrne went straight home, laid some planks on the steps, and drove the car onto the porch; because Segeen Wright had never yet spoken on a matter of professional competence and not been wrong. He was the one who had built the streets of the town with car-bouncing gutters across the roads at the comers, for drainage he claimed, but there was nowhere they could drain to, so they were always full of water. Lady Bird Alexander came over from next door to get the news: "Do you think they can hold the water, Judge?" — "Well, Mrs. Alexander, Segeen Wright says he can, and you know Segeen Wright. You can draw what inference you please." And she, exercising her famous barbed tongue: "I should think he could hold it out, Judge; he's held it in the streets for twenty years." It was harder to keep it out than in. It came gently at first, the long lanes sliding through the gutters like quicksilver, a reflecting dawn; then it built to a violence, a depth of roaring brown currents, which possessed, and for three months covered the land.

That was the difference. It had come with them as if it belonged, as if it had an old writ of ownership: "Let it be as the snake disposes." It was not only boys who felt their hearts on the river's side. One could not put a mill on the Mississippi, and a steamboat, which also worked with cogs and wheels, was in the water's grip, had gone down into the lair; it only fought against the stream by the power of fire. Uncle Steward was not aware of any satanic connections. He did not operate on the mudflat of moccasins where the only alternatives were sky and water, romantic drowning or transcendence. He worked in a society. His frame of values was perfectly clear. He had an instinctive love of battle, but that did not dignify his opponent. Like the old Hebrews, he was on God's side, and the snake was the snake. But Daniel's values were ambiguous. Prometheus, Faust, even Satan, were heroes; is was felix culpa, the cup well drunk and paradise well lost; and the ocean and river, the void and storm, were powers to be worshipped, even as you fought them.

In the dark of these speculations he lay outstretched, his eyes closed, invoking Lucy, sleep, or morning, whichever came handier . . . While the Mill revived around him . . .

There was always the low sound of water, like wind in the trees, but steady, where the laminar flow of the race shot down into the pit of the turbine, a roar which increased as you walked' down from the house toward the stone and red frame building beside the stream; it rose to meet you, a chambered waterfall. And then as you opened the Dutch door and penetrated the shadowy beamed space, and closed the door behind you, the sound grew muffled, was transmuted into the musical hum of the 35-kilowatt generator, converting that channeled plunge of water into ductile power.

When the eyes had accustomed themselves to the dusk, one looked around. It was also a place of sleep and dream, a vision from Ezekiel: wheels within wheels, the great weighted flywheel, larger than the main drive of a locomotive, was whirring round, spinning the governor by a separate belt, and the centrifugal balls, with all their cogs and gears; while the twisted belt of cemented leather, a foot wide and thicker and tougher than an elephant's hide, arched across the space, setting the D.C. generator croning at 900 r.p.m. Also from the central flywheel, all separate machines and gadgets could be turned by belts reaching through the murk, activating com grinders, lathes and power saws, and the bellows of a blast furnace.

Of all his achievements it was the one Uncle Steward loved most. His electronics plant in Philadelphia was of course something to be proud of, a thriving industry, which he had built up on his own. But this was his hobby; it revived the ideal of his childhood, the flint mill at Conowingo, which he used to visit in the summers long ago. It was archaic, quaint in a way, but not comical. It was too visionary for that. Like some self-invented, hand-made precursor of the machine age, it turned the raftered room into a hive of power. How often he must have stood there, his eyes sparkling, while all around him belts, gears and wheels sang his mastery, the voice of some country Price cousin or garden club visitor echoing in his head: "When this fellow Cope talks about engineering, you can tell he knows what he's talking about. He's got his hand on the throttle."

But suppose one went down to the dirt-floored basement, hardly above the water level and always damp, the earth cracked dry on top, but soft below, caking after the last rise, while the roar of water mounted. Then one began to wonder about the underground commitment on which the wheels of force rested. Catching a whiff of rotting wood, and noticing in the dark how the old props were sloughing off at the base from alternations of dry and wet — the mud floor yielding to the foot — one stared for cottonmouths or at least copperheads, recalling the Delta and nodding: "The secret is out — like everything else, built on the quagmire; give it a few years, it will be like Betsy Byrne's." Until the eyes adjusted to the gloom and one glanced up and saw the old oak beams, whole trees, solid, resting in stone walls, and under them, here and there, Uncle Steward's new pillars and props; and in the center, rearing through the basement to the floor above, giving support to the beams, to the great flywheel, and to the turbine shaft, was the massive concrete penstock, buttressed and reinforced like a bombproof fort, enclosing the water pit below, and above bearing and shielding the flywheel and dynamo. It was all mortised in the granite gneiss and solid for as long as a Cope could make it.

That pit was the core of the fabric, the last place to be explored. One could climb the penstock wall and stare down through a recess into a blackness of loud water, nothing but spray and roar, until the eyes adapted themselves again, and there it lay, the deepest foam pit. There too Uncle Steward had his road of access and control, the steel ladder descending from the trap above into the boiling socket, where the turbine, seated in the vortex and quivering like a wild stallion, gyred, turning the steel shaft, turning the flywheel, setting the belts and cogs and eccentrics and the fifty-horsepower dynamo into action.

It was here that Uncle Steward had descended after the great floods, or when the turbine had to be reflanged or the bearings replaced, or when water snakes had turned it into a snake pit, crawling in and being chewed to bits — he and his henchmen had gone down, lifting the wheel with a two ton hoist to unbolt the couplings, to roll back the turbine housing and draft tube, exposing the guts for replacing, cleaning, balancing, whatever was required, and repeatedly required, to keep the infernal forces in the service of the tree-shaded Mill.

Daniel and Lucy, even Adam Woodruff in the past, had peered or perhaps climbed down into that place, never without a touch of awe, a shudder beyond what the drop-leap of water, the noise and spray occasioned — Adam Woodruff himself, near as he was to being once-born. But Uncle Steward had trafficked up and down time after time, the smile in his eyes, the mustaches bristling, but with good humor — the cool competence of one who does not even know the forces of dark are tugging at him. He had wrestled with that old leviathan re-peatedly, until it had become a routine, and he had never yet betrayed any sense of having unveiled mysteries or penetrated any sorcerer's den. He did it as he did everything else, like one of the proprieties he was born to, that he had done before and would rise from the grave to do again.

If the Satanic commitment was there, Uncle Steward wasn't aware of it; and as Hamlet said, there is nothing either good or bad but thinking makes it so. The Mill remained an island of pastoral calm, the house decorous, the sheep grazing in the meadow. Like the nine-teenth century oil Uncle Steward had on the wall of his study, which he had loved since childhood, though perhaps it was tame art — an American river so romanticized you might have thought it the Rhine or an English lake — an idyllic scene barely hinting at the waterfall, far off, on the edge of the still horizon . . .

When Daniel had driven in from B.J.'s the phone had been ringing. It was Lucy, confirming the hour of his flight. So before he read her letter he had caught the new tone, the vibration of joy: gaudium. Her darker moods were occasionally committed to paper, but the voice was always gay. Especially when she phoned long distance — as if the operator had plugged her in on her girlhood, when she would call her parents from boarding school on first-days. You could remind your-self it was a woman, a mother, at the other end; but what you heard was the delighted child, the coloratura of laughter . . .

He drifts out under the ripple of the voice, lucent, evocative, as it takes up residence in the raftered dark room of the mill, voluminously enfolded, Gretchen at the spinwhorl in a shaft of sunlust singing: "The male is a furnace of beryl, the female is a golden loom." In moony night singing, noumena. Closed in the walls, the whirring dark, spinning with wheels, cogs turning and creaking, in the dry webwork she hangs, a lobe of luminous water.

He outside, by the wall and roof cut from her, mounts spirantly, a fire-drake, a pyrrhous ram, roots at the woundruff, shattering mullions, glass and bars — comet through crystal, beast onto beauty, comose in glaphyrous, combs the vaultings, cunous gynous. Hair of flame pubescent runs in the branches; in gouts of light, wood and stone flower, wax into radiance. She leafs up, crying, wavers, and becomes vapor, a wraithing. They are clouds, nymphalids, over sea and island, nubes nubiles, jubilant in marriage.

From dark bellies below, lightnings lunge into each, zygous conjunctive, sluice rivers of rain, infundate earth-furrows, cundle Gaie kyme: vines, fructuant, melons, mangoes, nuccioles, glandes, com copious, and gorbeilles of ficos in overy geardon. And again subliming, leaves into vapor, and her voice through the vapors: "Prince of fire and storms, tell me of your learning; Are we clouds of thunder, tumulus?" And his tongue's lightning: "Queen of waves and islands, and quell of burning: In cumular tumescence earth and cloud wreathe fructifying favors, such gods as we."

They fold long limbs to the twilight, gleaming devotive arms.

17 ~ The Graves

Daniel walked to the cemetery, dawn of the last day, an outward motion leading to a center. Laid out on higher ground along Rattlesnake Bayou, now drained, it had kept some of the original trees: swamp Spanish oaks with dark trunks, basket oaks, silver-gray, with broad leaves. Beneath them were later plantings of crape myrtle, jasmine, camellia.

Confederate soldiers lay almost as indistinguishably as the Indians who had hummocked the ground before them. The clumsy marble one, on a column, had been added in Daniel's youth. Judge Byrne, similarly elevated, and falling into somewhat the stance of the carved warrior, had delivered the panegyric. Daniel walked on, the dusk opening.

Then he saw the angel, standing as for an Annunciation, holding the lily, but with bowed head, and a look of incalculable yearning. It commemorated Gabriella de Rore, young bride of the hotel keeper. She had died long ago in childbirth, and the family had sent back to Italy for this angel of Carrara. It stood facing the Byrne lot, in the soft style of Pre-Raphaelite mystery, too sweet for the shadows of their swamp world. Daniel had wondered sometimes, as they put flowers there, what had been between them, the lonely Florentine and his own father, home from college, studying Italian with her, reading Petrarch, dreaming of a trip to Florence.

Daniel's family had gone to the cemetery every Sunday, as people did in the South. First they would lay flowers on the grandfather's slab, over which Judge Byrne never failed to wipe his eyes, a preservation of grief that seemed excessive to the boy.

Beside it was the small grave of the first son. He was to have been placed in the grandfather's arms, perpetuating the name. When the grandmother, incensed by the mystical distance of the bride, had broken off relations ("All right. He's a judge. He can understand. I have passed my verdict. Our Betsy has passed hers. And it's nothing but weakness in you, Daniel Byrne, that makes you not pass yours"), the grandfather, loving Octavia, had remained loyal. The namesake was to have been his reward. But the child died at birth, and before the sister could be cleared off the ways and a living Daniel brought forth, the old man had died too. So the infant grave received a special mourning. There was talk, in muffled sobs, how old this first Daniel would have been, and in what grade, or preparing for what walk of life.

When the grandmother died, she took her place by the grandfather, and it was hard for Octavia to commune with the old man, who had suffered so much in her cause; even his resting place was encroached on by the demoniac other. Octavia would bring flowers, but she preferred to stand back by the infant grave, while the children made a fair distribution between grandmother and grandfather.

Then her other son moved in, little Gerald, and for a time she had no thought for anything in the lot but him. And then her husband, like a fierce meteor, furrowed his way into the same ground. Now the space was so pre-empted with feuding remains, it was a question where the two left alive could find quarter, if this was still to be called a place of rest.

"Go measure, son," she had told him. "Betsy should be by her mother, and I at the other side of the lot, by little Gerald. I couldn't rest any nearer. Measure, and let me know."

So he had come — though he must have measured before, and told her, as he would tell her now, and she would forget, and ask at their next meeting, whenever he returned: "Have you measured, son? Is there room?" And he would come out once more to reassure her, getting up early to walk through the cool dawn, behind the house of his childhood, to the cemetery — as he walked now in pearly light under the great oaks, past the yearning angel, and came to the Cape jasmine bush by his brother's grave.

Before his father and brother were buried there, a gaudy spider as big as a fist had nested in the dark comer between the jasmine and the thorn. It was jet-black, with red and gold spots shining out like jewels. It had sat in the center of an elaborate geometry in which grasshoppers and night-flying insects would be balled up and sucked dry. It did not take much imagination for a boy to scale himself down to that size, and see the web in another dimension, what it eternally was, and by that act be ensnared, where the lurking presence came to the attack on bending wires.

Though sometimes he was on the spider's side. He had thrown horseflies there; and once when a wasp was entangled, he had watched the battle, impartial as a god. For a web is any texture hung over the abyss. It is a question of aspect, whether at any moment it will prove of darkness or of light.

He took a tape measure from his pocket and bent to his work, surveying the Todesacker, their plot of the dead.

As a matter of fact, his first paid job had been that; he had almost forgotten it. It was when he was ten or twelve, after trying to sell magazines and being refused, then trudging around with a patent window washer, scrubbing half the windows in town for a demonstration, and never making a sale, having to pay in the end for the one he had used — the cemetery was a relief after that, a real paid job, when the funeral parlor had got worried about burying one body on top of another, and had sent him down with an amateur surveyor to stake the lots and make a platt of everybody's holdings . . .

Forward and back, measuring. As the clocks at Woodruff Farm in the hush, the night after the funeral; or before his marriage, when he. would lie with Lucy on the sofa in the flickering dark teaching her to make love — the grandfather clock, ticking in one room, slow, the mantel clock in the other, higher and in double time, crossing the beat, measuring the spaces of their loves and dyings — so here, pacing and measuring, he ranged past and future, gathering births and deaths into the containment of now . . .

His mother's death also, the event for which he measured – a belated night ghost — was rising from that ground.

It had always been near her in spirit, the mystery she communed with. Spurge . . . For what child, real or imagined, had she written the poem Daniel had found among her discarded papers, in the style of another century, yet not a pose:

> Last year you walked within this quiet place
> Where shadows cross the sunlit earth.
> And kneeling in your reverend tender grace,
> You laid your hand upon the springing grass.
>
> It hides you now. In the same place,
> With eyes half weary of the light,
> Dreaming, again I see your face,
> Calm with the silence and the peace
> Of shadows on the sunlit earth.

Her death now was near in body also. Though that too had begun long ago. Once she had been a great walker, those early summers in the Ozarks. That had borne fruit in Daniel when he was at college. His letters became long accounts of walks and reading poetry, to which his father would reply with social advice, that he join a fraternity and make "valuable contacts," while his mother wrote:

> You know people can be knit together by the closest ties
> of blood and have no real affinity for each other; and when

occasionally with the tie of blood that of affinity appears, no
relation in life can be more rewarding. From your long letter
of last week, I have realized as never before how truly you
are the child of my spirit. I could enter into every experience
with understanding and joy. I suppose you are not aware of
it, but Wordsworth has been one of the great forces' in my
life. I can never forget the exaltation of first finding those
lines beginning: "For I have felt a presence . . . " *Walden*
also is a favorite with me, and has encouraged some of the
tendencies your father deplores.

But then, when he had memorized all the paths, and planned (his
father's son in that) which mountain views and forest springs and pilgrimage trees he would guide her to, when the family drove up in
June, she arrived too stiff with arthritis to follow him without pain.
Slowly the stiffness had increased upon her, until after the father's
death she was almost a cripple.

The new drug, cortisone, afforded a brief oasis. She experienced
a miraculous accession of strength, of joy even. It was then that
she moved to her new apartment, by the lake, built in the ruins of
Avon. At the height of that renewal, she joined a nature group for
a weekend in the Ozarks. They found her like a girl again, climbing
the slopes and beating through the thickets in search of wild flowers. Then came the reprisal. A routine examination on her return
showed that what had always been low blood pressure had gone
sky-high. Her whole metabolic type seemed to have been altered,
pushed over into a new equilibrium with its other syndrome. So the
drug had to be abandoned. Pain and stiffness returned, though not
crippling as before. The real incapacity now was the blood pressure,
and with it cholesterol, hardening of the arteries, a slow advance of
forgetfulness.

Even the mistake of a drug calls up latencies that were in us from
the first. She had always been forgetful. One could term it a defense

against the world. It was Daniel's trait too; he was almost proud of it. But in her, it went beyond defense; it was an assault, whether of love or war, by a darker power. Twice at college, under strain, she had experienced amnesia. She tried to leave class one day after an exam and did not remember where anything was, the dormitory, her room, or when she had another class. For days she was guided by a school friend down a maze of corridors.

Such hints were manifest whenever she was forced to make a new attack on the actual. It had seemed a protest sometimes against the organized bustle in which she was borne in her husband's wake. On their summer trips she might walk out from some hotel, only to get a breath of air, turn a comer and be out of reach, with no notion of how she had come. She would wander about or sit in a park peacefully watching the sunset until they came to find her, or, once or twice, until the police were called and tracked her down.

To her conscious mind, this refuge was partly a terror, a descent into the void, sheltering though it was. So she clung to routine, to the thin film on which the mind skates over its own nonbeing. As if going to the windowbox and watering the flowers, stirring up a bit of breakfast in the kitchenette and eating it at the garden bay, taking the known turn to the lavatory and back to the bookshelf, leafing through the old favorites, going to sleep in the same bed, the window open to the familiar noises: insects, lake water, wind in the trees, the mockingbird singing all night in the spring — as if only that recurrence kept her in touch with corporeal things.

And more often, coming to see her these last years, Daniel would mark lapses, when sitting by the window reading, she would simply look above the book, or through it, so deeply withdrawn that if you spoke to her or touched her shoulder she would start and give an involuntary cry. She had done that earlier also; it had vexed his father for her to startle that way, as if he were a stranger breaking in on her secret life; but it came more often now.

"Son," she would say, stopping in the middle of what she was telling, "you can't expect me to remember it. I'm losing what little mind I had." But if he stirred the right association, quoted from a German poem or Wordsworth, or spoke of birds, or something from her childhood, any of the things she loved, a joy would cross her face, and without thinking she would pick up the thread, go on with the story; and it would all come to life; she and her older sister, say, gone down to the bottom to pick hickory nuts, both riding the old farm horse with a bag slung over his rump; and the bag full now, swagging down on either side, Stella riding fore, Octavia, in her short dress, her legs long with growing and the knees bony, astride the crupper, her pigtails down her back, the dapple gray clomping up to the gate, which Stella, to save getting down, kicks with her bare toes; so it opens and they go through; but it strikes the clay bank and rebounds, carrying Octavia with the bag of nuts to the ground, that red earth . . . Or if Daniel had started her on poetry, she would take it up and go on quoting, until he would make the mistake of saying, as if to encourage her, "But you remember that very well"; or she would simply become aware of her own voice, and stop, the flow interrupted; she could not remember the next word: "No," she would say, "I used to know poetry, but it escapes me now."

Though what escaped her most were the things she had always disliked: mathematics and business, names, random facts. It was becoming impossible for her to balance her books. Not that she had ever done it with ease. Daniel's father had wanted an account of every penny — however few pennies might be saved that way. There were memories of the mother, still young and willowy, seated at the desk by the hall window, the pane cracked across a view of trees beyond, she in tears, bending over the scribbled account book, which had been done wrong and crossed out and redone, and the father, storming away, turned into a tyrant by incapacities his trying to help her had raised.

No, whatever mathematics she was to lose, it couldn't be said she had much to begin with; and the same with a sense of direction — with all practical skills. Though she complained of the loss, there was a kind of willful gain. She was following her bent, slipping into the pool of her quietness.

The road was clear. How many times Daniel was destined to come back he could not know, but each time the outward manifestation would startle him with its advance, would wring from him an involuntary alarm: "She is losing her mind"; until he would sit with her and they would talk of something, or better still, stop talking, letting the silence well up in her face, and he would reassure himself: "No, it's not that; it's not what she's losing; there is something else; she is finding her soul."

As with a spring that in drought has retreated into its source, you dig down and wait, and there is the bright trickle. She had learned it from *Walden,* how the temporal earth is suffused with another water; and there was a valley of her being where she remained kneeling under the beech tree, herself the face in the sky which was herself, mirrored in herself the pasture spring.

While the blood pressure remained ominous, and one asked when the stroke would come, thinking that surely would be the way — reaching into the future, but blindly, neglecting the other lot, which was already there, the need and portent of a harder passing.

She had always prided herself on her ability to bear pain. That was the stoic training of the hills — the father who would only say of the Civil War: "It was a bad time," the mother who kept the farm together, bore ten children and raised eight, and died herself of cancer, uncomplaining. Such was the death Octavia held before her, with fear, which is also a secret kind of martyr's desire, a last wager what the soul can endure. Like the time the dentist was hollowing out her tooth and wanted to know when he had reached the nerve, and kept poking it and asking "Does it hurt? When it hurts especially, let me know." And she, sweat standing on her forehead, but that look of mystical quiet unchanged (he told it all over town): "No, it's nothing really." There was something in her which had to prove itself in an ultimate pain, to teach a final lesson, which she could even have stated in an Emersonian way, that the soul in its last ditch stand has no longer anything to do with the challenges of body, any more than with memory, bookkeeping, its assumed skills and powers; or as Daniel would have put it: it is the vanishing vector as the finite function decays.

That would work out slowly. There were to be other visits, other summers — the smile of tender distance increasing on her, as if she had to catch a bird call way off, and would necessarily miss something of what you were about to say. Then her servant, old Lethe, would die — she was a walking miracle already — and the granddaughter, Ethyl, would drift off north; the apartment by the lake would become unfeasible. Daniel's mother would have to go, back to one of the downstairs apartments in the town house, where a neighbor could keep an eye on her.

And though the agent was still supposed to be looking after the rents there, she would always be forgetting and asking for payment, or sending mail away marked: "No such person known."

Or she would take her keys and enter an apartment, thinking it unrented, and there would be the young couple the agent had put in there, newlyweds, actively engaged on the sofa. So she would start, looking absent, and they would start, not looking absent at all; and she would withdraw with apologies, they too withdrawing, with something more like a curse. And if Daniel would fly down, partly to see her, partly to look after Aunt Bets, or whatever shacks he would inherit after her demise, but mostly in the hope of persuading his mother to come east with him, or failing that, as he was bound to fail, to keep the place rented — it would hardly appease the newlyweds to tell them: "It's not as if anybody had really seen anything;

because whatever you were doing, even if it was the most intimate thing imaginable, she would forget it at about the same time she closed the door; so it wouldn't be any more than if you'd been reflected in a mirror or a pool that would lose the image as soon as you turned away" — that wouldn't do any good; they would move out, and other tenants would have to be advertised for, over the growing obstacle of such complaints being noised around.

And whenever he came down she would have to go through the rigmarole of putting him up, with all the worries about where he was going to sleep and what he would eat — worries interminable, because the discussion would establish an orbit on which it would return again and again to where it started.

"But where are you going to sleep, son? On the sofa?"

"No ma'am, upstairs, in the old study."

"Isn't that rented?"

"No ma'am; that was left because of the attic stairs; it was never rented with the apartments."

"Is that so? But how can you sleep up there? Are there any beds?"

"Yes ma'am, two old box springs from the guest room."

"But are they comfortable, son?"

"Yes ma'am, they're fine."

"Do you have any cover?"

As if he would need cover anyway: "Plenty of cover, thank you ma'am."

"But you don't have a pillow."

"1 never use a pillow, Mother."

"Well, I'll get you some cover then." And she would begin pulling covers off her own bed.

"Don't bother, Mother, I've got plenty of cover."

"But I don't see any cover on the sofa. Where have you got the cover?"

"In the study."

"In the study! But where are you going to sleep?"

"Right there, in the study, ma'am."

"But there's no bed there."

"Yessum — the old box springs from the guest room."

"Is that so? Well, let me find you a pillow."

"Thank you, ma'am, but I never use a pillow."

. . . Through lines and creases, always more detached, the Gothic smile.

It was the same with anything she tried to fix for him. She would keep asking if he wouldn't like a cup of coffee, until he would weaken and say: "Yessum, thank you ma'am, I'd love some."

She would put on the water to boil, and then fuss around for half an hour locating the cups and getting them clean and laid out. Finally she would begin to search the pantry and kitchen shelves and every place else for the instant coffee. By that time Daniel would smell a queer hot smell, and jump up and find the water boiled away, and a little bit more and the pan would have begun to melt down. So he would grab it and burn his fingers and groan, just as she came into the room from the back porch, not having found what she was after, and not remembering what she had been looking for, but reminded by the act of search that maybe Daniel would like a cup of coffee; and she would face him, smiling in her gentle, wise way; "What about some coffee, son; wouldn't you like some coffee?"

"No ma'am," he would answer; "thank you ma'am, but I never drink it at all."

And now those queer hill ways that had plagued them when they were children, would come back to haunt her. She had always believed in laxative as a general tonic and restorative, a punishment too perhaps, so that whenever they quarreled as children, she used to say: "You're as quarrelsome as you can be. You must need a laxative." If worst came to worst, she gave them a dose of milk of magnesia.

She would get up in the morning now, complaining of diarrhea. He would hear her get out of bed repeatedly and go to the toilet. Then by afternoon' she would come drifting and stumbling through the room holding that big milk of magnesia bottle, headed for the kitchen.

"Where are you going with that stuff, Momma?"

"I've got to take some medicine," she would say. "I'm constipated."

"You can't be constipated, Mother."

"Well I am;" she would tell him. "1 haven't had an action for days, and it makes me feel terrible."

"Why you had diarrhea this morning; you even complained of it."

"That's impossible, Daniel," she would say.

"You're always thinking you're constipated, that's all and then running yourself into a diarrhea with that cursed magnesia."

"You never believed in medicine, son; but I take it only when I need it."

"Today's the proof, Momma. I was here, and I never get things mixed up. You had diarrhea a few hours ago. Now you've forgotten it, and you're ready to take medicine so you can have diarrhea again tomorrow. You'll wreck yourself that way."

Then she would make out a schedule and pin it to the bottle, and another above the toilet, to keep the thing straight, though of course that would come to nothing. She had other bottles all over the house and she ordered more whenever she couldn't find an old one; besides she could never be sure of the date, even if she thought to check the schedule.

The preserved sanctum of order within the ruins was going to be lost; the continuity that in the East could be maintained would be broken here; she would begin, like Aunt Betsy, to go down in a quirkish strange confusion and stubborn turmoil, her Southern, or perhaps only her mortal, heritage. Except as she moved toward it — what for the father had meant satanic confrontation, and for Betsy nothing at all, defiance drowned in incapacity — for her would appear an indefinable opening out, the mystery hinted at under the more absent smile . . .

Until it would come back to the hospital again. It would be spring. All their southern dyings seemed to come in the spring, as the northern ones were surrenders of the fall. This would be at Easter time. The rain would be falling, darkening the earth. He would never see the rain after that without thinking of her — how she had stayed on at home until she was too weak to move, and how the ambulance came to take her to the hospital for the terminal days; how the colored nurse (who had told him in the kitchen, sadly shaking her head: "I give my heart to Mrs. Byrne, as I never did to another; I hate to see her go") walked beside the stretcher as they carried her out, leaning over with loving protectiveness to cover the wasted face against the rain — and then the strong gesture with which Octavia had pushed the cloth away, kindly, but final — the farm girl walking in the rain on the clay hills: "No, I like it. I like the rain in my face."

It would be the hospital again, for a day or two, though unlike the other, waste visits there. He must watch for a presence action had always betrayed, an instant of subsidence when she would also be . . . nothing.

Watch — in the aseptic falseness of that place, and on the face hungered by long malignancy, the hardly skin-draped skull, the eyes under discolored lids like the hooded eyes of a bird, the teeth as in a mummy emerging from shrunken lips, and between snatches of pain — watch the lyrical softness take the features, and suddenly in the death's-head, see the girl again — running down pastures to the beech hollow and looking into the spring, infusing it with her image — melting into the water, flowing down from the source, through fields of flowers, the ideal phase of her love — as she sat with Gerald and read, the Song of Songs, he the heart's wooer, standing in his first form, the cypress by the water and the sun on the hills, before he scaled to the dragon, transfigured now, one with the son who leaned over her and the son who had gone before and would be calling her on — Father and Son and Son of Man, glowing on the hills in an ideal phase, engendering, a last outwardness, the dreaming smile.

What is the emotion stirred by the coexistence of the death's-head and the loving girl? A tearful lost poignance? That, but not that only.

He must learn again as he had learned before: extinction is no sure ground for anything but regret; there are no pat comforts; yet there is something, insubstantial, something the words "life," "comfort," "being," airily perpetuate, some web that sustains the tears. Like the Psalms she fell asleep reading, not wholly self-deception. It was not a question of survival after death, or of the grass here on the graves he was measuring, but of a sign, a blaze at the point where the dark is pierced.

While the lips move, the eyes closed, a dream quickens the nerve ends, and the hand reaching out takes the watcher's hand and grips it as pain rises on the cough. Then the voice, almost without sound: "I am waiting, son, waiting. Am I waiting patiently?"

And he, the sharpness schooled by her quiet: "Lord, you're a lesson to the heathen."

Her voice again, wry with pain: "Yes. I suppose that's some consolation."

In the end it would be the heart that would give her ease. The doctors had always called it weak, though it would seem strong. After the birth of Gerald she had been almost an invalid. That had occasioned putting a water elevator in the house so she wouldn't have to climb the stairs. But she had no sense of a machine and was in such fear of the thing that she hated to use it. There it sat, like a closet above and below, but serving for no storage, nor for anything else, until the children at risk of life and limb would sneak in, pull the chain, hear the hissing and splashing as of a huge flushing toilet, while the counter tank filled — and whoosh, the slow ride up or down in the dark, jarring into the hangar at the other end. It was the heart that would give her ease.

Daniel would be there, of course, having flown in from somewhere, his sister too, whom he had not seen since their father's death; she was brown with the sun and wind of the Argentine. They would be sitting by the bed, and the mother, as often with intuitive people, would know a few moments before it came.

"Have you measured the space, son? Is there room by your brother, in the comer, clear of the rest?"

Yes, he had measured many times. He had been measuring it for years, as he was measuring it now; and there was always room . . .

And now her voice, a ghost belated into the dawn — rising from the ground where she was not yet interred, the quiet musing voice — began her own ritual, not, from the Bible, not Christian even, but from the poem she had formed her soul around, and could not lose through all the other losses:

> And I have felt
> A presence that disturbs me with the joy
> Of elevated thoughts, a sense sublime
> Of something far more deeply interfused,
> Whose dwelling is the light of setting suns.
> And the round ocean, and the living air . . .

As if she could go on and on reciting — back in her early days, when she had turned her long wood walks to a service of poetic prayer. But she broke off. He leaned down, taking her hand. "It is too bad," she whispered, "that Gerald had to go at night, and alone." It was the first time in twenty years she had spoken of his dying. Or was it her son she was speaking of?

Then with a force the body never seems to have until it gathers all its life in a last act, a last betrayal and full surrender, fierce, unassuageable — her grip came on his hand.

And then the closing of the great hooded eyes . . .

He straightened up from measuring and looked over the graves. The angel had lost the finger of its lifted arm. He pictured someone a thousand years later digging it up, when all the works it anonymously copied were lost — what theories of an age of art would be based on its mournful softness. Now he could See into the shadow beyond the graves. An even larger spider than he remembered in his youth (though the standard of his measure must have changed since), and of the same species — perhaps the twentieth offspring, but more as if the old one had hibernated year after year and come back from the ground larger and glossier — was planted on an even more extended web, a web that pocketed all the space between the jasmine and the thorn.

The shafts of the sun went gold under the knitted oaks, shifting through the mist. He looked down at the tape measure where it lay on the ground, confirming what he knew and would assure her of, that there was room by her son for her, and diagonally across, for Betsy, at the grandmother's side, completing the array, whenever the time came.

He read the inscriptions, cleared off lichen and brushed the dirt back from the stones.

When he looked up again, the sun had reached the comer ruled by the spider. The gold and red were burning in the black body, and the web, outlined in dew, was glinting its commonplace of prismatic fire. Suspended over their graves, it had become a web of light.

18 ~ The Return

He rose again from the dead and ascended into heaven.

It was not that things below him were wrapped in cloud so much as that they had become cloud, had partaken of that substance. Down there he had thought it was clear, one of those rare crisp days in a Mississippi August. Only when he reached four or five thousand feet he saw what a vapor they had got used to living in, so that even the sharpest sunlight was muddy and brown. They broke through a line into the upper sky, and the horizon was mist, glowing in the sun, the pale translucence of the lower air. At first he thought he couldn't see anything; but there it was, shadowed, dim, the underworld, our human shore.

The Delta lay coiling like a plot of snakes: waterways, swampways, woodways, coils within coils, so plain but cunning, so serpentine in its involutions around the heart. The river stretched brown in the sun, huge as a boa constrictor and spawning on all sides, putting off lakes, and the lakes, bayous, the bayous throwing off shoots and whorls, bogs, sloughs, all assuming by common consent the double S curve, the flattened figure-of-eight, sign of infinity, or the interlocking waves carved on Roman coffins to suggest immortality — but what an immortality: in that ordinary sun-baked, hick town and cabin-dotted facade, earth's immortality of wildness, a fishnet of passions, each swallowing and giving birth to the other, a sentence that goes on interminably, phrase within phrase . . . It was his native place.

He had stayed three weeks and was going back east to the Quaker farm, the balanced ways, the spring and streams on bright rocks under sloping fields, the world that had received him; let it heal what the boa constrictor had broken.

For there is always time the arrow — as there is always time the wheel.

He had been climbing up east and sliding back south ever since he was a boy — since his father, driving them summers to places of a heritage he wanted to be part of, but could never go into orbit, and so fell back to the basin of their birth — had initiated the motion. The present journey was one of a sequence, of which you could not see the end or remember the beginning, hardly distinguishable, except that each would be stretched from the other by a somewhat different filling of events. Next time, Daniel thought, his aunt would have died, and after that it would be the will with the suits that would grow from the will, and then the apartments to manage, and then his mother and whatever must follow from that, until at last it would be his own carrion coming back to be buried in that ground.

For things do not happen at once but smeared indefinitely in time. The death he had come to assist in, "the business," as Savannah put it, "you got to finish off," was still hanging fire, hovering on 'twixt a balk and a breakdown, as the Old South did — and naturally, in the hands of the poor whites, the urgent breeders and schemers, who had nonetheless their qualities, who had learned from somewhere, misery or the Negroes, to get by on nothing and put up with everything, who could meet any situation, if not with an action, with a human, though passive, response.

Everything would remain, arrested in decay, waiting the next of his cyclical returns. The apartments would go on, patched and bungled, low bathrooms and screen doors dragging; some would stand empty until vandals had broken the windows and stolen the furniture, taken the iceboxes or cut the very pipes from the walls; and now and then, by the supreme exertions of his jackleg guardian, a roof would be patched enough to put on new paper and reactivate what was left of the plumbing, stoppling loose pipes with wooden plugs or leaky wine corks ("just to freshen hit up a bit"), and it would be rented to an indigent divorced woman with a passel of towheaded kids or a migrant worker drinking up his salary every weekend and falling behind with the rent. As with every declining state of life, all those holding operations of which life is made — except for the scarcely witnessable zero moment when the divine breath blows up the balloon, that thermodynamic balloon whose second law is to wither — like the nation and government around him, by the drift of negligence and incapacity for miracle — these would go on, everything held together by the hardest and at the expense of some expendable reservoir of power.

In this case the reservoir, which war had filled, blowing into one system at the cost of others, shifting and deploying the inexorable potential, was ten thousand dollars of government bonds, cut in half by inflation (while the stocks those cautious Quakers had speculated in went on multiplying), the wrong investment, but at least available — hoarded from the war-time salaries of the shiftless and needy on whom the management presently devolved.

The gains of crisis would be spent. The half-empty property could not pay taxes and repairs, much less Miss Betsy's living and medicines, the staggering cost of a modern and slow dying; and there was the upkeep of the Colesons, though they had volunteered for the job and were fond of the old girl, still, they were not likely to have taken her on as a charity. The bonds must foot the bill, a few thousand a year, maybe more; no doubt it was calculated to the last penny by the spinners who had allowed it to be gathered, just the amount to see her into the ground again; and Daniel would be left executor of a broken estate under an impossible will, holding in the end a few crumbling unmarketable colored houses, which he would want to keep anyway, since they were his last claim on that earth or its claim on him, the tie holding him to these life-giving grim descents into the land of the shades.

He could see that now, though yesterday he could not. This morning, a few hours before the flight, he had discovered two things, profit and loss: a packet with ten thousand dollars in government bonds, and beside it the insanely ambitious will.

He had followed his aunt's traces around the house and had reached her last stand. She had begun at the desk in the entrance hall. But even before the hall was shut off from the music room and darkened, she had filled that space and moved on, leaving only what Daniel's father might have called her jack-astral spirit sitting in bosomy youth answering one of the rapturous letters with which the desk was so burdened that only an immaterial presence could be accommodated there. She could not go into the front room; her mother had filled that with earlier deposits; so it was the drop-leaf cherry table in the sitting room that had to take the strain, flanked with bookcases and assorted boxes, to be heaped up slowly, until her hoardings there too displaced her. Then she moved back to the spare bedroom, now dining room, which had to surrender both claims. Eating was shifted to the kitchen, not a true kitchen anyway (that had been on the other side of the house), but a back porch glazed in and converted at the time she made the warrens. Shortly before the accident, the spare bedroom must have reached its limits; she had begun a migration to the kitchen table, and had moved some boxes of current papers out under the sink, where they looked like junk for discard. This was her final retreat; any further move would have brought her by the other door full circle into the dark hall where she had begun. ' Being the last, it had the desperation of all last resorts, since meals had also to be scrambled together and eaten on those same boards.

Daniel had gone to work on this cache after he got back from the cemetery, the last morning. He was ready to throw the boxes out entire — Christmas cards, advertisements, the usual junk — when, groping through the muddle, he heaved up a pack of brown envelopes tied together containing a whole series of war bonds. Then he really pawed through, and uncovered what, on examining, he would almost have sacrificed the bonds to have been rid of, the smeary half-illegible sketch of a will, which switched the whole affair onto a new and hardly predictable track.

Or was it too predictable? As the countdown of a rocket projected through the zero hour changes the sign, hinting at consequences, the rocket piercing not only space but time, a traceable likelihood until it withdraws into the unformed — he could not see the end of what that paper would stir up, but he could guess at the direction. It was a document so artlessly made and dubiously worded, a lawsuit seemed to lurk under every blot, fold and scratch; yet even if it had been clear, it was impossible, since it gave away three times the estate she had. And he, Daniel Byrne, was made executor of this infernal device, bond unspecified, to be responsible for carrying out its regal behests. For the third time and with increasing amazement, he read —

"I, Elizabeth Byrne, being of sound and disposing mind ..."

(His thoughts interjecting the jarring counterpoint: I don't want to shock her, but Betsy's off her rocker ...)

"... do make this my last will and testament.

"To Daniel Byrne, my nephew, when the bequests herein-after to be specified shall be paid, I leave the Byrne home, comprising my apartment and the two facing west, with all heirlooms and possessions..."

(Bottles, rocks, rusty keys, turds and cockroaches included without extra charge.)

"... the apartment house across the way with its appurtenant dwellings" (burnt-out trailers in the back yard), "six units in all ... "

(Gerrymandered flats unrented, a bathroom, as gossip once reported, split down the middle of the tub, with spigots stuck in at either end.)

" . . . nine colored houses" (three already sold before they were his), "good rental property, bringing him altogether an income of more than 500 dollars a month" (every month of Sundays), "this on the understanding he will live in the Byrne house and have freedom at last for his work."

(Freedom. One could burn the house of course to escape the clause, be like the old colored man standing in the field while the cabin of his childhood went up in flame, raising his hands to the sky, intoning what seemed a lament, until the overseer heard him: "Farewell chinches, farewell chinches," as his arms rose and fell.)

Specific bequests followed, a catalogue of relatives Daniel had not known existed, second-cousin Boones, Byrnes and Baines who had stayed in Ohio and Kentucky or moved to Texas and California — the people she had got her D.A.R. ancestries out of, and to whom she now tossed a thousand or five hundred each with a careless gesture: "Look what a Mississippi Byrne can throw around like chicken feed." Ten thousand disposed of there.

Then: "To the following dear friends, dearer to me than relatives, $1000 each." They were all accounted for, the cronies who kept their distance now, glad to leave things to the Colesons: the Impeccable, and Miss Mattie, even the alienated Patricia Towne Dudley (so maybe her daughter Patsy could cover those bare bu'bs). And by God Dr. Fisher was going to supplement what would no doubt be a final staggering bill for keeping her alive some last week of total unconsciousness in the hospital — oxygen and transfusions and a barrage of wonder drugs — with a fat bequest as well.

And here came the lesser friends, ten awards of five hundred each; and then the people who really needed something, old colored tenants, ranging down to tokens of fifty or a hundred dollars; then gifts for the church and cemetery, with an allowance for burial that would hardly have bought her a cut-rate plank marker.

— Daniel's head pounding as he added it up. Subtotal: 25,000 dollars cash —

And now, the ironies.

"To Daniel's sister, Hilda, since she is named for my mother, Hilda Boone Baine Byrne, I leave my D.A.R. files, with postage to ship them to her.

"To the Colesons I leave my kitty and $250 to look after her."

(It's a nice kitty — but how could Daniel's own aunt cheat him out of one of the appurtenances of his dwelling?)

At the bottom of the page, crowded in like an afterthought: "To Daniel's two wives, and for his three daughters, 5000 each, to be spent on their college education."

(What a wording! Well, it was about time Sibyl went to college, and how pleased she would be; but Lucy would have to fall back on graduate school.)

He turned the page and really staggered: "I wish Dannie to establish in the name of my brother, Judge Gerald Byrne, four $10,000 scholarships at the four Mississippi colleges, Oxford, M.S.C.W., Delta College and A.&M., $500 cash without interest to be loaned graduate students their last year and returned to the fund within three years after graduation, the notes to be signed by responsible friends of the students in case of default." (That would secure the capital, assuming there was any, but would a student with somebody to sign his notes need a loan scholarship, however often he had to graduate?)

On the last page Daniel learned where this cash was supposed to come from —

"I have agreed to sell through Mr. Laurence the four-apartment house on Walnut for $20,000 . . ."

(The haunted house Mr. Laurence had shown him years ago as being worth S3000, which they had sold since for $2500 to take care of bills and living.)

"The duplex and cottages on N. Sunflower for $ 15,000; the four shotgun houses on Cypress and Greenway for $25,000."

(Shotgun houses. That was because they were built with the doors all in a line from front to back; well, those doors were clean off now and the walls half sprung; you could have shot a cow through, if you'd had the breech to deliver her.)

The sale continued, house after house: "agreed with Mr. Laurence." Small wonder she would agree, at those prices, but had Mr. Laurence? It was a question that would drop his voice lower than the usual whisper. So if the source of the $100,000 distributed was now clear, it was only at the cost of it new obscurity: why in a matter as crucial as a will, and dated only a year ago, she had wanted to play make-believe with herself.

Daniel held the document in his hand. Conscience like the voice of God told him to destroy it. What stopped him was not respect for law, and it was not timidity; it was lack of knowledge.

As he trotted the three blocks to Mr. Hargreaves' office, he could mark the conversation, like a thunderstorm, gathering head before it occurred: the kindly old gentleman, his hands and voice shaking, his heart already signaling it could not hold out for another return — when Daniel would fly over the Delta as he was flying now, but south, descending again, in a legal confusion stemming from all this, Mr. Hargreaves having passed on, and Daniel groaning to B.J.: "I wish to God you were a lawyer. What's left but crooks, or guys so dumb they can't manage their own affairs, so they take to managing other folks' because they can't lose that way?" — the kindly old gentleman, and Daniel, resting his whole case in those trembling hands —

Whistles, groans, and then the voice: "I speak as your father's friend. Suppose this will were to disappear. You are forgetful, I am forgetful; suppose we should forget. There may be other wills. You tell me Miss Mattie spoke of one. But if that also could be ignored — You are leaving your aunt with the Colesons. By the time she dies you may be so circumstanced that even this will, curious as it is, might seem an asset. You would doubtless receive the houses. The condition on which they are conferred would not constitute a hindrance, if through no fault of yours the estate were short of funds. There would be a proration. The college clause, of course, is perplexing."

Mr. Hargreaves' quiet drawl, the legal language, launched themselves toward actualization in the sleepy court some future burning August: "I am afraid the court would interpret this as a clause testamentary, not discretionary; in fact, the wording: "I wish Dannie," so far from making the bequest less obligatory, raises question whether it would not be chargeable on the estate personally devised to you as well as on the estate not devised to you. It would be a battle of some interest."

Mr. Hargreaves waived the protest. "My professional curiosity. But what is to be done? In her state, I doubt if she can write a new will. It would be best for her to cancel the college clause. Could you persuade her to that?"

"How am I going to tell her to leave the money to me instead of to the colleges? I'd rather burn the will and dodge the problem. Besides, in an hour I have to catch a plane."

"Then leave me the will. I can explain your position. If she changes it, I will witness her intention, as well as the soundness of her understanding."

"How much would that be, Mr. Hargreaves?"

"I have done your aunt's business free, and your mother's, and I will do yours. I couldn't do otherwise, in memory of your father." Mr. Hargreaves appeared to wince. Did the mention of Judge Byrne remind him of his own diabetes and ailing heart? Or was it the thought of what he had undertaken, to go into the cat-fumed house and sit with the incorrigible Betsy to discuss how much money she had and how she should dispose of it? The burden of that encounter loomed in prospect, anticipating the event, which could be tomorrow, or next week, or now, back there, in the town Daniel had left in the haze . . .

The plane roaring through the blue over the gullied red slopes where the hills fell to the Delta — the comings and goings melted into a series, from the past half remembered to the future partly sensed, inseparable. As his mind, on the way out, had run back, gathering up the past, bringing it to bear on the present, in this going away everything reversed and .drove him forward to a future we are always reaching out to form, to incorporate in the now. It had been here, hanging over the insinuations of the Yazoo that he had thought all this going down, as he thought it now returning; and slowly again, as a water moccasin materializes on the mud bank by a snag where a moment ago you saw nothing, and you hear the slow suggestive hiss, Bud Coleson appeared in the memory and projected himself into the unformed, the destiny to which Daniel's aunt, by her queer insistence on hiring nobody but the cheapest, had been committed

— Bud Coleson, the man, and now the drawling voice: "Sure Daniel, we'll look after everything. Don't you worry." The Dickens bum with the heart of gold; well, it was the gold, at least, they were banking on.

Daniel closed his eyes . . . The weathered house, the rickety porch, his aunt in the shapeless housedress, beside her the gaunt Mrs. Coleson, the spit curl pasted down on her forehead, and the sweating fat Bud, pasty, cockeyed, grinning a little under the influence of liquor, and around them a litter of kids of every age, all waving goodbye.

So Betsy Byrne, who by her mother's pride had refused any available suitor as beneath her, would turn sobbing and go back into the filthy apartment, the side the Colesons had moved into; shunning the solitude of her own, to sit vacantly smiling at the television, while visitors would come from the alleys, and the whores Coleson would rent the house across the way to would drop in for a sociable beer and a few polite jokes with Aunt Bets, everybody's favorite, everybody's aunt.

And there would come loving weekly reports of incredible, faithful care, and the little snapshot made with a Brownie and a flash bulb, the picture which, as the Colesons said, his aunt so wanted him to have — like something taken of the destitute in the county home, the lost

strange face of the failing old creature, sitting with riffraff she no longer had the painful perception to distinguish from the friends of her
youth —the picture to be filed as a counterclaim to those overdressed
and overaspiring ones of 1905. And with the picture, the usual letter:

> Aunt Betsy is doing fine. Her feet have stopped swelling.
> Dr. Fisher give her another kind of medicine. We tell her
> it is Elvis Presley blood, she gits around so fast. It has help
> her a lot. The kitty had a operation. She can't give birth.
> We had to call the vet at night. One kitten was dead and the
> other died later. Slim taken the stitches out and Miss Byrne
> like to have had a fit. The cat ain't worth 10 c., but Aunt
> Betsy wouldn't take a million for it. Bless her heart.

And a footnote from the husband:

> The rents got most used up this month with repairs. A
> man paid me in advance for the vacant one on Bolivar, but
> he died next day, and I had to return it to the widow to
> burry him with.

Into this entourage, tomorrow, or next week maybe, Mr. Hargreaves
was obliged to intrude, asking if he could talk with Miss Betsy alone.

"No, Mr. Hargreaves, we don't have to be alone. Miz Coleson takes
care of me, and she might as well be around, in case I need something."

"Well, Miss Betsy, your nephew, Daniel, thought . . ."

"What concern is it of yours, Mr. Hargreaves, what Daniel
thinks? Have you come on business, Mr. Hargreaves? Does somebody want to buy some property? It's on the market; but I'll tell
you as I've told Mr. Laurence, I don't intend to give it away. It's
worth money, Mr. Hargreaves."

"No, Miss Betsy, it's not about property, it's about your will"

"My will?" She would stare in amazement as he drew the rumpled pages from his briefcase. "But what are you doing with my will, Mr. Hargreaves?"

Right there they would have reached one of those stalemates and points of total nonplus which crop up in human affairs. Mr. Hargreaves, however he might protest about Daniel's bringing him the will and telling him to see her, would not seem to be getting anywhere.

"Just give it to me, Mr. Hargreaves; I'll read through it. If there's anything I want your advice on, I'll let you know." She would stretch out her hand.

But for all his mild sweetness, Mr. Hargreaves was a man of conviction. Neither Daniel nor he could foresee how he would face Aunt Betsy; but when the time came he was going to face her, and by natural instinct, rise to the occasion. Tightening his grip on the will, he would stare her down, saying: "No, Miss Betsy, I won't give up that way. I've come in your interest and in Daniel's interest, and in the interest of your brother, who's dead. You know I don't charge you and I won't charge Daniel; so you have to listen. I'm a lawyer, like Gerald was, and this will doesn't make sense. Daniel can't execute it the way it stands. You don't want to hurt Daniel. But this property of yours has lost value. If you expect Daniel and your friends and relatives to get the money you've set down for them, you'll have to cancel these big scholarships, which won't work anyway, and you'll have to do it while I'm here, and put your initials by it, so it will be legal. And I don't intend to leave until you do, Miss Betsy, because it's for your good."

As when Daniel had met her once or twice head-on with what she must have waited all her life to be confronted with, the unyielding male conviction, she had yielded — so now: "Colleges? What colleges, Mr. Hargreaves? . . . ' I can't read, Mr. Hargreaves . . . Well, that *is* a lot of money. All right, I'll scratch it out. Show me where, because my eyes aren't what they once were . . . I'm writing, Mr. Hargreaves; I can't write any harder."

"While I'm here, Miss Betsy," he would add — "I hate to talk about this in front of Mrs. Coleson; but Daniel suggested you change her bequest to something more commensurate with the service she performs." —

Aunt Betsy could take so much and no more. "I'll think about it, Mr. Hargreaves; but there are some things I have to decide for myself."

Sharing in this interview was not likely to teach Mrs. Coleson anything she had not already known. She and the will had been hanging around the house together too long. But it would bring things to the surface. Neither Daniel nor Mr. Hargreaves could see into the privacy of those morning talks — Mrs. Coleson prettying Aunt Betsy up and wheedling her about the will; neither could guess at the hints of largess with which such arguments would be brushed aside: "Don't you worry, Mrs. Coleson, Dannie will look after you." How far Mrs. Coleson had mined and Aunt Betsy had undermined, not Daniel, nor Mr. Hargreaves, nor anybody else could have foreseen.

The plane rose from Memphis on the long lap east. Corrugations of hills stretched toward the Alleghenies far off, beyond the horizon. The voyage extrapolated itself like those sequential ranges, reached into the future, vistas opening through clouds. But where the flight cut one swath, the living spun a polyphony of threads, of which no voice could ever be brought to a resolving Farewell, told to pack up and clear off the stage. There would always be new entrances, weavings, the exits would only be rests.

No Dark Love this time was sitting by Daniel on the plane. It was a businessman, shuffling through a briefcase, preparing his sales record. But the absence was no guarantee against later incursions. Nobody escapes the dark while the sun wastes into space; nobody is safe from flame while lightning kindles in the clouds. The time might come when Sibyl would turn up in unavoidable distress, or their child, Octavia, incongruously bearing his mother's name in

Sibyl's body, but with blond hair and something of his own romantic recklessness, would arrive, an unmanageable teenager, sent by Sibyl as Daniel's half-uncle had been sent down the river seventy-five years before. And she might stay as short a time and be helped as little as that wandering Daniel.

In Chicago, before he and Lucy took up Woodruff Farm, the present Daniel had sometimes noticed a haggard brunette who used to walk the streets around the university, drunk, or sit on a curb smoking cigarette butts — a woman whose face and carriage implied a fall from some height. There were vanishing hints of appeal in the lean shoulders overflowed with dark hair. She was probably between asylums; and Daniel used to think, against his will, of Sibyl's confinement, and wonder if she could end so — a daughter of the swan become that Magdalene — wonder, and then check himself, calling the conjecture a fruit of the jealous wish. Because it was not likely. If nothing else, Sibyl had too much skill to get stranded that way. Young or old, sane or crazy, her romantic flights would hit the mark. She might sit up in her deathbed, gazing wide at the attendant doctor, realizing that here at last was the right man; and such was her power that no doubt the doctor would propose to her in the act of recording the dying pulse.

Octavia was another matter. She was too honestly impulsive, and had no practice on the ropes. As surely as the past grows to the future, she was going to wind up at the farm some winter after a crazy romance, elopement, a suicide attempt — sent by her mother, or in desperation run away. They would put her in school and she would do nothing, insult the teachers (by sure instinct puncturing the stuffiest), play hooky, fail out. Call that the dark center; yet around it is the glimmering penumbra, heart . . . rending: the lonely folk songs and blues she would learn or make up out of adolescent love and betrayal, enough to make a Puritan weep and love, the glory of her guitar playing, the abandonment of the life to form around her. And then a succession of beatnik boys, as if she was drawn to the wildest or they to her. So she retreats from the family. Scenes, scoldings, brief penitent returns. And night after night wondering — until some goon from the local base drives her up at one or two, and Daniel storms out in his dressing gown, blaming the boy, whom Octavia defends, kissing him goodnight: her fault entirely if any fault is involved. When Daniel has got her into the house: "But my Lord, Octavia, you can't . .". And she stands there looking at him with great brown eyes of hurt innocence — such pools of eyes as he saw twenty years before — such as Eve must have thrown on God in the garden: "Why did you put it there, and of such taste and color?"

It could not keep on that way; something would come up — Daniel's fellowship, say, for a year's study abroad. But one could not cut off from the commitment; they had to take Octavia if she wanted to go. Suppose he tells Lucy so. Then she will be the one to break down, worn by the long tension (not outward, but in herself — the conscious will and obligation against something stronger, the soul's exclusion of that seed of Daniel sowed in Sibyl's darkness); for all her kindly resolve, she must assume the stepmother role — have not the calm and cold always been allied?

Perhaps there was a sort of confinement from which Daniel had rescued Lucy, some gray limbo of restrained Patience (though she was halfway out without him); but if he had been her Orpheus, she had more materially been his Alcestis, and at greater risk. Like one who draws a poison by sucking it from the wound, she had stood, hardly aware of it, between him and night, protective. But if, as in the folk song, her tooth had been hollow, she would have paid for the office of guardian — and who is without some small cavities of that kind? It was a proof of her extraordinary wholeness that she had managed to sustain it with only the few dream-reminders of the pit she stood over. And now came something stronger, an almost epileptic seizure. "If Octavia wants to go, what can we do but take her?" It was Lucy who would give way, fall with palpitations and cramps, all the symptoms of heart attack, which did not yield until she was rushed to the hospital, though it was nothing but hysteria.

That too she would take in her stride, put it behind her, not be troubled by it. Still, it had occurred. You do not escape any encounter without a sign, a club foot or squint eye, the withering of some small member, a reminder you have tangled with the evil one.

In this case Octavia would bear the principal scars. If Lucy's seizure was an unconscious weapon, it was bound to succeed. So Octavia must be shuttled back to her mother, to be launched on whatever career of love, marriage and divorce she was slated for. The violence would come to roost somewhere. If Daniel had defended his present front yard, it was only by opening the back one to the onslaught.

As now, on the plane, returning to Lucy, he abandoned his aunt to the Colesons. For there were no conclusions, nothing but the old settling and resurgence.

This time not even the expected deaths had come off. They hovered between life and death, a universal dying. It was the others, Daniel's parents and Lucy's, Spurge and Little Gerald, the South, the North, Victorian England; it was Lucy and he who had died and were now to be quickened, in the palingenesis of all becoming . . .

Like Aunt Betsy, Uncle Steward had backed water. The first attack was a polite reminder. He might rise a few more times to fight floods, though at last even a clock man would yield. He was to manage his dying naturally, as behoved him, not wasting motion even in that. A few more years (Aunt Hannah had made a hundred) and it would strike — as he was turning with the shears from the rosebushes, asking Aunt Hester if they were . pruned enough; or it would be an October evening by the log fire, he standing there warming his backside, as all those Quakers loved to do, the women raising their skirts to admit the caloric; he would be reading Aunt Hester something about Thailand or Africa while she made notes for their winter trip, when without a sign or cry he would break off in the reading and fall, measuring his length on the floor:

So there would be another Germantown funeral, exhibiting more strongly than any the coercive power of Quakerism; not the original Quakerism, that secret garden of the mystics, but the practically managed orchard with its fruits of colleges, banks and factories. The qualities Lucy had loved in Uncle Steward would be lost in a host of tributes to wealth, strength and activity — a strong laborer in the Lord's vineyard. It was going to be such a funeral as even Nathaniel Pendle would be cowed by, and if the spirit did not move him to talk plain sense, for once would sit through silent.

The Mill, of course, would go on, the institution reaching beyond the span of however great a Miller. In that basement where each thing was in its place, there were instructions for every chore and process, all card indexed and filed: how much to mulch and when, when to plant and when to spray, how to repair the turbine and the power mower; it was a genetic capsule for the perpetuation of the organism. The sons who had taken over the family business would return on weekends, making entries of the old kind in the same log: "Oiled tower clock, pruned the nut trees, cemented two holes in the dam."

For the moment Uncle Steward had held his own against the downward current. He had paddled from the brink of the fall — as in the picture over his mantle — back into the landscape he had patiently preserved, had tidied and replanted after floods, the shallows of the river spread like a lake reflecting the afternoon, and on a foreground bank under an oak, children with fishing poles, not so much fishing as completing the ideal summer. Yet still, at the limit of the horizon, where the gorge rose and narrowed, was the drop from which he had returned, the roar, the lost landscape, the mists enshrouding . . .

Over forested gorges the plane rose to the divide. The flight stretched into the future, a sine wave to be plotted from the past out of which it flowed.

The withered sad face on the porch gazing at Daniel as B.J. drove him away generated the inescapable scene — the pallid smoothed features massaged and rouged to a refined waxwork covering the bones, vacantly peaceful after the mortician's work had ended, which would greet him sometime, after another return, in the chapel room of the amber-lighted funeral home — the whole figure absurdly childlike in its massive open silk-lined and lace-and-embroidery-padded black casket, that thousand dollars of plush Mrs. Coleson would have ordered before Daniel could get there to countermand it, the living propriety forcing itself on the dead, though the cost might keep her turning there like a barbecued bird. She would lie, a lost stern baby, the pastel skin over the brooding bones, almost seeming to justify the, creepy soft professionally voiced threat or assurance of the funeral parlor owner as he clinched the arrangements for a funeral in the style to which the Byrnes were accustomed (Daniel thinking, but why say it?: "Yes, but maybe the Byrnes have got wiser now; maybe they've learned something about values."), the creepy-voiced threat or promise: "She may be here with us now; she may see and appreciate all we're doing for her."

Though who should know better than this broker for the dead it was not really Miss Betsy lying there like a stern Puritan child, certainly not thinking or seeing — who better than he, in whose back chambers the disemboweling and skull-draining of the beautified remains had occurred — he who now murmured in sanctimonious tones: "Yes, I'm sure Betsy Byrne is here with us and sees and appreciates our care."

Why one could visualize the great face condensing out of the air, more like the grim duchess than the Cheshire Cat, except for the smile, the wide smile gloating over the puckered silk and plush-lined chrome-handled casket in which she would be displayed, delighted it was not some plain box of knotty pine — Daniel longing to take it up: "Yes, maybe she sees us, maybe so; but if she does, from where she sees, she sees our motives; she knows why you want her to have the plush casket and why I prefer the knotty pine." But why bother?

His eyes were closed. The plane's motion drove him forward. Having got as far into the future as the funeral parlor, it did not take much to penetrate another veil, and be in the country-style Gothic church after the impersonal beauty of the Episcopal ritual — a mixed gathering, the calmly controlled family (no more tears from that divided clan than from the stern-faced corpse itself), and sitting with them in the family pew, for they had become her family more nearly than the rest, the snuffling and red-eyed Colesons, sobbing like paid mourners. One could not even call it pretense. For what else but affection could have offered the all-suffering care, which none of her friends would have dreamed of and Daniel could not have borne up under, feeding her, cleaning her, scrubbing the floors after her breakdowns, prettying her up and joking her out of her blues, restraining those crazy impulses to go out and drive the patched-up car —

"Aunt Betsy," they would call her that now, "don't you go out today. It's too cold. You save yourself up for spring. I got a job laid out for you come spring. You gettin so strong now. You save up a little. I got you a job."

And she: "A job? What job? Where?"

And his slow drawl: "Oh don't you worry; I got you a job up Longwood way."

She insisting: "Longwood! What job?"

Then Bud: "Why hoein cotton, Aunt Bets, you gettin so strong now." He breaks into the loud po-white guffaw she can only fall in with, his laugh long and full, yet deferential, hers weak and bubbling, subsiding in tears.

So they will sit through the ritual, the sobbing emotionality of Mrs. Coleson against the dry-eyed dignity of Daniel, his mother, and the cousins who have come from out of town; until the Amen, when the pallbearers pick up the thousand-dollar heavy casket by the chrome bars, the old men, her brother's friends, hobbling as honoraries, their sons and nephews carrying the load. The Gothic doors swing open on the blubbering Colesons and the calm kith and kin, and the procession files out into the mist-filled Delta air, one of those spring days in winter, the soft sky and a glory of February sun; they walk across the road and through the graveyard to the family lot, under the blessing of the angel's wings.

Next was the torment of deciding what to do with the battered stained-oak hideous heirlooms. The old women, her friends who had consigned her living to the Colesons, would be there to offer advice, at least Mattie Crump and the brisk little woman Judge Byrne had heard the grandmother and aunt praise so much that he had called her the Impeccable. Miss Mattie is to be spokesman, being the oldest old maid in town now, one who taught Daniel Sunday school when he was a little boy, and she says: "But Daniel, that's the bed your father slept in."

He looks at the spraddly hunk of mahogany-stained wood with scrolls and gewgaws laid on with glue and nails, filling the attic and rising toward the ceiling: "I know that, Miss Mattie; I even slept in it once; but that doesn't make it a good bed. How could I ever get it up east, and what would I do with it when I got it there?"

"But Daniel, your father slept there when he was a little boy, and he loved that bed."

Then Daniel, like a little boy himself (one is always a little boy before such monitors): "But I don't love it, Miss Mattie. It's heavy and ugly and it's nothing but junk, and I'm going to get rid of it. I'll have to find some other way to honor my father."

"Daniel," she would say, "I hate to hear that. It's a fine old bed. And if you won't keep it, then I will, because somebody's got to save your father's bed from the junk heap. Now what about that clock? It don't run, but your grandfather bought it in Cincinnati for your grandmother when he was off up the River on one of his photographing trips . . ."

("Trying to sweeten the old bitch up," thought Daniel.)

" . . . and it lost its minute hand, because after your grandmother was blind, she used to feel of it to find out the time, and she felt of it and felt of it until the hand dropped off. But that's bound to be stored around here somewhere. You aren't thinking of letting that clock go, are you, Daniel?"

And he, outmaneuvered: "No, Miss Mattie, I'll take the clock; I'll take it in my own little paw and carry it up east on the plane, though it's not a fine clock and it won't run besides; but I'll tell my children how it lost its hand, and maybe when I'm old and blind, I'll knock the other one off."

They would go on, Miss Mattie and the Impeccable, shocked, offended, yet patiently pursuing the work, determined to get every piece of junk in the house adopted into the safety of a genteel home: "And what about this chest, Daniel? Look, it's full of letters — all those wonderful letters Betsy got when she was a girl."

While always in the background, going along with them like a bad conscience, would be the Colesons, Little Lilly "more leathery lean and incongruously sniffling, Bud grubbier plump and more smelling of whiskey, creeping around the walls with apologetic coughings, and their sweet giggling children running through at odd moments from their side of the house to pick up souvenirs, for naturally they would be living there, looking after the house as they looked after Miss Betsy. Daniel will be wondering how he can ever repay them. He offers them old furniture which Mrs. Coleson accepts with a shrewd sense of its value — she and Slim growing glummer as days pass and nothing but driblets appear, this pittance of the bequest they have looked for. Daniel talks to the lawyer, Hargreaves' rather vacant son, who tries to look wise in his father's chair, Daniel stressing what the Colesons deserve, young Hargreaves what they can legally claim, protesting: "You have no leeway. The estate won't cover the disposals actually made. So what can you do for the Colesons?"

"But I have to do something," says Daniel, thinking: "I'll pay them over the years, help the boy through college, something; but my God, to be saddled with them for life!"

He could sense the future well enough, if he could not see it in detail. From the moment he found that paper this morning, before he took it to Mr. Hargreaves, it was clear the estate would close bankrupt. The crazy will would absorb anything left to absorb — the gift to the colleges, or if that should be scratched out, the hearing for them to present their canceled claims, and the lawyer's fees for fighting those claims —

"And then, the last six months of required probation, while he would be at the artists' retreat in the great stone mansion in Vermont and the judge would just have gone on vacation for thirty days, and his own boat for the year's fellowship in Europe was scheduled to sail in August (some unknown future August like this on which he had made the descent and return), and the closing of the estate and distribution of the remaining assets set for the week before — then the Colesons would come into their own, as any study of the South or even its fiction might have warned him if he did not suspect, but he gave them the benefit of the doubt, seeing them devoted to Aunt Bets and helping her at the stipulated, modest figure, felt indeed his indebtedness, and resolved to find one way or another, wrestling with an estate already short of funds, to give them more than the comical legacy: "my kitty and 250 dollars to look after her" — the kitty already dead, so that $250 assured them, and the free use of her house for six months after her death, say $350, and the $300 check he would write Coleson as assistant in managing the estate (taking that responsibility on his own head), with the commissions Coleson had got for collecting rents and the rest, say a thousand in all, not to mention the furniture, by hook or crook they would have netted, in addition to the original payments, which was about right for the services rendered if commercial, and in so far as they were friendly, they would be hard to bill for — so his mind would be almost clear about them, but not quite, until they would free it altogether of any compunction or tenderness by suddenly coming into their own.

He would be in the studio room that morning in the elegant Vermont retreat, fighting it out to the bitter finish with some project that was never going to succeed, when he would be called to the phone and it would be his wife at the farm, telling him of a letter just opened from the lawyer, young Hargreaves, that the Colesons were suing for $12,000 for services claimed to have been rendered Miss Byrne on the verbal understanding they would be compensated out of the estate. And the Colesons' lawyer would of course be the old shyster his father had despised long ago when the fellow opened business in the town, and who had chased Daniel around later at the time of the accident trying to summon Miss Betsy into court — that same man with all his shyster skills and the judge on vacation and Daniel to sail with his family before court reconvened, he already a thousand miles away and supposed to go further.

So it would mean canceling the sailing and changing all plans and going down at the end of a baking August for another of countless returns, and this time the estate would be all used up and he would be in debt for his traveling. By the time he got there the evidence he had stored in the house, bank statements from years back and the rest, would have disappeared; but he would have the Colesons' letters about the care of Aunt Betsy with their monthly statements of collections and charges, which would almost throw the case out of court, though the new lawyer's fees and court costs and the thousand awarded to the po-whites by a derivatively po-white judge would just about polish things off, all but the Negro cabins, which he would hold on to for no reason except that he had determined on it; and perhaps the Colesons would not even have got the thousand (though he didn't begrudge them that) if he could have displayed a few of their letters which were lost. But he didn't have them. And even the ones he brought were wrinkled and water-blurred and curiously garbage smeared.

For that was the trick of all tricks an ironic future would play on him, that the phone call would come telling him of the Colesons' suit three days after he had sorted through all their letters, and feeling a deep devotion to them for their loving kindness, had chosen two especially tender in their warm illiteracy and marked them: "Keep for mementos" — yes, he would keep them always, reminders of poor people who had golden hearts — and had thrown the others away. Thrown them into the wastebasket of his studio at the Vermont over-regal mansion of a wealthy family now set up as artists' retreat; so he was destined to rush around, asking for the papers, and learn they had been taken by truck yesterday to the huge north dump in the scrubby woods and thickets under the last hill at the estate's edge. And he would tramp out in the sun of midday and spend his lunch hour grubbing — what a lunch that would be — walking first along the dirt road through fields and woods, the mosquitoes trailing in a cloud behind him, his handkerchief thrown over his head, keeping them off a bit by its flapping, but not enough, the bold ones crawling in under his ears and up his shirt sleeves, and worse than the mosquitoes the great deer flies, those three-cornered sons-of-bitches, buzzing around his head and settling in like dive bombers. And then through the woods would come the rotten whiff of the place he was looking for, and as he neared it the flies, growing thicker, would strike and sting, as if that was their Rhinegold treasure-trove to be defended to the last drop, not of their own, but of his blood — he thinking, "By God, if they're this bad before I ever get there, how am I going to stand it on the dump? Why, it may take me hours to find those damned letters."

Then the truck tracks would be ending at the ash and tin can and smelly maggoty ooze of the garbage slide, the dump of the whole colony for years, everything tousled and messed and soaked with the juice of the garbage — and Oh Lord, he had forgotten, it had rained last night; why there had been a downpour. But one thing he learned, one mystery worth a seer's interpreting: as he came toward the sloping wide hill of muck, the flies increasing and more furious, until finally after standing at the top looking fruitlessly down on all sides into the littered valley — nothing to be found at that body and soul's remove — he plunged over the slope, the muck yielding under his feet and bottles breaking on bottles — suddenly he noticed with a kind of wonder, the flies were not at him any more. They were flying around and lighting at his feet, sucking the rotten oranges or melon rinds or potato peelings drowned with spilled soup and the meat scrapings of plates, sucking or blowing them with maggot-producing eggs, but they were not stinging him. It was the calm at the whirlwind's heart, the confusion that comes on flesh in a universe of its own decay; why, in the reeking air, they could not tell the live meat from the dead.

So he was relieved of the deer flies, though the mosquitoes kept up a small running fire while he grubbed, with a stick first, and then finding it would not do, he could not separate the sodden waste papers of the whole mansion's discard one from another except with his hands, rummaging through with his hands, raking, and now and then in the vast rottenness finding a rain-run paper of that telltale baby blue with the illiterate pencil or ink scrawl and the salutation: "Dear Daniel," and the conclusion: "Sincerely, A Friend" — and weirdly enough she had been a friend, but he was purged of all that now, too joyfully purged of them and all concern on their part, raking with his ten fingers in the garbage, growling again and again, with the more than planter's arrogance he had been born to and tried to live down, and had been cautioned not to ignore or he would get fooled, and he had been fooled, yet he didn't mind, he couldn't have done it any other way and been the man he was; but it was over now, he was out of it, and he could rake in the mess picking out the blue scribbled pages and spitting through his teeth his furious satisfaction: "Trash, trash, garbage, trash, po-white trash, garbage, trash."

Except of all that future he could almost sense before it formed, or discern where it bided fore-formed in the ill-matched group he had left on the porch, or lurked in the scratchings of the will he had taken to Mr. Hargreaves — in all that future he could not see or guess what was occurring or would occur behind the barrier of the po-white crummy face and sallow skin.

For they had seen the will too. They knew the amount and wording of the ironical legacy, yet they undertook the care. And they would go on, believing in her like their own aunt, Mrs. Coleson writing the weekly letters: "I bought a new plastic cover for Aunt Betsy's mattress. She don't have any control over that. The Dr. says she can't help it. Sometimes she seems clear. Then she goes like a child: 'I'm going out now to find mother,' she says. Then I take her for a walk and after a while she comes back home same as before." Aunt Betsy would sit there while Mrs. Coleson combed her hair and petted her, she would smile her vacant smile, flinging out intimations of noblesse oblige: "You're so good, so good. But don't worry. Dannie will look after you when I'm gone."

In all his glimpses into the future (or his living it as it broke around him) he would never penetrate those worried gaunt sessions of husband and wife: "Can we count on Daniel; How do we know we can count on Daniel?" Down to that final one in which they broke apart quarreling, Bud slamming out for a drink, saying: "I don't want no part in it. You do better to stick with him. He knows what he owes."

And his wife: "He's goin to throw us off with nothin but some old furniture. He don't live here and he don't care. I been knowin it from the first day when he went off and left his own sick aunt for us to look after. Why didn't he take her up east with him? She was his kin, she warn't ours. Because he don't care. He wants to live easy. Look at the whole gang how they sat at the funeral. Why he even grudged her the coffin I ordered and would a paid for myself if I'd had to. You don't know nothin about him. He's goin to throw us off. And I'm goin to a lawyer."

So she would march out to the inevitable office of the only counsel in her ken, the shyster who had risen from her class to the ranch-home suburbs by just such lying inventions as the $12,000 claim he now cooked up, in which she swore under false dates and totally confused circumstances to years of service and expenses which had never been rendered or incurred, and which sank into oblivion the love and attentions she had in fact bestowed.

What Daniel, dimly guessing at a future where an infuriating suit would postpone foreign travels, could never focus on was the actuality before Coleson: drinking, squabbling with his wife, their girls ripening into slattems, he always blaming her (for the lawyer had taken them on spec at half the gain, and their share hardly covered moving and setting up in new and worse housing) — drinking, fighting, some jail — Daniel would not see it; he would hardly consider their fate again.

Of course, it was bound to be brought to his attention: Old Winnie would split her face in a grin and slap her thigh, telling how much they had stolen from Miss Betsy and from him. "Well; they can have it," said Daniel; "I hope they're rich now."

"Rich? They ain't got no thin, Misser Daniel. You go round comer Broadway and Persimmon mos any evenin bout four o'clock, thas where you find him."

"You mean he works there?"

"Work? No suh, thas where he drink. You see her too. Long bout five-thirty she come to git him. 'Haul up fum there,' she say. 'Who talkin?' he say, so drunk he cain't see. 'You better know me,' she say. 'Haul up fum there fo I bus this bottle on yo head.' I seen em. 'Doan hit him, Mrs. Coleson,' I tol her. 'Git in this car,' she holler, 'an drive me home.' 'I ain't fittin to drive,' he say. 'You drive anyhow,' she say, and slam de do. Thas where yo money gone, Misser Daniel; he drinkin it up."

But Daniel had another life. While Bud Coleson would sit with

Shorty Rowland, who had also rented .long ago from Miss Betsy, sponging a beer and saying: "He ditched us. Just like that. By God he was glad to ditch us. He told my wife he was glad when she sued him, because she got something and he found out where she stood. Same way he ditched his aunt when he went off and left her in that run-down house, with her and all the property for us to take care of, while he went back east to his precious wife and farm. Talk about low-down dealings!"

Descent and return, deaths, foreclosures . . . The house to be sold to payoff obligations — to be taken over by somebody who would patch it and paint it, try to rent it again, and go broke in turn, until some summer Daniel would walk by on his way to visit old Nellie (she by that time looking like the Cumaean Sibyl), and find the cycle completed, but to no age of gold —a low flat filling station, competing with two others at the same crossing, cementing the whole comer with concrete, brick and glass, and nothing as a reminder but the gnarled old crape myrtle tree the grandfather had planted, jagged as a storm-stunted cedar, jutting white bloom over the concrete runway by the gas pumps . . .

But that was all future. Now the plane settled through the calm evening. They were still out over the mountains. The man sitting beside Daniel had put up his briefcase and was talking to two across the way: threat of Russia, population explosion, yellow races, black races, creeping socialism: "What we ought to do is fling a few bombs around, let those Reds know we mean business; that damned conspiracy has taken the whole world."

In the old days Daniel would have spoken: *If you could learn once and for ail, we don't have the option to destroy the world because of wasting our chances in it . . .* Now the dialogue had moved inward, self-opposed — that trunk of old manuscripts Lucy taunted him he should bring along:

To perceive in the scope of its profligacy the history, that is the self-destruction of the West, is to glimpse no mere human folly, but one of those terrifying openings out of the organically wild and wasteful, the more dire for its satanic sense of direction . . .

Like the voice of old Loewenstein, and against it, Daniel's own:

Yes. But the private good: democracy, Woodruff Farm, Lucy, one's art? — Sequences of sunset, fruits of the general fall. It was energy again, the tragic field, vectors of leaf and flame, that backward rearing in the downward light . . .

A long descent through the dusk. Soon housing developments of the East would appear, breeding hutches. For the moment they were still over woods, first lights showing in a dark land.

There were no general solutions to a flux that had to be ridden and resisted at every instant, dealt with always afresh, that allowed nothing but moments of tentative answer.

The simplest case: to specify the mixture of father and mother which had produced in himself, Daniel, at least an operable blend, a life which gave him, with even some other people, joy. Allow the father a plus and minus: the plus, energy, ambition, what the phrenologist had called traits of the hustler; that had its minus which brought it to the ground, the insecure fever of such go-getting. Formulate similar antipodes for the mother: The minus was evident, incapacity to confront the world, her sensitive withdrawing which would have been pathological without its saving complement, the serenity that filled her solitude.

What has the formulation accomplished? Like dice or a pin-wheel, spin or roll: a man-child is conceived, Daniel, the father's drive, the mother's quiet, a sustaining power. Set the wheel spinning again, or if it should be coins, toss: the genes spar off, divide, coalesce: tails, tails — poor little Gerald. The mother's solitude, the father's unrest. What can he be but a child genius, praecox, allergic, asthmatic, neuralgic, a guinea pig for doctors to work on, to bore his sinuses and osteopath his bones, to scratch him for sensitivities and feed him a thousand pills? By puberty he will be a free-verse poet, a painter in the style of Nijinsky, resonating to a mad world, growing toward a moment of clarity in which he sees that nonbeing is preferable to this catabolic dependence. So he uses the medicines he is tied to anyway to remove himself, to clear out of the way.

Compare the budding of Woodruff onto Grafton. That dominance of the father had produced a prize child, Lucy; and by the same over-shadowing, a son breaking with what the father was, or under guise of a break, relapsing to the old money mills from which the father had fled. Also from Daniel and Lucy there was no telling what these charming letter-writing children, Hester and Mardie, might turn into.

It was not even clear that what he and Lucy were undertaking was a possible achievement. Any old saint, or Platonist for that matter, could have told Daniel that the fever of the Dark Love applied to all poking with the soul in that hole. Maybe he would have been wiser to have followed enervate Origin and cut it out altogether. But he was not interested in such wisdom. If he had learned anything from the Methodist barn of his childhood, it was Incarnation, and that there is a book in the Bible called Acts. Like Thoreau, he did not want to prac-tice resignation, unless it was absolutely necessary. And the only way to know whether it was necessary was to get on the romantic rollercoaster and see if it led to the same catastrophe. After ten years with Lucy, he was beginning to think that a happiness, kinder to our mortality than the ecstasy of monks in the Thebaid, was perhaps possible.

But the proof remained particular. All it indicated was that in the temporal descent, lights multiplying themselves over the dark land, there is an eternal rising from the dead, a pairing of poles, as simul-taneously converging from separate voyages, soul and body clasp in regenerative love.

The plane sank in the twilight. Lucy was to meet him at the airport. Then he began to worry. Not about the landing, but her long drive through weekend traffic. As they struck the earth, lurched, and lumbered up the runway, his eyes were searching the crowd at the lighted gate. But her trim form, so brisk and sure in its movements, the frank open face and deft hands, quick but placid, the unconsciously artful gestures — not there, not there. The span of the metal stair reached out. He was the first across half running, searching. She was not around.

Then at another gate, the wrong gate, small, looking lost and worried in the crowd (she had fretted about him, the delayed plane), she stood, hunting in the opposite direction, where another plane was unloading. His run dwindled to a tiptoe. He crept up behind her and catching her shoulders, touched his lips to her small neck where the mouse-blond hair was blown aside. And she turned, their eyes meeting and reflecting, both of them half in tears, whelming strange tears of joy; they held each other, but lightly, chastely, almost a brotherly caress, more eager to smile than kiss. Then peacefully their cheeks, only their cheeks, met.

No doubt later in the evening he would let loose with one of the ribald rhymes that popped into his head, something like a patter song from *Don Giovanni*, a dance, a rape, to be sung and acted in bawdy pantomime:

> When we would make love to ladies
> We must catch them by the titties;
> If they strike or do disdain us,
> Then we poke them . . .

Rhyme after rhyme . . . Lucy would draw herself up, like Aunt Hester for a moment, protesting: "Careful. Careful. My God. What do you think? Go on now. Leave me alone. I thought you were going to help me with the dishes" — spluttering and crying in her high coloratura: "My Lord!"

The tumultuous arch of flesh will become their resurrection, bawdy spilling out into its own pool of sacrament. As if the faith of

Lawrence had actually come true, and it was God himself who rose on Pillicock Hill.

The next morning Daniel would get up, daemonic as ever, as if he was going to die in a week and had lost all that time in Mississippi, and had every bit of his work to finish before the fatal day. He would rush around yelling about where his paintbrushes were; or maybe Lucy would have thrown out some of his favorite old rumpled ties in his absence, and he would storm to the trash bin to reclaim them; or it would be pocket papers he assumed she had made way with, until they would appear stuffed back somewhere in his own drawer.

He would get up into a world that did not give a damn for the work he was committed to: reading, note-gathering, drawing, writing, beating his head against the sheer recalcitrance of things, to break through into something not even Lucy understood, though she allowed it, with the winsome grudgefulness women show for the prepossessions of their lovers; he would get up tomorrow to assault what he had to assault. But tonight they were whole, the instant glowing around them like a jewel.

They touched cheeks only, laughing and in tears. They were together again; and Mississippi and the termite-eaten house and living in filth on terrible food, problems of past and future, the Colesons, Daniel's mother, Aunt Betsy, Sibyl, Sibyl's child Octavia, Uncle Steward, all the insolubles — palings of loss that enclosed the bright stable of their lives — were behind, before, far off, suspended . . .

They walked to the car and drove to the Quaker farm.

Fomite

Writing a review on social media sites for readers will help the progress of independent publishing. To submit a review, go to the book page on any of the sites and follow the links for reviews. Books from independent presses rely on reader-to-reader communications.

For more information or to order any of our books, visit:
http://www.fomitepress.com/our-books.html

More novels from Fomite...
Joshua Amses — *During This, Our Nadir*
Joshua Amses — *Ghatsr*
Joshua Amses — *How They Became Birds*
Joshua Amses — *Raven or Crow*
Joshua Amses — *The Moment Before an Injury*
Charles Bell — *The Married Land*
Charles Bell — *The Half Gods*
Jaysinh Birjepatel — *Nothing Beside Remains*
Jaysinh Birjepatel — *The Good Muslim of Jackson Heights*
David Brizer — *Victor Rand*
L. M Brown — *Hinterland*
Paula Closson Buck — *Summer on the Cold War Planet*
Dan Chodorkoff — *Loisaida*
Dan Chodorkoff — *Sugaring Down*
David Adams Cleveland — *Time's Betrayal*
Paul Cody— *Sphyxia*
Jaimee Wriston Colbert — *Vanishing Acts*
Roger Coleman — *Skywreck Afternoons*
Stephen Downes — *The Hands of Pianists*
Marc Estrin — *Hyde*
Marc Estrin — *Kafka's Roach*
Marc Estrin — *Proceedings of the Hebrew Burial Society*
Marc Estrin — *Speckled Vanities*
Marc Estrin — *The Annotated Nose*
Marc Estrin — *The Penseés of Alan Kreiger*
Zdravka Evtimova — *Asylum for Men and Dogs*
Zdravka Evtimova — *In the Town of Joy and Peace*
Zdravka Evtimova — *Sinfonia Bulgarica*
Zdravka Evtimova — *You Can Smile on Wednesdays*
Daniel Forbes — *Derail This Train Wreck*
Peter Fortunato — *Carnevale*
Greg Guma — *Dons of Time*
Richard Hawley — *The Three Lives of Jonathan Force*
Lamar Herrin — *Father Figure*
Michael Horner — *Damage Control*

Fomite

Ron Jacobs — *All the Sinners Saints*
Ron Jacobs — *Short Order Frame Up*
Ron Jacobs — *The Co-conspirator's Tale*
Scott Archer Jones — *And Throw Away the Skins*
Scott Archer Jones — *A Rising Tide of People Swept Away*
Julie Justicz — *Degrees of Difficulty*
Maggie Kast — *A Free Unsullied Land*
Darrell Kastin — *Shadowboxing with Bukowski*
Coleen Kearon — *#triggerwarning*
Coleen Kearon — *Feminist on Fire*
Jan English Leary — *Thicker Than Blood*
Diane Lefer — *Confessions of a Carnivore*
Diane Lefer — *Out of Place*
Rob Lenihan — *Born Speaking Lies*
Colin McGinnis — *Roadman*
Douglas W. Milliken — *Our Shadows' Voice*
Ilan Mochari — *Zinsky the Obscure*
Peter Nash — *Parsimony*
Peter Nash — *The Least of It*
Peter Nash — *The Perfection of Things*
George Ovitt — Stillpoint
George Ovitt — Tribunal
Gregory Papadoyiannis — *The Baby Jazz*
Pelham — *The Walking Poor*
Andy Potok — *My Father's Keeper*
Frederick Ramey — *Comes A Time*
Joseph Rathgeber — *Mixedbloods*
Kathryn Roberts — *Companion Plants*
Robert Rosenberg — *Isles of the Blind*
Fred Russell — *Rafi's World*
Ron Savage — *Voyeur in Tangier*
David Schein — *The Adoption*
Charles Simpson — *Uncertain Harvest*
Lynn Sloan — *Midstream*
Lynn Sloan — *Principles of Navigation*
L.E. Smith — *The Consequence of Gesture*
L.E. Smith — *Travers' Inferno*
L.E. Smith — *Untimely RIPped*
Robert Sommer — *A Great Fullness*
Tom Walker — *A Day in the Life*
Susan V. Weiss —*My God, What Have We Done?*
Peter M. Wheelwright — *As It Is On Earth*
Peter M. Wheelwright — *The Door-Man*
Suzie Wizowaty — *The Return of Jason Green*

www.ingramcontent.com/pod-product-compliance
Lightning Source LLC
Chambersburg PA
CBHW060727190726
48285CB00001B/109